I0527884

Abyss: Surviving the Zombie Apocalypse

SHAWN CHESSER

Copyright © 2017 Shawn Chesser

All rights reserved.

ISBN: 978-0-9980683-4-3

CONTENTS

ACKNOWLEDGEMENTS

For Maureen, Raven, and Caden ... I couldn't have done this without your support. Thanks to our military, LE and first responders for your service. To the people in the U.K. and elsewhere around the world who have been in touch, thanks for reading! Lieutenant Colonel Michael Offe, thanks for your service as well as your friendship. Larry Eckels, thank you for helping me with some of the military technical stuff. Any missing facts or errors are solely my fault. Beta readers, you rock, and you know who you are. Thanks George Romero for introducing me to zombies. To my friends and fellows at S@N and Monday Steps On Steele, thanks as well. Lastly, thanks to Bill W. and Dr. Bob ... you helped make this possible. I am going to sign up for another 24.

Special thanks to John O'Brien, Mark Tufo, Joe McKinney, Craig DiLouie, Armand Rosamilia, Heath Stallcup, Saul Tanpepper, Eric A. Shelman, and David P. Forsyth. I truly appreciate your continued friendship and always invaluable advice. Thanks to Jason Swarr and Straight 8 Custom Photography for another awesome cover. Once again, extra special thanks to Monique Happy for her work editing "ABYSS." Mo, as always, you came through like a champ! Working with you over the years has been nothing but a pleasure. I truly appreciate having a confidante I can trust. If I have accidentally left anyone out ... I am truly sorry.

***

Edited by Monique Happy Editorial Services
www.moniquehappy.com

Prologue

Despite measures taken to level the Winnebago on the spongy ground it sat upon, the cold bodies pressing against its thin metal skin caused it to sway and rock on its air suspension. The keening of metal on metal coming from the undulating awning increased as hollow concussions of bodies impacting the rear of the vehicle crashed off the walls of its gloomy interior. As the discordant banging trailed off, there came a scrabbling of nails on glass, and pale hands slapped the oversized rear window.

Standing in the narrow center aisle, jet-black Gerber in hand, Cade turned his head and met the lifeless stares of the sneering faces mashed against the glass. A quick headcount told him there were at least a dozen undead men, women, and children gathered around the back of the RV. And though the monsters leered with mouths agape and features collapsed and twisted with what could only be described as a mixture of rage and hunger, many among them looked vaguely familiar.

Slickened with freshly spilt blood, the vinyl flooring underfoot moved with a vigor that threatened to spill him to his knees. Worried that he'd fall and pull the writhing corpse down on top of him, Cade tightened his grip on the smooth skin of its neck and struggled to introduce the Gerber's honed tip into the thing's clouded-over right eye.

Every extra ounce of effort he put into what would be a killing blow was met with a pushback that inexplicably grew concurrent with the increasing tempo of the wallowing charnel house.

Off his right shoulder a metronomic thumping started. He tore his gaze from the snarling Z and regarded the narrow bi-fold door. It was vibrating with each impact then began to collapse and suck inward. *Did one of them wriggle through the tiny bathroom window?* Even the monsters assaulting the RV he had wrecked into the Hanna farmhouse hadn't been able to work the door latch to get to him. Sure, they'd finally succeeded in breaching the door through brute force, which, with his hands full and all, was what Cade really feared at this point. One more he could handle. A small army of them pouring through the side door he could not. As it was, this fresh turn was putting up one hell of a fight.

Where in the hell is Duncan, he thought, his wildly beating heart a caged animal trying to escape his chest.

He called out for his good friend.

Nothing.

He was all alone.

So he redoubled his efforts.

Sweat beads wetting his forehead, he inched the Gerber closer to the wildly roving eye.

As the RV continued to rock, the snarls outside rose to a crescendo.

A cupboard door popped open, spilling pots and pans at his feet.

Like a forge bellows, the small lavatory door flexed outward and then sucked back in on its own accord.

Adding to the stench of his own fear-laced sweat, the sour reek of the monster's final meal rose from deep within its shell and wafted over a picket of perfect white teeth, hitting him full on and starting a wave of bile rising in his throat.

Suddenly, the thing seemed to go limp and Cade watched three inches of razor-honed Gerber disappear into its eye socket. There was a harsh rasp as steel grated on orbital bone and then light was assaulting his retinas and he was lashing out with a sweeping right cross.

Bed frame ringing from the glancing blow, Cade came to and yelped as the wave of pain transited his arm from knuckles to elbow. He tucked his fist against his heaving chest and concluded the haymaker had been intended for the thing from his nightmare.

"You were having another bad one."

Though his eyes were still adjusting to the dim environs, there was no mistaking whom the voice belonged to. Nor was there any way he could mistake the silhouette looming just out of arm's reach for anyone other than his diminutive twelve-year-old, Raven.

"Thanks, Bird." He paused and rubbed his eyes. "But did you have to shake the bed to wake me?"

Raven gave him the look. Head tilting sideways, she said, "Either that or a splash of cold water. You lashed out and hit the bed. Better the bed than me."

"Good thinking, sweetie." He swung his legs over the bed rails and noticed Max. The brindle-colored Australian shepherd was sitting on his haunches, nearly lost in shadow. Head cocked sideways, the dog's liquid eyes—one blue, one brown—were fixed intently on him. And though far from the noise a zombie fighting to breach a bi-fold door might make, the hollow thumping of the dog's leg hitting the plywood floor as it worked to scratch a flea had seemed just that to a man in the throes of one hell of a nightmare.

"That's five in a row," said Raven, nodding an affirmative. "One every night since …"

"Come here," he said, arms outstretched.

"But you're all sweaty." She replaced the dagger and Glock 19 where she had taken them from: on top of a small table beside the doorway cut into the Conex container's metal wall.

Throwing a shiver against the still, fifty-five-degree air, Cade wrapped the wool surplus blanket tightly around his shoulders and drew his daughter in close. "Good thinking," he said, gesturing toward the "tools of his trade" sitting barely a yard from his bed. "But next time, instead of shaking my bunk to wake me, why don't you try calling my name. Or Daddy ..."

Raven lifted her chin from his chest and stared into his eyes.

"The movement and squeaking showed up in my nightmare." He described the terror he had just relived.

"I shook the bed because you were calling out for Duncan, that's why."

He stroked her hair. The same short movements he'd seen Brook employ.

"You wouldn't have heard me—" she began, her lip quivering.

"But *they* would have. I get it. We've been through a lot lately. There's no reason to think anyone is judging you. Because they aren't."

As if saying *Eff them anyway,* Max let out a low growl and laid flat on the floor. He stretched his front legs to full extension, resting his paws on his masters' bare feet.

"Maybe you should take the pills Glenda recommended."

Cade drew in a deep breath.

"They'll help chase the 'mares away."

"And dull my edge," he said. "I really can't afford that. Not until the road is snowed in."

Changing the subject, Raven said, "You promised some quality time outside the wire. You remember, don't you?"

He nodded. Reached for his Danners and loosened the laces.

"We're going?"

"Grab your pack and rifle and go tell the others. I'll meet you in the foyer in a couple of minutes."

Smile broadening, Raven plucked her daypack off the chair. She grabbed her Ruger 10/22 from where it was propped against the wall and turned toward the door.

"Not the Ruger," he said. "Take Mom's Colt. Think you can handle lugging a few extra pounds?"

Smile growing wider, she nodded. Swapping the longer rifle for the stubby close-quarters battle rifle, she hefted it and said, "Not much of a difference, really." She ejected the magazine and set it on the table. Only after she had cycled the charging handle back and forth to ensure the weapon wasn't "hot"—as she had heard her mom and dad call a loaded gun—did she reseat the mag and set the selector to Safe.

Good girl, thought Cade.

4

"See anything different about the magazine?"

Raven rolled the black rifle on its side and scrutinized the boxy metal magazine protruding from the lower well. Without meeting her dad's watchful gaze, she glanced at the similar desert-tan M4 hanging on a peg near the door. "This one is shorter," she replied, patting the side of her weapon. "And it's not plastic."

"Polymer," he corrected. "And it holds ten rounds, just like the Ruger. But these are a little bigger than the Ruger's and pack more of a punch."

"Mom let me shoot it a few times."

"With the suppressor attached?" he asked, gesturing at the short black cylinder affixed to the carbine's barrel.

Raven nodded.

"The smaller capacity mag should offset the extra weight up front a little. Not only does the suppressor save your hearing and quiet the gun a bit, it'll also reduce muzzle climb some. Suppressor, ammo, and optics, all total you're carrying a tick less than eight pounds. About the same as the backpack you used to lug to school."

Raven set the rifle aside to put on her parka. After drawing the zipper to her neck, she looped the single-point sling over her head.

"I already shortened it for you. How's it feel?"

Raven smiled and hefted the rifle, shouldering it a couple of times before swinging it around to her back.

"Good to go?" asked Cade, slipping a Motorola two-way radio into his cargo pocket.

"Good to go," replied Raven, scooping up her pack.

Cade rose from his bunk. He shrugged on a coat, donned his pack, and grabbed his rifle.

Raven stepped into the corridor.

"Go on ahead," said Cade. "Wait for me inside the front entry."

Raven shrugged, then set off on her own with Max padding close behind.

After pausing in the doorway long enough to see the two take the left toward the security container, Cade took his dog tags from around his neck. He rooted in a box on a shelf and found Brook's wedding band. It went on the chain with his dog tags and the chain went back around his neck.

Chapter 1

After latching the door to the Grayson quarters, Cade made his way down the corridor, negotiated the turn at the "T," and spied Tran hunched buzzard-like over the desk in the security pod. The slight Asian man was dressed in a gray sweatshirt and faded blue jeans, and had his boot-clad feet propped up on a faded red milk crate underneath the desk. His head was turned toward the flat panel where color images fed in from the multiple cameras about the compound filled up the half-dozen rectangular partitions. If Tran had heard Cade's approach, he didn't let on until his muscular frame was filling up the narrow entryway.

"Mister Grayson," he said in his usual sing-song voice.

"Busted," said Cade, a grin forming on his face.

Eyes still fixed on the monitor, Tran went on, "Dressed for a special occasion, I see."

Brow rising, Cade's smile melted and he met the man's gaze in the monitor's shiny surface.

The rolling chair squeaked as Tran spun the seat around.

"How's the road look?"

"I haven't seen any vehicles," responded Tran. "But I did count nearly a dozen demons moving in the direction of the roadblock."

Exactly what Cade had hoped to hear. "Is *she* nearby?" he mouthed, his eyes searching the monitor for any sign of the stocky middle-aged woman who called herself Bridgett.

Tran hooked a thumb over his shoulder. "In her quarters," he whispered.

Squinting against the light cast from the hanging sixty-watt bulb, Cade looked past the man and met Raven's eyes. She was standing on the threshold to the foyer and throwing him a questioning look. *Damn, how she resembles her mom.* A fresh wave of sorrow building, he said, "I need to talk with Tran for a minute."

Showing her impatience, Raven put her hands on her hips and turned away.

"The thing you wanted me to rig up is ready," Tran said under his breath. "It's not as slick a setup as Foley would have built, but I did my best." He went quiet for a beat. After looking over his shoulder, he added, "I really hope you're wrong."

"We'll see," Cade replied cryptically. "Hope for the best—"

"Prepare for the worst," finished Tran, shifting his gaze back to the monitor. "I see Old Man waiting for you topside."

Cade looked at his Suunto. *Seven forty-five.* He said, "I've been meaning to thank you for stepping up these last couple of weeks. Especially the last few days, considering the circumstances. Putting the gas additives in the fuel. Decanting water. Hunting and cooking. I'm kind of quiet—"

"Distant. Cold. Some would say unfriendly," said Tran. "But I can see past all that. You're a good man. A good father."

Cade hung his head. "Guilty as charged." He met the older man's gaze. "Stay frosty, Tran."

Back to watching the monitor, Tran reached up and plucked a Thuraya satellite phone from the shelf. "You should probably take this with you."

Patting his cargo pocket, Cade said, "No need. I've got a radio. Besides, we're not going to stray too far."

"Prepare for the worst?"

Reluctantly, Cade accepted the phone and stowed it in a pocket. "Turning hard-ass on me, huh?" He patted Tran on the back. "Want me to sign it out, too?"

"I figure you're on the up and up," answered Tran, flashing a smile Cade interpreted as an unspoken *touché.*

On the monitor the video feed of the state route went jittery and the camera aperture adjusted to compensate for the unusual glare coming off the road. "Better go," urged Tran. "It's starting to hail."

Perfect, thought Cade. *Opens up a whole new course of study.*

"Dad … let's get the show on the road," Raven called, parroting a line Brook would bray at her nearly every morning on a school day.

Cade clapped Tran on the shoulder. Then, ignoring a burst of laughter emanating from the Kids' quarters not far from the entry, he pushed aside the blackout curtain and led Raven through the metal door, up the packed-earth ramp, and around the camouflage blind.

Once out in the open, Cade ducked his head against the icy onslaught and trudged across the clearing toward Duncan. Creating a staccato ripping noise, BB-sized hailstones pelted the bill of his ball cap. They stung his cheeks and nose and found their way down his fatigue collar.

Emitting a little yelp, Raven took hold of her dad's slung backpack and pressed her face against its loose folds.

In just a matter of seconds the knee-high grass dominating the clearing began to bow and knuckle under weight of Mother Nature's untimely barrage. The hail continued falling in near impenetrable sheets, the pellets sticking and lending the flat surfaces of the vehicles in the motor pool a shiny pallor. The pair's boots squelched on the accumulation as they stepped from the grass and trooped across the makeshift airstrip's twin dirt stripes.

"I'd double time it if I were you," Duncan called from under cover of the tree line. "Not like the sun's comin' out any time soon."

As Cade and Raven finally made the tree line, the door to the Winnebago hinged open and Glenda Gladson emerged grim-faced and glaring at the sagging metal awning. It was white with hail on top and nearly brushed the top of her head when she stood underneath it. In her hands was a bleach bottle that looked to be empty judging by how she carried it: one finger through the neck handle and hanging limply at her side. Cade got confirmation of this when the fifty-seven-year-old widow chucked the gallon jug to the ground and it skittered lightly atop the matted-down semicircle of grass beside the RV.

Duncan looked groundward then let his gaze slowly follow the fresh footprints all the way across the clearing to the compound's hidden entry. "Still think we should have burned the 'Bago," he said, regarding Cade with one brow arched.

Cade nodded. *Message received.* He said, "Leave that for me to do, Glenda. I said I would get to it … and I meant it."

"We may be needing it down the road," said Glenda. "That's why I didn't want you boys to torch it."

Changing the subject, Duncan drawled, "Where are you taking my little Raven?"

Noting Glenda's glare directed his way, Cade said, "We're starting bushcraft one-oh-one. Basically, an entry-level course on how to move effectively outside the wire."

"Perfect weather for it," conceded Duncan. He wet a finger and tested the air. "It's pushing fifty degrees. Might even get to the ol' double nickel come noon. Means the rotters'll still be mobile." He removed his aviator-style glasses and started wiping them with a handkerchief. Finished, he leveled a knowing gaze at Cade. "About as *mobile* as a fella stuck in quicksand, that is."

Cade nodded. "Thanks for what you're doing," he said to Glenda.

Expression softening, she said, "Glad to. Jamie's been helping me." She smiled and glanced at Raven. "Besides, you've got your hands full with that tween of yours."

Eager to get on the move—or '*Oscar Mike*' as Dad liked to say—Raven shifted from foot to foot and tried catching his eye.

Shifting her gaze to Raven, Glenda asked, "Where's Sash? You two have been darn near inseparable since—" Catching herself before she finished the thought, she went silent.

Rescuing his loose-lipped damsel in distress, Duncan said, "Since you *saved* the day and a life by giving your dose of antiserum to Gregory. That's what Glenda was alluding to … *right?*"

Glenda pursed her lips and looked away.

10

Shooting the pair a look colder than the precipitation still falling in sporadic bursts, Cade said, "All of a sudden Wilson isn't comfortable with Sasha going outside the wire."

"Understandable with all that's happened lately."

Elbowing Duncan in the ribs, Glenda made a shooing motion at Cade and the youngster who was a spitting image of her mom. "Go and bushcraft," she said. "I'll have some hot stick-to-your-ribs venison stew ready by lunchtime."

"I owe you for all you've done for me and Raven since …"

Glenda shushed him and shook her head. "No, you don't. We're family here."

Cade made no reply to that. Instead, he consulted his Suunto, nodded, and led Raven in the direction of the feeder road.

Watching the pair slog off through the clutching grass, Duncan performed the sign of the cross over his chest and drew Glenda in close.

"Not that that's done anyone any good this last week," she said, wiping at the tear slowly tracking down her cheek. "For Oliver, especially."

Chapter 2

Walking at a measured pace, heads on a swivel and aware of their surroundings, Cade and Raven made the inner fence in under fifteen minutes.

Scaling the chest-high fence was going to be no easy task considering the hail clinging to it in places. After determining no dead things awaited them in the bushes flanking the road on the other side, Cade unslung his rifle and threaded it through the fence, careful to keep the muzzle pointed in a safe direction during the entire process. He did the same with Raven's carbine and then clasped his hands and offered them to her to use as a sort of stirrup.

"Can't we just open the gate?"

"Keys are in the compound," he answered. "Just pretend you're in boot camp."

Raven shook her head at the offered leg-up. Instead, grunting from displeasure more than exertion, she stepped up on the middle horizontal crossbar and hooked her left leg over the uppermost part of the gate. Then, making it look easy, she snaked her left arm across the top and pulled her small frame to the opposite side in one fluid motion.

"That move would have made my first drill sergeant proud."

Already scanning the road and steadily encroaching forest ahead for any kind of threats, Raven said, "What was his name?"

Following the same basic procedure Raven had, Cade hauled his five-ten, hundred-and-eighty-pound frame over.

"Why couldn't my DS have been a she?" he asked, wicking the accumulated moisture from his fatigues.

"I know how the world worked back then," she said, handing over the M4, muzzle to the ground. "And not much has changed now."

Save for telling Raven about the crazy Adrian woman who had killed Oliver—something that he was going to have to do, eventually—Cade had no rebuttal to that.

Bracketed on both sides by wet undergrowth and skeletal bramble runners, the pair began to walk the gravel feeder road, keeping to the grassy center strip where their tracks wouldn't show. A couple of minutes passed and Raven said, "Even in the zombie apocalypse I've noticed that the women are still doing the dishes and darning clothes."

The dishes part was your doing, young miss, he thought, but held his tongue on the subject. Instead, he said, "Who knows, maybe one day you and Sasha will be running the show here."

Raven slowed her gait. "What about you? Duncan? Glenda and the others? You all planning on dying on me, too?"

"Bird, I'm going to fight until I draw my last breath," he said softly. "It's what we Graysons do."

Raven said nothing to that. Just kept putting one boot in front of the other with metronomic precision, the crunching cadence the only thing rising above the encroaching silence.

***

They made better time getting from the middle gate to the main gate paralleling State Route 39 than they did on the first leg of the feeder road. Seeing the foliage-covered netting and dark wood lattice hanging from the hidden gate, Cade motioned for Raven to move to the shadows beside the road while he went forward to investigate.

Cade found the gate locked and undisturbed. He peered through a seam in the camouflage blind and saw the road running left to right along the fence line. Because of the recent deluge, it was one unending strip of white for as far as he could see in both directions—a mile or so in total.

Across the two-lane was the knoll where their dead were buried. Too many for him to count without giving it serious thought. Though he could see the three new graves in his mind's eye—Brook's, then Foley's, and finally Oliver's on the far right—there was nothing pointing to the fact that the unkempt patch of white and green and brown was a graveyard. There were no crosses or stones bearing names and dates. The important details were kept written down in a ledger in the compound. And, at present, the date of Brook's death was the only one he could recall. In fact, though it was just days removed, he'd never forget October 28th for as long as he lived.

He looked back to Raven. Though she was only a dozen feet away, he could read the question in her eyes: *Can we?*

With a subtle move of his head, he summoned her over. "Not now," he whispered.

"Why not?"

"You tell me," he said, craning to see the road.

A contemplative look fell over Raven's features. She stood shoulder to elbow with her dad, staring at the knoll for a long moment. Finally, she said, "Because our tracks crossing the road and going up the hill will be a dead giveaway if a breather comes along."

Suppressing a smile born of a father's pride, Cade nodded.

"This way," Raven said, striking off west while staying just inside the fence line. "I know a game trail we can follow to the far corner of the property. It dives deeper into the forest from there. Or, we can follow the road from there. It should be free of hail on the shoulders under the tree overhang."

That's my girl.

"My thoughts exactly," he said. "No telling when this storm system will pass. Better to be safe—"

"Than sorry," she finished, whispering the words over one shoulder.

***

Keeping up with Raven wasn't the issue. Dodging the small boughs and reaching bramble runners she was sweeping from their path with her rifle barrel was. Twice he was whipped across the face by the seemingly spring-loaded obstructions.

Raven whispered, "Why are we going to the roadblock?"

"Just keeping an eye on things," he replied, blinking away the sting from the slap of another incoming barrage of wet leaves. "That's all."

In reality, the reason for the increased vigilance of the past few days was the sudden arrival of a survivor with no known local ties and a very suspect backstory. That Bridgett was a self-professed loner and had purportedly driven through the area where Elvis detonated Bishop's nuke and showed no signs of radiation exposure set Cade's bullshit alarm a'jangling. Keeping to herself after undergoing a lengthy questioning session and then being offered a place to stay before moving on didn't help to endear her to the group. Which was why Cade had ordered everyone to keep their eyes on her. Save for visits to the pit toilets and when she was in her rack, she'd had little alone time.

Raven stopped and put her gloved hand on the corner fence post. To her right, the barbed wire fencing disappeared into the verdant forest. To her left the road entered a treed stretch and was lost from view rather quickly.

"What's in your pack?"

She made a pretty good drum roll sound with her tongue, then said, "Now for part one of bushcraft training." She shrugged her pack off, opened the top compartment, and removed the items from inside one at a time.

"An MRE and a couple of bottles of water ... that's good," Cade noted.

"I snuck an extra thirty-round magazine." She patted the backpack's still-zippered front pouch.

Cade nodded. *Good thinking.* "What's with the Stephen King paperback?" he asked, one brow arched.

"I brought it to read when you stop to rest your ankle."

"My ankle's nearly one hundred percent, you little Smart Alec. Good job on the packing. You can put it all back now. However," he said, his voice a near whisper, "next time might I suggest something *other* than a horror novel to read in your downtime."

Raven playfully stuck out her tongue then proceeded to return the items from where she had taken them. Finished, she stood and shouldered her pack. Then, letting her rifle dangle from its sling, she said, "Let me guess, part two of the bushcraft test comes when we get to the roadblock. I have a feeling you're going to make me help you cull any Zs that we find there."

"Do you have a problem with that?"

"Do I get to use this?" Raven patted her new rifle. "Or this?" She drew the knife from the leather scabbard resting against her right thigh.

"That," Cade said, indicating the item in her hand. He had personally liberated the blade from the quarry compound weeks ago with the sole intent of making it hers one day. The handle was fashioned from a length of polished antler. The blade was six inches long and tapered to a fine dagger-like point. If he had to describe it: two parts Daniel Boone (the leather and bone components) and one part Arkansas Toothpick (the blade, which was in a style said to have been designed by James Black of Bowie knife fame) would just about do it. It fit her to a "T," and though she had yet to use it against the dead, the time loomed nearer with each westward step.

Chapter 3

Tran was focused on the particular rectangle on the flat panel showing the Winnebago and small congregation of survivors—Bridgett now among them—when in his side vision something registering as a light-colored blur passed by the camera trained east down SR-39. By the time he shifted his gaze to the partition displaying the feed from the west-facing camera, a light-colored pickup had entered its field of view and was already retreating down the center of the hail-covered two-lane. Blossoming behind the truck was a turbid slipstream that obscured all but the fact that there were a pair of head-shaped blobs visible through the dirt-rimmed rear glass.

Still staring at the two panes displaying the tire tracks bisecting the once-virgin blanket of white painting 39, Tran plucked a Motorola from the desk in front of him and thumbed the Talk button. "Cade … Raven, Tran here. How copy?"

While waiting for the reply, Tran noticed a ripple of movement in the crowd of survivors topside. Then he saw Duncan, standing under the awning and wearing the ubiquitous white cowboy hat, pluck a radio from a pocket and bring it up to his mouth.

Expecting to hear Duncan's soft drawl, instead, Tran heard Cade say, "Good copy, Tran. What's up?"

Tran quickly rattled off the pertinent details. Which were basic, but all he could provide.

Topside, Duncan regarded the stunned looks on the faces of the others. There had been no mistaking the engine growl and hiss of radials carrying on the crisp morning air. After looking a question at the others, to a person, they all agreed the sound had come from the direction of the distant state route.

Hearing Tran hail Cade, Duncan took the radio from his pocket and was about to respond when Cade broke in over the channel.

Lifting his thumb from the Talk key, Duncan locked eyes with Glenda and listened intently as Tran described the vehicle and personnel in minimal detail. He was already rolling the volume up when Cade came back on and described where he was and indicated he could hear the vehicle drawing near.

Having opted to scale the fence and walk the road under cover of the double canopy, Cade and Raven were standing on the shoulder a mile and a half west of the corner post when the radio's muted warble sounded in Cade's pocket.

The chat with Tran lasted five seconds at most. Signing off with a curt, "I hear them coming," Cade regarded the jumble of hail-dusted logs making up the roadblock two hundred feet west of him. Pressing their element-ravaged bodies against the formidable head-high mound of fallen old-growth were the dozen or so shamblers Tran had reported seeing pass by the compound entrance earlier. Holding a finger to his lips, Cade motioned for Raven to come to him. Then, praying the dead couldn't hear the faint hiss of the approaching vehicle, he plucked his daughter off the shoulder, deposited her on the opposite side of the knee-high guardrail, and clambered over to join her.

Grabbing Raven's hand, Cade slowly backed away, eyes never leaving the Zs. As they melted into the wet undergrowth, the engine growl increased exponentially, which meant the person at the wheel of the unseen vehicle was taking advantage of the lack of hail and accelerating down the nearby straightaway. Looking to Raven, he said in a low voice, "They have no idea what's about to happen."

"What do you mean?" she asked.

Jaw taking on the familiar granite set, he said, "Just watch."

The engine roar didn't lessen one iota as the vehicle neared the end of the heavily wooded stretch of road. When the silver Toyota Tundra exited the forest and no downshifting was happening, it was clear to Cade and Raven that the driver had yet to realize the road ahead was blocked by tons of formerly standing firs and pines, let alone the small herd of walking dead trapped this side of it.

Just prior to the first high-pitched howl of automobile rubber trying to find purchase on the hail-slickened road, Cade heard the distinctive *click* of Raven throwing her rifle's selector to Fire. In the next beat, with the beefy 4x4 beginning to slew sideways a dozen feet in front of their roadside hide, Cade thumbed his rifle "hot," snugged it to his shoulder, and tracked the slow-moving train wreck through the M4's EOTech optics.

Voice raised to be heard over the cacophony, Cade said, "Don't open fire unless—"

"*Unless?*" interrupted Raven. "You meant *when*, right?"

As Cade let Raven's unexpected response sink in, the Tundra began to slow and right itself in relation to the centerline. "Fire *only* if I do," he finally reiterated. "And aim for the tires. I'll concentrate on the breathers."

By the time Cade returned his attention to the slowing rig, only a couple of seconds had elapsed and the Zs were fully aware of the approaching vehicle as well as the potential meal of fresh meat inside. In unison, the creatures whipped their heads around and slowly got their bodies to follow. The sudden about-face set twelve heads' worth of matted, ratty hair flying. In turn, the whip effect sent a spray of ice pellets airborne.

"Now?" asked Raven once the pickup had come to a complete stop broadside to the shambling zombies.

For a long couple of seconds the truck's throaty exhaust note competed with the usual noises created by a pack of Zs on the move: throaty rasps; feet (some bare, most shod in road-beaten shoes) slapping a cadence on the wet pavement. The sodden clothes draping their emaciated, rotting bodies swishing out a rhythm in tune with their clumsy gaits.

Before Cade could answer her, sharp reports of dead hands impacting the hood and passenger-side sheet-metal drew his attention. Soon, the four-door pickup was under full assault and rocking subtly on its lifted suspension.

Cade fixed a business-like gaze on Raven. "Fools rush in," he said. "For now, we observe."

Shooting him her best *I'm no fool* look, Raven hunkered down on her backside and braced the rifle's forestock on one upthrust knee. Peering over the carbine, she watched the pickup's driver-side window roll down a few inches. Then a cheek pressed the glass and a plume of blue-gray smoke roiled from within the vehicle.

Laughter followed.

In seconds the cab was filled up with smoke.

Peals of laughter sounded as the window pulsed down and more smoke billowed out.

When the front edge of the drifting cloud reached their hide, Raven crinkled her nose and said, "That smells like skunk."

Cade mimed zipping his lips. He turned an ear toward the idling truck, trying to pick up snippets of a muted conversation between the Zs' dry rasps. After listening hard for a spell, all he heard was a retort that conveyed how amazed one of them was at how close they'd come to crashing into the roadblock. Then, clear as day, he heard the driver say: "We better call this in."

The scrabbling of nails on the truck's sides continued for a few seconds. Then another cloud of smoke issued from the passenger's side window and rolled over the heads of the dead.

A minute or so after coming to the screeching halt, the truck began a slow roll backward with the dead in full pursuit. When the rig was about even with the spot in the road where Cade and Raven had crossed over the guardrail, the engine roared and it accelerated sharply.

"Looks like two women," said Raven, as she tracked the vehicle's right-to-left movement with her rifle.

Cade glanced at the pewter sky. It was once again pressing down on them, the clouds scudding by so fast they seemed to possess some otherworldly form of propulsion. He said, "Or long-haired men. Hard to tell in this light and behind that dark of a window tint."

"The voices were female," she insisted. "No doubt about that. Can we hit them now?"

As she uttered that last part, Cade detected equal measures of fear and confidence in her tone. Shaking his head *no*, he put a hand on the Colt's top rail and gently forced the muzzle down a few degrees. Remaining silent, he extracted the radio from a pocket, thumbed the Talk button, and conveyed everything he had just learned to Tran back at the compound.

As Tran came on to confirm the relayed information, a low rumble sounded overhead and the sky opened up again. With a new onslaught of pea-sized hail pelting the bushes all around him, Cade made it clear to Tran and anyone listening in that they were not to engage the interlopers unless it could not be avoided.

"Shouldn't we try to follow them?" asked Tran.

"No need," said Duncan, cutting in over the open channel.

"Stand pat," Cade said agreeably. "We'll be back in twenty or so."

"Dad?" called Raven.

"One second, sweetie," he said, flashing her his open palm as he watched the Tundra's driver perform a near-perfect Bootlegger's reverse—spinning the truck around in a one-eighty by applying a great deal of brake and a rapid hand-over-hand wrenching of the steering wheel.

"Dad?"

"Roger that," said Tran. "I'll be looking for you."

Cade watched the truck fishtail as it accelerated into the forested tunnel. Once he was certain the hasty retreat wasn't just to create some separation from the dead, he said, "Roger that, Tran," and pocketed the radio. When he turned to hear what Raven had to say, he saw that she was up and walking along the curving guardrail, the distance to the throng of jostling Zs already cut in half.

"We don't have time to do this," he called.

Leaning over the guardrail, shiny blade pointed skyward at a forty-five-degree angle, Raven replied, "Just one or two, Dad. I want to see what it feels like."

"Raven, don't——." He didn't get a chance to finish the admonition. The Arkansas Toothpick had already drawn blood and the female zombie was crumpling fast to the shoulder where it settled in a heap of sharp, bony angles. One eye socket leaked brackish blood and its lips were mashed against the blacktop, leaving the death mask in a permanent, lopsided scowl. The corpse's jean shorts rode up much farther than humanly possible and what was left of a tattered and torn tank top clung to its ribcage like an old and bloodied length of gauze bandage.

Not finished, Raven chided the nearest Z by telling it to "Come to Mama." Holding the blade loosely in her right hand, she caught its attention by waving her off-hand at the thing like a Toreador might a bull.

"Finish that one and come on," Cade said, exasperation evident in his voice. *Strong-willed, just like the one who bore you.*

A call from Tran emanated from the radio in Cade's pocket. "The pickup just passed the front gate heading back toward Woodruff."

Or Bear Lake, thought Cade. Ever since listening to Duncan and the other's accounts of their failed rescue mission north, he couldn't stop thinking about how poorly they had performed in the aftermath. How Duncan had balked when confronted with the fact that the job had been left unfinished. And now his gut was telling him the duo in the Tundra had some kind of a connection to the murderous cannibals Duncan had seen fit to let scatter into the wind.

"Send Lev and Seth to check the entrance. Have them go by foot and armed for bear."

"Copy that," said Tran.

"And, Tran," added Cade.

"Yes?"

"Have everyone roll their radio channels forward to the next one on the list."

"Will do."

Cade ended the call. Before stowing the radio, he changed the channel and sub channel to match the next one on a list he'd been keeping in his front pocket. Finished, he struck out ahead of Raven, moving fast and quiet, careful, as she followed in his wake, to not give her the same, constant wet-flora-to-the-face treatment he'd endured during their trek to the roadblock.

Chapter 4

Cade emerged from the underbrush a dozen feet from the fencepost bordering the westernmost edge of the property. He cast his gaze to the stretch of 39 running away to the east and was pleasantly surprised to see that instead of obscuring evidence of the truck's passage, the second cloudburst had merely thickened the ground coverage. In turn, the returning tire tracks were more pronounced, and thus much easier to follow.

"We've got to triple time it, Raven," said Cade, as he struck off for the feeder road at a steady jog.

Breathing hard, a dull ache emanating from deep within her still-healing punctured lung, Raven clutched the rifle to her chest and matched her father's pace.

***

Reaching the camouflaged gate, Cade didn't stop. In fact, he found another gear and kept it going for fifty yards or so before craning over his shoulder and clomping to a halt, straddling the strip of grass splitting the feeder road.

Just making the turn, Raven was moving sluggishly, one arm beating her side, the other clutching the rifle which looked to be battering her across the thighs with each labored stride.

Breath coming evenly, Cade jogged back the way he'd come. Stopping just short of his leaden-footed offspring, he motioned to Raven with a rapid wagging of his fingers—universal semaphore for *hand it over.*

She shook her head side-to-side. Gasped, "I got it."

"Not what your body language is saying." Despite her continued protests, Cade unclipped her rifle and relieved her of the backpack. Without a word, he turned and resumed his latest pace. Confident Raven could keep up sans the fifteen pounds he was now shouldering, he stopped and looked only when he arrived at the middle gate.

By the time Raven rendezvoused at the gate, only twenty seconds had passed. During that time, Cade had hailed the compound and had Tran pass on his hastily thrown-together plan.

A quick glance at his Suunto told him the driver of the Tundra already had a twenty-three-minute head start to wherever she was going. His best guess had them enjoying a luxurious thirty-minute lead by the time he and Raven reached the clearing.

***

Everyone save for Tran, Lev, and Seth were standing in a rough semi-circle near the Winnebago when Cade and Raven broke into the clearing. The RV's awning was nearly resting on Duncan's Stetson. Glenda was by his side, bolt-action long gun in hand.

At once Wilson and Taryn turned toward the sound of boots crunching on hail-coated gravel. Then, leaving Sasha behind, the pair strode purposefully in Cade and Raven's direction.

As hot and cold air collided high overhead, a low, ominous rumble rolled across the valley.

Gulping air, Cade slowed his gait and eventually came to a full stop, doubled over with his palms planted on his knees. Resting there behind the Raptor and F-650, he ran his gaze over the slowly dissolving congregation and picked up on a couple things of interest. First, their newest member, Bridgett, was on the periphery of the small gathering and was looking his way. Dressed in stiff new Levi 501s and sporting a flannel shirt complete with the obligatory down-filled vest riding over it, she stood out like a sore thumb among the others, who wore a smattering of camouflage and earth-tone articles of clothing. On the quick visual pass, he also saw that Duncan had the fully automatic Saiga shotgun slung over one shoulder. The weapon's curved magazine, stuffed with twenty shotgun shells—likely alternated slug, shot, slug, shot—protruded from behind the man's desert-tan, thigh-length jacket. That he wore a pair of rawhide gloves and had his black Model 1911 Colt pistol riding low in a drop-thigh holster all but screamed *I'm coming along.*

Looking sidelong toward the Winnebago—hands now on his hips and his breathing coming to him somewhat normally—Cade said to Raven, "I want you to stick close to Glenda while I'm gone. And keep an eye on the new one. I'm still not sold on her story."

"Me neither," said Raven. "She's got shifty eyes. And she eats *way* more than her fair share."

Seeing Duncan and the Kids stalking him, Cade wiped his brow and stood tall.

"What about this?" Raven patted her new rifle.

"It's yours. Take care of it." A quick glance confirmed the stubby Colt was still on Safe. As he went through the ritual of checking his weapon, he said, "I'll help you break it down and clean it when I return."

"Already know how. Mom taught me." She paused and smiled assuredly. "I'm pretty quick at it, too."

Throat closing up on him, Cade wrapped her in a tight embrace. Planting a kiss atop her stocking cap, he said, "She taught you well, Bird."

Mercifully sparing Cade from breaking down in front of the one who needed most to see him project strength, Duncan strode right into their personal space and asked, "Ford or ... Ford?"

The funny quip not producing so much as a half-smile, Cade shook his head. "I'm going solo ... in the F-650. And I'm going now," he fished the fob with the blue Ford oval from his breast pocket, "because the trail is getting hot."

Having just arrived on Duncan's heels, head cocked, Wilson said, "Hot? I thought trails usually went *cold.*"

"Eventually the sun is going to crack those clouds and the hail on the road is going to melt. When it does I won't have anything to follow." Cade watched Raven approach Glenda. Due to the fact that she was still pissed at being sedated the night Brook finally succumbed to Omega, his daughter's body language was a little chilly: crossed arms clutching her rifle to her chest.

Stiff-legged gait. Lips pressed into a thin white line. That Raven had been kicking things and cussing up a storm when she was barred from seeing her mom on the '*night of*' had made it necessary. Still, Glenda was in Raven's "dog house," a saying the twelve-year-old had only recently learned from hearing the older lady utter it in regard to one of Duncan's many minor transgressions.

"I've got a big dog in this fight," Duncan growled. With a firm set to his jaw, he looped around the F-650, opened the door, and hauled himself up and into the passenger seat.

Calling after him, through clenched teeth, Cade said, "Get out."

Duncan made no reply.

Cade opened the driver's side door to the sound of a seat belt clicking home. When he slid behind the wheel, he saw Duncan facing him, much of the same body language Raven had exhibited on full display: crossed arms. Mouth with a grim set to it. Eyes boring into his.

"I'm going," Duncan asserted. "You're gonna have to shoot me and push my carcass out."

Cade turned the key, setting the engine to rumbling. A pair of sounds caught his attention. Two subtle metallic creaks. One right after the other. A tick later, two solid thunks sounded behind him. One from either side of the truck.

"Look at what the cat drug in," said Duncan. Suppressing a cackle, he shifted his gaze from Cade to the back seat where Taryn and Wilson were stowing gear and buckling in.

Sitting with both hands gripping the wheel, arms tensed and ramrod-straight, Cade looked at the pair in the rearview mirror. "Two's company ... *four* is a crowd."

Taryn crossed her arms, sat back hard against the seat, and peered out her window.

After a split-second of eye contact with Cade via the mirror, Wilson pulled the brim of his boonie hat down low over his eyes and locked his door.

Cade regarded Duncan. "I can move faster and quieter alone."

"A fella can die that way faster, too."

Cade relaxed a bit and threw the transmission into Drive. Then, with an icy silence hanging in the cab, he carved a wide looping left turn in the tall grass and, without looking back at the folks seeing them off, spurred the Ford ahead toward the cut in the forest.

Chapter 5

Tran had just witnessed Bridgett peel away from the small group loitering in the clearing when the Ford F-650 filled up a partition on the flat panel and rolled to a stop a few feet from the middle gate. He watched Wilson exit the vehicle and stride around the truck's massive front end, momentarily disappearing from view.

A knock on the compound's main door drew Tran's attention to the gloomy foyer. Leaning back and craning to the left, he bellowed, "Be there in a moment." When he returned his attention to the monitor, the black truck had pulled through the gate and the redhead was securing it with a length of chain and padlock. A half-beat later the Ford was barreling down the feeder road. Still, he made Bridgett wait another minute while he snatched up the long-range CB radio and told the survivors in the truck that the road by the main gate was clear of rotters and breathers. Another few raps rang against the steel door while Wilson performed the same routine at the hidden gate fronting the glazed-over state route. Then, close on the heels of Bridgett's second subtle barrage, a new flurry of knocks—louder and more insistent—crashed off the security container's metal walls.

Once Duncan called back confirming the group was *Oscar Mike* (on the move in military speak) and Tran saw the truck disappearing from view eastbound on 39, he took Taryn's iPhone down from the shelf and thumbed in the unlock code. He tapped the screen a couple of times and replaced the device on the shelf, leaving it propped up lengthwise against some HAM radio manuals he'd prepositioned there.

Another flurry of sonorous bangs echoed throughout the underground compound. "Coming," he muttered as he rose up off the chair. With a little pep in his step, he covered the dozen feet to the door, getting there and throwing the lock before Bridgett had a chance to knock again.

"Shit, little man. I was freezing my tits off out there!" barked Bridgett just as soon as Tran had the door open. She loomed a head taller and stood there for a second looking down on him.

Ignoring the attempted intimidation, Tran brushed past her and locked them in. Forgoing any kind of greeting, he padded back to his post and found the woman standing before the monitor with her wide frame blocking his passage. After clearing his throat, he said, "Excuse me, I'd like to sit."

Tearing her gaze from the electronic items piled on the chest-high shelf running the length of the plywood desk, she looked down on him again and shuffled a few inches to her right.

Trying to make small talk, he asked, "What are the others doing?"

The cordial attitude Bridgett exhibited when around Duncan, Cade, and, to a lesser extent, Glenda, was nowhere to be found now as she sneered, "Most of them are standing around and jawing like a bunch of old women. The two Army dudes are out for a little *walk* in the woods." She chuckled at the last part.

"Lev and Seth," Tran said to himself as he ran his eyes over the monitor. "Lev's former Army. Seth is … not sure. I know he isn't former military. And your insinuation is all wrong. Neither one of them favors the company of men."

As if he sensed he was being talked about, Lev called on the two-way to let Tran know the outer fence was clear and the party was safely away.

"Rotters?" Tran asked.

"We haven't come across any inside the wire. There are more than usual outside, though. Saw a dozen or so east of the entrance … but they turned to follow the 650."

"Roger that. When are you coming back?"

"We're just going to walk the fence line for a while. Twenty or thirty minutes, tops."

"Copy that. Tran, out."

While Lev was signing off, Bridgett grabbed a folding chair from where it had been propped against the wall. With an unwarranted flourish, she snapped it open, spun it around backwards, and then plopped down hard on it. With her substantial backside sticking out one end and arms folded and resting on the flat metal back-rest, she completely blocked the narrow pathway through the Conex container.

"I hate to change the subject," she said, reaching across the desk and breaking herself off a substantial hunk of the MRE pound cake Tran had been eating. "But I'm gonna." She popped the purloined hunk of dessert into her mouth whole and chewed noisily.

Without looking away from the monitor, Tran urged her to speak her mind.

"You know, I'm tired of being a *watcher*. Just sitting on my ass and letting you all go merrily about your daily business is so boring. I'm a *doer* by nature, Tran my man."

Holding up a hand, Tran said, "Duncan and Daymon are allowed to call me that. Not you."

She went on, "Anyway, I just want to help. I know I asked you to go to bat for me yesterday ..."

Tran glanced at her for a brief second. "I may have."

"If you didn't, I'm going to jump the chain of command and ask the boss man myself."

Tran said nothing. On the screen before him, Glenda, Jamie, Sasha, and Raven were slowly working their way across the clearing. That they were arranged tallest to shortest wasn't lost on him. He couldn't blame the youngest—and shortest—of the group for wanting to be on the periphery; it was where he preferred to find himself—always had.

"Well, did you or did you not talk to your friend ... the one who's running the show here?" Bridgett swiped some more of the pound cake, adding it to the mouthful she was still working on.

Tran nodded and swung his gaze around to her.

Sending tiny pieces of cake raining down on the table, Bridgett blurted, "What the eff did he say?"

"I've been cleared to start training you." He rolled the chair back a foot and rose. "Sit here. Watch the monitors. You see *anything* on the road here, here ... or here"—he pointed to the three corresponding rectangles on the grid—"you pick up the two-way and let me know."

Taken aback by the sudden capitulation, she rose from the folding chair. "Where are *you* going?" she asked, settling her butt on the plush rolling chair.

"To relieve myself," he said, scooping up his Beretta and pocketing a Motorola. "Be right back."

"Happy squirtin'," she said to his back as he walked through the blackout curtain. "Want me to lock the door behind you?"

Tran paused in the foyer, hand on the door. "Of course," he said, the beginning of a smirk forming. "It's our new standard operating procedure. And you *better* keep out of dry storage. We're nearly out of pound cake."

In no time, Bridgett was at the door, wearing a guilty look. She pantomimed crossing her heart and said, "Hope to die. No more pound cake for this girl."

Hook, line, and sinker, thought Tran as the metallic *rasp* and *snik* of the lock being engaged reached his ears. *Time to bring the others up to speed.*

Chapter 6

In the F-650, Cade was keeping the speedometer needle hovering near the posted forty miles per hour. From the compound entrance to the partially overgrown feeder road leading to the upper quarry, not a word had passed between he and Duncan. Periodic glances in the rearview, however, told him that in the backseat Taryn and Wilson were having an entire conversation delivered via looks and hand gestures.

"Playing charades back there?" Cade finally asked, only to be met with a pair of guilt-ridden expressions. Taryn shook her head side-to-side. Wilson broke eye contact first. He removed his hat, placed it in his lap, and lowered his gaze.

"Let's address the thousand-pound elephant riding with us," said Cade, sweeping his gaze from the rearview mirror and settling it on Duncan.

"I weigh two ... two-twenty max, now," Duncan said. "All this running around and avoiding dead things is getting me back into fighting shape."

"Jenny Craig has nothing on the MRE weight-loss plan," quipped Wilson.

"Cut the shit," said Cade, slapping a palm on the wheel. "You all have been walking on eggshells around me since—"

"Since you had to put down your wife of thirteen years," interrupted Duncan. "You expect us to act as if nothing happened? She was a strong, capable woman we all grew to know and like. Hell, I loved her like a daughter. You're a pretty withdrawn individual, Cade. Out of all the men I've known over the years, yours was the toughest nut to crack. Sometimes I feel like I'm prying at a damn Brazil nut with a cooked spaghetti noodle."

Taryn and Wilson no longer wore looks of embarrassment. They were now watching wide-eyed and hanging on every word in the so-far one-sided conversation.

Cade didn't acknowledge Duncan's use of humor. Deep down he didn't begrudge the man for it, either.

"To be honest," Duncan added, "though we've been through a lot of crap together, up until I flew you into Idaho on your warpath to kill Bishop you had a barrier the size of the Great Wall of China thrown up between you and me."

Cade grimaced. "That obvious?"

Duncan nodded. "Oh, it's been coming down brick by brick since then. Really started to crumble when we fixed the roadblock at the Ogden pass and solved that problem. Hell, we were thinking alike as if we were a couple of Siamese twins when we took down Oliver at Glenda's place in Huntsville."

"Conjoined," corrected Wilson.

Though Duncan wanted to bonk the younger man over the head for continuing on with the political correctness bullshit, he instead swiveled around and shot the redhead a look that said *butt out*.

"And?" said Cade.

"And," continued Duncan, "ever since you set Brook *free* you've been stacking those terra cotta bricks back up. You keep on keeping to yourself like you've been … it's going to start rubbing off on Raven."

"I'm trying to prepare her for—" Cade began.

"For when you buy the farm," Duncan finished. "I get it. But I also have a feeling you've got an army of Guardian Angels watching over you. Mark my words"—he began to nod slowly—"you're going to be giving away Raven's hand in marriage one day. Have that first dance with her and all that jazz."

"Let's not get ahead of ourselves," Cade growled, his jagged knuckles gone white and looking like barnacles affixed to the wheel.

"Let us help you, Cade. Let us in. You need to learn how to *communicate*," said Duncan, the last word drawn out for an extra beat. "That thing you and Tran have going with Bridgett is brilliant. Almost as good as when me and Logan ran that good cop/bad cop routine on the Chance kid." He cackled and doubled over. "Priceless."

Grimacing, Cade said, "Tran told you?"

Duncan nodded. "He told me last night. Tran The Man and me are pretty tight. All it took was for someone to show a little trust in him. Newsflash … that boy is no longer working on his Pacifist merit badge."

"Doesn't matter who he tells," said Cade, a rare half-smile curling his lip. "I told him we're trying to catch our food thief. He was more than happy to help."

"If you're not trying to catch Bridgett stealing food …" Duncan looked out the window at the trees blipping by and caught a glimpse of the turbid Ogden River roiling along as it would for time immemorial. After a long moment spent in silent thought, he asked, "What the hell are you fishing for then?"

"Someone messed with Brook's sat phone two days ago. I found it unplugged and nearly out of battery."

"Sure you didn't just forget to plug it in?" Duncan asked.

Cade shook his head. "I was moving on autopilot that night. But I'm certain I powered it down and plugged it in before putting it up on that shelf."

Duncan exhaled sharply. "All this went down the very same day we let Bridgett out of quarantine." He knuckled the brim of his Stetson up an inch. Fixing a concerned look on Cade, he said, "I'm guessing no calls were placed on it?"

Cade glanced over. "Thankfully, no," he said. "It was locked. To set the trap I disabled the lock code on one of the other Thuraya last night."

"She *has* been acting kind of weird," Taryn proffered. "And now it makes sense you borrowing my iPhone. I thought that was unlike you when you asked. Raven has borrowed it more times than I can count. First time for you. Or anyone else for that matter."

Wilson parked his elbows on the seatback near Duncan's head. "Now that I think about it," he said in a low voice, "if that woman's not in her quarters or on the *crapper*, she's in the security container hovering over whoever's watching the camera feeds."

"We'll know soon enough via operation 'pound cake' if she's up to no good or just trying to stuff her gullet," said Duncan.

"If it turns out to be the former," Cade said, slowing to avoid a lone walker tottering out from the shoulder, "we'll get everyone together and quickly decide on an appropriate course of action."

While humming the first few bars of a once popular tune, Duncan sang, "Breaking rocks in the hot sun—"

"—I fought the law, and the law won," Cade finished. "How appropriate." His face broke into a rare smile that stayed put as he focused his attention on following the chevron-patterned tire tracks imprinted into the slowly disappearing sheen of white blanketing 39. Just as the lower quarry road and bullet-riddled sign announcing its presence blipped by and he was steering the rig into a sweeping left-hand turn, he spotted a host of splayed-out corpses blocking his lane. After braking hard and slewing the truck to the left to avoid running over the prostrate bodies—an unexpected action that elicited gasps from the backseat and sent Duncan scrabbling to get his hand to the grab bar near his head—he let his gaze wander the scene.

Judging by the tire tracks leading up to the grisly sight, whoever was driving the vehicle responsible had deviated only slightly, the calmly conducted maneuver causing the fading tracks to tick left, not unlike the blip scribed on a seismograph by a small, yet wholly unexpected earthquake. Clearly one of the rotters was down for good. Spread-eagled and unmoving on the centerline, its head surrounded by a spreading crimson miasma, the cause of death looked to have been a meeting of its mind with a speeding vehicle's high-rising grill. Clumped gray meninges and hair-covered skull spattered the road in a growing arc of gore from where its head had started the journey to where it had finally come to rest atop a pillow of plowed-up hail.

Flesh and bone being no match for rigid skid plates and knobby off-road tires, the other two had been reduced to crawlers after what Cade guessed had been a thorough tumble beneath the Tundra's undercarriage.

"I need to get something off my chest," Duncan said, bouncing in his seat as the F-650 rolled over one of the creature's outstretched arms.

Cade looked to his right and caught his friend worrying his new shotgun's nylon sling. "You drinking again?" he asked, concern evident in his voice.

"No," blurted Duncan. He removed his hat and ran an unsteady hand through his thinning, gray hair. "I wasn't compromised when I decided to take in the pound puppy. After I damn near plowed into her car ... which was surrounded by rotters by the way, I just flipped a coin in my head." He went silent again.

"And?" asked Cade, eyes locked on the winding road ahead.

Before answering, Duncan thought back to that late July day when this madness started. That day, sitting in his old Dodge with a clear view of the Columbia River and the glittering Vista House, he'd done the same thing. Only that time he had chosen to act against the results of his mental coin toss. And as a result, instead of continuing on to Utah alone, he had driven down to the stone and glass landmark perched above Interstate 84 and introduced himself to old Harry and the blonde twins (their names still escaped him)—which led to him joining up with the man to his left and eventually meeting the Kids in the backseat. What a trickster Fate was. If only he'd gone against the mental toss on the return trip from Bear Lake.

Taryn reached over the seat and gave Duncan's shoulder a soft squeeze. Rubbing his back in a platonic way, she asked, "You OK?"

"It was Bridgett's lucky day," was Duncan's response.

Free of the debris field, Cade mashed the pedal, hoping to get to the 39/16 junction before the sun threatening to break the clouds had a chance to fully emerge. Glancing sidelong at

41

Duncan, he asked, "Why'd you feel the need to give her a chance?"

"Because I had two dead bodies in the back of the rig I was driving ... Oliver and Foley," answered Duncan. "Couldn't see leaving a fellow breather to the mercy of those rotten things."

"There is no longer a *high road*," said Cade. He went on to tell the others what he'd done to the Chinese soldier who had not so eloquently told him and his team to go fuck their mothers. Described the gurgling noise escaping his throat as the Gerber ground through and finally rasped sharply against vertebra. "I didn't want to stop there. If I'd been alone, nothing would have kept me from removing that fucker's head clean from his body and hurling it into the trees. Not a thing."

"Everyone is an enemy," said Wilson. "Is that what you're getting at?"

Cade said nothing. It was way more complicated than that. Opening the stage for an argument on humanities was the last thing on his mind.

Duncan glimpsed a flash of color around the next turn. "Slow down," he implored. "We're coming up on where we left Bridgett's car."

Sure enough, the overloaded compact was revealed in tiny slices as the F-650 cut the corner at a crawl. The driver's side door was still yawning open and a pair of Zs stood wavering just a couple of yards from the inert vehicle.

When Duncan powered his window down, the competing growl of the engine and hollow roar of the nearby river came rushing in.

"The tire tracks continue on around the car," Taryn noted. "Why not stop to check it for supplies?"

Duncan craned over his right shoulder to get a clear look as the car and its undead protectors slid by. "I'd bet they did on the way in. Frick and Frack there are just enamored with the river."

Wilson said, "Think they're acting on past memories?"

As Cade steered the big Ford out of the turn, he intoned, "I've given up trying to figure out what makes them tick."

Chapter 7

At the junction with State Route 16, where 39 jogged left and became a narrow two-lane running east toward the Bear River Range, the trail the Eden group was following did indeed go *hot* on them. All that remained of the once-distinct chevron patterns created by the Tundra as it wheeled east were tiny rectangles of compressed hail.

Tendrils of steam rose from the glistening blacktop all around as a long east to west seam opened up in the gray cloud cover. Then, like some kind of biblical painting, bars of golden light arced down from the heavens, painting a broad swath of the countryside before them in muted shades of yellow and orange.

Cade looked to his right and studied the stretch of 16 that fed south to Bear River. There were no tire tracks or remnants of compacted hail that he could see. He looked northbound along the two-lane from the intersection through the gentle jog it took to the east.

Nothing.

Voice full of confidence, Duncan said, "They turned left."

Squinting against the glare, Cade said, "And you know this, how?"

"Transition lenses, my good man." Duncan pointed north. "I can see traces of the tracks in the runoff. They're real faint. Almost look like a pair of slug tracks at this point."

Cade flipped down his visor. Then, looking at Duncan, he gestured to the glove box. "Grab my Oakleys for me, please."

After handing over the black wraparound sunglasses, Duncan said, "You don't believe me?"

"I believe you," responded Cade. "But I gotta see to drive." He donned the glasses and wheeled left.

The state route heading north became Main Street as it cut through what passed for downtown Woodruff. Back In The Saddle Rehab was coming up on the right. Across the street from the ransacked two-story business was an auto body shop. Deposited on the sidewalk and frost-heaved parking pad by the force of the migrating horde was a colorful jumble of inert cars. They were dented and dinged and had come to rest at odd angles, some of them wedged tight against the bowed-in rollup doors. Just past Back In The Saddle's elevated front porch, half-straddling the sidewalk where the horde had shoved it, was an equally abused Cadillac. Missing most of its window glass, the American icon sat forlornly in the shadow of a two-story building whose upper windows were skewered through by the top crossbars of a crazily listing power pole.

Adjacent to where Center Street jogged off to the right, Cade slowed the Ford to walking speed and looked a question at Duncan.

"In the shadows," said Duncan, pointing. "See them?"

Cade perched his sunglasses on the tip of his nose and pressed his chin to his chest to see over them. A few feet beyond the Cadillac's stretched-out front end, where Main Street was cloaked in shadow, he saw that the tracks did indeed pick back up again. He lifted his foot off the brake and drove past the Cadillac, over the glass pebbles from the destroyed windows, and continued the slow roll under an entire block's worth of utility lines stretched to their limits by the canted power poles.

Cade said, "I lost them again at the next intersection."

Duncan said, "There's still a trace in the shadow of the tree up ahead. Keep going straight."

As Cade accelerated down Main, the Ford's passing totally obliterated any trace of the melting chevrons. Once they reached the intersection Duncan had pointed to, there was no more cover and the road was but wet pavement. Here the two-lane shot off in three different directions. North, beyond the intersection, Main Street ended and State Route 16 resumed its laser-straight charge out of town. To the left were three squat homes with big front

44

yards and long driveways. Rolling cans bulging with garbage never to be hauled away crowded the undulating sidewalk. At all four corners storm drains choked with months' worth of debris were underwater, the rapidly melted hail still feeding the burgeoning pools.

On the northeast corner sat the auto fix-it shop where Taryn had nearly fallen victim to the restrained and muted zombies. A block and a half east, on the left side of the street, stood the two-story rectory and quaint whitewashed church where Adrian's people had butchered a man, nailed him to the cross, and left him to turn.

Eyes fixed on the yawning door and rotting corpses spread out before it, Taryn said, "This corner brings back nothing but bad memories."

"Tell me about it," said Wilson. "I almost became a human pin cushion."

"Bunch of babies," Duncan shot. "Neither one of you had your tongue yanked through a gaping hole in your throat like Oliver did. A bullet didn't stop your heart and shred it into a dozen pieces as one did to Foley's."

For a long ten-count the group sat in absolute silence. If it hadn't been for the steady hum of the idling engine they may as well have been surrounded by the vacuum of space.

Wilson leaned over the seatback again. With his head and upper body cutting the air between Cade and Duncan, he said, "One of you please tell me you can still see the tracks."

Duncan sighed. "Not anymore. They die right here."

"No doubt they continue north to Bear Lake," stated Cade. "Hard for me to say, but I'm confident the women in the truck were looking for the people who threw the monkey wrench in their operation."

Head turned toward Cade, Wilson said, "I'd call killing their leader and burning down their compound a little more than a 'monkey wrench in their operation.'"

Cade leaned forward a few degrees and locked eyes with Duncan. "Lev and Daymon set the fires. They told you as much, right?"

"Saw it with my own eyes."

"Me too," said Taryn.

"Real big flames and smoke," added Wilson.

Still regarding Duncan, Cade said, "You saw all of this, right?"

Duncan nodded.

Cade looked into the rearview, then met Wilson's eyes, and finally settled his gaze back on Duncan. "Who here saw the Zs sink their teeth into—"

"Adrian," said Duncan, sounding deflated. "I guess I should have just given her a Columbian Necktie and been done with it. Hell, after all the killing … and what they did to the man in the church …" He slapped the dash, causing Taryn to jump. "I couldn't let her off that easy. Besides, she was locked in the stocks. *And* she had an effen broken leg. She was going *nowhere* under her own steam."

And the pickup trucks you let drive away without engaging? thought Cade.

As if reading Cade's mind, Wilson said, "You stopped Daymon and Gregory from lighting up those people fleeing in their trucks."

"OK, OK. I let them get away. In my defense, there were innocents inside the house next to the back exit."

"You didn't know that yet," said Taryn soberly.

Duncan leaned back and covered his face with the Stetson. Voice muffled, he drawled, "Crucify me for using a little discretion. Maybe I should have popped off a couple of nukes and killed everyone in a ten-mile radius."

Sparing his friend from any more scrutiny, Cade maneuvered the Ford into a wide U-turn, bouncing over two curbs and splashing muddy water everywhere in the process.

Voice still muffled by the hat, Duncan asked, "Where we going now?"

"South," said Cade. "Now take that hat off your face so you can show me the way to Daymon's new place."

Slowly, Duncan sat forward, allowing the Stetson to fall into his lap. "What do you have planned?"

Cade said, "Figured since we're already burning fuel, it'd make sense to kill a couple more birds while we're outside the wire." He met Wilson's gaze in the rearview. "For one of the tasks, the extra muscle that weaseled its way into my truck is going to come in handy."

"Keep going south," said Duncan. "I'll tell you where to turn. While you're doing that, why dontcha come clean about what you have in mind."

"I'm curious, too," Taryn said.

"Spill," demanded Wilson.

Ignoring the trio of questioning looks aimed his way, Cade wheeled the Ford back down Main Street in the direction they'd come.

Chapter 8

"You ate every last crumb of *my* pound cake," Tran bellowed over his shoulder. Seething inside, he plopped down on the rolling chair. Then, still shivering from the topside chill, he glanced to where he'd placed the iPhone. *Still there.* Because he had a hunch of his own that Bridgett had been fooling with the electronic devices, he scanned the satellite phones and radios on the shelf. All appeared to be arranged just as he had left them. Flicking his gaze to the desktop, he came to realize two things. First, Bridgett was a slob. There were sticky fingerprints on everything. The monitor. The HAM handset and headset, which she'd likely set aside so she could get her face close enough to his food in order to Hoover it straight off the wrapper and into her gullet. Then there was the legal pad on which dozens of call signs belonging to survivors scattered around the western United States had been scrawled. It had been folded back, leaving a fresh sheet in its stead.

The clang from Bridgett shutting the door was followed by a metallic *snik* of the lock being thrown. Then the laughter started up. It emanated from the foyer, deep and sonorous, bouncing off the low ceiling and growing louder as she emerged through the blackout curtain and into the light thrown from the hanging sixty-watt bulb. Without a shred of remorse to her tone, she said, "That I did, little man. That. I. Did. I ate it up. Every last crumb. My only promise was that I wouldn't get into the goodies in the dry storage, remember?"

Though Bridgett's tone said 'What the fuck are you going to do about it?' Tran left the bait alone. He simply smiled at her and said, "Thanks." Simple as that. Only *his* tone—much like that of a boss dismissing a subordinate—inferred that she was no longer needed and she should 'carry on.' However, the opposite was true. Tran was far from done with her. In fact, as soon as he had a moment to analyze the video evidence and catch her going to the dry storage and coming back with contraband, he was going to feed her more than pound cake. He was going to jam fucking crow down her throat. Make her eat a big steaming plate of the metaphorical black raptor right in front of the rest of the group.

The former pacifist suppressed a smile as the piece of work hitched up her pants, ran the zipper on the life-preserver-looking orange vest all the way up to the copious amounts of wrinkled flesh passing for a neck, and stormed out the door without bothering to ask how she did as a *doer* or voice any concern that the door be locked behind her. Hearing the door clang shut, Tran took his eyes off the swaying fabric curtain and regarded the monitor. In the partition showing the expanse of clearing fronting the compound exit, he watched the woman stalking off through the tall grass, cutting a straight line toward the Winnebago, which, at the moment, was sitting all alone near the far tree line. He kept his attention on the monitor long enough to see her hold a short conversation with Glenda and Jamie while taking a bowl of stew from the former. Bowl in hand, Bridgett then turned and threw something into the fire pit before stalking off toward the nearby tree line.

"Bitch," he muttered as he stood and plucked the iPhone from where he'd secreted it. Phone in hand and with Max on his heels, he brushed past the curtain.

Beating Tran to the door, Max pawed at the metal and whined.

"Gotta go potty?"

The dog eyed him and placed a paw on the door.

"Ok. But stay away from Bridgett." Then, half in jest, he added, "If you don't, she might end up eating you." He cracked the door and watched Max worm through the narrow opening and pad off.

After locking himself in, Tran walked back to the security container and took his seat at the desk. Confident he was the only soul in the subterranean redoubt, he typed the security code into the phone and selected the video icon. Waiting for the video to begin, he looked at the flat panel monitor and prayed for the alone time he needed to finish his mission.

Cade had the F-650 stopped in front of the rehab place, the engine idling. He looked left for a tick. The road east out of town narrowed and rose slightly before finally becoming one with the trees flanking the Bear River Range. The dark clouds from the recent hail-producing storm were just now swarming over the low mountains.

Swiveling his head forward, his gaze was drawn to the not too distant intersection where State Route 39 spliced into 16. The yellow snout and grimy undercarriage of the ever-present overturned school bus was clearly visible just beyond the incoming stretch of 39. Resting on its side, all but its abbreviated front end occupying the roadside gutter, the fifty-seat monstrosity looked more like a beached metal whale than the makeshift barrier it used to be. With its crushed roof and blown-out windows, it now served only as a reminder to what the undead hordes wandering the highways and byways of America were capable of.

Duncan asked, "Are we paying Daymon a visit or not?"

"Which way?" asked Cade.

"Left, if my memory serves."

Nodding in agreement, Wilson pointed at the nearby street. "There are a couple of nearly identical one-level homes up the road on the right. We see those, we know we're on the right track."

"I know the ones you're speaking of," Cade said, wrenching the wheel left and accelerating through the debris-strewn intersection. "I found medicine for Heidi there. Movies for Brook and the girls, too." He went quiet and stared across Back In The Saddle Rehab's rear parking lot as it was sliding by. Lying among the shimmering puddles dotting the pocked gravel expanse were a dozen twice-dead corpses. North of the prostrate corpses were another dozen of the walking variety, their clumsy footfalls finding puddles and sending sprays of muddy water airborne.

Soon the twin plats of land on which the pair of double-wide mobile homes sat passed by on the right. And just as before, on the left, farms setback from the road and the rusting farm implements marking them scrolled on by.

"Turn right here," said Taryn, her arm shooting across the seatback at a diagonal.

"It's unmarked," Cade answered, slowing and obviously hesitant to commit the large truck to a feeder road where turning around would entail a lot of jockeying of the wheel and perhaps taking out some barbed wire fence in the process.

"Half a mile in you'll find the driveway behind a rusty sheep fence," she said.

"It doesn't look like much," admitted Duncan. "And that's the beauty of it. You'll see."

"Who do you want to call ahead?" asked Wilson, mainly directing the question at Cade.

"Duncan, you have the honors."

After cycling the Motorola to channel 10-1, Duncan depressed the Talk button. "Daymon, Duncan here. Do you have a copy?" Figuring Daymon's radio was either parked on a base unit in the home, or buried deep in one of the man's pockets, he waited a few seconds, passing the time by staring across fallow fields adjacent to the paved secondary road.

Less than a minute had elapsed before Daymon's voice spilled from the tiny speaker. "Old Man! Well I'll be damned. Figured Captain America would come calling before your mangy carcass darkened my doorstep. Good thing I remembered the old standby channel, eh?"

"I'm not alone," said Duncan. "Cade and the Kids are here, too."

There was a long moment of silence. Then, the statement obviously directed at Cade, Daymon said, "I'm sorry I ran out before you returned. I had no idea the severity of the situation." There was nothing jocular about the delivery. Daymon's voice was soft and the words came across as sincere to all in the F-650's cab.

Duncan handed his Motorola to Cade who thumbed the Talk button and drew it to his mouth. "You have no reason to apologize," he insisted. "You were outside the wire with Duncan and the others. No way you could have possibly known. In the end, only Glenda and Duncan knew the truth about Brook's dose of Omega antiserum coming from the bad batch."

"Heidi is listening," said Daymon. "She wants to know how Raven is taking it."

Cade looked into the rearview mirror. "Raven cussed God and kicked a lot of inanimate objects for the first half of the first day. Then she ran a path in the clearing the latter half of the day. Probably ran a half marathon all total."

Heidi asked, "How is she now?"

"About as good as can be expected for a twelve-year-old who just lost her mom," Cade replied, his gaze locked tight on the road beyond the galvanized steel gate.

Duncan flicked his eyes to the wing mirror. *Clear.* He gestured for Cade to press the Talk button and leaned near. "Let's finish our jaw session inside the wire," he drawled, head turned in the radio's general direction. "Gate's chained up and secured with a lock. You gonna come and let us in?"

"No need," Daymon said. "Go to the fence post on the right. At the middle rung, reach around to the back side. Opposite the hinge you'll find a loose plug of wood. Work it out and you'll find a key to the lock behind it. If there's any rotters watching … make sure you put them down and hide the corpses before you do anything."

"We know the drill," said Cade. "Be there in a bit."

"Copy that," answered Daymon. "On your way in, leave my *watchrotter* be."

Shaking his head, Duncan shouldered the door and stepped to the steaming blacktop.

Cade turned toward the backseat. "Watchrotter?"

Taryn grimaced.

Squirming in his seat, Wilson said, "You'll see."

Chapter 9

Head bowed and iPhone held close to his chest, Tran watched the covertly collected footage from start to finish. Save for pausing the video a couple of times to check topside activity on the flat panel to his left, the happenings on the tiny screen held his attention all the way to the ten-minute mark when he reentered the security container and Bridgett brushed past him in a blur of hunter orange and bad vibes. Still in disbelief at all the newcomer had been able to accomplish during his brief absence, Tran rolled the video back to the 3:23 mark, hit the Pause icon on the glass screen, and scrutinized the image frozen there.

By the time the captured footage had reached the point in time indicated by the digitally rendered numbers, he had already witnessed enough to know that Bridgett was their food thief. In fact, the second she had come back through the blackout curtain after locking him out she had blown by the iPhone and was out of frame again and moving fast (a conclusion buttressed by the rapid clomp of boots picked up by the microphone) in the direction of the dry storage Conex. A tick later she was back, her face filling up the screen, a mud-brown MRE pound cake package clamped between her teeth. And though Tran couldn't see much of her vest because she was crowding the lens as she retook her seat, more than likely its inner and outer pockets were bulging with more of the same.

He watched with rapt attention as she shoveled the last of his pound cake into her mouth. Finished with the big pieces, she ripped the foil bag open along the seams and licked the silver lining clean, probing the corners with her tongue to get at every last speck of the moist yellow cake. But she hadn't stopped there.

Barely coming up for air, she tore open another pound cake package and went to town on the contents.

Though he was never drawn to the programming on Discovery Channel during Shark Week, he had seen the commercials. What Bridgett had accomplished in a matter of seconds was on par with one of those Great Whites going to town on a hapless harbor seal—minus the crimson-frothed water, of course. And sticking with the Shark Week theme, the woman's eyes rolled back into her head and copious amounts of drool sluiced from her mouth and ran down her chin as she chewed slowly, obviously savoring her ill begotten gains.

After hiding the second foil package in a pocket, the confirmed food thief stood and inspected the satellite phones—picking each one up and thumbing it alive and regarding the lit-up screen before moving on. Tran had shaken his head as he saw her fish the unlocked bait phone from the shelf and sit back down with it clutched in her hand. A little confused as to what she was trying to accomplish, he watched her power it on and push buttons and then scribble something on the yellow legal pad on the desk in front of her. Then, without warning, she bent over and was out of frame for a short while.

Three second rule, thought Tran as he watched her pop back into view, chewing and swallowing what he figured was a dropped morsel of cake.

What Bridgett did next further added to the mystery. As she wiped the drool from her chin onto her left forearm, she reached in the iPhone's direction with her right hand. As she did so her arm stretched and distorted until she got ahold of something below the shelf the iPhone was positioned on. In the next beat, she donned a pair of headphones and plugged them into the jack on the HAM base unit sitting atop the desk beside the monitor. The second she powered on the unit and her hand went to the frequency tuning knob, Tran knew exactly what she was doing. And when he heard her utter a few muffled words and then go quiet, presumably to listen to someone on the other end, a cold finger of dread raked its nail up his spine.

As Bridgett continued the seemingly one-sided conversation, Tran's gag reflex was activated by the sight of her digging deep into her nostrils and extracting big hairy nuggets which she promptly deposited into her yawning mouth. The booger mining went on uninterrupted for some time, with her dividing her attention between the monitor to her left and speaking in hushed tones into the boom mike affixed to the headset.

Now, with the reason for Bridgett's actions still a mystery, he stared at the tiny iPhone screen, squinting hard to read the writing on the yellow pad. *Nothing.* The angle of the page in relation to the iPhone had rendered the faint pencil scrawl illegible.

Though it was clear to him Bridgett was up to no good, he didn't know exactly how to go about exposing her for one action without letting on he knew about the other. As a result of this added wrinkle, his idea of confronting her about the thievery and feeding her the much deserved helping of crow was off the table.

Tran shifted his attention from the phone clutched in his palm to the monitor on his left. In one of the panes Raven and Sasha were running back and forth along the dirt landing strip. Now and again, bounding deer-like, Max would elevate above the tired-looking grass for a split second then disappear from view as he fell back to terra firma. In the distance, above the tree line bordering the motor pool, the dark cloud cover was beginning to break. Bars of sunlight lanced down at a steep angle, hastening the melt and starting a steady trickle of water to spring from both sides of the RV's aluminum awning. Obviously finished with the diversionary tasks he'd heaped upon them, Glenda and Jamie sat underneath the awning on folding camp chairs, both clutching ceramic bowls, the steam from their contents wafting around their faces.

Venison stew, thought Tran, a low rumble sounding in his stomach.

The long-range CB on the shelf came to life with Duncan's voice. "Tran, my man. We're just outside of Woodruff where the trail went cold. How's things at the compound ... specifically the outer gate?"

"Road's clear, now," said Tran. "I did see a couple of rotters heading east after you all left."

"Good to hear," Duncan replied. "We're just rolling up to Casa de Daymon. Gonna cross some T's and dot some I's before we come back. Keep your eyes peeled and holler if anything comes up."

"Duncan ..." Tran said, his voice wavering.

"Yeah? I'm still here."

"I need to talk to Cade ... privately."

In the F-650, Duncan looked to Cade. Then, with a mischievous twinkle in his eye, Duncan radioed back to Tran. "I already told Cade what I know about your little conspiracy."

There was a long moment of silence in the cab. No white noise emanated from the radio. Only the keen of hardy ground-hugging bushes raking the Ford's slab sides could be heard as the pickup negotiated the rather narrow feeder road.

Coming upon a lone Z crowding the right shoulder, Cade wheeled the big rig left. Then, with the screech of the abomination's nails raking the passenger's side sheet metal, he gestured for the radio.

Relinquishing the CB, Duncan quipped, "Hands at ten and two."

Eyeing the Z warily in the rearview, Cade spoke into the radio. "Cade here. It's OK, Tran, you can speak freely."

And Tran did. He spilled about everything that was on the recording. From Bridgett's attitude toward him to her disbelief at being allowed to sit in for him, to her using the Ham radio, to how she bolted from the compound without giving a thought to having him lock the door behind her.

"Where is she now?" Cade asked.

First Tran spoke of her affable demeanor prior to being allowed to sit in for him. Then he described how that had taken a one-eighty once he returned. He left out the insults and how he had yearned to embarrass her in front of the others. However, he didn't hold back when describing how she had left the compound in a tizzy and stalked across the clearing toward the RV. He told

Cade how she paused and spoke with Glenda and Jamie just prior to throwing the unidentifiable item into the fire pit and walking away.

"Where is the heifer now?" asked Duncan, unexpectedly finding himself on the receiving end of one of Taryn's *oh no you didn't* glares.

"Seeing as how the portion of my pound cake she scarfed was little more than an appetizer," said Tran, "I assumed she was just going topside to help herself to a bowl or two of Glenda's stew."

Assumed, thought Cade. *Like I assumed you'd keep the cards closer to your chest.* "Where are the others?" he asked in a measured tone.

In the compound, Tran glanced at the monitor. "The girls are throwing the ball for Max in the clearing. Glenda and Jamie are taking an early lunch. I don't see Bridgett, now. Maybe she took her stew with her to the latrine."

Still holding the radio near his mouth, Cade regarded Duncan. There was no twinkle in the Delta operator's eyes. His jaw had taken on the famous granite set. Steering one-handed, he held the pose for a couple of seconds. "Lev and Seth," he finally said. "Where are they now?"

"They're walking the perimeter," answered Tran.

Cade stopped the truck a dozen yards from where the road spilled out into what looked to him to be a motor court. To the left was a regulation-sized basketball court fashioned from poured cement and marked with the appropriate lines. To his amazement, opposing ten-foot backboards sprouted on the baseline at each end. Still gawking at the spread he would have never guessed was here based on the gate and road leading in to it, he thumbed the Talk key and said, "I have a hunch Bridgett isn't what she says she is. Call Jamie and tell her what you told me. Have her fill in Glenda, too. I want Jamie to shadow the girls. Stick to them like glue—"

Tran interrupted. "Lev and Seth?"

"Talk to Lev. Tell him everything. Have him and Seth backtrack to 39. Tell them to approach Bridgett as if she's armed and dangerous. Have them tell her she has to answer to the group for her suspected involvement in the disappearing food problem."

"What do they do with her if she cooperates?"

"Have them take her to dry storage. No zip ties, though. Keep her thinking she's in trouble *only* for pilfering food. Do *not* mention the video."

"And if she runs or happens to resist?" asked Tran.

"No need to bring that up with Lev," said Cade. "He'll know what to do. Hit us with a SITREP as soon as you know anything."

"Copy that," said Tran.

There was a click and the CB in Cade's hand went silent.

Seeing the stone and timber mansion bracketed by a pair of trees standing sentinel at the terminus of the gently curving drive, Duncan said to Cade, "You think she's armed?"

Wilson said, "The weapons are all locked up. I made sure of that before we left."

Duncan regarded Cade. "Unless she takes one off of one of our people, she's only got her hands."

Cade brought the F-650 to a slow rolling stop underneath a portico at the top arc of a circular parking pad made of pavers laid down in a herringbone pattern. The cover made of stone, iron, and roughly hewn timbers extended out from the home a good thirty feet and sheltered the stairs and massive wood front doors from the elements.

Cade threw the transmission into Park and said, "What's to keep her from finding an axe, sharp stick, or rock to use as a weapon?"

"Or her fists," said Wilson. "She's big-boned. And muscled under the flab, too. I've seen her cutting wood. Wouldn't want to be on the receiving end of one of those swings."

"If she tries to rabbit, Lev and Seth will know how to handle her," Cade said bitterly. He killed the engine and in his side vision picked up the movement of one of the ten-foot-tall doors swinging inward.

"The man of the house," said Duncan, gesturing toward Daymon, who was already descending the stairs, smiling and brandishing an M4.

Chapter 10

"*Bridgett* ... really? How in the *hell* did you come up with that gem of a name, Iris? You couldn't have pulled a *Heather* or a *Mysti* or even a hippy dippy name like *Crystal* out of your fat ass? You're a *Doer* now, girl. You've gotta think quickly on your feet. Much quicker than that or you're going to find yourself demoted to Watcher and wasting away in barns and attics again. Is that what you want?"

Iris didn't answer her own question, because that's what crazy people did. And that's what she was going to be if she had to go back up into another spider-web-filled steeple and share space with the bats in the belfry. In fact, she'd rather be dead than serve one more watching session in a barn reeking of cow shit and moldy hay. She hauled her frame over the newer-looking fence she'd just come across. The taut length of wire chafed her inner thigh as she rolled over the top. There was a tearing sound followed by a puff of white feathers as equal parts gravity and her own inherent clumsiness sent her crashing to her back on the soft ground. With goose feathers raining down on her chest and face and the ground all around her, Iris rolled over onto her ample stomach and pushed up to her knees. Using the fence for support, she rose and looked down at her chest. Fine little feathers flocked every square inch of the torn vest where the leaves had wet it. Brushing the vest front with both hands, she took one step forward in the direction of the watery sun and felt the ground give way and, as if she'd stepped from a curb unexpectedly, her boot punched through what looked to be a purposefully assembled collection of leaves and twigs. A fraction of a second later, with her heart lurching in her chest and the determined expression morphing into a clown mask of confusion, she felt a pain like no other. It was as if her leg from the knee down was receiving acupuncture treatment from a sadist wielding a dozen white-hot fireplace pokers. Though blindsided by the initial breath-robbing wave of pain, she still had the wherewithal to know to bury her face in her vest collar before releasing the howl trapped in her chest.

Biting bloody furrows into her lower lip, Iris plunged her fingers into the soft topsoil, tensed her left leg, and drew up on her right with all the strength she could muster. Which was more than enough to start behind her eyelids a brief but furious display of fireworks that preceded her plunge into the deep, dark chasm of unconsciousness.

Bear River, Wyoming

As the mud- and gore-stippled pickups Alexander Dregan had been tracking crested a rise and entered a straight stretch of Wyoming State Highway 89 half a mile south of the Bear River community, he put down the binoculars and scooped up the Dragunov sniper rifle. He hacked once, spit the bloody wad of phlegm over the edge, then snugged the scoped weapon to his shoulder. Resting its lengthy barrel on the lip of the sandbagged six-by-six plywood guard tower, he peered through the high-powered optics and parked the crosshairs on the lead truck.

The driver, a Caucasian man with sandy hair and wearing a panicked expression, struggled mightily with the wheel as the truck wallowed and shimmied the entire length of the steep, water-slickened downgrade. Sitting in the passenger seat with a black carbine in hand was a much younger man—Hispanic, guessed Dregan, judging by the brown eyes, light brown skin, and jet black hair. Pressed to the man's cherubic face was a pair of binoculars that appeared to be trained on the school bus blocking the entrance directly below Dregan's perch. How the man could keep the field glasses trained on anything the way the truck was bouncing on its tired suspension baffled Dregan. That he was interested in the walled community told the volunteer sheriff the small convoy had no intention of holding course and continuing across the nearby Utah state line.

Between the driver and binocular-wielding passenger stood a kindergarten-aged girl. Blonde pigtails snaked from under a pink stocking hat. Face scrunched into a mask of terror, the kid had one small hand splayed out on the truck's dash and was clutching the fabric of the passenger's winter parka with the other.

In the bed of the copper-colored Dodge, a trio of bodies lay prone among a hodgepodge of camping gear. The three waifish forms lolled with the truck's every move. The pale, waxen skin of their slack faces, clenched hands, and unshod feet stood out starkly against the jumble of colorful nylon sacks likely containing tents and rolled-up sleeping bags.

The second pickup was a silver Chevy still wearing a paper dealer plate in the front license frame. The middle-aged driver and his front seat passenger were both Caucasian, the latter a pimply-faced teen. The three sharing the rear bench seat were kids: boy, girl, boy. The kids all looked under ten and bore expressions identical to the little girl's in the lead truck. The Chevy's bed was also crammed with gear and bodies. However, unlike the Dodge, these three bodies—all women who looked to be in their thirties—were alive and sitting upright. Eyes narrowed against the cold slipstream screaming around their heads, they all stared intently, fixated on what Dregan had already concluded was their ultimate destination.

Now on high alert, Dregan continued watching through the scope and barked orders into a two-way radio, instructing the men at the gate and adjacent guard tower to fire at the first sight of a weapon being brought to bear. He drew his eye away from the scope and relaxed his grip on the weapon. He regarded the young man to his right and opened his mouth to speak, but before he could form a word another wet cough wracked his body. Bloody bubbles formed on his lips. He swiped at the froth with his sleeve and drew in a deep breath.

"Are you OK?" the fair-haired twenty-something asked.

Dregan nodded. Then, words competing with a hollow rattle, he said, "Watch for weapons. And make sure the ones in the back of the first truck are not infected. If they are, enact proper protocol."

Still training his black carbine on the approaching vehicles, the young man simply nodded.

Dregan set the Dragunov aside, grabbed his trusty AK-47, and cast his gaze to the state highway where the trucks showed no signs of slowing. Though he had picked the pair of trucks up a couple of miles out, their headlights a dead giveaway, their ultimate destination wasn't clear until the overloaded Dodge tore into the right turn at a high rate of speed, sending the bodies in back rolling hard to the left and a plume of blue-black smoke lifting off the right-side tires. The second truck didn't slow either. If anything, it seemed to accelerate, the passengers clinging to the bed rails in back nearly paying dearly for the abrupt maneuver.

Dregan said, "I'm going to the gate," then descended through the cutout in the floor and trundled noisily down the telescoping aluminum ladder.

A dozen miles north of Bear River, Cade was shouldering open the F-650's massive door. His boots hit the pavers and he couldn't resist walking out from underneath the portico to run his eyes over the mini mansion. It was multi-storied and featured a multi-pitched roof. He marveled at the sturdy bi-fold storm shutters. Unlike the for-looks-only adornments on most McMansions he'd come across, these solid metal items were attached to hinges beside every window on every level and appeared to be fully functional. And taking cues from the homes in mountain communities such as Aspen or Jackson Hole, the two-story affair here in rural Utah was all hewn lumber, iron fittings, and quarried stone. The materials and colors chosen by the former owner blended seamlessly with the scenery backstopping the place. *Natural camouflage*, Cade thought approvingly as he retraced his steps to the Ford.

Smile creasing his face, Daymon lowered his rifle, padded to the bottom of the stairs, and motioned for Duncan, Taryn, and Wilson to exit the vehicle.

"Had to get another *watchrotter*, didn't you?" Duncan said as he shut his door and joined Taryn and Wilson near the steps.

Daymon's smile faded. "Did you recognize her?" Seeing no recognition on Duncan's part, he met Taryn's gaze.

Eyes going wide, Taryn nodded and said, "Yeah. She is familiar to me now that you mention it. She was one of the twins from the Bear Lake compound, right? One of the ones that had been walking the ramparts by the gate?"

"Yep. I found her wandering Woodruff last night." He looked to Duncan. "I still don't think leaving them in the stocks was the right decision. This kind of proves it. Leads to more questions probably never to be answered."

"I agree with Daymon," said Cade. He was rounding the F-650 and had heard the entire exchange. "If the Zs had gotten to her while she was still confined to the stocks, your pet would be a walking skeleton."

"*Watchrotter*," said Daymon, leveling his gaze at Cade. "She's not my *pet*. I may be a sick puppy ... but I'm not *that* kind of sick."

Cade nodded agreeably. "But you knew what I meant."

Wilson put his hand on the pistol on his belt. Fingers caressing the smooth leather holster, he said, "For one, how'd she become infected? Second, who freed her from the stocks before she became infected?"

"Wasn't Mom ... or Adrian, whatever you want to call your rotter's former boss. She was in no kind of traveling shape when I locked her in her own torture device." Duncan shouldered his Saiga shotgun. "Her leg was broken badly and she was bleeding out. Just like she let Oliver bleed out. Only slower. No way she deserved the quick way out."

"I concur," said Cade, remembering how he had sent Pug out of this world. "But you still should have stuck around for proof of death."

"Undeath," Taryn corrected. "Even more fitting."

"If wishes were fishes," said Duncan. Changing the subject, he looked to Daymon. "Where's your better half?"

"She heard you all were at the gate and decided to raid the pantry of the good stuff. Come on inside." Seeing the look of apprehension settle on Cade's face, he added, "It'll be OK. The watchrotter is *not* my only line of defense. The grounds are seeded with motion sensors. Our six is fairly well-covered by trees. As are our flanks."

Cade craned and gestured at the dormers sprouting from the home's steel roof. "What about an attic?"

Daymon shouldered his rifle and stepped aside to let the others enter through the open door. "It does indeed have an attic," he answered, brow knitting. "There's also a panic room off the master bedroom. Neither of which I want to see the inside of. I'd put a bullet in my head before reliving that day in Hanna."

Knowing precisely where the man was coming from, Cade said nothing and mounted the stairs.

Chapter 11

Bear River

The one thing Dregan disliked most about visiting the guard towers to check on his men was climbing back down the rickety ladders. The ascent wasn't so bad because he could take his time. Coming down, however, with his near three-hundred-pound cancer-addled frame causing tremendous strain on his leg and arm muscles, always got his wind up. Which was no good considering his lung capacity was strangled by the fast-growing tumors that were hurtling him to an early death at an ever-increasing pace.

Now on the ground, his wind slowly returning, Dregan strode purposefully toward the gate.

Seeing Dregan approaching, the gun-wielding group of men and women who had been expecting him formed a ragged line and snapped to attention.

Still following Pomeroy's rules, thought Dregan, eyeing the wavering formation. "At ease," he barked. "I'm your sheriff, not the provost marshal of this damn place."

After the recent flyby of the black helicopter and subsequent presidential phone call to Judge Pomeroy, the job of watching over the citizens of Bear River had been returned to Dregan. So, with a renewed sense of purpose, the self-proclaimed Natural Gas Baron of Salt Lake City had made a solemn vow to himself to spend his remaining days on earth making the town of nearly five hundred not only a safe place for his sons Gregory and Peter going forward, but also a thriving community where the rule of law was respected and its citizens held a vested interest in keeping it that way. Gone were the expulsions for petty crimes. The literal interpretation of the biblical tenet 'An eye for an eye' that Judge

Pomeroy had employed with impunity before President Clay's intervention was also a thing of the past.

Mandatory service had become the great equalizer. Men who once only manned the towers and patrolled the streets looking for work for Pomeroy now helped with the laundry at the washhouse. Conversely, once relegated to the tasks the men felt themselves above, the women now found themselves taking up arms and sharing in the most important security duties.

Dregan racked a round into his AK, confirmed the selector was on Safe, and approached the deputies standing in the shadow of the concrete-laden bus serving as the main gate. He picked two from the group—David Hunt, a heavily tattooed man of about thirty whom he knew had once seen combat, and a bespectacled woman named Joan MacLeod who was nearing middle age and carried with her a reputation of being a tough-as-nails survivor.

Though he doubted it needed saying, he looked to the pair and did so anyway. "I'm going to see what our callers are up to. Cover me ... but keep your rifles at a low ready."

The pair nodded a silent affirmative.

Dregan moved closer to the bus's open driver's side window. As he did, the heavyset balding man at the wheel greeted him with a nod.

"I want a man-sized hole," he said to the driver. "Nothing more."

Eyes narrowed, the driver leaned forward in his seat. A tick later, there was a metallic rattle of the engine turning over. A deluge of blue-gray exhaust poured from the rear of the vehicle as the big diesel roared to life.

As the bus began to reverse, Dregan stood by the front bumper, holding his hands a shoulders-width apart. Slowly but surely, the bus's springs creaking in protest, a sliver of light appeared beside the concrete freeway noise barrier, dwarfing Dregan on his left.

Dropping his arms to his sides, Dregan said, "That's good." Then, wasting no time, he hefted his rifle and moved on through the opening with both of his deputies in tow.

Keeping the AK's business end trained on the copper-colored pickup, he hollered, "Close the gate." Next, he looped around front of the pickup, keeping his eyes on the driver's upthrust hands. Seeing MacLeod fanning out to his right, and Hunt doing the same on their left flank, he ordered the outsiders to leave their weapons behind and step out of the vehicles.

Opening his door by the outside handle as instructed, the driver of the lead truck began pleading for the gate to be reopened. "We need to get inside," he insisted. "They're coming."

Dregan covertly sniffed the air. Knowing the answer, he asked anyway. "Who is coming?"

The man was standing on the packed earth beside his truck. "The dead," he whispered, his voice hoarse and tired-sounding. "Fucking thousands of them."

"At *least* ten thousand," added a woman who had just climbed from the second truck.

Dregan watched her go to her knees, hands still reaching for the sky. Through the entire process of throwing her leg over the silver truck's bed, issuing the warning to no one in particular, and assuming the position usually reserved for gangbangers and wanted felons in the old world, the fifty-something woman never took her eyes from the feeder road running away from the entry west by south.

Once everybody had exited the pickups—thirteen total—Dregan ordered they be checked for weapons and bites. Through the whole ordeal, the woman watching the road chanted the same two words: *They're coming.*

"Clear," called MacLeod, her rifle now aimed skyward.

"We're good over here," said Hunt.

"Everyone on their knees," ordered Dregan. "I want to see your hands behind your heads, fingers interlaced." He walked over to the occupants of the first truck and asked them where they were going in such a hurry.

The driver from the first truck indicated they had camped the night before a dozen miles south of Evanston and were set upon by the horde at first light. He went on about how they hastily broke camp and put some distance between them and the dead until the Chevy overheated from a punctured hose and they were forced to stop and search for a compatible part to get going again.

Hoping the unfortunate breakdown had happened some time ago and very far south of here, Dregan asked, "When and where did you break down?"

Brows knitted, the man unlaced his fingers and looked to the south. "Four miles back. My brother tried to lure the pack away. To save the kids, mainly. They got him, though. They got my brother, Doug." Tears welled in his eyes. "There was no way I could save him. There were just too many."

"Wasn't anything left of him, Larry," the woman called from a dozen feet away, her voice all nasally and insistent.

Larry shook his head. Cheeks wet with tears, he said, "He bought us enough time to get the rigs moving, but—"

Seeing the man freeze up, Dregan crouched down and pressed him for more.

The man raised his head and met Dregan's gaze. "Those things are on the hunt now. They move much faster when they have prey in their sights."

"I know how they operate," Dregan said. He rose and looked to the tower he'd just vacated. The shades used to cover the opening on all four sides during a lockdown—semi see-through bamboo mats—were already in the down position. He plucked a radio from his vest pocket and called for the southwest tower to report in.

"Armstrong," came the reply.

"Anything new to report?"

There was a long pause on the other end, during which Dregan heard the man's ragged breathing. Then, overcome by a pain unlike nothing he'd yet to experience, Dregan doubled over and palmed his knees. Holding that pose, he took a few shallow breaths—gulps really—counted to ten, then hinged upright and found all eyes in the immediate vicinity locked on him.

Waving his hand at his deputies—universal semaphore for *It's nothing, I'll be OK,* he thumbed the Talk key. "Armstrong … do you see evidence of anyone or *anything* pursuing these folks at the gate?"

Up in the tower, thirty-year-old former pizza shop owner James Armstrong pressed the binoculars to his eyes to ensure that what he was about to report to the man in charge of security was not a byproduct of his sometimes-overactive imagination.

Sure enough, from the far rise roughly two miles out to the bend in the road a quarter mile further south, all he saw were bodies in motion. Rotten and ashen living corpses of men, women, and children who used to be fathers, mothers, brothers, sisters, neighbors, perhaps even his dead kids' school mates. Hell, he thought, some of them may have even noshed slices of his famous New York style pizza before the cruel hand of fate consigned them to spend the rest of their days hungering for the flesh of the living.

He focused on one particularly tall specimen at the head of the lurching train of hard-driven hunger. The near seven-footer wore a button-up shirt that was plastered to his jutting breastbone by a miasma of fresh-looking blood. The thing had eaten well recently and clearly it was still hungering. Hanging by a long strand of corded jaw muscle, the abomination's dislocated lower mandible bobbed to and fro like an infant working a Johnny Jump Up. And like a kid in one of those bouncy suspended contraptions, the movements the tooth-studded jaw bone made were chaotic and non-stop.

Pepperoni or Hula-Lula, Armstrong mused crazily. *None of the above,* the raspy undead voice in his head answered. *I'll have a trip through the Flesh and Organ Bar, thank you all the same.*

As the undead leaders of the pack approached the point in the distance where road and horizon parted, the entire horde came into view. Moving in a stilted, half-in-the-bag manner that was strangely hypnotic, the river of marching corpses crested the hill, then picked up speed and flowed snake-like down the decline.

Armstrong swallowed hard and set the binoculars aside. He drew the radio to his lips and depressed the Talk button. Let it hang there in front of his silent, gaping mouth for a long second as he tried to think of how to accurately describe what he was seeing. Finally, unable to fully put into words the magnitude of the juggernaut filling up all three lanes of the passing zone, he said in a near whisper, "Sheriff ... you *need* to come back up here and see for yourself."

Chapter 12

Eden Compound

A piercing scream rolled across the clearing, causing the half-dozen birds perched on one of the Black Hawk's drooping rotor blades to take flight unexpectedly. The laughter and joyful sounds that had been keeping Glenda company were all but drowned out by shrill cawing and a furious flapping of wings as the raptors sought higher station in the bare trees crowding in on the motor pool.

The matriarchal figure jolted upright and fumbled the ladle into the stainless-steel stock pot. Narrowly avoiding a splash of hot venison stew to the face, she snatched up the rifle leaning nearby and craned around the RV's rear quarter to see what was afoot.

Fully expecting to see a stray rotter emerging from the forest's edge, instead, Glenda spied Max stretched to full extension, front paws on Raven's shoulders and the twelve-year-old's crimson-cheeked face on the receiving end of a thorough tongue bath.

"Ewww … dog spit!' wailed Raven, her words rising over the noisy birds.

Nearby, Sasha, also flush in the face, was laughing and holding a yard-long branch aloft. In the next beat, she began wheedling Max by shaking the branch near his muzzle and calling his name repeatedly.

False alarm, thought Glenda, as she was struck with an overwhelming sense of gratefulness. Cradling the long gun in the crook of her arm, she walked a few feet to her left and saw Jamie, twenty yards from where the unfair game of keep away was unfolding. She was sitting atop the group's lone Humvee and actively panning a pair of binoculars over the far tree line. Satisfied all was as it should be, Glenda made her way back to the al fresco kitchen.

"Glenda," a familiar voice called from behind her. "You save me some?"

After turning to see Lev, all decked out in woodland camouflage and carrying a black carbine, step from the nearby tree line, she smiled and said, "Of course I did, young man. There's enough for everyone."

Rifle held at a low ready and head moving on a swivel, Seth emerged from the forest close on Lev's heels. "What about me?" he asked, one hand loosening the rubber band securing his long hair in a tight ponytail.

"I made extra with you in mind, Seth," she said playfully. "Wouldn't want the compound's eyes and ears to go into a shift change on an empty stomach." She wiped a bit of splattered stew from her denim shirt, then extinguished the Weber's burner. Giving the pot a stir, she went on, "Grab a couple of bowls and get some before it goes cold."

Steam rose from the shiny thermal liner as Seth peeled off his black parka. He propped his AR against the RV and grabbed a pair of bowls from the abbreviated counter affixed to one end of the stainless-steel grill.

Meanwhile, hovering near the stove and eyeing the stew hungrily, Lev had plucked his radio from a pocket. He cleared his throat and thumbed the Talk button. "Anything new to report?" he asked, quickly relaxing his grip on the Motorola.

Tran answered, saying the compound was empty and locked tight and stressed that he hadn't seen Bridgett show up on the cameras since her brief pow-wow with Glenda and Jamie.

As soon as Tran broke the connection, Jamie jumped onto the open channel and noted that she'd been sitting in the motor pool for some time and hadn't seen the woman, either.

"Did you boys check the latrines?" asked Glenda as she accepted the bowls and spoons from Seth. "After I ladled her some stew, she headed into the trees and struck off in that general direction."

Lev shook his head. "We just came from there. Both were empty. As was the shower stall. I'm thinking she looped around behind us and made for the road."

Always applying a glass-half-full outlook on things, Glenda pressed, "Now why would she go and do that? She got a taste of what the security shift is like. Maybe that motivated her to find another way to pitch in. She could be filling water bottles over by the collection barrels."

"Save for begging me to let her sit and learn the routine at the security desk, I've *never* seen her take the initiative on anything," said Seth, his eyes fixed on the steaming pot of stew.

Lev stared off toward where the feeder road spilled into the clearing. "My money says she just grew tired of Cade and Duncan's rules and decided to boogie."

Glenda regarded Seth. "Where's she going to go?" She motioned with the ladle at the clouds overhead. "And in this weather to boot."

Lev nodded toward Raven's purple and white mountain bike sitting on its side a dozen yards away. "We know she's got food. But she's got no wheels. That will be a *big* problem if Old Man Winter decides to up the ante on the hail and go all in with another snow event like we saw last week."

Seth had been standing by the stove, bowls in hand and listening to the exchange. Without a word as to why, he set the bowls down hard on the stove and looked first to Lev, then back to Glenda.

"What?" said Lev.

A knowing look settling on his face, Seth arched one brow and strode over to the fire pit.

Standing with the stew-filled ladle hovering in midair and the bowls now an arm's reach away, Glenda watched Seth kneel by the fire pit and pry a hunk of charcoal from a blackened piece of firewood.

Head tilted dog-like, Lev said, "What's up, bro?"

A twinkle in his eye, Seth displayed the finger-long piece of charcoal. "I have an idea," he said, a smile curling his lips. "Be right back."

Men, thought Glenda. *Can't live with them, can't kill them.* After watching Seth for a moment, she cupped her hands in front of her mouth and hollered in the direction of the airstrip. "Raven. Sasha. Jamie … food's ready!" She turned toward Lev. He was standing, hands on hips, watching Seth cut a laser-straight path through the grass toward the compound entrance. "Cade's expecting an update," she said, the long-range CB thrust in his direction.

"Right away," Lev said, accepting the radio and walking away to find some quiet. With a head full of unanswered questions troubling him, he adjusted the volume and placed the call.

Bear River

Dregan didn't need to climb any rickety ladders or set foot in one of the guard towers to see *anything* with his own eyes to know the kind of danger they would all soon be facing. Though his head was pounding and the churn in his guts had loosened his bowels so that his adult incontinence pants required changing, his sense of smell and hearing were not compromised. There was no mistaking the sickly-sweet stench of decay carrying on the wind for anything other than what it meant. Nor was there any denying what the fleshy slap of bare feet meeting asphalt and rasps of first turns coming from the nearby highway meant: The horde was back. And it was drawing nearer by the minute.

While Dregan looked on, the two deputies who'd accompanied him outside the gate frisked and disarmed the adult survivors who had inadvertently led the dead to Bear River's doorstep. Despite the fact the mercury was hovering in the mid-fifties, Dregan ordered them all to strip down to their undergarments. Starting with the kids, each person was checked thoroughly for bites, females by Deputy MacLeod, males by Deputy Hunt.

Covering his deputies with his AK, Dregan watched them perform thorough head to toe inspections on every survivor before allowing them to stand together.

Seeing his deputies getting to the last of the adults, Dregan motioned toward the bus with his free hand and bellowed, "Roll the gate!"

"Done," said MacLeod. "No bites or major open wounds on the females."

Deputy Hunt finished with the last of the males. After gently steering Larry to where the others were congregating, he regarded Dregan with tired-looking eyes. "Good to go."

Satisfied that his deputies had vetted the outsiders to the best of their ability considering the circumstances, Dregan made a sweeping motion with his rifle toward the gap in the gate. "Take them to quarantine," he called out. "Get 'em clothed and fed before you begin the debriefing period." He regarded the shivering group and simultaneously felt contempt for the undead and an overwhelming sense of guilt for the dignity-robbing ordeal he had just been forced to put those fleeing the horde through. But it couldn't be helped. He'd already learned the hard way the unacceptable number of casualties just one infected inside the walls could inflict on the living. To let a *hot* outsider into Bear River with the specter of a long siege looming would erode the modicum of trust he'd built back up among the people, while at the same time emboldening Judge Pomeroy's many supporters.

The man with the sandy hair calling himself Larry shuffled from the group, near nude and barefoot. Exuding an air of authority belying his appearance, he asked, "What about our belongings? Our weapons? The trucks?"

"Screw all of that," shouted one of the women, tears carving white channels down her dirt-smudged cheeks. "What about our dead?"

"The dead are the lucky ones," answered Dregan. He glanced anxiously at the lurching creatures beginning to amass at the mouth of the feeder road. "The dead have to remain outside with the trucks. You'll get your weapons back after we get to know you all a little better."

"Teresa, Ned, and Cloe are going to turn," said the woman with the grime-streaked face. "What about them?"

Dregan said nothing. He turned and ordered Hunt to police up the weapons. Letting his rifle dangle from its sling, he pulled a long buck knife from its leather holster. Under the watchful gaze of the outsiders, he strode to the lead truck and leaned over the bed. Two of the three corpses were beginning to stir: a boy of about ten and a tween girl. The eyes darted under heavy lids and their stick-thin bite-riddled arms twitched minutely. Without letting on that the transformation had already begun, Dregan uttered a short prayer and then performed the necessary task the loved ones for obvious reasons had not.

Face devoid of emotion, he turned and spread his arms wide as if he were giving the little band of survivors a much-needed group hug. Then, like a sheepdog working a flock, he made shooing motions with his arms and herded them all toward the gate.

As Deputy MacLeod crabbed past the mangled grill and bumper, the school bus's diesel engine came to life. By the time the group was through, Deputy Hunt was doing the herding.

Dregan stopped and stole one last glance at the pickups and was reminded of his family's escape from Salt Lake. Pressing his palms to his eyes to staunch the forming tears, he stood there for a moment bracketed by the group's vehicles and the idling bus. Coming to some kind of conclusion, he fished his radio out and strode through the gate, already barking out orders at the driver to close it up and issuing others instructing his deputies to begin shoring it up against the dead now streaming unimpeded up the feeder road.

Once inside the wire—a universal term soldiers called the inner sanctum of a base of just about any size so long as there were fortifications sufficient to keep the enemy outside—Dregan hailed Gregory and Cleo and ordered them to meet him in Judge Pomeroy's chambers.

Chapter 13

Iris came to hearing the name she hated being called being repeated over and over. Now and again one of the searchers—the long-haired guy named Seth, judging by the slightly nasal quality to the braying voice—would bellow *"Bridgett!"* and make an appeal for her to show herself. The plea would always arrive ahead of the promise that she would not be punished for stealing food.

"We just want to talk to you," called a second male voice she couldn't match to a face. "That's all ... *just talk.*"

The pain in her leg stifled the rising chuckle brought on by the absurdity that anyone would believe some bullcrap like that. *Maybe in the movies or on television,* she mused. *This Doer ain't biting. Hell no!*

She dragged her sleeve across her forehead, wiping away the sweat beading there. Then she leaned over and gently removed a few handfuls of decaying leaves from around her knee, grimacing as each movement sent new tremors of pain surging through her body.

Iris paused for a moment then continued clearing the leaves and found that the next layer was mostly wet clods of dirt shot through with reddish-brown clay. Adding to the mud already caked to her palms and trapped underneath her nails, she plucked out most of the debris filling in around her trapped leg. After succeeding in getting through the secondary layer without passing out, she learned that the hole was not home to a bear trap as she had suspected, but was instead bristling with a half-dozen sharply pointed sticks, each one protruding from the walls and floor at a different angle. She also saw that not only was her calf pierced

81

through by at least two of the sticks, but her shoe was shot through with one as well.

After digging furiously for a couple of minutes at the wall on the right side of her leg, the blunt ends of the sticks began to release from the mud holding them.

Thank God for the recent rains, she thought, as the stake piercing through her jeans and into her calf from the left side began to break free from the wall. With the sweet endorphins flooding her system and dulling the pain, she had no way to gauge the damage done until she freed herself from the grips of the diabolical trap.

"Why did you Eden fuckers allow me inside your precious compound?" she hissed through clenched teeth, ahead of a soft, sad chuckle. *Who had been fooling whom?* Though she had convinced their older leader to save her from the purged and take her in, she never felt welcomed by the younger man. The one with the permanent hard-set jaw and calculating gaze they called Cade. He was a Doer in a Watcher's body. And she had a strong suspicion that he was the group's de facto leader the moment she saw him interact with the others.

"Fuck me," she said softly. "I've been played."

Her first thought upon having this epiphany was: *This isn't happening.* Then she asked herself: *are you really going to give up after completing the tasks you were given? Hell, Iris, you convinced the women sitting by the RV that you were going to the latrines, then doubled back out of the camera's reach with all of them none the wiser.*

She put a hand over her mouth to hold the laughter in. *Back in a minute*, she remembered telling them, all the while stifling the urge to laugh and call them both *cunt whores* to their faces. Then inform them of what they really were: *purged waiting to happen.* Then drive the dagger deeper by laughing in their hope-filled faces and mock the death of the man they called Oliver who *did* get purged that night she successfully completed her first official mission as a Doer.

After so many successes was the Doer about to be undone by a bunch of sharp sticks?

"Fuck no," she muttered. "I'm a *Doer* now."

***

Two minutes after having her great epiphany, Iris freed her leg and lay flat on her back and stared straight up through the gnarled boughs and branches. Afraid to assess the damage, but mostly afraid of what it might mean for her future as a Doer, she stayed prone for a long time, watching dark clouds scud by and listening hard to detect the search party.

Nothing.

Five long minutes and she had heard nobody braying her pseudonym.

Unable to further ignore the throb in her leg reminding her that she was going nowhere without tending to it, she arched her back and regarded the fence she had scaled prior to stepping in the shit that got her here. It was basically three strands of heavy gauge wire strung between steel T-posts commonly found at most builder supply stores. Incidentally, she concluded it was of the same construct as the fence and swinging gate under constant surveillance of one of the half-dozen video cameras supplying a steady stream of moving images to the monitor in the underground compound. The realization of which brought on epiphany number two.

You are a Doer now, Iris. Suck it up.

And she did suck it up—literally—in the form of a lungful of cool, damp air. Which she held in to counter the solar flare of white hot pain that came when she sat up and gazed down the length of her leg. The denim from her knee down wore a morass of blood and mud. There were numerous quarter-sized tears in the fabric. And like the tail on one of those dinosaurs whose name she couldn't pronounce—ankylo-something or other—one branch had pierced her Achilles tendon while two more, as thick as her thumb and twice the length, protruded from each side of her calf. Jiggling one of the sticks in her calf told her that they were two separate pieces. A good thing, she figured. The through-and-through, however, she feared was going to be a bitch to remove. Lastly, she inspected her shoe. Somehow the upthrust stakes had missed her foot entirely, the only damage occurring when one had skewered the sole and exited above the inside arch.

Dodged that bullet, she thought even as she steeled herself to remove the ones she hadn't. The two in her upper calf slid out with little trouble, but lots of added pain. Panting hard from exertion, and with a remembered vision of some movie star performing battlefield surgery on himself in a setting eerily similar to this, she took hold of one end of the stake wedged between her Achilles tendon and whatever bone it was attached to. Hell, she wasn't a nurse. There had been two in the compound. The older one, Glenda, was a self-righteous, tee-totaling bitch. Always so fucking positive. What she needed was to be locked up for a few months. That'd show her what powerlessness really was. Doubtful if her higher power would see fit to stick around in the *hole* with her. Because, from experience, Iris knew that the only company one had while in solitary was of the *Me, Myself*, and *I* variety. One week-long stint last spring had been enough to nearly drive her mad. Thank God the purge happened when it did, ensuring she would never again be locked up with only herself as company.

Anger coursing through her, she yanked the stake free without thought of the ramifications. There was a nuclear explosion of pain behind her eyes. Then she rolled her head to the right and vomited up pound cake peppered with undigested nuggets of venison from the stew she'd recently inhaled.

A byproduct of the lightning bolt of pain was an inadvertent scream which she quickly stifled with her dirty tartan sleeve.

Leaving the splinter- and dirt-filled wounds in her calf to be dealt with later, Iris tugged up on her pants leg, releasing a torrent of blood that spilled over her shoe and onto the carpet of decaying leaves.

Pulling her sock down, she inspected the wound to her Achilles. There were two holes, one on each side, and they were pulsing with blood. To staunch the flow, she tore off one of her tartan sleeves at the elbow and wrapped it twice around her ankle, tying it off with as tight of a knot she could produce. In seconds the ligature staunched the flow of blood. Next, she undid the button on the other sleeve, pulled it over her hand, and dabbed at the other wounds with it. Determining she wouldn't be bleeding to death anytime soon, she looked up and cast another furtive glance at the fence. Nothing moved in the general direction of the compound. She drew a breath, cocked her head like a dog, and again listened hard. *Nothing.* There were no harried voices of people hunting for the source of the stunted scream. Save for the steady patter of drips landing on the forest floor and distant cries of a pair of bickering ravens, all was quiet.

Countering the pain with thoughts of sweet revenge, she rose from the ground and stared at the bloody sticks and collapsing pit, taking one of the former and stuffing it into a back pocket. Face twisted into a hate-filled mask, she said, "Cade and Duncan, this is all your doing." Then, biting her lip to distract from the dull throb radiating upward from her heel, she took a tentative step, placing the majority of her weight on her injured leg. When she didn't immediately end up on the ground in a worthless heap, she smiled and hissed, "Better watch your asses, Doer one and Doer two. Because Iris is coming back with reinforcements."

Chapter 14

Casa De Daymon

Daymon led the callers inside, closing the door after Taryn. "I like the new do," he said. "Are you happy you hacked it off?"

"I'm not," Wilson interjected before Taryn could answer.

Stepping out of the way of the door's wide swing, Taryn said matter-of-factly, "It needed doing."

While Daymon was throwing the dual deadbolts, Taryn punched Wilson in the shoulder and shot him a look that said: *I'll talk for myself, thank you very much.*

Casting his gaze counterclockwise around the grand foyer, Duncan noted the lavish finishes as well as the framed photographs and high-end art dotting the walls. Tiled with sand-colored tumbled travertine, the nearby stairway curled up and away to his right. Left of the entry near the base of the stairs was some kind of sitting room. Through a set of open pocket-doors he saw Shaker-style oak furniture with cushions wrapped in saddle-brown leather. A soot-stained fireplace clad with smooth, gray river rock and capped off with a live-edge wood mantel dominated one interior wall. Affixed to velvet-wrapped mounts, a dozen different animal heads stared down from the walls, their beady glass eyes seemingly passing judgment on the displayed opulence. Two types of deer framed the ugly mug of a razor-tusked boar: a common whitetail (ears perked forever), and some species of prong-horned African deer. Positioned high up on the far wall, complete with upthrust horns and dangling shaggy black beard, was the enormous head of an American Bison.

Whoever owned this place had been a busy little beaver, Duncan reflected as he glanced at the ceiling directly overhead.

Suspended there by a long chain anchored in the center of a carved wood medallion was a massive crystal chandelier complete with hundreds of multi-faceted prisms all cut into delicate-looking tear drops. He imagined when the switch on the wall was thrown a mosaic of light would speckle the battleship-gray walls and splash a stepping-stone-like pattern across the highly polished walnut floors.

Instead of turning and addressing the rest of his guests after locking the door, Daymon reached out to a keypad on the wall nearby and punched in some numbers.

Seeing a light on the panel flash red and then go to solid green, Duncan whistled. "You wired this place for solar already?"

"Not my doing," Daymon answered, a sly grin forming. "The owner had the solar panels installed behind chest-high parapets."

Duncan raised a brow and worried one side of his mustache. "That's why I didn't see them the first time you brought us here."

Content to just soak up the intel, Cade kept his mouth shut and ears open and looked down the hall toward the back of the house where, judging by the sounds of slicing and dicing going on, Heidi was in full command of her new kitchen.

Leaning against the wall supporting the staircase, Wilson asked, "Wouldn't the panels be visible from the ground farther out? Reflect the sun? That'd be a dead giveaway, wouldn't it?"

Daymon shook his head. "I can walk to the trees and still not see them. Because they're south-facing and installed at a shallow angle, if you're looking at the house beyond the trees you'd be hard pressed to see them *through* the trees."

Duncan poked his head into the sitting room. Seeing the booze-filled decanters on the bird's eye maple coffee table, in his best Robin Leach, he said, "Lifestyles of the rich and famous. Caviar dreams and champagne wishes."

Having just returned from the short side trip to the end of the hall, stopping now and then to analyze the people and locations on display in the nicely framed photos hung here and there on both sides, Cade found himself casting extra scrutiny on one particular photo of a smiling family of four obviously taken during better times. The example of days gone by was wrapped in a gilded frame and occupied a place of prominence where anyone heading down the hall would see it first.

Seeing the Delta operator examining the photo, Daymon said, "I've been wondering where they are now, too."

The exchange got Duncan thinking about the old television programs of the same name. Lord knew he'd been guilty of wondering what had become of certain people. Though he loathed the boob tube before the dead began to walk, strangely, it was mostly celebrities' whereabouts that piqued his interest. That loudmouthed coffee-swilling guy on MSNBC who kind of rode both side of the tracks. Where was he? Did he become rotter bait? Or the salt-and-pepper-haired late-night opinion fixture on FOX. Was he still throwing his NERF football somewhere? Or was he forever ambling around Manhattan in a tattered three-piece-suit and leather loafers in dire need of a resole job? Duncan knew going down this rabbit hole always took him full circle to the small number of people he'd called friends before the shit hit the fan. Sadly, Aunt Matilda and Charlie Hammond both went to meet their maker within a day of each other at the very onset of all this madness. "Who's '*they?*'" he asked, more to staunch the thoughts of loved ones lost than because he actually gave a rip about the class of people who lived in places like this.

"A very wealthy family from Salt Lake. First couple of trips through the house I glanced at the pictures but didn't make the connection. After going through a filing cabinet in the upstairs office I came to learn that this house belongs"—he paused and grimaced—"*belonged* to the Hollah family."

Nobody spoke.

"Manny Hollah?" Daymon pressed. "You know ... the dude with the gold chains who owned a dozen dealerships along the Wasatch front. He sure looks a lot older in the pictures scattered about the house than he did in those goofy commercials." He tried to imitate the catchy jingle, butchering it badly. Then he spouted one of Manny's many tag lines: "Give Manny a hollah if you wanna save some dollahs?"

Blank stares from the others.

"We finance *anyone* the law allows?"

Nothing.

"If you don't come see me today, I can't save you any money."

Crickets.

"I've a feeling *none* of us got those commercials where we lived," said Duncan. He walked over to one of the pictures and peered at it over his glasses. "If ol' Manny Moolah had any sense, he and the woman and kids in the pictures are holed up in a mansion just like this on the west slope of the Wasatch. Trying to get through Salt Lake and past the National Guard's roadblocks would have been a fool's errand. Hell, Logan squirted north from Salt Lake early on. The stories he told me—"

Daymon was nodding when he interrupted. "South Salt Lake was a shit show," he said, his voice low and wavering slightly. "I tried to get to my Moms' house and had to turn back. That's why I doubt Manny even contemplated trying the long end-around to get to this joint."

"If he did … he probably died trying," proffered Wilson, his own harrowing flight from Denver to Springs still fresh in his mind as if it had happened yesterday.

Cade stepped from the shadowy hall and regarded the group. "Poked my head in the kitchen," he said. "Heidi's making Spam and hash browns for us." He settled his gaze on Daymon. "Why don't you give us the nickel tour while she's putting on the finishing touches?"

Before Daymon could reply, a voice was emanating from the radio in Duncan's pocket.

"Duncan here," he answered. "We're at Daymon's place. He's listening in."

"Roger that," Lev said. Then, skipping platitudes, he launched into a lengthy situation report.

Hearing about Seth taking the charcoal from the fire pit and having a good hunch what the man had been up to, Cade looked to Duncan. "Have Lev go inside and check on Seth."

Duncan lifted his thumb off the Talk button. Speaking directly to Cade, he said, "For what? So he can look over our budding artist's shoulder and critique a still life?"

Cade explained exactly what he would do with said hunk of charcoal if he were in Seth's shoes.

"Dang, Captain America," said Daymon. "Someone has been watching *waaaay* too much CSI."

Cade said nothing.

Someone's fart shattered the still and echoed about the foyer.

Cheeks reddening and on the receiving end of another of Taryn's sharp elbows, Wilson cast his gaze toward the ceiling and ignored the incredulous stares being directed his way.

Shooting the redhead a harsh look, Duncan said, "The nickel tour. And some gas masks, please."

"Nickel tour commencing," said Daymon. "Gas masks are in the panic room." Breathing through his nose, he shouldered his rifle and beckoned for his visitors to follow him up the staircase.

Chapter 15

Iris kept within the tree line and limped east, the still ascending sun playing peek-a-boo with her through the swift-moving cloud cover. After freeing herself from the trap, she had sought to distance herself from the vicinity as fast as her bad leg would allow, stopping only to clear her eyes of sweat and tears. Initially the pain had been so near to the surface any weight she put on her toes nearly knocked her out on her feet. Eventually, however, the throbbing subsided and the waves of pain that came with it were supplanted by a creeping numbness. In a matter of minutes, the undergrowth thinned and she was on a game trail and trekking along eastbound at a fair clip.

Keeping pace with her on one side was a dense thicket that looked to have been a source of food for whatever species of four-legged creatures which frequently transited the west/east running trail. What leaves that hadn't already fallen victim to the changing seasons were now nibbled down to nubs. And further proof the trail was used often, every few feet she would spot tufts of light brown fur trapped on the rusty barbed wire fence opposite the rambling thicket.

Beyond the fence was a knee-high ditch. Bordering the ditch and dotted with clumps of vibrant green moss and beaten-down grass was a wide gravel shoulder. Running parallel to the shoulder was a two-lane road divided by a double solid yellow. *Must be near a hill*, she thought, pausing again to rest. Only place besides a blind corner UDOT would think it prudent to forbid passing on a rural road usually closed in the winter. With all the stupid asses texting and driving before the purge, she mused, the powers that be would have been better off putting up a sign saying: Pass a car here and you'll likely come grill to grill with an eighteen-wheeler hauling logs and your decapitated head will take a tour of your backseat. *Can't fix stupid.* A wide grin parted her pursed lips and she cackled, startling herself. *But you can purge 'em.*

Soon the trees closed back in on the game trail and clumps of grabby undergrowth slowed her advance. Didn't matter, though. At this point she couldn't feel anything of her leg from the knee down. It felt as if she was swinging a hock of ham to and fro.

Eventually Iris came to a fence identical to the one bordering the road and had to make a decision. Confident she'd hear engine noises long before a vehicle was upon her and be able to go to ground and cover herself in leaves just as she'd done in the past, she stepped on the lower wire strand with her good foot, forced the bad leg through, and ducked her head between the parted strands. On the other side, she scooted into the ditch on her butt and scrabbled up the opposite side on all fours, the dead weight of her right leg carving a deep, bloody furrow in the ditch's muddy wall.

Parched and out of breath, she sat on the shoulder of the paved two-lane and took an MRE pound cake and bottle of water from her vest pocket.

The sun was really breaking through now, causing curls of steam to rise like dragon's breath from the road's ruddy surface. As she ate and drank, a pair of ravens took station in a tall fir across the road. "Go to hell, you black buzzards," she said, tossing the empty brown wrapper in their general direction.

Finished with the water, she chucked the empty bottle at the wrapper and then shuffled around on the roadway until she was again on her hands and knees. With considerable effort, she hauled her two-hundred-pound frame off the road. After swaying in place for a long ten-count with the birds cawing at her the entire time, she cupped her hands and shouted, "I'm not roadkill." Then, to prove the declaration, she took a few tentative steps along the soft shoulder.

Through trial and error and after bloodying both knees and one elbow she found that if she took one step forward with her left foot, then swung her dead leg forward *pendulum-like* and let it drop to the road like a fleshy anchor, she could keep her forward momentum up without adding more road rash to the growing collection.

***

After trudging the road for some time with her head down and fully absorbed in the awkward and exhausting task walking had become, she caught a whiff of death riding the wind at her back. Dropping anchor so to speak, she planted her feet a shoulder's width apart, turned her head, and walked her gaze up the road to the apex of a right-hand turn she guessed to be a quarter of a mile back. There, trundling the center line in her direction, was a pair of purged. Barely clothed, their pallid bodies stood out starkly against the tree- and foliage-cluttered backdrop. The steady breeze out of the west that had helped to alert her to their presence also stood their fine wisps of hair on end, making it seem as if a couple of drunken, mad scientists were stalking her.

Better than a hostile search party, she conceded, letting her gaze roam the fence, ditch, and length of road she'd just traversed. On the fence where she had wormed through, a scrap of orange nylon from her vest was stuck fast to one of the rusty barbs. And starting on this side of the fence on through the ditch and all the way to where she was standing, a meandering trail of feathers marked her progress like breadcrumbs. While the feathers in the ditch and on the grass beside the shoulder didn't really draw the eye in, the ones stuck to the drying road were impossible to miss. To solve the problem she quickly removed the vest and turned it inside out.

Seeing that the purged were gaining ground on her, she zipped the vest to her neck and struck out east again.

***

Iris plodded ahead, stopping only when she came upon a bullet-riddled sign rising up beside the eastbound lane. On the sign were the driving distances to Woodruff, Randolph, and Bear River.

95

With a renewed sense of purpose, and a good hundred-yard lead on her pursuers, Iris put her hand in her pocket and caressed the smooth surface of the two-way radio she'd pilfered from a milk crate underneath the plywood desk. Replacing the batteries with the fresh ones she'd taken from the storeroom would have to wait. For now, she was content with the knowledge that the electronic lifeline was in her possession and it had lit up and emitted a soft hiss of static when she had powered it on inside the compound.

A few more miles and I'll put you to use.

A crooked grin formed on her face and then she let loose with a tortured cackle that sent the nosy ravens winging away for good.

Chapter 16

Daymon stood on the travertine-tiled landing at the top of the stairs and waited for the others to join him. The massive expanse spread out before him was five-sided and shaped like home plate on a baseball diamond. Roughly twenty feet to his fore and offset a few feet to the right, two walls came together to form its point. The tray ceiling overhead was finished with ornate crown molding. Running from the stairs to the far wall on Daymon's right was a waist-high rail of dark wood and gleaming white balusters. And dead ahead from where the stairs spilled to the landing was a shadow-filled hall leading away to the rear of the upper level.

"Your new nickname," said Duncan as he mounted the final step, a little winded, "is Daddy Longlegs."

Daymon grinned and ran one hand provocatively from hip to knee. "They get me where I need to go in a hurry."

"And your new nickname is Tree Sloth," said Cade as he prodded Duncan to move aside. "I've seen a double amputee summit a set of stairs faster than you."

"I really do miss the back and forth banter between you two," said Daymon.

"Enough to go back to sleeping underground?" quipped Duncan.

Daymon threw a visible shudder. "Not in a million years."

Once Taryn and Wilson made the landing, Daymon began the tour by pointing to the pair of doors on the far-right wall. "Manny's kids' rooms are three times the size of anything I ever had. Their televisions and electronic toys ... top notch newest shit. I thought I walked into a Best Buy first time I set foot inside

97

there." He gestured to the wall between the widely spaced doors. "Behind that is a huge Jack and Jill bathroom."

"Where's the other egress?" asked Cade.

Daymon led them past the closed doors. At the far end of the tiled landing was a hall branching off to the left. "This feeds to another stairway."

Cade nodded approvingly.

Wilson asked, "Is it as big as the one up front?"

Daymon shook his head. "Nope. It's utilitarian. Just a couple runs of stairs that turn in on themselves and come out near a mudroom and pantry."

"What about fields of fire from this level?"

Smiling, Daymon looked to Cade. "Delta Boy is always thinking two steps ahead."

"Three or four, at least," said Duncan, clapping his friend on the back. "Isn't that right?"

"I've been known to have a game plan," Cade responded. He paused and looked over the railing. *Long drop.* "I've also been known to improvise," he added, already thinking of ways to shore up the front doors.

"This way," said Daymon, leading them back the way they'd come. "I think you'll approve of what our car dealer's done with the place." He came to a pair of closed doors to the left of where the walls formed the tip of the landing and threw them open with a flourish. Flicking the lights on, he said, "Behold the guest room. Hell of a footprint, eh?"

Cade padded into the room ahead of the others. The carpet underfoot was thick and bounced back quickly, the imprints his Danners made disappearing as he crossed the room to the window set over a massive California king bed. He skirted left of the bed and pulled aside the heavy curtains. Though they weren't blackout items like the ones at Schriever, they were still a dark shade of gray and looked up to the task.

"We never bother with the shades," said Daymon. "No need. With the shutters closed you could fire up a disco ball and no light is gonna escape."

Curious, Cade found the mechanism—a thin rope working an overhead pulley—and drew the curtains open. Sure enough, only four clusters of light—pinpricks, really—infiltrated the closed storm shutters, one at each corner by the hinges. All in all, looking at the back side of the matte-black shutters was like staring into a mine shaft.

Cade asked, "How easy are they to open?"

"Step aside, kind sir," said Daymon, obviously happy to show off the *whats* and *hows* of his new above-ground digs. "Throw these latches—" he reached up and simultaneously thumbed two levers away from each other—"then you haul the two window panes open, push, and voilà." Daymon did indeed push on the shutters, which caused them to swing open swift and silent, allowing a chilly draft ripe with the smell of death to pour into the room.

Cade covered his nose and edged closer to the window.

Spreading his arms in front of the open window, Daymon said, "From here you can pick off anything that moves behind the house." Gesturing to his left. "You've got a wide-open field of fire from the garage on past the breezeway and all the way to the fence line." Pointing at the firs bordering the house on the opposite side, he added, "Solar-powered motion sensors over here alert us to anything approaching."

Arms crossed, Cade said, "Distances?"

"I haven't had a chance to pace off distances yet—"

Interrupting Daymon from the opposite side of the divided picture window, Wilson said exactly what Cade and Taryn had to have been thinking up until now: "What the eff is with all the rotters in the pasture?"

Cade's second glance had already told him more than the first. Down below, perhaps fifty yards from the rear of the house, were no less than twenty of the dead things. Four were fresh turns that showed little signs of decomposition. A pair of males clinging to the fence were horribly burnt. In places their blistered dermis was sloughing off, which left charred flesh and bone exposed to the elements. The remaining Zs were very badly decomposed first turns. Recent precipitation had left their hair plastered to their scalps and what passed for clothing—just soaked scraps of graying fabric—clinging to their emaciated bodies. Even across the distance he could hear their hoarse, dry cries riding a wind gust which threaded its way through the cyclone fence keeping them at bay.

"More watchrotters," conceded Daymon. "I think some of them may have been friends of Adrian's."

Taryn said, "A few do look pretty fresh."

Duncan said, "Wishful thinking. If they came all the way here from Bear Lake, they would show a lot more road wear than they do."

Closing the shutters, Daymon said, "Before we go to get what you came for, I want to show you the panic room."

Wondering what the heck a "panic room" was, Wilson and Taryn exchanged glances.

"Thought you weren't going to be caught dead in there," drawled Duncan.

"I was joking. I can handle the panic room. The attic …that's a different story. No way," he said emphatically, his mini dreads whipping along with the side-to-side movement his head was making. "No *effin* way you're getting me up there."

Daymon led them from the guest suite to the set of double doors nearest the top of the stairs. He hinged these doors inward slowly while saying, "I'm still not at all comfortable staying in this opulence. It's like one of those Presidential Suites at the Bellagio in Vegas."

Envy evident in the tone, Wilson asked, "You've stayed in one?"

"Nope," answered Daymon as he led them past the foot of the massive California king bed. "But I did see *The Hangover* about a dozen times. That Zach what's-his-name dude is one funny cat."

Ignoring the banter, Cade let his gaze wander the rectangular room. At twelve o'clock to the entry, flanked by a pair of antique nightstands, was a bed that looked capable of sleeping four comfortably. It was unmade, the comforter and sheets nearly spilling off onto the carpeted floor. Evenly spaced above the bed's ornately carved mahogany headboard were four large windows. The drapes were burgundy with gold thread and parted to reveal the backsides of shutters identical to the ones over the windows in the guest suite. Remembering how glitzy Vegas had appeared on the outside, Cade thought: *Presidential Suite indeed.*

Pausing by the foot of the bed, he looked left through a hall where a pair of cream-colored double doors stood open. Lit up by light spilling through a skylight, the floors gleamed white—Italian marble, he presumed. At the rear of the room, also splashed by diffuse light pouring in from overhead, was a clawfoot tub and a walk-in shower surrounded with thick glass panels.

While Daymon went on about how many pair of shoes Manny Hollah and his wife had been keeping in the closet of their *vacation* home—all, unfortunately, three sizes too small for Heidi and not even in the ballpark for him—Cade fixed a stare on a strange alcove twenty feet to the right of the head of the bed. Centered equidistant from the windows and wall and pushed back into the dead space was a gilded chair upholstered with fabric the color of United States currency. Above the pale green chair and centered perfectly on the wall was an expensive-looking oil featuring hunting hounds and men on horseback. Affixed to the wall above the painting was a tiny spotlight not currently illuminating anything.

It wasn't the chair or painting that piqued his interest. They were aligned with everything he'd seen so far: over the top. It was the unnecessary placement of the wall in relation to the guest suite next door that got him thinking. To the casual observer, the items were placed there to fill in what appeared to be twelve useless square feet of an already humongous room. But Cade knew better. While Daymon led the group from the studio-apartment-sized walk-in closet to the spa-like bathroom, Cade padded in the opposite direction toward the alcove.

Chapter 17

Barely slowing during the transition from side street to driveway, Dregan whipped the Army surplus Chevy Blazer onto the cement parking pad fronting his three-story home. Stopping hard a foot shy of the fortified garage door, he threw the transmission into Park, killed the tired engine, and glanced up at the front door and pair of windows flanking it.

The blinds were drawn shut.

Elbowing the camouflage SUV's door open, he thought: *Good boy, Peter.*

A quick conning of the house across the street told Dregan that his son, Gregory, had beaten him here from the gate. A lone Humvee painted in woodland camouflage—soft-edged brown and green shapes shot through with black—was nosed in against a two-car garage. Unlike Dregan's home, the front door to his son's home was on the ground level at the end of a narrow, paved walk bordered by beds of flowers that looked to have been dead since summer.

The door hinged open and Gregory's six-foot frame filled up the doorway. Shod in black leather boots and wearing a red flannel shirt over tan work pants, the thirty-three-year-old was dressed for the job he had chosen for the day.

Dregan waved his boy over and stepped from his rig, grunting from the exertion. He watched Gregory descend the short stack of stairs, stroll down the walk, and cross the road in his direction. The younger man's pace and long strides belied the fact that he was also living on borrowed time. At least he was if all that the old fella, Duncan, of the Eden crew had to say about the Omega antiserum failure rate could be believed. A stark reminder

103

of the zombie attack that nearly killed him, Gregory still wore a bandage on the side of his neck.

A vision of Brook unexpectedly entered Dregan's head. It wasn't the picture of her rage-filled face peering up at him over the barrel of her Glock. This appearance had her kneeling in the mud, his bleeding son by her knees. She was cradling his head in her lap, smoothing his hair back, urging him to fight to live. The anger-torqued expression was gone. In its stead, the woman wore a stoic, business-like countenance as she stuck the cylindrical device to Gregory's bare skin and administered the government-made antiserum. The visage in his mind's eye was a hundred and eighty degrees removed from the one wrapped in righteous fury the day he led a posse to the Eden compound to complete one mission: extract a pound of flesh for the murder of his daughter Lena and her new husband, Michael. He thought: *We all know how that one turned out.*

He shook his head and reached a hand out to his son. Delivered a firm handshake and invited him inside.

"Sure you can handle the ladder?"

"I've got cancer, boy. I'm not dead like one of those things."

"Yet," answered Gregory. "What do you want to say to me that you couldn't say over the radio?"

Dregan said nothing. He put one hand on the semiautomatic pistol riding on his hip and looped around back of the Blazer. Satisfied the pistol was secured, he stepped to the telescoping aluminum ladder serving as stairs to his home and wrapped his hands around a rung just above his head. Hand over hand, he climbed the ladder in silence.

Standing at the base of the ladder and spotting for the elder Dregan, Gregory proffered, "We can rebuild the stairs for you."

"No need," said Dregan. "This place will belong to Peter before long."

"He's days away from thirteen. He ought to come live with me or … Uncle Henry."

After taking hold of the wooden porch rail and hauling himself off the ladder, Dregan shot Gregory a look only a son

104

could decipher. "Climb," he ordered, then turned and entered his home.

***

Dregan was sitting on the low-slung couch in his front room, still catching his wind after the arduous climb. Perched on his knees was a TV tray. On the tray was a smattering of pills, a once-white handkerchief dotted crimson, and a half-full bottle of water the color of weak cherry Kool-Aid.

"Henry is out of the question. He's too old. *If* he recovers from the flu that he's battling, he'll be hard-pressed to take care of himself in the coming years."

Gregory said nothing to that. Better to not bury the man prematurely. As he closed the door to outside and turned to face his father, Peter came bounding down the stairs, leaping the final three. Blond hair flying free, Alexander Dregan's youngest son landed on the floor facing his father and froze in what was obviously some kind of pre-determined pose. His left arm was thrust out wing-like, parallel with the floor. His knee on that side was splayed out, while the other, along with his clenched right fist, was planted firmly on the carpet. Head bowed low and speaking through the locks cascading before his face, he said, "Superhero landing."

"Have you been drinking?" asked the elder Dregan, exasperation showing in his voice.

"He's being a kid, Dad."

Still in character, the arm held aloft now wavering slightly, Peter said, "That's how Iron Man lands, Dad."

Dregan locked eyes with Peter. "Is that what you were watching when I came inside?"

Peter peered through his hair and fixed his blue eyes on his dad. "Yes," he said matter-of-factly.

"I'm glad you weren't watching some Chuck Norris movie," Dregan said, beginning to laugh. "You might have given your old man a knuckle sandwich."

Now on his knees across the coffee table from his dad, Peter said, "That, or tore your spine out of your body and beat you to death with it."

Dregan's laughter turned to a coughing bout, prompting him to snatch up the kerchief, fling it open, and deposit a spritz of fresh blood to the Rorschach pattern already dried on there. "I'm afraid the big C has already got me on his dead pool, my boy."

"Better than Deadpool having you on his dead pool," replied Peter.

Having no desire to explain who the Merc With A Mouth was to a man who barely had a grasp on the heroes of the Golden Age comics, Gregory sat on the couch and regarded Peter. "Baby brother ... you need to go back upstairs and finish watching your movie."

If the elder Dregan was wondering who this Deadpool was, he didn't let it show.

"I already know the monsters are coming," said Peter, a twinkle in his eyes. "I saw them from my room. They're in the field and some are already crowding against the north wall."

"Movie. Now," ordered Dregan, his voice going hoarse.

Peter's hair brushed his shoulders as he shook his head. "Seen it twenty times already." He rose and plopped down on the nearby loveseat. "If I'm old enough to live here alone, aren't I old enough to know what's going on?"

One brow arched, Gregory shot his dad a look that said: Can't argue with that.

"Eavesdropping is not good," said Dregan, his Slavic accent suddenly more pronounced.

"That's what I'd have been doing if you sent me upstairs."

"OK. Last thing I want to be remembered as is a hypocrite." Dregan sat back on the couch and regarded Gregory. "Does your Hodges friend still have the rig that brought him here?"

Gregory nodded.

"Does it run?"

Gregory shrugged. "If it doesn't," he said, "I'm pretty sure I can make it."

Peter asked, "What are you going to do with *that* big ol' thing?"

Dregan said, "Teach you to drive in it."

Gregory laughed at the visual. "I'll put blocks on the pedals and he can sit on a phone book."

"They stopped printing those, didn't they?" Dregan said soberly.

Now Peter's back was pressed hard against the loveseat. "No way," he said vehemently while shaking his head for added emphasis.

Gregory was beginning to laugh. Drawing in a deep breath, he said, "You'll *never* get a girl to date you driving that thing."

Face going pale, Peter rose and shot both men a death glare. "I'm going to my room," he pronounced, already stomping toward the stairs.

"Now, where were we?" said Gregory with a twinkle in his eye.

"Will Hodges. I need his wheels in running order as soon as possible."

"What if he doesn't want to part with them?" asked Gregory. "He told me over beers at the RAT that it's all he has left of his old life. Why he keeps it under tarps in his driveway."

Dregan grunted and another round of spasmodic coughing commenced.

There was more blood. Much more this time. The cough was phlegm-addled, the crimson spritz now nearly black and swimming with what looked to be pieces of diseased bronchial tube.

"Whatever it takes," he growled. "Get it."

Chapter 18

From the far end of the master suite, Cade watched Daymon stride from the master bathroom. Stretched tight over the lanky man's jeans and white thermal underwear top was a gold Adidas two-piece tracksuit. The cuffs of the sleeves and ends of the pant legs fell way short of reaching his wrists and ankles. The zippers to the legs were run up to mid-calf on Daymon. The nylon fabric made a soft, swishing sound as he walked. Strung around his neck and gathered into a thick knot just below his sternum were a dozen gold chains that swayed and clinked together. Some of the chains were braided rope-like and looked strong enough to suspend a boat anchor from. Others were delicate and fashioned in an intricate herringbone pattern. When Daymon passed under the lintel and entered the master suite, the entire mess weighing him down glittered brightly in the light of the overhead recessed lighting.

It was apparent to Cade when Duncan came into view that the joker had also raided Manny's closet. Over his jacket, he had donned a dark brown thigh-length fur coat. It was beyond fluffy and the lapels bunched around his neck. Made from the same type of fur—beaver, Cade guessed—and pulled down low on his head was a rounded-at-the-top Russian Ushanka hat.

Daymon spread his arms wide and the words "Straight pimpin'" rolled off of his tongue as he stepped onto the pile carpet. A half-beat later his jaw was falling open and he was gaping at Cade, who was sitting on the gilded chair and watching the show from afar.

In no mood to smile, Cade merely shook his head. Nothing Daymon or Duncan did these days came as a surprise to him. It was as if humor was their coping mechanism and the entire zombie-filled world their stage.

Arms now crossed, but still staring wide-eyed in Cade's direction, Daymon said incredulously, "You found it."

Sure enough, the wall at the end of the alcove behind Cade was standing open. "Hiding something in plain sight works some of the time," said Cade, hooking a thumb over his shoulder. "Just not with something that big. Especially when the square footage isn't utilized in the suite next door."

"Good find, Sherlock," said Duncan. "But how pray tell did you get the door to open?"

"The switch is behind the fake Monet. Pretty obvious if you know there's a hidden room." Cade rose from the chair. "I bet even someone with your eyesight would have eventually sniffed it out like you did those cowboy boots in Hollah's closet."

Glancing down at the ochre-colored ostrich-skin items, Duncan said, "Good eye, *Sherlock*. They're broke in and they fit me. Can't ask for more than that."

"Doesn't matter if someone finds the switch *after* you're inside," Daymon said. "Once all eight bolts are thrown, nobody will be able to get to you."

Wilson said, "So what's to stop them from blocking both doors and burning the house down with you trapped inside your precious panic room?"

"There's a second hidden egress," said Cade.

Appearing stunned, Daymon said, "Where?"

Cade removed his ball cap and ran a hand through his lengthening hair. Replacing the cap and tugging it low, he said, "In the panic room next to the door leading to the back stairs is a shelf with one book on it. A book by Charles Lutwidge Dodgson." He said the hard-to-pronounce name slowly.

"Alice in Wonderland," said Taryn.

Cade nodded. "I didn't get the correlation until I tried pulling it down and the whole thing sucked inward, revealing a passage."

Duncan shed the throwback to the Soviet Union's Cold War era and tossed it on the bed. "So where's the rabbit hole go?"

"Gorbachev speaks … and in English," quipped Wilson.

Cade answered, "The *rabbit hole* leads to another stairway that takes you down underneath the house to a locked door. I stopped there. Figured I'd let Daymon earn his nickels."

Scowling at Wilson's Russian dictator insult, Duncan removed his glasses and looked at himself in a nearby mirror. Pulling the hat down to within an inch of his bushy silver eyebrows, he said, "*Da*, Wilson. I can see the resemblance. You weren't even a stain in someone's underwear when ol' Gorby was spreading his seed around the world. How'd you pull that out of your keister?"

Wilson said, "Advanced world history. Senior year."

Shaking her head, Taryn shed her full-length mink. She tossed it onto the bed on her way to the window. Though the shutters were closed, she stood there, looking at them. After a moment contemplating something, she turned and faced the others. "I bet the tunnel comes up either inside the garage or somewhere real close by."

"I'd tend to agree," said Cade. "It's what I'd do if this were my place and money was no issue."

Duncan got rid of the fur hat and put on his Stetson. He regarded Daymon. With a click of his boot heels, he said, "Well, Auntie Em … you gonna give us the rest of the tour or will I have to demand a refund?"

"I want to see where this new passage goes," replied Daymon. "If it does end up in the garage—"

"We kill two birds with one stone," finished Cade, just as Lev's voice leapt from the CB riding in Duncan's coat pocket.

Duncan retrieved the radio and answered with a curt, "Go."

Lev came back at once. Without detailing the technique Seth had used to be able to read the imprints left on the yellow pad, he told Duncan that they had deciphered what Bridgett had written on the top sheet.

"Don't leave us hanging," interrupted Duncan. "Cut to the chase."

Gaze never leaving Duncan, Daymon padded toward the windows, crossed his arms, and leaned against the wall by the nightstand.

Lev said, "There are two numbers at the top. Thirty-nine and sixteen."

"That's gotta be the junction near Woodruff," said Duncan, "Go on."

"Three o'clock p.m. was written just below that," Lev said, the sound of crinkling paper coming over the open connection. "And underneath the rendezvous time is a long string of numbers." He proceeded to rattle them off rapid-fire.

A look of confusion on her face, Taryn regarded Wilson. She mouthed: *What do the numbers mean?*

Wilson shrugged and shook his head.

Duncan thumbed the Talk button. "Anything else?"

"She wrote the word 'Doer' around the edge of the page a couple of dozen times."

"How long did you leave her alone in there?" asked Duncan.

"Wasn't me," Lev said, irritation in his tone. "It was Tran here."

In his mind's eye, Cade saw Tran sitting next to Lev in the security pod and slowly slumping down in the rolling chair. Trying to become one with the fabric. And, truthfully, Cade felt sorry for lying by omission, for putting the man in the middle without all of the information up front. "Let me have that," he said, motioning for Duncan to hand over the radio. After taking possession, Cade walked into the panic room and came clean to Tran about what he had hoped to really accomplish by leaving Bridgett alone. When he turned and stepped over the threshold between the panic room and master suite, he saw that everyone was looking his way. Beginning with Taryn and ending with Duncan, he met each gaze and held it for a second. Finished speaking to Tran, he signed off and addressed the elephant in the room. "My plan backfired," he said, eyes narrowing. "I figured if Bridgett wasn't who she said she was she would just call whoever sent her and tell them she was somewhere west of Woodruff."

112

Duncan said, "She was blindfolded and bound when I brought her in."

Daymon slid to the floor and sat cross-legged. "We didn't drive around to confuse her, though. Doesn't take a rocket scientist to figure out the approximate location of the compound."

"Approximate is only good when you're talking cruise missiles or tactical nukes," quipped Duncan. "We'll be OK so long as we limit the comings and goings for a few days."

"Won't matter once it snows," said Taryn. "It sticks and stays ... *nobody* is going to be out and about."

Daymon glanced up from his spot on the floor and exchanged a knowing look with Cade.

Cade said nothing. His jaw had taken on the familiar granite set. His eyes suddenly seemed black as coal. Some kind of decision-making was going on behind them. Finally, he sat back down on the gilded chair. "Those numbers Seth revealed," he said, in front of a pregnant pause, "are the *exact* GPS coordinates to the Eden compound. She got them off the unlocked sat phone, wrote them down, then used the ham radio and relayed them to somebody." He buried his face in his hands. "I didn't think she had the smarts."

Wilson mouthed: *What the fuck.*

Taryn approached Cade and placed a hand on his shoulder. "We'll just have to be ready for them when they come."

"Whoever *them* is," shot Wilson.

Daymon looked about the room. "*Or* ... you take the initiative and hit them at the rendezvous."

Cade sat up and fixed a gaze on Daymon. "Take it to them on our terms," he said, rising up from the chair.

"But we have no idea how many we're dealing with," noted Taryn, voice filled with concern.

Wringing his boonie hat with both hands, Wilson said, "And what do we do if Bridgett's *friends* show up with the kind of numbers that make an attack on our part a death sentence?"

Duncan said, "Surprise is a force multiplier. We could call Lev and Jamie. Have them bring the Hummer and set up west of the junction and cover us with the Ma Deuce. There's still plenty of linked rounds for her."

Cade shook his head. "That'd leave the compound severely undermanned. More so than it is now."

Wilson said, "One thing in the positive column is the road block west of the compound." He nodded at Daymon. "Now that they know about it there's no way they're going to be able to flank us from that direction."

"And with Dregan's people watching the state route from Bear River," added Taryn, "I doubt they'll be coming from the south, either."

"Leaves us one direction to cover," said Duncan. He began to pace. His boot heels left impressions in the pile as he approached the set of double doors leading to the landing. He stopped at the threshold still on the cream-colored carpet and turned around to face the others.

Brow raised, Daymon asked, "What's brewing in that head of yours?"

Duncan replied, "I know we just cashed in Brook's chit with Dregan—" He grimaced at his choice of words and buried his face in one hand.

Outwardly unaffected by the slip, Cade said, "I was thinking the same thing. Given Dregan's cancer and his boy's suspect health, I doubt we could get them to go on another hunting expedition. However, if we got Dregan to loan us the Hummer with the Mk-19 and a few high explosive rounds—"

"—we wouldn't need the extra personnel," Duncan finished, just as two other voices called out. One followed a burst of static and emanated from his back pocket. The other was a woman's and had originated downstairs judging by the way the words "*come and get it*" caromed off the ceiling and filled the landing behind him.

Duncan fished the CB out and said, "Come again?"

More static, then Tran said, "Dregan just called. Bear River is under siege."

Thinking the worst, Duncan asked, "Breathers?"

"Demons," Tran replied. "The horde is back."

Taryn's mouth formed a silent O.

Heidi called up again. "Fooood's ready."

"They're going to be taking it to go," Daymon called down, his words competing with the ones still spilling from the tiny speaker.

In less than a minute, Tran had relayed all that Dregan had told him—along with one request that was more like a special favor.

Wilson's head was instantly filled with visons of the legions of dead circling the Viscount Arms in downtown Denver. He could almost smell the stink rising off of them as his chest grew tighter and breathing became a chore. "With that many rotters a few miles south of here," he gasped, "do we really have time to do that?"

"Tran said Dregan used the word *siege*. I'm pretty sure that old warhorse isn't into mincing his words. And taking into consideration what he said about survivors showing up at the gate ahead of the horde and that they had to call people back from outside the wire ..." Cade paused and stared at the floor by his boots. Looking up he added, "Tells me the Zs already know there's meat behind those walls. With those kinds of numbers, it truly is a siege in the making."

"And they ain't going anywhere anytime soon," Duncan said. He removed his glasses and pinched the bridge of his nose. "And I hope those walls hold until the dead grow tired and move on."

"Could take a while," said Cade. "And about that special request of Dregan's ..." His face went stony again. "That was going to happen anyway. Brook asked me to do it ... posthumously."

A confused look settling on his face, Wilson turned and regarded Cade.

Meeting the younger man's stare, Cade said, "She left me a death letter."

"What's a death—"

Taryn clamped a hand over Wilson's mouth. In quick succession, she looked to Duncan and then Cade. "We've come this far," she said, swallowing hard and letting her hand fall away.

Duncan swung his gaze to Cade. "If we're going to fulfill Brook's wish, then we better collect what we came here for and *di di mau.*"

"And Bridgett and her ilk?" said Wilson. "They know where we live now."

We deal with them after," Cade said over his shoulder as he disappeared into the panic room.

Chapter 19

"I'm coming home," Iris whispered. "You'll see, Mother. I *am* a *Doer*." She stopped rocking for a moment and swiveled around on her butt to face her pursuers. Purged number one was male. The only reason she knew this was because of the continual appearance of the shriveled-up piece of flesh hanging between the atrophied legs propelling the mindless husk in her direction. With every step the beast drew nearer, its flaccid penis would make another appearance through the foot-long tear in the crotch of its pants.

Tiring of the uninviting game of pee-pee peek-a-boo—*hell,* she thought, *my old Ken doll had a bigger schlong than Mister Flippety-Flop*—she pushed herself up to her knees and withdrew the sharpened stake from her back pocket. Now able to see the purged female staggering along behind the male, she picked a spot on the road to take them on, to rid herself once and for all of their continuous ogling and lusting.

"Break's over," she called out across the distance. "Come and get some."

The words alone spurred the zombies into finding another gear.

Dragging her leg along, Iris made her way across the stretch of leaf-covered state route she had chosen to engage them—one at a time, hopefully. She passed the dotted centerline and continued on another half-dozen feet before squaring up on the opposite shoulder.

Closing to within an arm's reach of their prey, the creatures' raspy hisses morphed into guttural snarls.

"You sinned," Iris said. "I'm going to grant you final rest." Breathing as if she'd run a marathon, when in fact she'd barely limped a couple of yards, she spun the makeshift weapon in her right hand so that its point faced the ground, and extended her left arm.

***

Lasting a minute at best, Iris's battle for survival had been far from epic. Moving barely a step faster than the purged, she jammed the stake into the female's temple, then backed away as the twice-dead thing slipped from the blood-slickened length of branch and crashed to the road in a heap.

Moving a little faster than the fallen female, Mister Flippety-Flop got a hold on Iris's vest and drew itself in. Bad mistake. She was already bringing her weapon up to her face to meet the attack. All it took once the stake was horizontal to the ground and taking up the space between her face and its snapping teeth was to simply to position the sharp tip before one roving eye and let its forward momentum do the rest.

The result was a hollow pop followed by a spurt of foul-smelling liquid that dribbled down the front of her vest.

Spent and grateful she had upheld her promise to Mother, Iris fell to the ground still in the clutches of the male purged. The latter half of the minute she spent pulling the stake from its eye socket and getting herself rolled over onto her back.

Now all alone on the stretch of road, she removed her vest and stripped the shirt from the male purged. The former she balled up and tossed into the ditch. The latter she shrugged on and buttoned to her neck.

Before moving on, she replaced the batteries in the radio, chucking the old ones into the ditch with the vest.

She powered on the radio and set the channel from memory. *Moment of truth.*

She pressed the Talk button and asked if anyone could hear her.

Nothing.

Knowing she was still out of range and hours from the time she was told to be at the junction, she powered down the radio and renewed her trek east.

Casa De Daymon

The F-650's cab smelled of hash browns, fried Spam, French roast coffee, and Frank's Red Hot by the time Cade closed his door and fired up the engine. In the back seat, both Taryn and Wilson were holding plastic Hollah Chevrolet promo cups and shoveling spoons heaping with Heidi's concoction into their mouths. In the passenger seat next to Cade, Duncan was clutching his red *Hollah to Save A Dollah* cup in a two-handed grip and purposefully inhaling the steam wafting from it. A smile on his lips and prescription lenses fogged, he took a tiny sip and declared the java simply delightful.

Still blown away that the panic room's hidden tunnel had indeed fed into Hollah's vehicle-packed multi-car garage, Cade flicked his eyes to the rearview and settled his gaze on the Arctic Cat snowmobile shoehorned lengthwise into the F-650's bed. With every rut and pothole the truck's oversized tires found, the lime-green Sno Pro 500 shimmied and shook, the movements stretching the already taut nylon tie-down straps and causing the metal ratcheting hardware to vibrate spastically.

"It's going nowhere," promised Cade in response to brief eye contact from Wilson. "The packaging said the straps are rated up to five thousand pounds."

"If you say so," replied Wilson as he gestured to the cup of hash mixture still balanced on the center console. "You going to eat that?"

With the keen of Daymon's watchrotter's nails dragging along the truck's flank standing the hairs on his neck up, Cade handed the hot-to-the-touch promo cup back to Wilson, the smell of the red-pepper-infused hot sauce radiating from it doing nothing positive for his appetite.

After driving roughly a quarter of a mile, Cade slowed the F-650 and parked it a dozen feet from the sheep gate. On the opposite side of the gate were the trio of Zs he remembered seeing in the distance on the main road before they turned in. The child Z with the Pokémon tank top had ventured into the

119

roadside ditch beside the gate and was mired ankle-deep in mud. Opening and closing its black hole of a mouth, the lone female of the group swayed before the gate like a stalk of wheat in a lazy breeze.

Anticipating the meal of fresh meat the mere sight of the vehicle promised, the male first turn, having just finished the long trudge from the main road to the gate, cut a hard left and unwittingly slammed its emaciated body full bore into the fence post beside the gate.

Newton's Third Law, which states that for every action there is an equal and opposite reaction, instantly came into play. The action part of the equation was the violent collision which started the Z's head whipping forward. A half-beat later the second component of the timeless truth in physics had the Z rebounding off the post and crashing to the ground as if on the receiving end of a Mike Tyson overhand right. Cade knew the Z wouldn't be feeling the brain-jarring impact to come; still, he couldn't help but wince when the rotter's skull met the road square on. Even inside the truck's enclosed cabin the hollow thud was heard by everyone.

"I never get used to that sound," said Duncan as he elbowed open his door and stepped from the truck. "There's nothing else in the world like it."

Reminded of the Viscount Arms and the very necessary atrocities he'd committed there with his Todd Helton Louisville Slugger, Wilson said, "Yes there is," and threw a shudder.

Taking Wilson's statement into account, Cade looked the others in the face one at a time. "Duncan gets gate duty," he said. "Taryn, the adults are yours to cull." And though he knew the story of Wilson braining his neighbors with his prized bat and then leaving their undead toddler to rot in the enclosed downtown Denver apartment, he still tasked the redhead with putting down the undead little boy stuck in the mud.

Sink or swim.

Duncan nodded and stepped from the truck.

"No problem," called Taryn as she jumped out and drew the Tanto-style blade from its sheath.

Cade watched Wilson follow Taryn out and tracked them all as they made their way to the gate.

Once Taryn reached the gate, without pausing, she grabbed a fistful of the female zombie's hair and buried her blade hilt deep into its brain.

In the next beat, Duncan had the gate unchained and was swinging it wide.

With no hesitation, Wilson strode through the gap. *He's not a boy, he's not a boy, he's not a boy* was running through his head as he planted his boots on the crumbling edge of the ditch just out of reach of the tiny rotter's straining fingers. Batting the pale, stick-thin arms away with his free hand, he leaned in and thrust his blade into the grade-school-aged rotter's left eye. Viscous black liquid spurted onto his hand and continued to sluice from the wound. Little runners of the brackish fluid snaked over its alabaster cheek, down its bite-ravaged neck, and then was absorbed by the tattered shirt collar.

When Wilson withdrew the blade, the twice-dead boy pitched sideways into the fence but remained standing. Flicking his gaze to the sturdy hiking boots still stuck fast in the mud, Wilson muttered, "Just my luck," and lashed out with his right foot.

The vicious kick landed and started the upright corpse listing sideways. Gravity did the rest and the boot nearest Wilson came free of the mud with a wet sucking sound.

Watching from the truck, Cade said, "Good work, kid," then swung his gaze to the right just in time to see Duncan step around the gate and plant an ostrich-skin boot on the sternum of the still-prostrate male Z.

Stepping over the female rotter's corpse, Taryn said, "That's my job, Old Man."

Staying clear of the snapping teeth and kneading fingers, she dropped to a knee. Then, having already slipped into the numb fugue state she wore like a security blanket whenever she faced culling even one former human being, she added the blood of another released soul to her black blade.

Chapter 20

Three minutes after locking the gate and heaving the twice-dead corpses over the opposing fence, the Eden survivors were on the move. At the T junction Cade slowed and steered left without thought of the new load in back. As a result, there came a chirping noise and a loud thump when the Arctic Cat's rubber paddles broke loose and the five-hundred-pound snow machine juddered across the bed's raised ridges and came to rest against the passenger side wheel well.

"I've got to cinch those straps tighter when we stop," said Cade.

"Gotta stop driving like a moonshiner high on his hooch," quipped Duncan.

"Burn rubber, Captain America," said Wilson, then promptly regretted it.

Content to stay out of the testosterone-fueled banter, Taryn stared out the window and took in the rural scenery scrolling by.

***

A minute after turning at the T they were nearing the pair of houses set back from the road Cade had talked about earlier. At the bottom of the gentle dip in the road were about a dozen Zs. Upon seeing the fast approaching F-650, the small band of first turns performed the same kind of slow, clumsy pirouette Cade had seen them do a thousand times since the early days of the outbreak. Steering wide around them, he sped up and flicked his gaze to the homes he'd already cleared. Since he'd been there last, someone had marked the doors with big white Xs. On the right, a cluster of rusted-out cars in one yard caught his attention. As did the X scribed on the barn doors behind them.

"Adrian's crew has been looting," observed Taryn.

123

Duncan adjusted his Stetson. Said, "We got our share of it back."

"Didn't come without consequence," Cade said quietly.

Duncan shifted his body away and joined Taryn in soaking up the view out the window.

Cade drove and said nothing more until they reached the jog in the road before the 16/39 junction. There he braked gently and stopped the Ford dead center in the two-lane. To the left were about twenty Zs. To his right, Main Street began its short run through what passed for downtown Woodruff.

Cade said, "Volunteer to secure the load?"

After casting a nervous glance at the dead things, Wilson volunteered.

"Quickly," said Cade.

Wilson hopped out, leaving the door partially cracked open behind him.

Cade regarded the rearview mirror and watched the kid go to work.

After sitting in silence for a minute or so, Duncan looked to Cade and said, "That's the second test you've given the kid in the last ten minutes."

Cade nodded but said nothing because Wilson was finished with the task and climbing back inside the rig.

As if the previous topic of discussion had never occurred, Duncan swung his gaze around the intersection and said, "We could set up the ambush here. Winch that Cadillac across the road by the auto body shop. Maybe roll out some of the little cars from the lot across the street and push them against the Caddie. I volunteer to set up shop upstairs in Back In The Saddle with a rifle."

Wilson said, "One of us could lay up in the body shop office."

Taryn said, "I could probably squeeze through the gap in the rollup doors."

"We," said Wilson. "You're not going alone."

124

She shot him a sharp look. "And you're not calling the shots."

Wilson bit his lip and latched his seatbelt.

"First things first," said Cade. "I have a promise to keep." He dug his satellite phone from his thigh pocket and handed it to Duncan. "The unlock code is my birth date."

"I've heard through the grapevine that you're thirty-five," drawled Duncan. "But I'm no mind reader."

"One, one, seven, five."

"You're a New Year's baby," gushed Taryn, throwing her arms over the seatback. "So am I."

Cade shook his head. "I was born *November* of seventy-five."

Taryn slumped back into the passenger compartment, muttering, "The year is off anyways ... by *seventeen*, to be exact."

Duncan took his eyes off the phone's tiny screen and regarded the moaning mass of dead flesh making first contact with the Ford's bumper and chest-high grill. Grimacing, he said to Cade, "November the what?"

A smattering of hollow thuds and low resonant gong-like sounds entered the cab as Cade started the rig moving against the undead phalanx. As he wheeled left on Main, the monsters fell behind and once again the survivors were left with silence and the troubled thoughts brought about by the sight of the dozens of sneering faces that had been pressing the glass.

Finally, as the overturned school bus where Brook had gotten bit slid by on the right, Cade answered, "November eleventh I'll be thirty-six."

Duncan cackled. "Armistice Day. Somebody forgot to tell the dead about the war to end all wars."

Wilson said, "I thought that was Veterans Day."

"It is," conceded Duncan. "Good old WW Two proved Armistice Day wrong. So the powers that be changed it to honor the past and as we've all learned since, the future fallen."

"Always hated being the center of attention on that day," admitted Cade.

Duncan said, "I can see how that'd be tough on a budding Eagle Scout."

Cade didn't respond to that. Instead, he pointed over the wheel. "We've got a mini horde."

"Looks like fifty or more. Probably all first turns," said Duncan. "Better slow down."

The speedometer needle dropped and hovered at twenty as Cade halved his speed.

Duncan reached up and wrapped his fingers around the grab bar by his head. "Gonna play icebreaker?"

"No other choice," Cade admitted as he slowed even more to study the shambling mass and find what might be a point of least resistance. Seeing no obvious chink in their rotten armor, he gripped the wheel tight and aimed the truck for a disemboweled specimen straight ahead and equidistant to the roadside ditches.

Remarkably, motoring along at barely walking speed, the Ford entered the moving roadblock and parted the undead mass evenly down the middle. The target Z was swallowed up under the truck much like its guts had been before it joined the ranks of the undead. Then the chain reaction created by the truck's wide bumper started the Zs spilling to the ground, many ending up at the bottom of the roadside ditches, hands clawing for the rig as it passed them by.

The cabin went strangely quiet and nobody spoke as Cade negotiated the numerous dips and rises the road took before straightening out a few miles south of Woodruff. Once the fence and top half of the Thagons' farmhouse and barn came into view, everyone save for Cade seemed to perk up a bit.

Though Wilson was full from Heidi's cooking, he couldn't help but think about Helen's, which in every way was far superior.

Taryn said, "First left at the break in the fence."

Cade nodded and braked.

The white fence bordering the grazing pasture to his left followed the contour of the land, which took on a slight rainbow-like arc from the road to the flat where the house and barn were perched. The paint was faded and scaling off. Suggesting the zombie horde had come into contact with it sometime in the past, some of the posts were leaning away from the road. Once the Ford ground to a halt, Cade looked to Duncan. "Check and see if we have any movement up there."

Duncan lifted the binoculars off his lap and trained them on the property. After a few seconds spent panning them back and forth, he said, "Upstairs window is open. I can see the curtains moving a bit. Other than that, nothing is stirring. Nothing living. Not even a mouse."

"How about vehicles?" Cade asked. "I remember Brook mentioning that Ray drove a pickup like the one her folks had when she was a girl. A baby blue Chevy, I believe."

"One detail I left out of the Bear Lake excursion," Duncan replied with a wag of his head. "Dregan gifted Charlie Jenkins' Jackson P.D. Tahoe to old Ray. As we speak, that decrepit blue rig you're talking about is dripping oil on a driveway up north. If anyone is home, either they parked the Tahoe out of sight behind the house, or it's stashed inside the barn."

Cade scanned the road ahead with the binoculars. Handing them back to Duncan, he consulted the mirrors. Nothing was moving on the road for as far as he could see. Which was good, because it lessened the chance of their presence leading to the zombies taking notice of the house on the hill.

Cognizant of the fact the rotten meat missile they had just parted on the state route had already about-faced and begun their indefatigable search for the truck he was presently sitting in, Wilson said, "Are you sure these folks need checking on? After all … they're notorious for not monitoring their radio."

"Or turning one on in the first place," added Taryn. She leaned forward and told Cade and Duncan about finding the blood trail leading to the Thagons' door. That had been the same day Oliver disappeared. That had also been the day she found herself staring down the barrel of Helen's rifle. Though the blood on the farmhouse stoop turned out to have been from a rabbit Ray had butchered, the side trip had proved to her the old folks could handle themselves. And with the rotter mega-horde currently just a few short miles south at Bear River, popping in to check on the geriatric dynamic duo was nowhere near the top of her "*to-do*" list.

Duncan craned around and shot a sour look at the backseat passengers. It said: *Give the man some slack, he just lost his wife.*

"Has to be done," Cade said gruffly. "Stay in or get out. Your choice."

Wilson shot a furtive glance at the road behind the truck. "Getting out," he said.

Taryn agreed, but added, "Let's make it effin quick. I don't want to have to wait the horde out in the barn again."

"You and me both," Cade said soberly. He took his foot from the brake and let gravity pull on the truck down the hill. At the bottom of the decline where the dingy white fence parted, he committed to the turn and fed the engine some gas. The transition from asphalt to the feeder road was like driving over a cattle crossing guard. The entire truck shimmied as the tires tackled the washboard ruts left by two weeks' worth of inclement weather. After slewing right, then left, all the while threatening to spill the tethered Arctic Cat from the bed, the F-650's tires bit into the mud and forward momentum was established.

Piles of gravel lining both sides of the narrow road suggested to Cade that Ray had had it graded regularly and likely topped with fresh rock afterward to prevent against seasonal runoff. Regular having gone out the window three months ago, it didn't surprise him that Ray had let the road go.

Taryn noticed Cade's head panning the road and detected a definite change in his body language. He was going *frosty*, as she'd heard Brook describe the zone he went into when facing certain *situations*. "The Thagons will recognize this vehicle," she said, trying to put him at ease. "Besides, they don't shoot first."

"One of them usually gets the drop on you, though," said Wilson. "Lord knows *I've* stared down the barrel of Ray's rifle before."

"Ray's a hell of a shot, too," added Duncan as he tightened his grip on the grab bar by his head.

"Better slow down," said Taryn, thrusting her arm between Cade and Duncan and pointing to the looming curve in the drive. "Beyond the rusty combine there the road is washed out pretty bad."

Duncan said, "*This* isn't bad?"

She said, "Compared to what's ahead? No. There's a drop of at least eight inches and the wash broadens out to where it's between fifteen and twenty feet across. The Raptor ate it up. With the snowmobile back there … this rig, not so much."

"Ray said they'd get the tractor out and fill it in come spring time."

Duncan looked at Wilson over his shoulder. "When did the old boy tell you that?"

"After he took the shotgun from my neck," he answered. "We're best buds now."

Knuckles going white as the Ford dipped into a particularly deep rut, Duncan said, "I think we should stop here and go the rest of the way on foot."

Cade made no reply as he brought the pickup to a lurching halt a foot from the heavily eroded roadway. Still mute, he rolled the shifter into Park and set the brake. He popped out of his seatbelt, sending it sailing home. As his hand went for the keys, his eyes roamed the two-story house looming over the gravel parking area fronting the wraparound covered porch. Like the fence, the paint on the house was scaling off. Large sheets hung off the clapboard siding here and there. After stilling the engine, Cade dumped the keys into a cargo pocket and his hand went for the M4 pressing against his left leg. It was within easy reach, angled down out of sight with the telescoping stock collapsed and the suppressor kissing the firewall.

Clicking out of his seatbelt, Duncan whispered, "I'd take that as a yes."

Still, Cade remained quiet. The way his eyes never left the farmhouse told Duncan the Delta operator sensed something was amiss.

Duncan slumped low in his seat and cast his gaze on the house. "Whatcha got?"

Cade said, "At first I thought the window was left open. It's not. It's been shot out. See the bullet pocks on the walls? There's also broken glass on the porch roof."

Hefting the Saiga and clicking his door partway open, Duncan said, "No, I don't see those details ... but I'll surely take your word for it. What's the move?"

Chapter 21

The first detail Dregan noticed when he pushed the door open to the bedroom his son had claimed weeks ago were the curtains covering the far window. They were shut, as they should be. However, he noticed a thin strip of light infiltrating where the drapes had been left open. Colorful tanker trains with eerie plastic smiles chugged here and there on the curtains. Peter had the toy versions of the trains when he was still dawdling around their house on the cul-de-sac in Salt Lake City. Always fascinated with anything mechanical—especially the jet airplanes whose flight paths took them directly over the subdivision several times daily—Peter had worn deep grooves into the wooden tracks playing *choo-choo* with Thomas and Percy and Henry.

Now, edging into his teens, Peter was into any movie that he could get to play on his scrounged laptop computer. He'd stay glued to the thing until the battery went dead and then bring it back to life with a portable solar charger Dregan found while out foraging. *Wash, rinse, repeat*, thought Dregan as a mother of a cough slowly worked its way up from the far recesses of his failing lungs.

"Peter," he said, gently nudging with the toe of his boot the blanket-swaddled form stretched out lengthwise on the floor. "You need to make sure the curtains are all the way closed before night."

A grunt was all he got from the boy.

"Did you finish your movie?" he asked.

Voice muffled by the comforter, Peter said, "Battery died before the killer shark did."

Dregan yanked a corner of the bed cover, exposing a shock of blond hair which he promptly tousled with his mitt-sized right hand. Meeting the boy's ice-blue eyes, he nodded toward the shelf full of toy trains and said, "Why don't you play with Thomas and Friends then?" What started as a belly laugh dislodged the cough Dregan had been fighting hard to suppress. His body was wracked by an unstoppable coughing fit, the laugh all but drowned out by a rising tide of bloody mucous.

On the receiving end of a glare from his son that said: *Are you kidding?* Dregan fished out a square of fabric torn from an old tee shirt and turned it a dark shade of crimson by spitting the contents of his mouth into it.

Face nearly the color of his hanky, Dregan wiped his mouth and tucked the soiled fabric into his jacket pocket.

"Done smoking?"

Dregan's body seemed to deflate as Peter's words registered.

"Cause it's not doing you any good."

"I know, boy. It's been three days since I finished my last pack. Now that Greg seems to be recovering from the bite, I'm not as stressed. Don't feel as if I need one every waking moment."

Peter sat up and cast a furtive glance at the window. "You must not have looked out there lately."

"Correct," he said. "Not since we lost the woodcutters trying to make it to the gate. Has anything changed?"

Peter looked at his dad with those eyes. They were watery and glittered like twin sapphires. In a low voice, he said, "Only thing between our stretch of the wall and the roamers in the field is the graveyard fence."

Dregan shuffled past the beanbag chair and parted the Thomas curtains a couple of inches. Peering out with one eye he saw that Peter was right: The dead were now amassed six deep around the newly erected fencing. A dozen yards behind the monsters was the doomed woodcutting crew's pickup. It carried most of a full load of split logs and sat low on its springs. So low that the long grass nearly brushed the handles on the open passenger side door. In his mind's eye, he saw the old step side come in from the south and pass the feeder road at a high rate of speed, taking out dozens of walking dead in the process. As the corpses went tumbling to all points of the compass, the blood-red pickup abruptly faltered and fishtailed wildly. He recalled shaking his head and saying "No" as the pickup's rear end broke hard to the left, then swung back to the right. He cursed and punched the wall as the driver lost all control with the vehicle's grill nearly square with the sloped embankment directly across the field from Peter's window.

Still etched into his memory were the driver's and passenger's faces—the color of driven snow—as the pickup left the road, bounced through the ditch, and continued on for another fifty yards, dragging fence posts with barbed wire still attached. The truck had churned muddy furrows into the field before finally coming to a violent, juddering halt a stone's throw from where Dregan was standing now.

As a result of the sudden stop, the load had shifted and cut firewood rocketed through the rear window, gravely injuring both the driver and passenger. Before Dregan could order up a rescue team, the first of hundreds of undead that had followed the stricken truck in from the road reached the crash site and began to worm in through the broken rear window.

An hour removed, the screams of the dying men still echoed in Dregan's head. What was left of the passenger still lay on the circle of crushed grass where the dead had dragged his kicking and flailing body before stripping it clean of its flesh and organs. The driver, however, was still in the truck. Having been killed mercifully by a headshot delivered by one of the snipers positioned in the tower north of Dregan's home, the corpse's pale hands still clutched the wheel even as the monster sprawled across the bench seat continued to feed.

Rattling the elder Dregan from his vivid walk down memory lane, Peter asked, "What are you going to do about them?"

Still holding the curtains apart, he said, "I'm working on a plan, Peter."

"What kind of plan?"

Dregan heard the question, yet couldn't take his eyes from the perimeter wall. He was focused on the spot where the continuous run abruptly doglegged around a large bog where sinking the multi-ton panels into the ground hadn't been an option. It was at that point where the dead were beginning to pack in the tightest—dozens deep by his estimation. Hundreds of bodies were pressing against each other, their combined weight being focused at the point where the south-running length made a near ninety-degree turn to the west. Hundreds more were mired in the bog and fighting mightily to free themselves from the sucking ground. Dozens more of the abominations were trapped on the outer periphery of the bog and had already been trampled by their own kind. Stark white legs and arms jutting from the bottom of the pile continued to kick and claw the air, the crushing weight of their undead brethren inconsequential against their unrelenting desire to reach the nearby prey and feed.

A long hard look at the jog in the panels told him a few were beginning to bow inward. If something wasn't done before nightfall, he feared that the dead would be flooding through a breach before he could put into motion the plan stewing on the back burner of his mind.

Peter joined his dad by the window, peeled the curtain back further and repeated his question. "I don't think you heard me, Dad. What kind of plan?"

"It depends upon whether your brother gets back to me with good news or not. I'll let you know when I know. I promise you that." He took his son's head in both calloused hands, bent down, and kissed him on the cheek. "I love you, boy. Now put on your boots and grab a jacket … today is take-your-son-to-work day."

Peter stole one last glance outside. His eyes fell on the roamer tangled in a length of barbed wire attached to a three-foot-long fence post. It was still trudging across the bog. However, since he'd seen it last, it had somehow gutted itself, the rope of slimy gray entrails now one with the splintered wood and tarnished wire.

After saying a silent prayer for the soul of the man whose husk remained behind on Earth, Peter smoothed the curtains to the wall and arranged them so the two halves overlapped each other in the center of the window. Greatly troubled by the sheer number of soulless human shells still shuffling north on the state route, he turned to retrieve his shoes from the floor and spotted his dad stooped over and leaning against the doorjamb. Underneath the stretched fabric of his long black duster, his broad back heaved as a fresh bout of coughing wracked his body. In that moment, the towering figure he had always thought of as invincible seemed defeated.

Holding a hand up to silence the forthcoming query, Dregan buried his face in the crook of his arm and hacked uncontrollably. The fit was the worst to date. It lasted a couple of minutes, a softball-sized black stain on his jacket sleeve the end result.

"Let's go," he wheezed, and then led Peter out of the room.

Chapter 22

Thagon Homestead

Sixth sense jangling crazily, Cade grabbed the binoculars off the seat, shouldered open his door, and stepped from the truck. *Cover is your friend* sounded in his head as he slowly backed away from his open door and hauled open the rear passenger door. Danners ankle-deep in muddy water, he ushered Wilson and Taryn from the cab, she toting an AR, the gangly redhead pressing his black Beretta to his leg. Stopping the latter by placing a hand on his shoulder, Cade leaned in close and told Taryn to take cover by the tailgate.

"What?" Wilson asked, sounding irritated, his eyes flicking to Cade's hand.

"Only good use for that pistol if we get into a gunfight is to use it to fight your way to your rifle." He reached across the seat and dragged out an M4. "So holster the Beretta and take this."

Heeding the unsolicited advice without a word to the contrary, Wilson aimed the rifle at the ground by his feet and backed up slowly to where the others were huddled.

Crouched next to the F-650's rear tire with two open doors between him and any possible incoming rounds, Cade raised the binoculars to his eyes and trained them on the upper story. With two far-from-clean panes of auto glass in the way, the image was a little blurry.

Head craning around the rear bumper, Duncan said, "Whatcha got?"

"The upper window on the left has been shot through … half a dozen times," Cade replied. He walked the field glasses to the right. "Same with the other window up top. Looks like the lower pane is gone completely." He rose and steadied the Steiners on the truck bed rail to get an unimpeded second look.

"And …?" asked Duncan.

"The lower half of the right window isn't shot out … it's open," Cade answered.

Just then the curtain in the window in question was ruffled by the wind, revealing a black cylindrical item. It was angled down and moving toward the windowsill.

"Gun," whispered Cade, causing everyone to duck. He dipped down behind the bed and passed off the Steiners to a waiting hand. Then he deployed the 3x magnifier to augment the EOTech holographic sight atop the M4's top rail and snicked the selector to Fire. At the back end of a long two seconds, he shouldered his rifle in one fluid motion and brought its stubby suppressor to bear on the upper story.

"Why aren't they—" Wilson began.

"—shooting at us?" Cade finished. "I don't know." With the Oliver incident not too far removed, he held his fire but kept the window in his sights, hoping for a target to identify and engage if warranted.

Steiners trained on the house, Duncan said, "I have eyes on the first floor."

"Copy that," replied Cade, still targeting the upper right window, his rifle barrel unwavering.

A minute passed.

Nothing.

The wind kicked up, ruffling the curtains. Cade saw nothing but a dark void behind them. "Show yourself," he growled as the two halves again went slack and came together in the middle. Though no match for the Steiners, he was certain the optics atop the rifle were sufficient to have revealed the muzzle to him had it still been present. *Maybe they're outgunned and retreated out back.* With neither the manpower or combined experience to surround the house, that was a risk Cade was willing to take.

As if reading Cade's mind, Taryn said, "My side is still clear."

Wilson chimed in. "Our six is clear to the road, but we got rotters coming from the south. The ones we passed on the way to the drive are nearly to the turnoff and they're eyeballing the farm."

"We've got some time before Bridgett is set to rendezvous," Duncan said in a low voice. "I'd rather spend it setting up our ambush than watching the paint peel off this house."

Cade lowered his M4. "I'm going forward," he said through gritted teeth. "Cover the windows."

Wilson and Taryn edged around Duncan, who was already shouldering the SAIGA.

Cade flipped the 3x magnifier away, leaving just the quick acquisition sight atop the rail. With a sidelong glance at Duncan, he asked, "You have slugs in that thing?"

"Every other."

"Make them count."

Duncan said nothing.

Taryn and Wilson were crouched low and directing questioning looks Cade's way.

Meeting Taryn's gaze, Cade instructed her to keep her weapon trained on the breezeway between the house and nearby barn, the latter of which he explained was an unlikely place to spring an ambush since the massive double doors were shut and secured with a length of chain wound multiple times through the iron door handles.

Wilson crunched down his boonie hat with one hand. The M4 was clutched in the other. "What do I do?" he asked.

Cade pointed to his eyes with two fingers splayed into a V then quickly gestured to the feeder road with the same hand. "Keep watch on our six," he said, eyes full of intensity. "I doubt if the Zs will catch up with us." He flicked his eyes back to the Thagons' home for a second then brought his gaze back to bear on Wilson. "But if they do, I want you to do them quietly with a blade. Think you can handle that?"

"He has to," replied Taryn, her eyes flicking to her man.

Absentmindedly feeling for the knife on his hip, Wilson nodded and accepted the job with a sincere air of confidence.

"I'm going to start running for the house at one," Cade said, beginning to tick down from five with one hand.

At the count of three, he had risen and was skirting the near side of the truck in a combat crouch.

When the count reached two in his head he was passing the front bumper and moving at a brisk pace. A half-beat later the count was over and he was sprinting toward the house in a serpentine pattern—changing direction every few feet to throw off anyone who might be drawing a bead on him.

Keeping his M4 trained on the front door, he came up on the short stack of steps with a full head of steam. At the last second, however, when anyone watching would assume he was about to mount the steps, cross the half-dozen feet of wooden porch and introduce his hundred and eighty hard-charging pounds to the front door via a strategically placed boot sole, he abruptly peeled off to the left.

Using the shrubs fronting the railing for concealment, he made his way to the far end of the porch where he snugged his rifle to his shoulder and quickly swept the muzzle to the right. Seeing nothing but scraggly, low bushes huddling against the house's cement foundation, he made his way to the far northeast corner, went to one knee, and peeked around the corner. Nothing there save for more bushes and a sort of sunporch bumping off the far corner of the house. The all-encompassing windows were weatherproofed with opaque plastic that looked to have been riddled with gunfire. And giving the porch a life of its own, every time the wind kicked up from the south, the plastic sheeting would expand and contract, like lungs drawing a breath. Adding to the intermittent rustle of sun-aged plastic, someone or *something* inside the house was making a hollow knocking sound. He heard three or four taps, then silence. A few seconds passed and the sound was back.

Cade waited there for a few more seconds and learned there was no pattern to the number of taps, nor was the interval of silence between them constant. He envisioned the Thagons bound and gagged and crammed inside a closet. Then his mind went to the worst-case scenario: that the house was booby trapped with dead things like the rehab place and fix-it shop in Woodruff had been.

Cade tuned out the wind and foreign sounds and cleared his mind of the *what ifs*. He deployed the 3x magnifier, shouldered the M4, and surveyed the landscape to his left through the augmented optics.

The first hundred yards or so consisted of overgrown pasture land dotted intermittently with crumbling mole hills. Bordering the pasture, a wire fence ran left to right. A handful of yards on the far side of the fence, backstopped by the low mountain range of the same name, was the Bear River. Usually just a creek, it was now swollen with runoff from the early morning hail that still blanketed the foothills all around. The fast-flowing water made the long grass submerged along the river's banks whip rhythmically to and fro.

After determining the perimeter clear of threats, Cade retraced his steps, stopping in front of the first window he came to. Both panes had been shot through. He counted more than a dozen bullet holes, most of which were outgoing. This told him that Ray and Helen had recently engaged someone from inside. And if he had to make a guess, it was the same people coming to pick up Bridgett at the 16/39 junction. Cade noted the time on his Suunto. Decided that as long as the dead encircling Bear River stayed put, he and the others would have plenty of time to decide how and where they would take the fight to Bridgett's crew.

Rising slowly from a crouch, Cade cupped his hands and peered through the quarter-inch vertical seam between the drawn curtains. Though the interior was gloomy and shadowy around the edges, he could still see that the dark wood floor was polished to a luster. The room's far wall bore paper that looked to have been hung in the fifties. Wide stripes in muted pink and seafoam green drew his eye to the coved ceiling, which was bordered by fancy crown molding and home to a light fixture sprouting six upturned brass sconces, each with a trio of crystals dangling from its conical base. Here and there the wall was marred with quarter-sized craters created by incoming bullets.

Suddenly the sounds were back. A steady *tap … tap … tap*, followed by a resonant *bang*. Still, he saw nothing moving inside as he noted the furniture, every piece of which looked to be from the sixties and would have fetched high dollar in Portland considering its burgeoning hipster community. The pair of low-slung couches, upholstered in avocado-green fabric, were pushed against the far wall. Strangely, one of them was left blocking the open doorway leading into what was clearly the kitchen.

Chapter 23

The Thagons' kitchen was illuminated by the light coming in from the sunroom. The only thing moving in the kitchen were golden dust motes and a lone housefly. The counter was strewn with tin cans. Some of the cans, clearly empty, lay on their sides, jagged metal ringing what looked to be hastily pried open lids.

Doubtful Helen would have left a mess of that magnitude, he was thinking as he drew back from the window and retraced his steps to the wrap-around porch.

Going to a knee out of sight of the front door, he made eye contact with Duncan and through a series of hand signals told him to send the Kids over one at a time—Wilson first.

Grinning because of the way Cade had silently designated Wilson—one hand caressing an imaginary afro—Duncan motioned the redhead over and sent him on his way. Keeping his SAIGA shouldered and trained on the upstairs window, he watched the spry youngster cover the seventy feet from the truck to the front porch running a poor man's version of the serpentine pattern Cade had utilized. Once Wilson was on the porch and leaning against the wall by the right-side doorjamb, Duncan relieved Taryn of her rearguard task and sent her across the open ground.

To Duncan's amazement, nobody sprang from the window to shoot at the brunette as she zigged and zagged her way to the stairs. That's the way he would have done it if the circumstances were reversed. Taken a page from old Carlos "White Feather" Hathcock's book. Ninety-three confirmed kills didn't lie. Copying a tactic the famed Marine sniper had employed to pin down and decimate an entire NVA platoon, perhaps the shooter upstairs was just waiting for the group to get separated before putting one of them down in the open ground. Wound the female and let the others wring their hands deciding what to do next. Surely the men would feel compelled to save her. Then again, if someone *was* up there watching and waiting they had no idea that the first man they had let go across open ground unscathed possessed a lethal set of skills they likely had no counter for. *Or,* the pessimistic voice in Duncan's head added as he rose and began a loping sprint for the door, *maybe they're allocating their rounds for the wizened old dude.*

Duncan put his head down and clomped off toward the house. There was no fancy footwork. No cute head fakes to throw off a would-be sniper. He didn't deviate left or right whatsoever. His only goal was to reach the stairs without falling down and making an ass of himself. And he succeeded, albeit out of breath and holding his side when he hit the porch and pressed his back to the doorjamb opposite Wilson.

Keeping his carbine trained on the curtain-shrouded picture window to his left, Cade threw his right leg over the top porch rail and clambered onto the porch. The weathered boards creaked as he went to his knees and swung the rifle around on its sling, letting it dangle vertically near his spine. In order to keep from presenting a silhouette for anyone waiting behind the drawn curtains, he dropped to his stomach and commando-crawled past the window. Once clear of the window, he quickly rose and crept the remaining twenty feet to where the others were waiting.

"Just like they taught you in boot camp," Duncan mouthed to Cade as the Delta operator formed up across the door frame from him.

Cade said nothing. He did the fingers at the eyes thing again and then pointed at the porch, directing the others to look down.

Dots of what looked to be blood meandered across the worn boards from the edge of the doormat to the short stack of stairs.

"That's the rabbit's blood," Wilson whispered.

Taryn nodded, showing her agreement.

Cade swiped a finger through a pencil-eraser-sized drop. Though it appeared dry—almost black and possessing a matte sheen—the arc of dark red left behind after he was finished proved otherwise.

"Hell," said Duncan, his mouth near Cade's ear, "it hailed this morning. This close to the mountain range, good chance they got rain, too."

Cade shook his head slowly side-to-side. Then, with Wilson and Taryn both subtly nodding to show they agreed with Duncan's theory, he reached out and stuck two fingers into the black mat by his knee. Left them there for a two-count and then held up his hand to show the others the result of his experiment. Slowly, as gravity's pull kicked in, crimson tails sprang from his blood-slickened fingertips. As the others looked on, the runners reached his knuckles where the creases there provided a new path for the still very wet bodily fluid to congeal.

"Still convinced it's from Ray butchering a rabbit days ago?"

Fingers slowly kneading the M4's forestock, Wilson swallowed hard and said, "What do we do?"

Taryn looked to Duncan, then swung her gaze to Cade and let it hang there, obviously awaiting an answer.

"I'm going in solo," said Cade. "Same as before. Duncan watch the house. Taryn the barn—"

"—and me, our six," Wilson finished and swung his rifle around, training its lethal end on the feeder road.

Cade nodded as he looked each person in the eye, then turned to face the door.

Knock and wait to see if there are Zs, or go in unannounced?

Choosing to go the latter route, he turned the knob and pushed gently on the door to test its swing. It moved freely a quarter of an inch, proving it was unlocked.

Still muffled and hard to place, the knocking and banging began anew.

Cade cocked an ear and listened until the noises subsided.

Unsure of which approach was less likely to get him into a gunfight with a squatter, or shot at by the couple he was supposed to be protecting, he motioned for Wilson to swap places with him so he could get a better feel for the home's interior layout before proceeding.

State Route 39

The blood-crusted nylon chafing Iris's neck was beginning to be too much to handle for even her—a seasoned Watcher used to enduring discomfort for days on end in cramped attics and church steeples. For seemingly the hundredth time in the last ten minutes, she stopped to adjust the collar of the shirt she'd liberated from Mister Flippety-Flop. Holding the stiff fabric away with one hand, she attacked the tiny raised bumps dotting her upper body with the other. They were concentrated mostly in her underarm area and between her breasts and were beginning to bleed from her constantly scratching and picking at them.

After going at her chest and neck for some time, reluctantly she pulled both arms inside the soiled sleeves and went at both pits with all the vigor of a coonhound trying to dislodge a burrowing tick.

You're a mess, Miss Doer, she told herself as a new pinprick of pain flared on her left temple. Before she could thrust her arms back through the sleeves and scratch *that* itch, a series of new attacks erupted down below, confirming to her that the unidentified insects inhabiting the shirt were now in her hair—upstairs and down.

For a brief second, she entertained the thought of stripping off the shirt and going on in just her bra and blue jeans. One glance at the dark clouds overhead quickly dispelled that notion. They were fat with moisture that could come down in the form of rain, hail, or, even worse, given a steep enough temperature drop, snow.

What she needed, she told herself as the feeding frenzy in her pubic region reached an untenable level of discomfort, was a vehicle and a razor—not necessarily in that order, unless the snow started up this second.

Before resuming the trudge east in search of a set of wheels, she jammed one hand into the front of her pants, pinched a tuft of pubic hair between finger and thumb, and yanked hard.

"Fuck me!" she wailed and drew in a breath. Still grimacing from the unexpected shock, she exhaled sharply and drew the sample into the light of day.

After placing the wiry black tumbleweed into her palm and sifting through it with her pinky, she closed one eye and brought it to within an inch of her face. Seeing nothing moving in the tangle, she brushed her palm off on her pants leg and went back to the well. Face screwed up in morbid concentration, she ripped and tore and came up with a fistful of short n' curlies which received the same inspection that garnered the same result: Nothing to see here, move along.

And she did, cursing and hollering and begging God to make the radio in her pocket come alive with the voice of one of her own.

Chapter 24

After finding the Thagons' front door unlocked, Cade had stepped across to the side opposite the handle and gently elbowed Wilson out of his way.

Now, back pressed against the house's exterior, he leaned forward a few degrees and peered through the two-inch gap between door and jamb. From this new vantage all he could see was one arm of a winter coat hanging on a coat tree to his left. It was close enough for him to touch. It was also bent at the elbow and obscured everything in his line of sight save for the blood-spattered rug on the floor. Simultaneously, he shouldered the door in a couple more inches and moved the sleeve aside with his free hand. *Better.* He could now see past the coat and beyond the foyer. But the sliver of light lancing in wasn't sufficient to cut more than a few feet into the gloom. Triggering the tactical light affixed to his M4's side rail illuminated a formal dining room, in it a table and chairs oriented lengthwise. Because of the angle, the white cone of light failed to reach further into the home. However, based on what he'd seen through the side window, he knew the sitting room full of chairs and sofas lay beyond. And through basic deduction, he placed the stairs to the second floor off to his right.

Knowing that swinging the door all the way in could lead to him unintentionally springing what Wilson had taken to calling a *rotter trap*, Cade called the old couple by name, then cocked an ear and listened hard.

A beat later the creaking noise was back, followed at once by the steady tapping. With the door now cracked open a hand's width, it became obvious to him that the tapping noise was emanating from the kitchen area dead ahead. The creaking, however, was coming from somewhere upstairs. Maybe even the room directly above the foyer.

Glancing at his Suunto, he said, "Give me five minutes." He regarded Duncan then patted the Motorola in his pocket. "I'll radio once I've cleared the place."

Eyes narrowed, Duncan said, "Holler if you need us."

Cade made no response. He was already focusing on the task at hand. Going into the *zone*, as he called the heightened state of awareness achieved by pushing anything that might come to be a distraction to a secure place in his mind and locking it down.

Keeping his M4 trained on the center of the heavy wooden door, he gave it a good shove and stepped aside. Unlike the fix-it shop where Taryn had almost lost her life days ago, there were no tethered Zs waiting for him on the other side. Brushing past the winter coat and its grabby lifeless arm, he made his way silently over the threshold and closed the door at his back.

The temperature inside was no different than out. The sickly-sweet stench of death rode the drafts coming in through the breached windows. It was so thick here it seemed to Cade as if he was slowly being choked by tendrils of carrion-infused air.

Swinging the M4 to his right illuminated a staircase complete with wide wooden handrails. Sandwiched between an ornate bannister and a wall covered with floral print paper was a flight of stairs that climbed from right to left. The leaded window set above the base of the stairs was covered with newspaper, the words on the individual pages impossible to make out from afar. Moving closer he discovered that the yellowed pages had come from an Ogden Standard-Examiner dated the Monday after the dead rose. The subtext below the paper's masthead read **Serving Northern Utah Since 1888**. Cade shook his head. *A one-hundred-and-twenty-three-year run brought to a grinding halt by a man-made virus.* The headline below the subtext screamed: **Salt Lake City Teeming With Walking Dead**. The declarations **State of Emergency Bypassed - OMEGA VIRUS Forces President Odero To Suspend Habeas Corpus! - Martial Law Declared**, were all below the fold in smaller font. Cade had seen these words flashed on the television and repeated on the crawl before leaving Portland that last Saturday in July. Never before had he seen them *all* confirmed on the front page of a widely distributed newspaper.

He moved the beam from the stairs and illuminated a squadron of newborn houseflies buzzing lazily around the dining room. The table was set for three: plates, service, and coffee cups. Salt and pepper shakers and ceramic urns presumably meant for cream and sugar sat equidistant between the plates. The plates looked to still have food on them. Intermittently, one or two of the flies would break formation and land on the morsels, loiter there briefly, then take flight again with their newfound bounty.

Deciding on a counterclockwise recon of the main floor, he swung his rifle back to his right and took a couple of paces toward the back of the house. The hall ahead of him was now more than just a black tunnel. It ran for twenty feet or so then spilled out into the kitchen. The walls on both sides shared the same vertical-striped paper he had spied from outside the sitting room window. Pictures featuring a middle-aged couple in happier times hung on the left wall. The right wall, cut off at an angle at the top to accommodate the open staircase, featured photos of alpacas—hairy creatures with long snouts and swooping necks. Hanging on wide straps of ribbon from the necks of the hooved beasts were shiny oval medallions—most of them gilded.

This set Cade at ease. Regular county-fair-attending country folk didn't strike him as the shoot-first-and-ask-questions-later kind of people. Then that supposition started a chill to creep his spine, for the ask-questions-first type of folks weren't long for this cruel world.

At the hall's terminus to his fore was the door to the sunroom. It was inset with a square window that was weatherproofed with the same blurry plastic as the outside windows. The door was cracked open a hair and sucked in and out intermittently much like the plastic sheeting on the sunroom had. This revelation erased the newfound calm brought on by the photos of the Thagons and their prized stock.

He heel and toed it down the hall, stopping before a door on his right he guessed hid an under-stair storage area. He tried the handle, finding the door unlocked. With no hesitation, he pulled it open and illuminated the interior with the tactical light. Finding nothing but cobwebs and dust and a large plastic bin with the words *Board Games* written on it in cursive, he closed the door and moved on to the kitchen.

Pausing before the door to the sunporch, he braced it with his toe to limit its swing, then poked the M4 through the three-inch gap. Seeing only a rusty propane tank and his and hers rubber galoshes on the floor, he closed and locked the door.

Awash in the high-lumen beam, he saw that the kitchen was as barren as the sunporch. Aside from the opened cans on the counter, the kitchen had been emptied of everything. The cupboard doors hung open. There were no cans or boxes, only imprints in the dust where they had been.

The floor was covered with shards of broken china. The light-blue pattern on the pieces matched the settings on the table.

As Cade shifted his attention from the mess on the floor to the sitting room beyond the kitchen, the tapping resumed. And it was coming from behind the door at his back.

After turning a slow one-eighty with most of his weight on the balls of his feet, he trained the M4 on the door and tried the brass handle.

Locked.

Tap, tap, tap.

Cade crouched to inspect the lock and saw the rounded end of a skeleton key protruding from the keyhole.

Tap, tap, tap.

He drew a deep breath and turned the key. A solid *click* greeted the effort.

Tap, tap, tap.

What he wouldn't give right now for one of those camera on a stalk things Adam Cross carried with him on every mission.

Tap, tap, tap.

"Helen, Ray," he called, rattling the door.

152

Tap, tap, tap.

Like fingers drumming a tabletop, thought Cade as he decided to investigate.

Standing opposite the door's swing, he crouched down, turned the knob, and flung it open. Rifle snugged to his shoulder, he stepped clear of the door and brought the muzzle online. The moment the beam from his tactical light pierced the dark, three things were revealed, none of them good. The room was small and contained a shallow, blood-stained sink. A mirror hanging over the sink bounced the beam around, which let him see the freshly turned Z to his right. Thankfully it had been placed on the small porcelain toilet and tied down with a yellow nylon rope. Though the thing had blood-rimmed craters where its eyes should have been, and bloodied holes where ears used to hang, the wispy shock of silver hair and roadmap of wrinkles creasing its ashen face convinced Cade that he was looking down at Ray Thagon— one-half of the couple he was here to check in on. Though the fresh turn was unable to stand, it *could* reach the wall to its fore with those bloodied fingertips. And as Cade watched it squirm against its bonds, it paused long enough to lean forward and recreate the sound that had drawn him here in the first place.

Tap, tap, tap.

Like fingers drumming a table, indeed.

Even robbed of the sense of sight, somehow, the undead thing knew he was here. That much was clear. Because from that moment forward the scrabbling at the wall continued without pause until Cade moved closer and planted one of his Danners on the abomination's wrists, effectively trapping both arms against its legs.

Drawing his Gerber from its scabbard, Cade said, "They made you face a Z or two before torturing you, I see."

There wasn't much fight left in old Ray's bite-riddled body as Cade shifted his weight forward. Just some grabbing at the folds of his bloused pant leg with those gnarled and bloodied fingers.

"I'm sorry I have to do this, Ray," he said, choosing an eye socket to receive the tapered point. "If Helen's gone before you,

you'll get to see her soon." Voice cracking a bit, he added, "And when you see Brook up there … let her know we miss her terribly." Then, a hot tear streaking his cheek, he slowly introduced the combat dagger to the struggling creature's brain. There was a little resistance, then a barely audible pop and the job was done.

"Senseless savagery," muttered Cade as he withdrew the blade and swung his gaze to the mirror. What he saw there worried him: bushy beard, gaunt cheeks, dark bags under sunken eyes. All in all, it showed him the sum of several difficult days and sleepless nights spent trying hard to adjust to his new normal. Also reflected back at him was writing on the same wall old Ray had been scratching at. Though the writing was reading backward, the four letters **ADRI** still held meaning to Cade.

He backed away and closed the door on the way out. He retraced his steps to the hallway, then took three deliberate strides through the kitchen, paying the broken china underfoot no mind. He didn't bother to open the refrigerator. No need. There was no electricity. Hadn't been any since late July. And he had a feeling this rural part of Utah would forever be off-grid.

After shoving the couch away from the doorway feeding into the oblong sitting room, he wove through the coffee-table-and-armchair maze, passed under the arched room divide and emerged at the far end of the dining room an arm's reach from a buzzing cloud of flies.

Batting the pests away with his free hand, he trained the light on the table. On the plate nearest him was a pair of human eyeballs. *Ray's eyeballs.* The pupils were fixed and dilated. The irises were but thin green bands flecked with gray.

"For fuck's sake," he muttered under his breath. With the lifeless eyes seemingly tracking him, he cut around the end of the table, keeping everything atop it illuminated.

The second plate was home to an inches-long slab of meat. As Cade neared the chair pushed against the table, the flies covering the plate took flight, revealing the fleshy lump for what it really was: a bloated and rotting human tongue. Minus the flies and center stage in the antiseptic glare thrown by the tactical light, the tongue was nearly as white as the plate it lay upon.

Cade grimaced as he realized that the bloody ears on the third plate, when paired with the body parts arranged on the other plates, made up a grisly trifecta.

See no evil.

Speak no evil.

Hear no evil.

He looked at his Suunto. Barely two minutes had elapsed since he left the others to wait for him on the porch.

A gust of wind buffeted the old house. In response, the creaking overhead began anew.

Leaving the others to wait on the porch for his all clear call, Cade bypassed the front door and scaled the stairs. Landing his footfalls to where he guessed the treads were nailed to the stringers—mainly to the sides near the kickboard—he made it to the midpoint landing without making a sound. Using the same technique, he turned the corner and started up the next run.

Stopping halfway up the run, he peered down the long hall. Muddy boot prints ran the length of the hardwoods. Viewed at eye-level, the jagged-edged chevrons left behind looked like mountain ranges on a topo map.

An open door on his right revealed a small bedroom. Facing each other farther down the hall were another pair of doors. At the end of the hall was a rectangular window. More of the Ogden Herald was plastered over the glass there. To Cade's left was a partially open door. And through the six-inch gap came a cold draft carrying the stench of death. Following the caress of air on his cheek, the creaking started anew.

Wood on wood.

Then there was a hard to place rustling noise.

The curtains?

Or is something or someone moving around in there?

Keeping his rifle trained on the open doorway, Cade crept up the remaining stairs. Eyes roaming what little he could see of the room's interior, he cut the corner by degrees until it was crystal-clear to him that what he had seen poking through the curtains when he was out front of the house was not a weapon. Far from it. In fact, the floor of the hall Cade was standing in could benefit from a few passes with the object in question.

Leaving the macabre sight behind, he hustled down the hall, methodically clearing the rest of the rooms along the way.

Chapter 25

Though the Z tied to the rocking chair was dressed in the type of sensible polyester clothes an old person might wear, one look at the clumps of dark hair clinging to its cream-colored skull confirmed it was not Helen. As Cade ranged around to face the writhing creature, it was obvious to him that the undead woman had taken her last breath well before reaching middle age. The bold, black tribal tattoos encircling her bare biceps screamed Nineties kid. After doing the math in his head, Cade figured her to have been just north of thirty when she left the realm of the living.

Both of the Z's claw-like hands were gripping the chair's armrests and secured in place with silver duct tape. An ordinary broom had been run through the zombie's trunk from behind, the entirety of its worn bristles still sticking through the slat in back of the chair. The broom's worn yellow handle had punctured the blouse-like top on the way through. The tip, wrapped with more silver tape, was nearly horizontal to the floor.

Cade pushed on the chair's high back, causing it to lean forward on curved rockers. Which in turn caused the handle to stab through the curtains and the confined Z to whip its head around wildly.

Back to back, Cade did two things. First he fished out the Motorola and broadcast the all clear to the trio waiting on the porch. Then he said a silent prayer for the soul who used to inhabit the rotting shell in the chair and pushed his dagger through its temple.

He leaned in closer, parting the high collar with his blade. There was all kinds of damage to the Z's throat and neck area. So much hacking had been done there that he could see the white glint of bone amid the shiny muscle and crusted blood. Definitely not the same kind of operation Duncan and the Kids had described having been performed on the Zs at the fix-it shop. And judging by the meat still left on all four of its extremities— this corpse had been treated nothing like the man crucified in the church.

Who would show this kind of disrespect to a female corpse? A man?

Cade shook his head. None of this made any sense. If only he could wake up in his bed in Portland with a nightmare-induced knot in his gut and the Beatles' *Here Comes the Sun* playing on the clock radio. Feel Brook nestled close. Hear Raven stir and then jump out of her bed and come running. What he wouldn't give to have the sound of Duncan's heavy footfalls in the hall at his back turn out to be his daughter's bare feet slapping the wood floors back home and come to and find he was in the middle of one long nightmare brought on by bad Pad-Thai.

Duncan filed into the room ahead of Taryn. "Whatcha got?" he asked.

Like a game show contestant displaying a particularly nice prize, Cade stepped back and with a sweep of his arm gestured at Rocking Chair Girl.

"I have no idea," he said as he crossed his arms over his chest, trapping the slung M4 in a tight embrace.

"Seen it before," said Taryn. "Someone has done the backroom surgery thing to silence it. Looks like a rush job, though." She regarded Cade. "What did you find downstairs?"

"It looked to me like maybe we spooked someone just sitting down to eat," said Wilson. "Even though it was pretty dark down there, I could have sworn I saw food on the plates set around the table."

"That wasn't food," said Cade glumly.

"What was it?" replied Wilson, the words coming out slowly.

"You don't want to know."

Taryn squared up with Cade. She asked, "What *else* is down there?"

Cade locked eyes with the young woman. "You don't want to know," he repeated, adding a slow side-to-side wag of his head for effect.

Undeterred by the swift change in the Delta operator's body language, Taryn produced a headlamp from her pocket and snugged it on. Working the switch, she said, "I'm going down to see for myself." Without pause, she brushed past Cade and issued Wilson a preemptive stare that could only be construed as a silent order for him to vacate the doorway.

Duncan watched her go then started to pace the floor. Boots clomping a rhythm on the bare wood, he said, "Someone put her here to deter breathers from snooping around."

Wilson nodded at the broom-brandishing rotter. "Who's *that* thing going to stop?"

"Someone very timid," Cade said. "Someone unused to conflict."

Creak.

Duncan stopped pacing and looked toward the ceiling.

Wilson went wide-eyed. He whispered, "Think that's a watcher?"

Putting a finger vertical to his lips, Cade nodded. Then he pointed to the ceiling with the same finger.

Duncan looked a question at Cade.

Cade mimed for Duncan and Wilson to stay put, then mouthed, "We do nothing until Taryn returns." He turned toward the doorway.

Duncan gripped Cade's shoulder. He whispered, "Where are you going?"

"To see if I missed anything important."

Chapter 26

Though the pair of hinges on the thin plywood door had been oiled recently, constant exposure to the elements ensured a nerve-jangling screech when Raven exited the makeshift outhouse. There was no moon cut into the door's face to let in ambient light. There was no shingled roof rising over the four slab sides to make it appear to be anything but what it was. Instead, to keep the occupant dry as he or she did their business, a blue tarp had been stretched tightly over the top. Standing out against the thin, sun-bleached ripstop material were dozens of rusty staples dripping ochre tears down plywood walls already gray and warping from several years' worth of changing seasons. At the bottom edge of the mud-spattered walls, as if recoiling from the morass accumulating there, the layered wood was beginning to separate and curl away from the soupy ground.

"Your turn," Raven said to Sasha, holding the door open for her.

"You give it a shot of Lysol?" the redhead quipped.

Not quite getting the gist of the fourteen-year-old's barb, Raven remained silent and closed the flimsy door after her.

Voice muffled, Sasha said, "At least you warmed the seat for me. Thanks for that."

"You're welcome," Raven said as she sidled up to the scavenged washbasin hanging off the side of the outhouse. She swiped one finger across a withered sliver of soap and tipped some water from a plastic bottle to wet her hands.

A habit learned only recently, she checked her surroundings as she lathered up. Holding a silent vigil, Max sat on his haunches a few feet away. Behind the Shepherd, through the grove of trees and across the wide expanse of wind-whipped grass, Raven could see slices of the motor pool and most of the Black Hawk helicopter. The same wind moving the grass was making the tarp draping the helicopter pop and crack with regularity. Regarding Max again, she said, "That's a good boy. Always watching our six." She turned to pluck the plastic bottle from its perch on the shelf above the sink. In doing so, her gaze swept the shaving mirror hanging on a nail to the right of the shelf. And in that split-second glance she saw her own visage for the first time since putting her mother into the ground. The person looking back from the depths of the small oval drugstore-find looked nothing like the young girl in that last school photo her dad carried in his pocket at all times. Though distorted slightly by the viewing angle, she still noticed that her jaw was clenched, the muscles there small knots full of tension. Her eyes, brown and watery and identical to her mom's, held no hint of happiness. And to complete the apocalypse-induced transformation, the pigtails she had worn in that school picture as well as every other snapped from kindergarten to fourth grade were gone. In their stead was an unruly shock of brown hair held in place by a navy-blue stocking cap, the front of which was snugged down to within a fraction of an inch from her furrowed brow.

Hands still dripping water, she forgot all about drying them and lashed out at the stranger staring back at her. Thrown on a shallow upward trajectory, her right cross shattered the glass and sent the mirror spinning around the nail like an out of control Tilt-A-Whirl.

The instantaneous spritz of blood left the wall and triangles of broken mirror speckled with a constellation's worth of crimson dots. Raven yelped and kicked the base of the outhouse, causing Sasha to shriek and issue forth a spate of salty language.

Welling with emotion brought on by the sudden reminder of her recent monumental loss, Raven clenched her left hand into a fist and initiated an opposing blow meant to erase every last sliver of mirror in the mangled chromed frame.

But that blow never landed. Just as the fast-twitch muscle fibers began to unload their pent-up energy, the swing initiated with a twist of her hips was redirected down and she found herself wrapped up in a vice-like embrace. Arms pinned firmly to her sides, she struggled and craned to see her attacker.

That Max wasn't coming to her aid hit her blindside. Wind rustled the firs all around, sending a barrage of trapped rainwater hurtling toward the ground. In an instant, the gentle patters became a full-blown assault on the tarp.

Tuning out everything—Sasha's renewed queries from behind the outhouse wall. The creaking of the trees overhead. The water sluicing down the wall to her fore—Raven lifted her boot off the ground and searched for some toes to land the heel on.

"Don't," ordered a disembodied female voice.

Raven heard the word, but its meaning and context didn't register. The primal part of her brain responsible for fight-or-flight instincts had already kicked into high gear—instantaneously producing endorphins, dopamine, and a handful of other chemicals and funneling them directly into her bloodstream. A millisecond after the stranger had made herself known, the only thing driving Raven was an inborn desire to survive the unexpected encounter.

Without further thought, she arched her back and stomped down, missing the intended target completely. In the next beat, the stranger was spinning her around forcibly and a face she recognized was inches from her own.

"What's gotten into you?" hissed Jamie, clamping down hard on Raven's wrist and drawing the dainty hand near in order to inspect the self-inflicted damage.

"I thought you were *her*," gasped Raven.

"What the *eff* is going on out there?" asked Sasha, her voice several octaves higher than normal.

Speaking loud enough to be heard over the wind and through the quarter-inch plywood, Jamie said, "It's just me. I surprised Raven, that's all."

Still watching with the kind of indifference only a dog could convey, Max yawned and flopped down onto a bed of semi-dry pine needles.

"I'm not her. And I forgive you for trying to stomp my toes flat," Jamie said as she raised Raven's right hand so the girl could get an eyeful of her own bloody knuckles. "But I do want to know what *this* is all about?"

Eyes downcast, Raven said softly, "I saw my mom in the mirror."

Jamie released her hand. "You're mad at her?" she said. "For leaving you and Cade all alone?"

"No," Raven replied softly. She looked up and met Jamie's gaze. "I'm mad at myself for seeing what was happening to her and not making a big deal out of it. She wasn't getting better after she got the shot of antiserum. She was slowly getting worse. Withering away in front of my eyes. I noticed it every time she had me give her a back massage." She swiped a forming tear, leaving a streak of crimson from cheekbone to chin. "Bottom line ... I should have said something about it to my dad or Glenda."

"It's not your fault," Jamie said, getting her face level with the girl's. "You're by no means a medical professional. And neither one of them, Cade or Glenda ... hell, *none* of us for that matter could have stopped what Omega started."

"Not even God?"

Now Jamie was getting misty-eyed. "Nope. Not even the Big Man upstairs," she conceded.

The door creaked again as Sasha stepped from the outhouse. Still cinching her belt, she said, "Don't worry, Raven. I sprayed enough Lysol for the two of us."

Jamie forced a smile. Pinching the bridge of her nose, she said, "You're *both* too young to have shits with stink worth worrying about."

Raven's eyes lit up. "Oooh," she exclaimed, and left it at that.

As she wet her hands with water from the bottle, Sasha looked at the others' reflections in the remnants of the mirror and said, "You've been following us all morning, Jamie. What gives?"

Clamping her bloody hand under her armpit, Raven answered for Jamie. "Probably following my dad's orders."

Jamie nodded.

"What happened to this?"

Grimacing, Raven produced her right hand.

Sasha's brow inched up, but, strangely, she held her tongue.

"C'mon," said Jamie. "Let's go see Glenda and get you patched up."

"Wait," blurted Raven, grabbing a fistful of Jamie's jacket sleeve.

Seeing the confused look settling on the young girl's face, Jamie said in her most big-sisterly tone, "What is it, honey?"

"I'm bleeding somewhere else."

As if she'd been kicked in the gut, Jamie exhaled sharply.

Raven's eyebrows pulled together and tears welled in the corners of her eyes.

In spite of everything, Jamie had to smile. "It's going to be all right, sweetie." She wrapped her arm around Raven's slight frame and pulled her along toward the compound entrance.

Chapter 27

Iris guessed she'd made another half-mile of forward progress since donning Flippety-Flop's shirt. Two times since that awful decision she had heard the telltale rasps of the purged on the march. And both times she had wisely gone to ground in the roadside ditch and remained there until the shuffling processions passed her by. Two first risers were about all she was confident enough at this stage of her career as a Doer to take on solo. Roaming bands of purged the size of which she had just avoided were way out of her league considering she had yet to receive any formal firearm or edged-weapons training.

Then there was the dead weight of her leg. Still numb from the knee down, it was getting harder and harder to swing around and plant so she could affect the next step with her good leg. Up to this point, the times she'd spilled over onto her face numbered in the teens. And as a result of her many skirmishes with gravity, her palms and elbows and knees resembled ground chuck and were bleeding profusely.

Then it happened again. On her feet and plodding ahead one second, crashing helplessly to the unforgiving asphalt the next. Only in this instance her reaction time was a half-tick too slow. Her hands were still near her sides when the road dealt her a near knockout blow that sent her bottom teeth clean through her lower lip, adding a flap of shredded flesh to the growing list of bleeding body parts.

Lying there on the road in the middle of Utah, she felt the last vestiges of resolve wriggling free of her pain-clouded mind. With a shroud of darkness threatening to close around her and send the stars dancing before her eyes on their way, Iris dug down deep, both figuratively and literally, and managed to pluck the radio from her pocket. It was all she could do to roll the volume up and thumb the Talk button. After a short rest, during which she drew a few deep breaths, she inched the hand grasping the radio across her chest, placed the plastic speaker grill near her mouth, and uttered a horribly garbled plea for help.

At that moment, in the Thagons' farmhouse eighteen miles by crow, Taryn was backing away from the cramped powder room with one hand covering her mouth and nose. The sight of the kind old man sitting on the toilet, horribly disfigured by the combination of torture and Omega's effects, had started the first tell-tale trickle of bitter saliva leaking from the glands in back of her throat. She stumbled down the hall and grabbed a chair at the dining table for support. Standing there weak in the knees, she took a few deep breaths to quell the initial gag response, then took a seat at the head of the table.

She sat there for a second, eyes closed and trying to conjure up an image of Ray. Anything to displace the one currently burned into her mind and psyche.

As Taryn opened her eyes and inclined her head, the narrow cone of light from her headlamp painted a pair of walnut-sized orbs sitting on the plate at the far end of the table. Swinging her gaze left illuminated the tongue and scattered the few remaining flies feeding on it. Still unsure of what she had just seen, she looked down at the plate on the table in front of her.

Immediately recognizable from her viewing angle were a pair of ears. Not dainty things you'd see on a pop singer or cute little baby. These ears were stretched by what had to be several decades spent under gravity's unrelenting pull. Stiff gray hairs stabbed up through canals crusted with blood dried to reddish-black.

The scream formed deep in Taryn's lungs was usurped by the chain reaction started earlier in the bathroom. Her body shuddered and the headlamp bobbed. Shadows danced about the room as she heaved her meager breakfast onto the horrors plated so carefully on the fine china before her.

And at the same moment Taryn was pushing away from the table downstairs—equal parts disgust and fury building within her like some kind of unstoppable fission reaction—Cade was finishing his second, more thorough recon of the rooms upstairs.

Ignoring the retching noises echoing in the stairwell, he returned to the room where Duncan and Wilson were waiting and motioned for them to follow.

Cade led the silent procession across the hall to the room he had cleared just prior to summoning them all upstairs from the front porch.

At first glance there seemed to be nothing to the room. Opposite the door, abutting the wall below a window covered with blackout curtains, was a low desk. Filling up the desk's knee-hole was a simple, low-backed wooden chair. Atop the desk was an old sewing machine. On the floor in the center of the room was a wooden ammunition box, its lid hinged open and revealing that it was empty. Stenciled on the sides of the box in black were words describing its contents as 5.56 ball ammunition—definitely U.S. issue, Cade had concluded at first glance.

Discarded in the single closet located on the far wall left of the entry were a half-dozen ripped-open MRE packages and an equal number of cellophane sleeves—the type which new Army M4 rifles leave the factory sealed in. And positioned against the wall just inside the door to the left was a chair matching the one at Helen's sewing station.

Cade crossed the room and parted the curtains covering both east-facing windows. He turned and pointed to the attic access panel inset into the ceiling directly above the chair that had been left pushed against the wall. In the light of day, the panel was impossible to miss. Around the panel's edges were faint, finger-print-sized smudges. And on the cream-colored wall below the panel, one well-defined handprint seemed to be waving at them all.

"Well lookie here," declared Duncan over the sound of boots scuffing the stairs outside the door. "I do believe we have someone *treed*."

Taryn entered the room, still dragging her sleeve across her lips. She stalked to the windowsill adjacent to the desk and took a seat on the narrow ledge. The sunlight streaming in cast her shadow over the debris strewn about the scuffed and gouged wood floor. Glaring at Cade, she said, "Treed?"

"Kind of like how your old boss had you trapped in his office at the airport," he explained.

"Treed means you're trapped and you know it," Wilson added.

Hefting the Saiga, Duncan stabbed its gaping barrel skyward. "And that, my friends, adds a degree of difficulty to our next move."

Chapter 28

When Duncan mentioned her old boss Richard Less, aka *Dickless,* Taryn had gone silent and glanced out the window at the pasture and fast-flowing stream beyond. A tick later she visibly started and flicked her gaze to the ceiling. "Anyone else hear that?"

In unison, like hounds on the scent of a coon, Duncan, Cade, and Wilson went stock-still and looked up at the ceiling.

Seconds crawled into the past. Half a minute later the nearly imperceptible sounds were repeated.

Directing his whispered question at Taryn, Cade said, "What'd you hear the first time?"

Voice barely a whisper, she said, "Same thing. Static."

He mouthed, "Then?"

Taryn made a face. She whispered, "A woman's voice, for sure. She said 'Help' ... I think." She screwed her face up again and thought for a second. "And I could have sworn I heard 'State Route thirty-nine,' too."

Cade nodded in agreement. Still whispering he said, "Time to flush them out." He looked to Duncan. "Any ideas?"

Duncan patted his shotgun.

Cade shook his head. "Verbal encouragement, first."

Wilson said, "Have Taryn do it."

Taryn shifted her glare from Cade to Wilson. "You bastards picking on the fairer sex now?" She swung her gaze back. "First *he* lets me go downstairs without warning me about—"

"What?" asked Wilson. "What's down there?"

"There was no stopping you," said Cade. "And being put on the spot like that, I didn't have the words to describe what they did to Ray. That was Ray ... wasn't it?"

Taryn nodded.

"What did they do to him?" asked Wilson, his voice taking on an annoying, pleading tone.

"No time to explain," said Taryn. She looked to Cade then flicked her eyes back to the ceiling.

M4 trained on the ceiling left of the access hatch, Cade backed to the wall and motioned for the others to follow his lead.

Seeing this, Taryn hesitated for a second. Which was enough of a window for Cade to whisper instructions to her.

Taryn nodded in understanding. Then she cupped her hands around her mouth and bellowed, "We know you're up there!" Then, lying, she added, "And we don't mean you any harm." Fact was, she wanted to jam her Beretta into the mouth of the person responsible for killing Ray and personally pull the trigger. Watch the person's eyes bug out. Hell, maybe even shoot them out one at a time to get even for the *see no evil* treatment that'd been inflicted on the corpse downstairs. Whether the damage had been done post-mortem or not, she didn't give a shit.

But there was no response. No utterance of surrender. No shuffling of feet of someone preparing to flee the punishment they most definitely had earned. Not even another static-filled peep came from what they'd all agreed had probably been a radio of some kind receiving a transmission at the worst moment possible.

On the bright side, she thought as she drew in a breath sufficient to deliver loudly enough her next sugar-coated overture, the call going unanswered likely meant the attic dweller was just hoping they'd go away without incident.

"Come down now—" Taryn began.

"Or we will shoot holes in the ceiling until you do," finished Duncan, adding an exclamation point to the threat by cycling a round through the Saiga.

The verbal threat worked wonders. Or was it the *schlak-schlak* sound of him expelling an unfired shell through the breach? He didn't ponder the thought for long, because a half-beat after the

172

hollow-sounding footfalls began retreating to the north side of the attic, he poked his head into the hall and said, "Wait for it."

Following Duncan's lead, Cade craned around the door frame just in time to hear a panicked string of curse words and see a slender leg come plunging through the ceiling ahead of a puff of plaster dust and falling debris. Shades of the Hanna farmhouse, he thought. Only this leg had a feminine quality. Even clad in pants made from a strange tan and black camouflage pattern, there were definite womanly curves to it.

Exhibiting a burst of speed belying his age, Duncan bolted down the hall. Three strides removed from the sewing room door, he was wrapping the leg up in his arms and twisting the foot counter to where the ankle bones wanted it to rotate.

There was a yelp of pain and more plaster rained down.

"Shoot the knee," feigned Duncan, even as he applied more pressure to the ankle laterally and added his own bodyweight to gravity's natural pull. In response to his efforts, there was another explosion of plaster and the leg's owner let out another shrill yelp. With lumpy insulation raining down on his head, Duncan barely avoided a mouthful of boot as the person's other leg plunged through the ceiling and scythed the air an inch in front of his face.

Just a couple of steps behind Duncan, Cade saw the shower of white powder and let his rifle hang on its sling. Already on the move and witnessing the second leg blast through, he lunged forward like a receiver going for an errant pass and ended up arresting the pistoning leg just as the knee began hammering against his friend's temple.

Cade walked his gaze up the camouflage fatigue pants and lower-half of a dirty and tattered thermal top to where the rapidly widening hole was still calving debris. He saw the opposing faces of two ceiling joists through the shifting insulation. He also saw that the woman's thin arms were hooked over the top of said joists. This revelation led him to conclude her hands were busy holding on for dear life. Too busy to effectively bring a weapon to bear and achieve any kind of accuracy.

"*Pull,*" Cade bellowed. "She can't hold on for much longer."

Though his glasses were fogged and he was beginning to look like a flocked Christmas tree, Duncan saw two things happening in his side vision. Taryn was glued to the hallway wall and advancing with her rifle aimed roughly a foot over his head. Which amounted to center mass on the writhing body in his grasp. And visible behind Taryn, Wilson was crouched at the top of the stairwell and training his M4 toward the landing below. Even in that brief snippet of time and seen through dirty lenses, Duncan could tell from the young man's body language that his attention was undivided. Wilson was watching their six without having to be prompted.

"Quit fighting," hollered Taryn. "I *will* put a bullet into your spine. See how running from rotters goes without use of your legs."

At the same moment the word "spine" rolled off Taryn's lips, the fight went out of the woman and her upper body slipped free of the hole. Since her legs were still being held by Cade and Duncan, her head and chest crashed hard into the floor. As the resounding thud filled the narrow hall, both Cade and Duncan went sprawling onto their butts and came to rest with their backs to the wall, Cade on one side, Duncan the other. Each man had retained his grip on one of the woman's legs and instinctively hinged over sideways to get at her flailing arms.

Coming to rest with most of his weight and the slung M4 crushing down on the woman's bony pelvis allowed Cade to let go of the woman's leg and grab hold of her left wrist. He drew her near and planted his elbow down hard on where he guessed her carotid snaked past her collarbone.

Duncan was on the opposite side and face-to-face with the woman. From his vantage, he figured her to be in her thirties. Set above a hawkish nose, her jaundiced eyes met his.

"Quit yer bucking," he said.

A light went on behind her eyes. "I saw the big black truck," she spat. "You're the ones who stole Mom's supplies."

Duncan said nothing. He didn't have the energy to argue the case.

She cracked a mirth-filled smile. Her teeth were rotting, the stench carrying on her hot breath. On her plaque-whitened tongue was a red capsule. Her eyelids flickered and she closed her mouth. Lips pressed into a thin white line, she crunched down on the item Duncan had caught a fleeting glimpse of.

"We know where you live," she said, eyes rolling back under heavy, dark lids.

Feeling the woman relax, Cade let up on the pressure he was putting on her neck and got up to his knees. Still holding a wrist with one hand and keeping her leg immobilized with his leg, he made a face and looked to Duncan. "You smell that?"

"What'd you fart?"

"*Seriously?*" Cade said, "It's almonds. I smell almonds."

"All I smell is this one's ass-breath. Got some of those plastic handcuffs of yours handy?"

The woman's eyes widened. She said, "Not my fault."

Duncan looked at her over his glasses. "Who killed the old man?"

"Adrian did," she answered, the words coming out a little garbled.

Taryn pressed the M4's muzzle to the woman's sweaty forehead. "Who's Adrian?" she hissed.

Recoiling from the cool steel, she said, "Before the dead came, Adrian called the shots on the inside." A tick later the woman's eyelids fluttered and closed.

Cade shook her back to consciousness. "How'd you get *outside?*" he pressed.

Between labored breaths, she answered, "Once the food ran out Adrian cut a deal with the warden to go outside and forage for more. For everyone, she promised."

Duncan asked, "Then what happened?"

"The head screw let his guard down." She smiled again. "And then we killed them *all.*"

Knowing she was slipping away, Cade began firing questions at her rapid-fire. "Where is Adrian now? How many of you are there? What weapons do you have?"

The woman opened her eyes and tried focusing on him. When she finally attempted to speak, all that the effort produced was a thin rime of foam that coated her lower lip and then rolled down her chin.

Out of the corner of his eye, Duncan saw Wilson craning to see what was happening.

Blood trickled from a half-moon the rifle barrel had cut into the woman's forehead. Taryn applied more pressure and said, "Tell us everything you know, bitch."

"She's swallowed poison," said Cade, sweeping the barrel aside with his hand. He looked to Duncan. "Help me get her to her knees."

While Duncan helped to haul the dead weight off the floor, Cade was fishing a pair of pre-fashioned flex cuffs from a pocket.

As Duncan let her down and kicked her feet apart, Cade was securing the woman's arms behind her back. Then, after squaring up with her, he gripped her left shoulder with his left hand. With Duncan still steadying the woman, Cade made a fist with his right and twisted his upper torso clockwise away from her. Finally, without a word of warning, he uncoiled and let fly a roundhouse that landed just south of the woman's sternum.

The whoosh of his fist cutting air was answered a beat later by a sharp grunt as every square inch of air was forcibly expelled from the woman's lungs. The grunt morphed into a guttural groan accompanied by a spray of spittle and more frothed saliva.

"No dice," said Duncan as he jammed the Saiga's barrel into the woman's mouth.

Taryn gasped. "I was just playing bad cop. I wasn't going to shoot her point blank."

Duncan held the shotgun steady with one hand while he jammed two fingers down the captive's throat. He rooted them around in there for a few seconds, but failed to produce the desired effect.

"She's dying," Cade said soberly. He shook her by the shoulder hard enough to cause the stocking cap to slip off her head. Which in turn caused her greasy blonde hair and a few assorted items to spill out, among them a couple of cigarettes and a dirty hypodermic needle.

"I saw her bite down on some kind of pill," conceded Duncan. "Looked like a Tylenol cold capsule."

Cade stood up quickly, taking the limp form along for the ride. He wrapped his arms around her from behind and applied the Heimlich to no great effect. All he got from his efforts was a fresh whiff of the almond-tinged air leaking from her gaping mouth.

"I'm no Quincy, M.D.," said Duncan, "but I'm pretty certain she's dead."

Cade lowered the body to the floor. Went to his haunches and checked for a pulse.

Duncan began wiping his glasses with a cloth. "Is she gone?" he asked matter-of-factly.

Firm set to his jaw, Cade regarded his friend. Through clenched teeth he said, "Helluva way to flush her out, Duncan. Kinda went off script, don't you think?"

"Gotta admit it *was* pretty effective."

Cade made no reply to that. Instead, he looked to Taryn. "See what's going on out front." Then he stared up into the gloom.

Remembering the Prairie Fire call he'd received what seemed like a lifetime ago from Cade, who had also gotten himself *treed* along with Hoss and Daymon in a farmhouse attic in Hanna, Utah, Duncan said, "You got it in you to go up there?"

Cade said, "I'm not Daymon."

"Want me to get you that chair, then?"

Cade looked at the jagged hole. "I'll go up through the hatch. If there's someone else up there, that'll leave one less direction for me to take fire from."

Reporting from the other room, Taryn said, "The rotters are almost to the truck."

Cade was already standing on the chair and pushing up on the attic access panel with the M4's barrel.

Poking his head into the front bedroom, Duncan said to Taryn, "We'll cross that rotten bridge when we get to it. Keep your eyes peeled for breathers. I'm going back to spot for our attic rat."

Taryn had shoved the corpse and rocking chair aside and was kneeling at the window with her rifle's muzzle poking through the ripped plastic. "Copy that," she answered back, her eye never leaving the 3x magnifier deployed atop the M4.

Slipping between rooms, Duncan paused long enough to instruct Wilson to go downstairs. As the redhead moved out, Duncan called after him. "If anyone shows their face, you be sure to shoot first and ask questions later." When he turned around he dropped to one knee and fumbled inside the woman's back pocket for the item he felt pressing his gut as he had held her down to the floorboards. Extracting it and seeing that it was exactly what he was expecting made his gut clench.

With equal measures of repulsion and giddy anticipation fighting for dominance in his head, robotically, he slipped the find into his inside jacket pocket.

Chapter 29

"There you go, Raven," said Glenda. She wore a pained half-smile and was cradling the girl's right hand in hers. The way the white gauze was wrapped over the knuckles and across the palm made the scene look like something out of a Rocky movie. "All better now. Just keep the dressing dry. Maybe stay inside the rest of the day and read a book or something."

Max was sitting on the floor and looking inquisitively at the goings on.

Speaking to Max, Raven said, "Looks like Sasha's your chief ball thrower from here on out."

Max's stub-tail began to thump against the wood floor.

Regarding Glenda, Raven said, "So no bike riding?"

"Nope."

Looking on from the top bunk, Sasha said, "You've been known to crash that purple thing with *two* good hands."

Raven made a face. "Not true," she said. "If I remember right it was *you* who instigated that."

Changing the subject, Sasha said, "Perfect time to practice your off-hand shooting. Then maybe you can call yourself *Wyatt Junior.*"

"I'll never be as good a shooter as my dad. Besides, he says you can't give yourself a nickname. It has to be besto—" Face screwing up in thought, she looked to the metal ceiling.

"*Bestowed* is the word I think you're looking for," proffered Glenda as she zipped closed the small emergency medical kit and placed it on a nearby shelf. "I call those senior moments. And speaking of your dad ..." She reached back to the shelf and came away with a thick envelope from which she selected a thinner, sealed envelope. "He asked me to be the guardian of these while

179

he's gone. Your mother left behind some handwritten notes to be given to you as you get older. As you hit certain milestones, so to speak. Getting your monthly check is one of those milestones. And this is the note your mom wanted you to have in case she—" Glenda's voice trailed off, leaving the painful words unspoken.

Raven took the envelope with trembling hands, then looked to Sasha for support.

Sasha's mop of red hair bobbed as she nodded. "I got mine around your age. Maybe a little sooner. My mom was working a flight from Denver to Seattle and then Anchorage. All I had was Wilson."

Raven and Glenda both grimaced.

"You'll live," Sasha added. "Maybe you'll even turn a little bitchy like I do now and then."

"Now and then?"

"OK. Most of the time," Sasha conceded.

Raven tucked the sealed envelope into a pocket. "Won't I need—"

Sasha took Raven's uninjured hand and pressed a dainty packaged item and a neatly folded piece of paper into her palm.

"Those instructions there," she said, lifting her brows. "The pictures speak louder than the words."

Sasha slumped dramatically against the metal wall. Her head was bowed and shoulders rolled forward.

Raven rose from the bunk and placed a steadying hand on her friend. "What is it?" she asked.

Sasha said, "That injury of yours just got you out of dish duty. Probably for a couple of weeks, too."

Glenda wagged her head side-to-side. "Nope," she said. "Two days ... max. Once the wounds on your knuckles begin to knit, I'll put fresh butterfly stitches on and you'll be good to go."

Brows knitting together, Raven said, "But it'll get wet. Won't they fall off?"

"I know we don't get bread from the store anymore," said Glenda, a twinkle in her eye. "But we've got plenty of plastic bread bags. Previous owner of the RV squirreled them away everywhere. Some of us who remember hearing stories of the Great Depression make things stretch. Believe it or not, repurposing was cool before it was *cool*."

"What good is a bread bag?"

Sasha was smiling now. She liked where this was going.

"You wrap your injured wing with the plastic and duct tape it in place," said Glenda. "Then the dirty dishwater won't be a problem."

Feminine pad and instructions in hand, Raven stalked off to the Grayson quarters.

Thagon Home

Being careful to step only on the north\south running joists, Cade made his way past a trio of plastic Rubbermaid bins sporting writing denoting their contents. Two bore the words **X-Mas Ornaments** and one was marked **Halloween**. That the Thagons took the time to decorate their alpaca ranch for *that* holiday blew him away.

Strands of gold and silver garland snaked from the open lid of one of the Christmas boxes. It was looped through the ceiling support above the box and wound around the beam all the way to the north-facing dormer where the top half of a faux Christmas tree had been propped up against the bare wallboards. Tinsel and ornaments adorned the perfectly symmetrical branches. Clearly the woman lying dead downstairs had had some time on her hands.

Beyond the boxes to Cade's fore was the west-facing dormer he figured to be the watcher's favored perch. With a commanding view of a substantial stretch of the north/south-running state route, it was exactly where he'd set up shop for an extended overwatch. And though he hadn't been privy to the layout in the attic above the church rectory in Woodruff, he had a good idea that what he was looking at here was much of the same.

A milking stool sat before the dormer whose two-by-two window was split up into four panes with milled wood dulled gray with age. Three of the magazine-sized panes were clouded over with an accumulation of dust and cobwebs presumably decades in the making. A softball-sized porthole to the outside had been rubbed through the grime coating the upper left pane. The narrow sill below the window was home to hundreds of shiny black husks. A closer look revealed them to be mostly exoskeletons sprouting spiny legs all locked together in the customary dead-insect repose.

A square of plywood was nailed to the floor before the window. It was barely visible underneath the quilts and blankets and pillows piled up against the window. Written in black ink, the word ADRIAN decorated the unfinished wood header above the window. The letters were big and rounded and connected in spots. It looked almost like graffiti on a subway car, but not quite. And the longer Cade thought about it, the more it struck him as the style of writing a middle-school-aged girl would put on a Pee-Chee folder to proclaim allegiance to the crush of the week.

He peered through the portal and saw the Zs streaming past the Ford. One of the shamblers was caught on the open tailgate, its tattered shirt slowly ripping away as it continued to march in place. He watched the driver's side mirror get folded forward as the telescoping stalk gave way to the half-dozen first turns filing through the yard-wide gap between fence and truck.

He looked around for a radio, but found only a couple of MREs and some plastic bottles full of clouded water likely collected from the stream cutting through the pasture. The MREs he'd take, the water could stay.

Before moving on, Cade went through the bedding. He found nothing of interest. However, moving the rat's nest and pillow off of the plywood exposed the framing below the window sill. And wedged between the vertical two-by-fours was an old-fashioned long-range CB radio. It was powered down and cool to the touch, which struck Cade as odd until he realized the watcher was just that and would be the one sending intel, not necessarily receiving it. Which made sense tactically considering batteries were quickly becoming worth their weight in gold. He powered it on and heard only the faraway white-noise hiss of an open and unused channel. There was no kind of chatter from the convoy he envisioned heading toward the rendezvous at the 39/16 junction. He hovered his thumb over the side-mounted Send key. Thought about depressing it and issuing a challenge to whomever was on the other end of channel 22. That notion quickly dissipated as he realized they'd lose the element of surprise by his doing so.

Chapter 30

Cade was just powering off the CB when he spotted the dog-eared corners of several sheets of paper. They were folded up on themselves and wedged into a crevice behind where the CB had been. He grabbed a corner and wiggled until the item was free of the hiding spot. One glance at the front page under the light coming in through the dormer windows told him what he had. And it was exactly the thing he was hoping to find.

Cade stuffed the item into an inside pocket and turned toward the hole punched through to the second-story.

Duncan called out, asking him if he'd found the radio.

"Affirmative," said Cade, seeing only Duncan's head (sans cowboy hat) jutting up through the attic hatch. In the dim light the flare off his friend's aviator glasses completed the strange *Max Headroom* floating head effect. "Thing is, my gut tells me it's not the one she just received the call on."

Illuminated from below, Duncan's ghostly-looking head bobbed ever so slightly.

Cade stared across the expanse, but said nothing. Figured he'd allow the man time to think.

Finally, after a long ten-count, Duncan said, "Why don't ya come back this way and start moving north of where she went through the floor. First reaction when you lose your legs is to throw your arms forward. I'm an old drunk, I should know. Had my share of Pete Rose stumbles. Maybe Skinny Minnie here fumbled it over yonder somewhere when she broke through."

Cade picked his way across the open joists to the jagged opening. Then, keeping both boots and one hand in constant contact with the joists, he began to make his way toward the

Christmas tree, probing the insulation with his free hand as he went.

"Make it quick," urged Duncan. "Taryn says we have lots of company."

Cade said nothing. He was up to his elbows in insulation—a good deal of it airborne. Much like the flies he'd disturbed downstairs, fine particles he was sure were seeking a new home in his lungs clouded the air around his face. A dozen feet from the north dormer his hand brushed something smooth. It was about the size of a pack of cigarettes and when he brought it into the dim light of day he saw that it had a nylon wrist-strap dangling from it. The word Cobra was painted below a front-facing speaker grill. Dominating the top two-thirds of the black plastic case was an LCD screen glowing a muted green and displaying a bunch of different icons surrounding the numbers 31-3. A tiny skeleton key above the numbers told Cade that both the main channel and sub channel they represented were locked in. Resisting the urge to thumb the side-mounted Talk button and try to trick the person to repeat their garbled transmission was an exercise in willpower.

Cade turned toward the attic access and underhanded the radio in Duncan's direction. The thing skittered off a joist, caromed off of Duncan's temple, and came to rest atop the fluffy insulation a foot from his face.

"That what I was supposed to find?"

Wriggling one arm through the portal, Duncan took hold of the errant projectile and looked it over. "Set to channel thirty-one, three, huh? And it was powered on?"

"Affirmative," answered Cade. "But the volume was rolled all the way down." He made his way back to the newly created hole and stood there peering down between his legs at the floor below. The corpse was nowhere to be seen. However, the spot on the floor where he had to land was littered with debris from the woman's forcible removal.

Never one to take the easy way out—nor the high road, for that matter—Cade knelt down gingerly before the hole and said,

"Look out below." A tick later he was gripping the joists and lowering his five-ten frame through the opening. Once he had reached full extension, he let go of the joists and dropped the remaining eighteen inches to the floor. A hollow thud sounded when his one hundred and eighty pounds alit atop the uneven pile of lathe and plaster and insulation. While not a picture-perfect landing, he stayed upright and started to fan away the fresh cloud of fine white dust he had inadvertently kicked up.

A beat later there was a similar hollow thump from the other room and Duncan peered through the door. He looked to Cade then gestured toward the stairs with the Saiga. "Wilson needs us." In passing, he poked his head into the front bedroom and ordered Taryn to follow him.

Downstairs, Wilson was standing in front of the picture window and peeking through a thin vertical seam in the center of the curtains. "They're interested in the barn for some reason," he noted, peeling the curtain aside to allow Cade a look.

"Whatever the case, they need to be dealt with," Cade said, drawing his Gerber from its sheath. "I count roughly twenty. Sound about right?"

"Twenty-one," answered Taryn from the foyer. "We got lucky. I saw a real big group move on past the drive a couple of minutes ago."

"Direction?"

"North."

"That's bound to continue until the entire horde tires of Bear River and breaks one way or the other."

Wilson let go of the curtain. He stared at Cade. Said in a low voice, "*If* they tire of Bear River."

"If they don't," said Cade, "those folks better pray the temperature drops below freezing pretty soon."

Duncan and Taryn circled around the dining table. She went to the window, pulled on the curtain, and peered out. He put a hand on Wilson's shoulder and said, "That may not even be enough. At least right away. Get too many of them rotters crowded in against the walls and gates and they freeze there. No way to drive through them. Nor can you wade through them all on foot."

"I already did the math," Wilson said, shaking his head. "If this horde is even half the size of the one that followed me and Sash out of Denver, it's going to take every one of Bear River's citizens working round the clock for days to kill them all."

"Flu's still burning through the folks there," said Duncan. "Dregan's son said his Uncle Henry and half of the population is down with it. The other half is walking on eggshells hoping not to catch it."

Wilson said, "So then you have what, a couple of hundred people killing and clearing?"

"That's backbreaking work in and of itself," added Cade. "And when you're done culling them a week later, you've still got several hundred thousand corpses you have to dispose of."

Wilson shuddered. "Then you've got a festering Mt.-Everest-sized biohazard on your hands. Can't begin to imagine what that many corpses would smell like."

"You leave a handful lying around for even a day or two and your fresh water supply will be unfit to drink," said Cade. "Then you've got no choice but to use precious fuel to boil water to drink."

"It ain't going to come to that," said Duncan. "Dregan's a crafty fella. I'm sure he has something up his sleeve. Besides ... we have more pressing matters to attend to *here*."

"Thinning the herd and searching the barn," said Cade. "Any ideas on how to go about getting both done quietly?" He shifted his gaze from face to face. In the gloom, each one of them looked to have aged considerably since he'd first met them, Duncan more so than the young couple.

Without missing a beat, Duncan said, "I was hoping we could use one of those screaming jobs you brought back with you, Mister I Saved the Constitution and Bill of Rights singlehandedly."

Simultaneously Taryn and Wilson looked questions at Cade.

Shaking his head, Cade said, "Wasn't just me. I had help in D.C."

After picking her chin off the floor, Taryn said, "I'll find the gate to the pasture and lure them inside."

Wilson said, "And I'll close it behind them."

Talking excitedly, Taryn added, "And then I jump the fence back to safety."

Grimacing, Cade said, "Looks good on paper. But the moment one sees either one of you the song of the dead begins. There are a few first turns mixed in. You get them all excited and the fresh ones start to moan—"

"More will start streaming up from the state route," finished Wilson.

Duncan ran his hand through his thinning hair. He said, "Then for sure we're up shit creek without a paddle." A strange look settled on his face.

"What is it?" asked Taryn.

"Anyone seen my Stetson?"

Cade said, "Where'd you last have it?"

If I knew that it wouldn't be lost, thought Duncan. He said, "Upstairs. I pushed the sewing desk over so I could watch you without doing any climbing. Think I may have left it on the chair."

"Spare your knees," said Wilson, already heading for the stairs. "Wouldn't want you to leave your lucky hat behind,"

"Left mine in the Sequoia outside of Boise," Cade said to no one in particular. He was staring out the part in the curtains.

"The Trail Blazer cap you had on when we met?"

Cade nodded.

"I didn't peg you for a sports fan," said Taryn.

"I didn't peg you for a world class dirt track driver," replied Cade.

Feeling left out, Duncan asked, "Which of my many attributes have I impressed you two with?"

In full stereo, Taryn and Cade said, "Duncanisms," and both cracked a smile.

189

Duncan's cheeks flushed crimson. He said, "And hearing that makes *me* happier than a puppy who just discovered his peter."

Shaking her head, Taryn said, "That's a hell of a visual."

Cade checked the time on his Suunto. Changing the subject, he said, "We need to get a move on. We still have the rendezvous to deal with."

"First things first," said Duncan. "We need to take care of those things out there."

Wilson returned from upstairs, Stetson in hand. He saw the other three rooted in virtually the same spots as where they'd been when he left. They were now wearing sheepish expressions and looking at one another conspiratorially.

Wilson handed over the hat. He asked, "What'd I miss."

Shifting his gaze from Taryn to Wilson, Cade said, "Willingness."

Duncan studied the redhead for a tick. "Definitely moxie," he said, suppressing a grin.

Taryn was silent for a long two-count. Finally, she said, "Heart."

At a loss for words, Wilson simply shook his head and waited for Cade to dole out marching orders.

Chapter 31

Crouched low and moving silently behind Wilson, the group exited the farmhouse single file through the front door and fanned out, Duncan taking up position to the left of the stairs, and Taryn to the right.

Bringing up the rear, Cade pulled the door closed then crossed the porch and made himself as small as possible behind the picket of balusters Taryn was crouched behind. First thing he noticed was how strangely still the air outside was. He guessed the temperature to be in the mid-fifties. *Calm before the storm*, came to mind as he swung his rifle around to his back where it could hang out of his way. While letting his gaze roam the barn doors where the dead were amassed, he mated the black suppressor to his Glock 19 by feel. *Just in case.*

Seeing Cade go to his pistol, Wilson drew his Beretta and was in the process of sheathing his blade when a hand gripped his wrist and a familiar voice quietly drawled, "As a last resort only."

On the opposite side of the stairs, Cade was telling Taryn to go whenever she was ready.

Clutching her black Tanto-style blade, Taryn stepped from cover, descended the short stack of stairs, and made a bee line for the near corner of the barn where her quota of rotters were pressing in against the massive doors.

Saiga slung diagonally over his chest and holding his black, single-edged blade at the low ready, Duncan nudged Wilson on the back to get him moving.

So far, so good, thought Cade. The predetermined order of movement was going off without a hitch. Most of the early success could only be attributed to whatever it was inside the barn that the dead were so attracted to.

After nodding at Cade, Duncan followed Wilson off the porch in as close to a running crouch as his knees would allow. Pacing a half-dozen steps behind Taryn, both men followed her until they neared the far side of the gravel parking area where they all peeled off on divergent tangents.

Glock in one hand, sleek black Gerber in the other, Cade leaped from the porch. Arms and legs pistoning, he sprinted for the furthermost corner of the barn where the parked F-650 and random pieces of rusted farm equipment had created a sort of funnel a handful of Zs were still negotiating.

By the time Cade was passing the point where the barn doors came together, Taryn was ripping her blade out of the first of her chosen targets and deftly sidestepping the falling corpse.

To Taryn's right, Duncan was grabbing handfuls of greasy, insect-infested hair and introducing his blade to lifeless flesh with assembly-line precision.

As Cade bypassed Wilson's position, two things happened. First, the adrenaline flooding his system slowed the action around him to a crawl, making it seem as if as he was moving at normal speed while everything and everyone was caught up in some kind of slow-motion replay. Then from the corner of his eye he saw the redhead grab a towering specimen of rot and decay by the shoulder and move to insert his blade into the base of its neck. Strangely, however, the Z spun away from the killing strike and in the blink of an eye the two were tangled up and pirouetting around like a couple of drunks engaged in a three-legged race. Even more troubling than the shocking display of agility was that this one seemed to be matching Wilson in strength—something that Cade hadn't seen from a Z as *seasoned* as this.

Sink or swim, thought Cade as he continued on, splashing through puddles and sending loose gravel skittering away with each footfall. Finally reaching the west corner of the barn behind a full head of steam, he jumped into the fray. Two lightning-quick flashes of the Gerber had the pair of Zs facing away from him crashing vertically to the ground where they became but static tents of ashen skin misshapen by jutting, sharp-edged bones.

Parrying grabbing hands with the pistol, Cade waded deeper into the pack of Zs, ramming his black dagger to the hilt into the nearest monster's eye socket. Grimacing from the stench of carrion polluting the still air, he crabbed right a couple of steps and brought the butt of the polymer pistol down squarely atop a grade-school-aged Z's head. There was a sickening crunch of collapsing bone and the tiny thing was sent on its way to the ground quivering from a final death twitch.

Cade was spinning around to engage another Z when in his left side vision two things became clear to him. Bringing him an instant feeling of relief, he saw that Wilson was indeed *swimming*, having vanquished his overly capable foe and was moving on from yet another kill sprawled on the ground near his feet. Then, starting a cold ball to form in Cade's gut, came the realization that the remaining dead were now aware of their proximity to fresh meat and beginning to moan and rasp and turn in his direction.

In the next beat, a male Z oblique to Cade was staring side-eyed and reaching out for him with its skinless, claw-like hands. Sidestepping the clumsy swipe, the Delta operator landed a devastating one-two combination. The former being a left forearm to the Z's neck that stood the thirty-something upright and rigid. While the latter—coming from down low and sweeping blindingly fast on an upward right-to-left arc—was delivered in the form of a perfectly aimed and timed dagger strike to the temple.

As the twice-dead creature did the slow slide from Cade's blade, from out of the south a wind gust roared over the farm. To Cade it sounded like Murphy voicing his displeasure at the leg up Mother Nature just gave to his outnumbered group. *Fuck you, Murphy.* In Cade's line of work advantage came in many forms—most often when least expected. And he wasn't about to look this gift horse in the mouth.

On the sloped pasture at the group's backs the withered grass whipped violently to all points of the compass before bowing due north in supplication to the sudden arrival of the carrion-rich gale.

In the lee of the barn and sheltered from the rising tempest cutting around the huge structure, the small group found themselves in a strange bubble of calm. The normal properties of how sound travelled were momentarily altered. Which Cade quickly decided to use to their advantage. Telling the others to disengage and back away, he sheathed the Gerber and brought the Glock to bear on the nearest Z. Pistol steadied in a two-handed grip, he caressed the trigger once. The muffled report sounded and a millisecond later the 9mm Parabellum was bridging the gap between muzzle and pasty forehead and a shiny brass casing was tracing a graceful arc away from the ejection port. Even as the creature's face was collapsing and a mist of brackish blood bloomed around its head, Cade was tracking the suppressor left and dropping the first of Wilson's remaining two Zs with a bullet to its temple. With twice-dead rotters falling domino-like in the wake of accurate fire, Cade continued sweeping the polymer pistol right to left.

Without blinking and devoid of remorse, he pumped single shots into the snarling creature's faces, the screaming slugs plowing into eye sockets and opened maws and foreheads, leaving behind entry wounds surrounded by shredded dermis and shockwave-pulped flesh and bone.

Though clearly audible to Cade and the others, he was all but certain the residual noise of the rapid-fire gunshots escaping the cylindrical suppressor was being carried safely north of them by the wind.

No way it could have reached the road a quarter-mile west of the barn.
Or so he hoped.

"Give me room," he called, pointing an elbow to where he wanted the others to go.

Counting eight undead things still navigating the phalanx of prostrate corpses, Duncan reached out and grabbed Wilson with his free hand. Seeing Taryn already heeding Cade's command, he reluctantly backpedaled away from the barn with the redhead in tow.

"This way," Cade said to the staggering brood. Waving one arm over his head, he lured the Zs around the barn's east side and trudged into the oncoming headwind. Raising his voice to be heard over the intermittent wind howl and calls of the hungry dead, he continued hollering and gesticulating at them until he reached the midpoint of the barn's looming wall where a lone clouded-over window was located. Noticing Duncan shooting a *what the eff are you doing?* look in his direction, Cade took an abrupt ninety-degree turn and backpedaled a path through the grass. A dozen yards from the barn he felt the gravel drive under his boots and sensed the farmhouse crowding him from behind.

Seeing that the others were now at a safe angle to the right of the barn, Cade stopped, planted his feet a shoulder-width apart, and promptly punched a third eye into the forehead of the first of the eight Zs following him.

He let them come.

He let the Glock speak seven more times.

He looked over the bodies of former Americans and felt a rising anger. Not at them. It wasn't their fault. It was the evil in men that had gotten the Omega ball rolling. It was the evil in the Adrian woman responsible for Ray's gruesome death. And Cade was certain the horror yet to be discovered behind the closed barn doors was going to trump everything he had seen to date.

Slide locked open and smoke curling from the suppressor, Cade headed back to where the whole conga line of death had begun, along the way sourcing another magazine and swapping it for the empty.

"*Wyatt,*" said Taryn, the word drawn out long and colored with an equal measure of awe and contempt. "Fitting. But we're not a bunch of stiffs. I was down to just two."

Cade said nothing. Time for talking would come later. Instead, he looped around the leaking bodies lined up perpendicular to the barn wall. He stepped over dead things wearing twisted death masks and edged past the others on his way to the F-650. Stopping by the driver's side front fender, he craned around the bent-forward driver-side mirror and was rewarded with an unobstructed view down the length of the drive.

Chapter 32

"We still clear?" asked Duncan. Even with the wind beginning to subside, he was forced to cup his hands around his mouth and yell to be heard.

Cade tore his eyes from the lolling heads of the dead things traipsing north on the distant state route. "We dodged a bullet," he called back. "Squall came at just the right time. Helped drown out their moans." He racked a fresh round into the Glock and started off toward the barn doors.

"The gunfire, too," Duncan answered, his brow crinkling. "That was some fast thinking."

"Damn fast shooting, too." added Taryn.

"You never let us have any fun," chimed Wilson as he looked to Taryn for support.

Stopping a few feet from the permanently stilled flesh-eaters, Cade looked to Wilson, saying, "Killing should never be fun. If it ever crosses the line from a dark deed necessary to survival and becomes something you actually look forward to ... then you're treading dangerously in the territory sociopaths live in."

"Yeah. Like Adrian," said Wilson. "I was just busting balls." Embarrassed, he looked away.

"Saw a friend in 'Nam lose his way," said Duncan. "Disappeared into the jungle one day never to be heard from again."

Cade said, "Smacks of *Apocalypse Now*. His name Kurtz?"

"If I was the eyerollin' type," drawled Duncan. "I'd be rollin' them somethin' fierce about now."

Taryn and Wilson exchanged bewildered looks.

Cade knocked lightly on the barn and scrutinized its looming face.

Both doors were nearly as wide as they were tall and decorated with big white Xs fashioned from one by six planks. Victim of harsh winters and the relentless high-altitude summer sun, the paint was faded and cracked, the fissures curling up at the edges. In places, blood and flecked bone and clumps of hair still rooted in festering flesh clung to the weathered boards.

Cocking an ear to the door, Cade said, "Hear that?"

One brow raised, Duncan nodded. "Sounds a lot like a kitten's mewing."

Wilson turned away from the barn. "So how come we didn't hear it when we were hiding behind the truck earlier?"

"Because we were all fixated on that gun-barrel-turned-broomstick that kept poking through the curtains," answered Duncan. "I sure as hell thought maybe Ray or Helen had snapped and was up there drawing a bead on us."

Taryn said, "You think Helen is in the barn?"

"She's still not accounted for," answered Cade.

Looking at Cade, Taryn said, "Whose tongue was that in the house? Ray still had his. Not much else, though."

"Let's find out." Cade asked Duncan to watch their six for rotters. Then he made a fist and pounded three times on the left-side door. Not too hard. Hard enough, however, to silence the mewing and start a shower of fine dust to fall from the top of the door.

Hoping to draw anything dead and ambulatory to the doors, he tried again. Same method. Same number of strikes.

As soon as the reverberation from the solid blows subsided, the mewing returned, still distant and muted.

Leading by example, Cade holstered the Glock then bent over and grabbed the wrists of one of the Zs. He dragged the body a dozen feet from the barn and let the limp arms thump to the ground.

***

Five minutes after Cade started the process, with help from Wilson and Taryn, they had the doors clear and the dead bodies stacked waist-high a dozen feet downwind from them.

Standing before the barn, Cade looked to Wilson. "You did good with that big Z. You want honors here?"

Playing it cool—but still feeling the feathery bat wings of dread caressing his stomach—Wilson shrugged and said, "If you insist." From a jacket pocket, he fished the tiny Maglite he'd employed while standing watch on the stairs in the house. Flashlight clamped between his teeth, he unwound the chain slowly and parted the doors, leaving just enough of a gap between them to shine the narrow beam through.

M4 held at a low ready, Cade said, "What do you see?"

"Nothing I can attribute that creepy ass noise to."

Duncan said, "No dead things in traction waiting to be sprung on us?"

Wilson said, "Not that I can see."

The wind had gone calm again. Just intermittent little gusts that ruffled the partially drawn curtains in the farmhouse's upstairs windows.

Taryn offered to run *point* as she'd heard the men with military training call the guinea-pig-like role of being the first person walking in a patrol line or entering a structure needing to be cleared. Last time she had taken this kind of initiative she still had waist-length hair and Oliver, Foley, and Brook were still alive. Nothing for the rotters to sink their grimy claws into now, she mused. Nothing much for Wilson to grab hold of either, she quickly lamented.

Cade backed off the door a couple of steps. Looked to Duncan for input.

"Knock yourself out," was Duncan's reply.

After handing Taryn his suppressed Glock, Cade snugged the M4 tight to his shoulder and trained the muzzle where the doors would soon part.

Patting Wilson on the shoulder, Duncan said, "Haul them open, *killer.*"

Wilson made no reply. He wrapped both hands into the opposing handles, leaned away from the doors, and tried pulling them apart.

The left door moved a few inches in its track, but quickly seized up behind a noise sounding like a carpenter's planer being dragged across wood.

Borrowed pistol held in a two-handed grip, Taryn stepped forward, ready to enter as soon as Cade said to. *Time to get back in the saddle and ride, girl,* she thought to herself as a low amp current of fear started her heart to hammer. Last thing she wanted was to be stuck doing the kind of monotonous jobs always foisted upon Tran, Seth, and the late James Foley.

"A little help?" Wilson said to no one in particular.

Slinging the Saiga, Duncan stepped forward and took hold of the right door handle.

Wilson grabbed the left handle with both hands. "Ready?" he asked.

"Go," Duncan said.

The right door moved first, sliding a few inches and restarting the noise of something overhead grating against wood. Once the doors were open evenly, the previous noise was replaced by the squeal of metal on metal and the tension on the doors disappeared entirely.

What happened next caught each of them by surprise.

Missing the movement above the door due to the bill of his cap, Cade was aware of the falling body only when it was arrested a yard from his face and barely a foot off the ground.

Catching a glancing blow on her shoulder from above, Taryn yelped and was sent sprawling to her left. As a result of the pain lancing from her shoulder to her wrist, her hand involuntarily opened and the Glock was separated from her grasp.

Duncan was still gripping the handle when an object ejected from the hayloft door above caught him squarely on the top of his head, knocking the Stetson one direction and his senses the other.

Spared injury, but shocked all the same by the sudden appearance of a ghastly figure complete with bruised and bloated facial features, Wilson let go of his hold on the handle and was carried onto his back by his own spooled-up momentum.

In the next instant, Cade was flicking his rifle to Safe and rushing to check on Duncan, who was on his back and twitching like a fish on land. Feeling a pulse and seeing his friend's chest rising and falling underneath the thick jacket, Cade turned his attention to the person hanging from their neck by a taut rope. Though at first blush the body that had been ejected through the sliding hayloft door a dozen feet above him along with a basic wooden chair looked a lot like one of the undead, from where he was kneeling he could see that its bare, varicose-veined legs still possessed a slight pink hue. Even as he was wrapping his arms around the hips and lifting up to relieve the noose of tension, he was calling for Wilson to use his Gerber to cut the rope.

As Cade waited for the redhead to act on the command, he walked his eyes up the body in his grasp and came to realize it was a woman. And she was elderly. And her skin was still warm against his cheek. Which meant she was alive, or had been a few seconds ago before Duncan and Wilson's simple act of forcing open the lower doors had somehow started the upper door moving in its tracks. Which in turn, he guessed, had sent her and the chair that had clocked Duncan careening into space.

Wilson righted the chair and placed it beside Cade. After slipping the Gerber from the sheath, he jumped up on the chair and began sawing at the rope with the dagger's serrated edge. As he worked, he was casting furtive glances at Taryn who was by every definition of the boxing term—*down for the count.*

Cade felt a slight jerk and then he was supporting the woman's entire body weight. Which felt double of what he guessed it to be because there seemed to be no life left in her. "Check on Taryn," he called to Wilson as he let the body to the ground and laid it out flat, cradling the misshapen head gently in one hand as he did so.

Examining the woman's face, it became clear to Cade that she was dead or very close to it. Her eyes—*at least they were still in their sockets*—were bugged out and the pupils fixed. She was making no sound and the color was draining from her cheeks.

Sounding hopeful, Wilson said, "She's just shaken up."

Out of his right eye, Cade saw Duncan beginning to stir. Without looking over his shoulder, he barked at Wilson, "Get over here then. I need your help."

One atop the other and fingers interlocking, Cade placed his hands on the woman's narrow ribcage and began chest compressions.

Skidding to a stop, Wilson went to his knees. First he looked at Cade, then the woman, then swung his gaze back to Cade. "What do *I* do?"

Matching chest compressions to the one-hundred-beat-per-minute tempo of the Bee Gees ditty looping through his head, Cade said, "Tilt her head back and make sure she hasn't swallowed her tongue."

Wilson did the first part and was sticking his fingers in the woman's open maw when he recoiled and said, "We have a problem."

Coming to realize whose tongue was inside on the plate, Cade said, "Start breathing for her then."

The anticipated complaints didn't come. Instead, Wilson hunched over and drew in a lungful of air. With no hesitation he planted his mouth on the woman's blood-rimed lips and transferred the trapped breath. He continued the process while Cade hammered away right next to him.

Though Cade's knuckles were beginning to ache and his shoulder and forearm muscles were burning from the roughly two-hundred chest compressions he'd already administered, he kept *Stayin' Alive* playing on repeat in his mind.

The two men kept this up for what seemed like an eternity. When they finally stopped, Cade declaring her dead after failing to find a pulse, only five minutes had elapsed since her sudden and wholly unexpected gravity-aided entrance.

From his perch on the nearby chair, Duncan said, "Dollars to doughnuts her neck is broken. Fall probably did a number on her brain stem, too." His hand subconsciously went to the tennis-ball-sized goose egg growing on his head. "No coming back from that."

Cade spun around and went from a kneeling position to sitting cross-legged. "That's what I figured," he said, shifting his gaze to the hayloft door. There was a taut length of white rope cutting the space horizontally. A new item, judging by how clean it appeared.

Taryn was on her feet now. She braced herself by taking hold of the chair back. "Another trap set by Adrian's people," she said, grimacing.

Looking side-eyed at her, Duncan said, "That was no trap. It was a message."

Voicing what Cade had already noted, Taryn said, "That tongue in there is hers. She wouldn't talk. And that's why she lost it."

"Brook said Helen was one tough cookie." Silently scolding himself for another slip of the tongue, Duncan grimaced and looked away.

"Brook had a lot of good things to say about this couple," Cade said in a near whisper. "Her note to me was almost two pages. That forced dinner she had with them left a great impression." He clenched his jaw and clasped his hands behind his head. Looking to the north, he added, "They didn't deserve this."

Wilson was standing in the gaping opening and staring into the barn.

Voice taking on an ominous tone, he said, "There's more."

Chapter 33

They all filed into the barn behind Wilson. And just in the nick of time, too. Because the sky decided to open up and pea-sized hailstones thudded the ground and raked the fallen corpses with machinegun-like efficiency.

Even as Helen's thin cotton night clothes jumped and rippled from the sudden bombardment, her open mouth was filling with the frozen precipitation.

A few yards beyond the prostrate bodies, the F-650 was also taking a heaven-sent beating. With each crystalline explosion created by hail striking its windshield and sheet metal there came a furious, gunshot-like report.

The damp air inside the barn was heavy with the sweet stink of carrion and rotting hay. And as the cacophony from the fusillade hitting just outside the doors rose to a crescendo, to Cade, the hail banging and booming off the tin roof overhead began to sound like a hundred blacksmiths hard at work straightening metal. Or, on second thought, bullet-proof South Dakota soil reducing a stealthy black helicopter to a mess of twisted metal and shredded carbon fiber. Pushing that hellish memory from his mind, he activated the tactical light on his M4. Swept the muzzle over the walls and saw miscellaneous pieces of tack hanging here and there. Gardening tools were propped in a nearby corner. Adorning the walls was an assortment of porcelain-coated signage harkening back to the time before lighted reader boards and neon migrated from the big cities. The products advertised on the differently shaped and brightly colored signs ranged from *Mobil Oil* to *Yankee Girl Tobacco* to *John Deere* tractors, the latter of which was represented in the barn by the real thing. Covered with a thin coating of dust, the hulking green piece of machinery essential to most every rural enterprise sat silently in a far corner under a translucent canopy of wispy cobwebs.

After finishing the clockwise visual recon by shooting the others a *nothing to see here* expression, Cade studied the ladder running up a nearby support beam. Letting his eyes travel its length, he saw that it led to a three-by-three trapdoor installed between one pair of the dozen or so rough-hewn four-by-six timbers running horizontal to the barn's front doors. The trapdoor was open. By the light infiltrating the parted loft doors he could just make out the rafters and dull underside of the tin roof above. Without a word, he let his rifle hang by its sling and began to scale the ladder.

Without missing a beat, Wilson blurted, "I'm coming, too," and hustled up after.

The closer Cade came to the top rung the more the odor of death was affecting him. By the time he stopped short of the opening to look and listen, his eyes were beginning to water and he had to breathe through his mouth to keep from gagging. A long ten-count with Wilson waiting impatiently a rung below his Danners told Cade all he needed to know. Save for the steady drum of hail from the passing storm, he heard nothing to make him think anything living or dead awaited him. Holding in a breath, he swept the M4 up, poked it through the opening one-handed, and climbed another couple of rungs. Head and shoulders inside the loft, he thumbed the tactical light on and panned the sterile white cone in a smooth right to left arc. Seeing the beam refract off of something liquid and shiny at the end of the sweep, he let it linger for a tick then quickly jerked it away and began to dry heave.

Down in the barn Taryn had already turned toward the once-gray field of gravel fronting the parted doors. Outside the hail was still hammering everything in sight. In less than a minute, the landscape for as far as she could see had gone from mostly earth tones dashed with the warm colors of autumn to a blanket of white shot through with shades of gray.

The upturned faces of the rotters drew her attention back to the foreground. Sunken eye sockets white with hail lent the impression a half-dozen Orphan Annie's were staring blankly back at her. Mouths left yawning by a sudden second-death also brimmed with hail, the excess sloughing off and piling neatly on the ground around their heads. Unmoved by the surreal sight, she glanced up at Wilson on the ladder and indicated that she was content to hang with Duncan and help keep an eye on the driveway.

Wiping an errant rope of drool on his sleeve, Cade leveled his gaze to the wall a half-dozen yards to his left. There, partially obscured by shadow from the overhead beams, were two people. Even in the dim light he could see that they both had been crucified in a spread-eagle position. The rusty heads of what looked to be railroad dog-spikes protruded several inches from their palms. Down below, the same style spikes had been driven through their ankles until the flat, bent heads had come to rest against the pale flesh there. Both of their heads were touching the steeply pitched roof near where the rafters met the wall. The inky dark permeating the angled recess made it impossible to see their faces, which in turn left Cade in the dark as to their gender.

From ankle to groin and wrist to breast the corpses had been skinned and stripped of flesh. Ribcages devoid of all internals gaped down on him. All that was left between their legs were gaping holes with pelvic bone and unidentifiable reproductive organs on full display. Though Cade had never seen this level of wholesale savagery in person, he'd heard fellow soldiers describe the torture houses they'd come across in Fallujah, Iraq, where drills and flame and all manner of blades had been employed on Iraqis friendly to the American-led invasion.

The floor in front of the corpses was covered with hay. On the periphery, it was dry and yellow with the gray wood floorboards clearly visible. Below the corpses, the hay was mixed with drying blood. Like little black bergs in a shiny crimson sea, a number of baseball-sized clumps had formed where the hay had continued to soak up the blood leaking from the crucifixion wounds.

Cade averted his eyes and peered down the ladder at Wilson. "You have a full stomach?"

"If I was going to *uneat* I would have already done so inside the house," admitted Wilson. "If that woman upstairs and the shit on the plates in the dining room didn't make me go praying to the porcelain gods, I doubt that whatever you see up there will."

"You're good, then?"

Voice full of confidence, Wilson said, "I'm good."

Without another word on the subject, Cade scaled the final few rungs. He approached the corpses and turned toward the trapdoor, training the tactical light on the opening so he wouldn't miss seeing the redhead's expression.

A beat later Wilson emerged from below and swung his gaze to his left. Face twisting in disgust, he whistled low and slow and said, "Fuck meeee."

"You still *good?*"

Wilson shot Cade a sidelong glance. He nodded and said, "This is just like the scene in the church. Were these two still alive … er, I mean undead?"

"No," said Cade, shining the light on the bodies. "This is exactly how I found them."

"Consider yourself lucky, then. *Ol' Chatter Jaw* from the church is still visiting me in my sleep."

Cade thought: *Lucky my ass. I just had to put down my wife.* Purging the memory, he swept his arm in a wide arc from the open hayloft door to the vertical seam of light infiltrating the closed doors opposite them. "Does the handwriting look like what you saw in the church?"

Wilson didn't answer. He was inching closer to the shorter of the two corpses and craning his head sideways to better take in the scene that looked to have been torn from Marquis de Sade's twisted mind. A pitchfork had been forced into its buttocks from below. Barely an inch of splintered wood from the broken-off handle remained in the rusted, iron head. Thanks to the hollowed-out chest cavity, he could see that all four curved tines had travelled upward and came to rest near parallel to its spine.

Like some kind of sleuth, he craned to get a closer look at the other corpse. Barely visible and hanging phallic-like between its skeletal legs was what could only be a rat's tail. It was flat and curled like a J. Upon closer inspection, he saw that the rest of the mummified rodent was wedged inside the pelvic cavity.

"Why the eff would someone take the time and go through all the trouble?"

Cade illuminated the writing on the wall to the right of the unlucky duo. He said, "For the meat, first off."

"And why didn't they do the same to Ray and Helen?"

He thought: *They introduced Ray to the Zs first. Then to encourage him to talk before he turned, threatened to do the same to Helen.* But to spare everyone the horrible truth of the matter—infected meat was not edible—he simply said, "Do you like mutton?"

Wilson shook his head. "I don't even know what that means."

Cade said, "Never mind. Is the writing familiar to you?"

Wilson took a couple of paces back from the crucified pair. Let his gaze travel the loft walls, pausing for a half-beat each time Cade illuminated the Bible verses scrawled there in what looked to be dried blood.

Voice rising from down below, Duncan said, "What's the stink from?"

To Wilson's chagrin, Cade dropped the light to a pile of clothes he'd spotted earlier. He stirred them with a toe. Seeing what looked to him more like smeared pitch than dried blood on the wrinkled flannel and denim, he called down, telling Duncan he had a strong feeling the rendered corpses were those of a woodcutting crew gone missing from Bear River the day before.

Duncan called up the ladder again. "Wrong place, wrong time. That's too bad." He paused for a moment then asked, "What's with the writing you guys were talking about?"

"Come up and see for yourself," implored Cade.

"If Glenda had a twin and the two of them were up there begging me to frolic with them, I still wouldn't climb that rickety little ladder."

Taryn said, "I heard that, Duncan Winters."

Rubbing his shoulder, Duncan said, "I'll totally deny it if you tell her. Three against one here."

Wilson said, "Two."

Cade added, "You're on your own on that one, buddy."

"Give an old fella a break, will ya?" begged Duncan, dragging the chair to the bottom of the support beam. "Can you read me a bedtime story?"

Standing over the trapdoor, Cade peered through the opening and caught Duncan's eyes.

"Well?"

Cade nodded and disappeared from view.

Chapter 34

Raising his voice so it would carry between levels, Cade said, "All right, Old Man, where do you want me to start?"

"What's it say on the wall the woodcutters are nailed to?"

"That's the east wall. There's a verse attributed to *Matthew 6:19*." Cade cleared his throat and went on, "'Do not store up for yourselves treasures on earth, where moth and rust destroy, and where thieves break in and steal.'"

Expecting a response, Cade paused. The tin roof seemed to have warmed a bit. It pinged a couple of times; whether the sound was from the introduction of sun to the oft-stressed panels or errant hailstones, he couldn't tell.

Not sure what to make of the uneasy silence, Wilson just continued to stare at Cade through the gloom.

"Well?" Cade finally said, eyes downcast as if he could see Duncan through the hay-strewn floor.

"That verse has more to do with Ray and Helen than the dead folks up there. Ray told me he and the *missus* had a stockpile of supplies and weapons they took from fallen National Guard roadblocks those first days of the outbreak. Said they had MREs and ammo and batteries and weapons. I'd bet the house this is the baddies up north wagging their finger at the Thagons for having all the toys and not sharing."

Cade said, "I concur."

Duncan said, "OK. How about the wall facing our allies to the south?"

Wilson had his flashlight out and was already lighting up the far wall. His beam wavering slightly over the second set of doors servicing the loft, he said, "This verse is from Jeremiah 5:17. 'They will devour your harvest and your food; They will devour your sons and your daughters; They will devour your vines and your fig trees; They will demolish with the sword your fortified cities in which you trust.'"

Duncan remained silent.

Cade said, "That can't be about the Zs. They don't utilize weapons."

Duncan said, "That's a warning directed toward Bear River. Adrian's saying when the time is right her people are going to march south and take what she perceives to be hers."

"That's bullshit," Cade hissed. "*Nothing* is hers. And if she wants to fight for it … then a fight she's going to get." His ears were hot. The warming tin near his head had nothing to do with it.

"All those white Xs on the doors in Woodruff and Randolph," said Wilson. "The watcher scribing her name in the church rectory. Lord knows how many are out there. Could be one in every attic for all we know."

Wearing a knowing look, Cade said nothing.

"I wouldn't go that far," said Duncan.

"Still a bunch of bullshit," added Wilson, nervously shifting his weight from foot to foot.

Duncan said, "I couldn't agree with you more." He was standing now and pacing the dirt floor below the opening. "Those fuckers tried to justify their cannibalism by quoting the Bible and scrawling it on the church walls. Now they're broadcasting their next move. And to add injury to insult, they know to a certain degree where the compound is located."

Wilson regarded Cade. Brows knitted, he said, "This bitch is unhinged."

"You think?" replied Cade, tongue firmly planted in cheek.

"I'm afraid to ask," Duncan called up. There was a long pause. Finally, voice devoid of emotion, he did just that. "What message is directed toward our compound?"

Cade lit up the wall and read the passage. "*Ephesians 4:28*. 'He who steals must steal no longer; but rather he must labor, performing with his own hands what is good, so that he has something to share with one who has need.'"

There was no pause this time. Duncan said, "*That* is Adrian's *fatwah*, so to speak. A declared death sentence on *us*. And I have no doubt she'll try to make good on it."

Cade dropped his chin to his chest. *Loose ends.* After a couple of beats he said, "Especially now since she knows precisely where to find us."

Wilson crunched down his boonie hat with one hand. "And where to find her U-Haul trucks filled with supplies."

Though he'd driven one of said U-Haul trucks, Duncan made no reply to its mention. Instead he moved on, asking, "What's on the front loft doors?"

"Not a thing," Cade answered back. The air around his head was warming. And he was growing tired of breathing through his mouth. He said, "I've seen enough."

***

At the bottom of the ladder, Cade turned toward the open doors and called Taryn over.

Duncan pushed off the chair and stood on unsteady legs.

Together they waited for Wilson to finish coming down the ladder.

Once everyone was standing in a ragged semicircle, Cade said, "Adrian, or her people, didn't need to leave another verse on the north wall."

Taryn looked a question at Cade.

"Ray and Helen didn't talk," he said.

"And you know this, how?" asked Wilson.

Standing between Taryn and Wilson, arms crossed, Duncan wore a knowing look and simply nodded as Cade laid it all out for them. "Because Ray lost his eyes and ears and then, finally, when he didn't talk—"

"They made her watch as the rotters fed on his arms," said Wilson, finishing the thought for Cade.

213

"My guess," answered Cade. "That's a fate worse than death. And when Ray still didn't divulge the compound's whereabouts, they left him there to turn—"

Duncan interrupted. "And *then* they made Helen climb to the loft and sit in the chair and watch as they butchered the woodcutters."

Arms crossed, Taryn asked, "And why didn't they write a verse on the doors behind her?"

"Because she didn't talk. And it had nothing to do with her being the strong woman Brook described. It was simply because she had nothing to tell. She didn't know where the compound is. So her and Ray died for nothing. Thanks to our mole at the compound, Adrian and her people found out where we are anyway." Finished talking, he ground his teeth and faced north.

Duncan saw Cade go rigid and a thousand-yard stare take over his features. In that moment, it was clear to the Vietnam veteran that his friend was teetering on the precipice of a deep, dark abyss the likes of which few emerged from unscathed—mentally or physically.

Without a word, Cade stalked off toward the house. Ignoring queries from Taryn and Wilson, he mounted the steps, pushed through the door, and continued into the dark guts of the house, his steady, purposeful gait never slowing. He went straight to the bathroom and hauled open the door. Using the Gerber, he sawed through the ropes used to secure the once undead Ray to the commode. Before standing, he pulled Ray's corpse toward him and adjusted its weight on his shoulder. Once he'd found a good balance point, he rose and backed out of the tiny powder room. Bracketed by the back door and dead refrigerator, he spun a careful quarter-turn and headed for the flat light streaming in the open front door.

On the way back down the main hall, Cade chose a photo off the wall and plucked it from its hook. In the picture, Helen and Ray were standing before the white fence with the north run of the Bear Mountains and a wide expanse of lush, green grass behind them. The pasture was home to a dozen alpacas, the majority of them deep in the background. However, one cheeky young specimen was cutting into the photo, its head taking up space near Helen's ear. The couple wore toothy grins. From that brief glimpse Cade got as he selected the photo from the half-dozen others on the wall, he was sure at that moment in history no two people on Earth had been happier.

Without pausing to assess how they were hung, he yanked the set of curtains from the dining room window as he passed on by.

At the front door, he angled his shoulders a few degrees right and squeezed through the opening designed for an average-sized person at the turn of the century. Careful to not bang Ray's head on the jamb, he spun a one-eighty and closed the door behind him.

At the truck, under three pairs of watchful eyes, he laid the drapes out on the gravel and very carefully placed Ray Thagon lengthwise on them.

Mute since making the decision he was acting upon, Cade placed the photo on Ray's chest and crossed the corpse's arms across it. He about-faced and trudged from the truck to the barn where he knelt and scooped Helen up in his arms. Boot prints glistening in the rapidly melting hail, he retraced his steps to the truck and gently laid Helen's corpse beside her husband's.

There on the splayed-out burgundy fabric the pale corpses looked nothing like the couple in the photo. Secure in the thought the two of them were together again in a better place, Cade blanketed them both with the drapes and said a silent prayer.

Rubbing a knot out of his shoulder, Cade looked a question at Wilson and Taryn.

Message received.

***

Three minutes later—with Wilson and Taryn's help—the snowmobile was moved to one side of the truck's bed and the shrouded corpses occupied the narrow space beside it.

"Forty-five minutes," were the first words Cade had uttered since leaving the barn to go back in the house. He remained silent even as he backed the F-650 down the feeder road. Like a ship at sea, the big Ford listed and shimmied as it negotiated the rutted road.

Though the going down the road was trickier in reverse, they made it to the state route without pitching man or machine from the bed.

As Cade wheeled across both lanes, parting a throng of Zs in the process, he asked Wilson to look at their load and tell him what he saw.

Wilson threw an arm over his seat back and lifted his butt off the seat. Craning hard, he let his gaze roam the contents of the crowded bed.

The keening noise of fingernails raking the truck's flanks reverberated throughout the cab.

Sitting down hard, Wilson met Cade's eyes in the rearview mirror. "Ray and Helen are still snug as—"

A glare from Cade cut the inappropriate comment off at the knees. He said, "Just the facts."

A sheepish look on his face, Wilson went on. "The Thagons haven't moved from where we put them. The snowmobile shifted toward the open gate a bit."

"What's a bit?"

"Half a foot."

Cade slipped the shifter to Park. "Do we have to get out and adjust the load?"

Wilson began to speak, but was cut off for a second time by Duncan.

Looking at Cade, Duncan said, "Time's a wastin'."

Ignoring the faces pressing against his window, Cade calmly plucked the Motorola from a pocket and thumbed the Talk button. "Eden, Cade here." He crossed his arms on the wheel and dropped his forehead, resting it on his knuckles as he waited for the response. Which came three seconds later.

"This is Tran," came the familiar sing-song voice.

Cade brought Tran up to speed. He left nothing out. Not a single gory detail. He wanted everyone there to be filled in, too.

Verbatim, he stressed. Because he wanted everyone there to be as pissed-off as he was about the new atrocities that amounted to little more than a cherry on the sundae of death and destruction Adrian and her followers had already wrought on anybody unfortunate enough to have come into contact with them. Finished describing the way the Thagons' bodies had been desecrated, he passed on instructions for Lev and Jamie. The two were to arm up and rush to Woodruff in the Raptor.

"What if they come across Bridgett along the way?" asked Tran.

Cade lowered his head again and tapped out a cadence on the steering wheel.

"She's not going to let them see her," said Duncan. "She'll go to ground the second she hears that growling engine."

Cade lifted his head and met Taryn's gaze in the rearview. "That's what I'm counting on. And if she does what any good soldier would do, the rest should fall into place nicely." He nudged the transmission to Drive. Then, with the hollow bangs of palms slapping sheet metal seeing them off, he motored north toward Woodruff and the rendezvous he knew was sure to be a bloody affair.

Chapter 35

At the 39/16 junction, Cade pulled the F-650 hard to the side of the road opposite the tipped-over school bus. He took the Glock from the seat beside him and dumped the magazine. He racked the slide and let the live 9mm round fall into his lap.

"Chamber's empty," he said, handing the suppressed weapon and fresh mag over the seatback to Wilson.

Wilson took the Glock and, much to Cade's surprise, pulled the slide back an inch to check for himself. "It certainly is," he reported back.

"Quiet and fast," Cade said over his shoulder.

Wilson seated the magazine and cycled a round into the chamber. "We got this," he declared as he scooted across the seat and followed Taryn out the rear passenger-side door.

"Be careful," Duncan said over his shoulder half a beat before the door thunked shut behind his head. He looked to Cade, one brow cocked. "Think it registered?"

"Hope not," admitted Cade. "*Careful* is for building scale airplane models and working on pocket watches."

"Wilson was scared," Duncan added, his tone betraying a trace of worry.

Cade flicked his eyes to the side mirror where he could see the two walking parallel to the dashed centerline which was just beginning to show through the melting hail. Staggering along the 16 a few hundred feet ahead of the kids were the Zs he'd just steered the Ford through. *Fifteen or more*, he guessed. *Plenty enough to keep them busy.* Happy to see the young couple placing a few feet of separation between themselves, Cade said, "I hope he is afraid. A good measure of fear never hurt anybody."

"It wasn't the lock up all motor function and cause you to shit your pants kind of fear I detected," said Duncan, ahead of a chuckle. "But I could smell it coming through his pores."

Cade thought: *Sink or swim.* The new mantra. If he went down to man or Z, he wanted Raven in the company of as many seasoned survivors as possible. The *swimmers* of this new world. With fond thoughts of Raven trying to surface from the dark place he stowed them while outside the wire, he fished his backup Glock and the Steiners from the center console. The former he placed on the dash. The latter he used to scan the tree line west of 16. Seeing nothing moving there, he swept the binoculars to the right a few degrees and glassed the foreground a short distance away. He panned right to the point where the intersecting State Route 39 entered the forest and snaked away to its eventual terminus at Daymon's roadblock a couple of miles past the compound. He didn't expect to see Bridgett on foot there, and she wasn't. Her getting to the junction by now would be akin to someone finishing a half-marathon in record time. However, as low a probability as it seemed, he half-expected to see an abandoned vehicle that hadn't been present when they passed earlier on their way to check in on the Thagons. But with no way to jump or push start one of the many vehicles still sitting idle at the lower mining concern or in the drives of the half-dozen unoccupied homes scattered along 39, the latter scenario was almost as farfetched as Bridgett having any kind of long distance runner's pedigree.

Duncan asked, "What do you see?"

Cade lowered the binoculars. "Not a thing moving," he said. "Road and tree line ... both clear."

"No rotters?"

Cade hooked a thumb over his shoulder. "Just those."

Shifting his gaze to the passenger side wing mirror, Duncan watched the action happening at their six while he worked at rubbing the knots from his tweaked shoulder. He winced as Taryn waded into the dead. Saw her stiff-arm the first emaciated specimen and quickly drop it with an upward arcing knife strike to the temple.

Opposite Taryn, the redhead was also meeting the monsters head on. He had the borrowed Glock in a two-fisted grip, its suppressor tracking from monster to monster and jumping slightly as spent brass arced away toward the roadside ditch. The young man looked at ease as he crab-walked through the throng wielding the weapon with a kind of efficiency Duncan had yet to see him exhibit. And contrary to the *Objects In Mirror Are Closer Than They Appear* warning etched onto the mirror below the reversed image, the puffs of hot gasses leaving the suppressor were hardly discernable.

Cade had dropped the binoculars to his lap and was watching in his mirror, too. "Must be the added weight of the suppressor," he said. "Kid's tracking smooth and keeping the sights on target."

Duncan grunted. "He's got it, all right. But he didn't argue your 'only good use for a sidearm in a gunfight is to get to your battle rifle' gobbledygook."

"No breathers in sight," noted Cade as he hefted the Steiners and resumed his left to right visual recon, keying in mainly on the area surrounding the spot where four arterials came together in a sort of twisted X.

Just about where Woodruff started and State Route 16 became Main Street was the auto body shop Cade was already familiar with. He halted his sweep there for a closer look at the vehicles in the lot. Most were wedged in tight against the bowed-in roll-up doors. The few cars that had avoided the undead horde's previous northbound surge would be of no use for what he had planned. West of the cinderblock building, where the uneven, frost-heaved expanse of blacktop curled around back, he spotted a black tow truck backed in close to the wall that piqued his interest. Though not sure of the make and model, he guessed it to be either a Ford F-350 Super Duty or Chevrolet's equivalent. Emblazoned on the passenger door in gaudy-looking gold-leaf outlined with red striping were the words WOODRUFF AUTO BODY.

Cade supposed it would suffice for what he had planned.

Sitting nearby on four flat tires was another American-made pickup. Its glass was intact, but clouded over. The once-white factory paint was streaked vertically with dirt and moss. In the bed were a dozen tires all jammed in at crazy angles.

"Those will both do," said Cade. He regarded Duncan and ran the hastily concocted plan by him.

"It could work," Duncan agreed. "So long as they don't see our tire tracks."

"If they get that far then Murphy has already made an untimely appearance."

"Then that means we don't have to worry about dragging the rotters off the road," Duncan stated, glancing over his shoulder at the young couple. "Looks like a dozen down. Only a couple left standing. They do good work."

"We'll see about that," Cade said cryptically, a tick before a burst of white noise filled the cab. Going to his thigh pocket, he pulled out the radio he had taken off the attic watcher. It was powered on but not the source of the electronic squelch. He went to the other pocket and retrieved his Motorola—which by then was broadcasting Taryn's voice. She sounded winded as she requested help to clear the dead off the road.

"No need," answered Cade. "Come on back. We're moving out."

***

Wilson was at Cade's window a minute later. He looked in and started working an invisible crank—universal semaphore for *roll your window down*. Which Cade did at once saying, "How many did you shoot?"

"I don't know," said Wilson. "Eight, maybe nine."

"How many bullets did it take?"

"More than eight."

"Wrack your brain then pick a number you can live with."

Duncan flashed a questioning look at Cade. "Hell are you playing brain games for?"

Cade looked to Duncan and held up a hand.

Taryn opened the door behind Duncan and jumped in.

Cade swung his gaze back to Wilson. "How many?"

"Nine," he replied, confidently.

"You sure?" Cade said, palm out. "Give it to me. We'll see."

Tentatively, Wilson handed the Glock butt first through the open window.

Without pause, Cade pointed the suppressor at the firewall between his feet and cycled the slide back and forth until the unspent bullets tumbled out and it locked open. He inventoried the rounds and leveled a gaze at Wilson.

Wilson's Adam's apple bobbed. Unconvincingly, he said, "Nine." Then he asked, "Was it nine?"

"Twelve," Cade said, brows knitting in the middle. "Keeping a good mental shot count might just save your butt one day."

Sheepishly, Wilson said, "Copy that," and climbed into the idling truck. Then, trying hard not to succumb to the urge to spew hot vomit onto the backseat carpet, he looked to Taryn and said, "I didn't feel overwhelmed one bit back there. Did you?"

Seeing Wilson's hand palsy as he reached to close his door, Taryn leaned across and lent him a hand. "You did fine, Wilson," she said, wrapping her extended arm around his waist. "*We* did fine ... didn't we, gentlemen?"

Before doing anything, Cade found Taryn in the rearview. Shifting the Ford into Drive, he locked eyes with her and winked.

Chapter 36

Having covered less than a mile since the run-in with the pair of zombies, Iris came to a full stop on a short straightaway between opposing curves. She wavered there for a moment, listening hard. At first she had attributed the subtle hum off her right shoulder as belonging to the Ogden River which she knew snaked through the woods somewhere below the nearby embankment. Now she wasn't so sure. It seemed to be getting louder and there was a throaty roar comingling with the rushing water sound. By the time something clicked in her pain-addled mind and she became keenly aware she was hearing tires hissing against the hail-covered state route—the white noise and exhaust note had grown exponentially and the low growl of an engine hard at work joined the chorus.

Panic rising like water in a flood-swollen creek, Iris ran through her options—none of them good.

First she looked to the scrub brush encroaching on the two-lane's left shoulder. *Too far.* Then she stole a quick glance at the guardrail to her right. *Too high.* Besides, if she were to get over the thigh-high obstacle, the tumble to whatever lay below would probably kill her. She looked at the road by her feet. Barely visible through the sheen of hail was the solid yellow centerline. *Not much room for error.*

Though the last thing Iris wanted to do at this point was play dead in the middle of the road in the likely path of a rapidly approaching vehicle, she had no other option. That the vehicle was approaching from the west, where she knew the road was blocked by dozens of fallen trees, meant it couldn't be carrying anyone friendly to her.

Seconds after first detecting the vehicle, she started to feel the vibration from the engine and rumble of the exhaust in her chest. In fact, the vehicle was closing with the nearby corner at such a high rate of speed that the thrum of its tires came across like an angry swarm of hornets about to alight on her back.

So she did that last thing on her mental list. She went limp mid-limp and let gravity take her to the hail-slicked roadway.

The spot where she came to rest—good leg locked straight, bad cocked at a crazy angle—was less than ideal from a survivability standpoint. But it was too late to do anything but tense every muscle in her body and hold her breath.

The vehicle was just rounding the corner as the repercussions from the voluntary freefall threw Iris's mind into a desperate fight against the tractor-beam-like tug of unconsciousness.

Cursing herself for getting caught out in the open and ending up prone so dangerously close to the middle of the road, she closed her eyes and listened to the wicked thrumming of rubber on cement envelope the space all around her. Her eyes involuntarily snapped open the second the wall of air being pushed ahead of the speeding vehicle hit her body full on. Then she was shocked into a fit of screaming when the follow-on blast of icy slush thrown from the oversized tires slapped her in the face, stinging her cheek and ear and neck as if the imaginary hornets had been riding the slipstream.

Her screams morphed into an animalistic howl as she drew back her right hand and saw that the offending tires had turned it into a swirl of broken digits. The soft flesh on the sides of her shattered fingers had split lengthwise from knuckle to knuckle under the immense pressure exerted on them. An instant pulse of blood began to sluice from the gaping, mouth-like fissures and pool with the water on the road.

Iris rolled to her side and did two things simultaneously. She pressed her head hard against the road and arched her back. As she did she rolled her eyes up into her skull and caught a split-second glimpse of the retreating vehicle as it rounded the far corner and disappeared from sight.

She relaxed her body and began to chant the words *dirty white pickup, two people*. Wavering on the edge of consciousness, she grasped her pulped hand with the good and dragged it to her bosom. After a series of rapid breaths failed to chase the encroaching shroud of blackness from her peripheral vision, she closed her good fingers around the bad and squeezed with all her might.

An explosion of stars chased away the dark. Endorphins flooding her brain provided the clarity necessary to do what she had been meaning to before this series of unfortunate events had rendered her crippled and broken in the middle of the road in fuck-it-all Utah.

After fishing the two-way radio from a pocket and finding it unscathed from the fall and subsequent hit and run, she brought it to her mouth and thumbed the Talk button. Hand shaking like a drunk in dire need of a maintenance nip, she spoke into the radio. But instead of spewing the boilerplate identity and wait for a response, she repeated her mantra aloud, then resorted to begging for someone to respond. Even taking her dire circumstances into account, she hated how it all sounded. However, with winter nearly here and nightfall coming increasingly sooner, the specter of having to spend the night alone in the wild scared her more than any beating the display of weakness might bring.

Spent from the exertion of extracting the radio and then placing the thirty-second call, her lips parted into a half-smile and her eyes flickered. Then, as if an invisible hand was working the drawstrings of consciousness, darkness slowly encircled her field of vision until all that remained was a single pinpoint of light lingering behind high, watery clouds.

"That was damn close," said Lev as he instinctively leaned forward and rolled the volume down, silencing the heavy metal track in the process.

While he was killing the tunes, Jamie was whipping around in her seat. She got her shoulders squared with the tailgate and craned just in time to catch a fleeting glimpse of the dead thing. And in that split-second snapshot in time, she saw that it was rising up, its body arching off the blacktop at an incredibly awkward angle. "He was playing possum," she said as she turned back to face forward.

Skeletal trees and undergrowth beaten down by recent weather were whipping by on both sides. Far off, flanked by fast-moving clouds, the finger of rock rising over the quarry was just coming into view.

"I've heard Cade speak of seeing the Zs do some strange shit," said Lev as he steered the Raptor out of a sweeping left-hand turn. "Working doorknobs. Pretending to drive. One even stalked him at the helicopter crash site in South Dakota. First time I can remember seeing it firsthand, though."

"So I wasn't seeing things?"

Lev shook his head. "Caught it flopping like a fish in my side mirror. That little bump we felt back there makes me think I ran over part of him."

"Maybe you ought to slow down a bit. And try staying in your own lane. Do that and we won't be changing a flat and exposing ourselves to whatever might be wandering the road."

Lev said nothing. Instead, he let his foot do the talking and eased up on the gas, shaving at best two miles per hour off their forward speed. Shooting Jamie a smartass smirk, he reached for the volume control.

"Nuh uh," said Jamie. "I'm done with Metallica. Whose is that, anyway?"

"Not Wilson's," he said with a grin. "I have a feeling he's a Maroon Five or Dave Matthew's Band kind of guy. Sensitive music for sensitive folks."

With a tilt of her head, Jamie said, "Who, then?"

"Who has two arms full of dragon and skull tattoos?"

Jamie rolled her eyes and hit a button on the head unit to select the next disc. While it was going through some out of sight mechanical chore, she fixed Lev with a serious stare. "So Cade shares all that stuff with you?"

Lev nodded.

"He doesn't say a word around me. Well, I take that back," she conceded. "He does offer up a gun or knife tip now and then. Unsolicited, of course."

"*Of course*," Lev said, mimicking her. He playfully squeezed her leg. Which drew a pretend punch to the arm from her.

"Eyes on the road, Gropey Groperton. We're coming up on the quarry roads. There's usually some dead things hanging around just after the curves."

Hands locked on the ten and two, Lev bled a little more speed. They were traveling east at just five over the posted limit when the Motorola on the seat between them came to life with a hiss of white noise followed at once by a disembodied voice.

"Cade here," the voice said. "We're waiting."

Lev looked to Jamie. Said, "Ten mikes out."

She relayed the message. Thought about mentioning the seemingly self-aware rotter, but released the Talk key instead.

A click of acknowledgement emanated from the radio's speaker and that was it.

The Raptor's powerplant roared and there was a whoosh of exhaust as Lev matted the pedal. A tick later the bullet-riddled sign announcing the lower quarry flashed by. Because Lev had them going nearly double the speed limit in a short amount of time, they both failed to see the overgrown road servicing the upper quarry. Approaching the next curve, Jamie reached for the grab bar and said, "We're going to die before we meet up with them."

"We're not going to make it in time to help set up if I don't push it."

Jamie said nothing as the truck listed hard to the right and the nose dipped on her side, Lev steering aggressively through the curve. On the next long straightaway, he opened it up and acquainted the speedometer needle with the north side of seventy miles per hour.

Chapter 37

Cade released the Talk key and pocketed the Motorola. While he had wrestled with the decision to tell Lev and Jamie that he had just heard over the watcher's radio that the woman calling herself Bridgett had just spotted them and called it in, he ultimately decided nothing would be gained by sending them on a fool's errand searching for her. It'd surely be the metaphorical needle in a haystack type of folly. Burning gas and time for what? To capture and then interrogate a woman who likely knew little more than the one he took the radio off of.

That time would be better spent setting the stage for his next act. Only this wasn't a play. Big life and death stuff was about to happen in the general vicinity of Main and Center, and he wanted to get started on the preparations.

After killing the engine, he left the ignition locked in Accessory mode. Then he issued instructions to Taryn and Wilson and watched them pile out and scamper west across Main Street toward the auto body place. Pleased to see they were moving quickly, their rifles held at low-ready, he sat back against his seat and drew a deep breath.

Sitting in the truck parked a dozen feet north of Back In The Saddle Rehab, Cade rehashed his plan with Duncan. After a few moments of spirited back-and-forth conversation, tweaks were made and Duncan volunteered to do the "heavy lifting" and shoved open his door.

Pebbled glass and melting hail crunched under Duncan's boots as he stepped to the road. He let his eyes roam the wrecked Cadillac straddling the sidewalk a yard from his open door. The black land yacht was a four-door model of indeterminable age. He flicked his gaze to the road and saw that both driver side tires were blown out. Figured it probably happened when it hopped the curb and made acquaintance with the nearby tree it was wedged up against. *Good luck moving this tank*, sprang to mind as the sun broke from the low clouds and made the window glass on the ground sparkle like a thousand diamonds. Peering inside the car, he saw the deflated airbag hanging limply over the horn ring. A long dead corpse sat behind the wheel, rotting away. Its hands were in its lap and, mouth wide as if belting a primal scream in death, its head was hinged at an impossible angle over the seatback. Blood, pooled and dried to dark crimson long ago, sullied the rain-sodden leather seats and once-beige carpet.

"What do you think?" Cade called through the open door.

Duncan looked up. "Didn't end well for this one."

"The *car*," exclaimed Cade. "Think it'll budge?"

Remember, glass half full, Duncan told himself. "I will make it happen," is what he said as he looped around front of the idling Ford. Wasting no time, he unclipped the tow hook and, with Cade working the winch controls from inside, spooled out twenty feet of cable. He set the shotgun on the car's wide trunk then went to his knees—a monumental feat for a man closer to sixty than fifty and with one arm working at half strength. He gripped the bumper and let himself down easy until he was laid out flat on his back parallel to the long length of chromed Detroit steel.

Out of sight somewhere Taryn and Wilson were encountering dead things. There were shouts of warning first. Then calm, cool conversation reached Duncan's ears. The new *glass half full* mode of thinking had him imagining the pair drawing blades and then coordinating and carrying out a successful cull.

Hearing the sounds of battle subsiding, Duncan shimmied further underneath the car. Working by feel and suffering a couple of scraped knuckles, he finally got the hook and cable threaded around the axle and cinched tight. As a heavy silence descended on the rubble-strewn stretch of Main Street, he rolled out from under the car and reversed the complicated process he'd used to go prone.

Snatching the Saiga off the trunk, he turned and gave Cade a nod. Then, moving gingerly, he mounted the curb and took up station behind a listing telephone pole where he figured there was no chance of the car kneecapping him if it shifted unexpectedly once tension was applied to the cable.

Cade flashed a thumbs-up and reversed the Ford slowly until the cable was stretched tight.

Duncan looked north up Main Street. *All clear.* He gazed across the street. Saw that the Kids were nowhere to be seen. There were no screams which led him to presume they were searching the auto body place for keys. Cade gunning the F-650's V-10 dragged his attention back to the task at hand. "Do it," he mouthed and backpedaled a couple of more feet until his back was pressed against the two-story building rising up behind him.

Metal groaned as the Ford and Cadillac moved in unison— the former under power, the latter rather reluctantly.

The Caddie's left side mirror sheared off and went spinning away through the broken glass. A half-beat later the car was free and turning on axis and coming off the curb. Duncan recoiled as the passenger side front fender scythed the air barely a foot in front of his legs. As the weathered radials scribed a black arc across the sidewalk to his fore and bounced off the curb, he flashed Cade a thumbs-up.

Inside the Ford, Cade grimaced as the car narrowly missed cutting his friend off at the knees. Seeing the car come to rest in the road parallel to the curb, he jockeyed the F-650 around so that the cable was slack and the oversized rig was positioned to finish the job. Dropping the transmission into Park, he returned the thumbs-up and then pointed to the car's crumpled front end.

Taking the cue, Duncan stepped off the curb, grumbling and trying hard to not let on how his aches and pains were truly affecting him. He went through the motions of unhooking the tow cable and when he finally hinged up, holding the hook, Cade was standing there with his gloved hand extended.

"You're moving like someone beat you," observed Cade.

"That obvious?"

Cade nodded and took the cable. "I got this," he insisted. "Heater's blasting inside. Get in and do the driving."

Head hanging subtly, Duncan made his way to the truck and clambered aboard. While Cade was hooking the cable to the Caddie's front axle, Duncan was eyeballing the auto body shop. Nothing moved in the lot. Nothing moved beside the structure to the north. Studying the cinderblock wall facing the sidewalk, he saw that nothing moved behind the opaque windows there, either.

The Kids were nowhere to be seen and the radio remained silent.

Remember, old man, glass half full.

Reluctantly, Duncan took his eyes off the building long enough to check the mirrors. In the rearview, he saw a dozen man-sized forms. Judging by their stilted, head-lolling gait they were definitely of the undead variety. And though the mirrors made determining true distance difficult, he was confident they hadn't yet made the 39/16 junction. Which was a good thing because neither had Lev and Jamie who were set to arrive any moment now.

A bang from the hood area caused Duncan to jump. He looked over the steering wheel and saw Cade, one hand flat on the hood, the other making the universal gesture (finger upthrust and cutting a circle in the air) that every person who had spent any time soldiering instantaneously took to mean: *Let's get this show on the road.* Or, the saltier version which Duncan had had screamed at him more than once during boot camp decades ago: *Unfuck yourself, Private Winters, and find another gear.*

Which he did. Reverse gear in fact. And as agreed upon ahead of time, he backed the Ford south down Main until the cable was stretched tight against the Caddie's driver side panels.

Seeing that Cade had learned from the recent near miss and was standing a few yards beyond the car's front end, he tromped the gas and steered hard left.

Initially the engine protested and the rear tires spun on the damp pavement. Once the off-road rubber found purchase, the front of the Caddie jerked left and the car swung around, blocking both lanes, its flattened tires again leaving black marks on the road.

Seeing the cable go slack, Duncan eased off the gas and braked, stopping fully with the Ford's back tires against the curb and its rear bumper crushing into the hedges bordering the auto body shop's featureless facade.

Cade dragged a finger across his neck—*kill the engine*—then went about the task of unhooking the cable.

After shutting the truck down, Duncan elbowed the door and stepped to the road. Peering down Main, he saw that the dead were now past the junction and loping their way. Regarding Cade, he said, "We've got company."

Finished freeing the hook from the Cadillac, Cade looked at his Suunto. "That's OK. We've still got a few minutes until they're an issue. Besides, Lev and Jamie should be here any minute. They'll see them and do what needs to be done."

After pulling his sleeve up and seeing only bare wrist, Duncan said, "Left my watch at the compound. How long until the rendezvous?"

"Thirty-two minutes."

Climbing back into the truck, Duncan said, "We better get a move on, then." He paused before starting the motor. "You still plan on adding the little rice burner to the mix?"

Cade nodded and started spooling the cable around his elbow and wrist. Then, as Duncan fired up the big truck, Cade unceremoniously tossed the wound-up cable and tow hook onto the Ford's expansive hood.

Chapter 38

Across Main Street from Back In The Saddle, behind the body shop, Taryn and Wilson were hiding the twice-dead corpses behind a stack of balding radials that would never make it to the tire recycler or end up on a rope tied to an oak in somebody's front yard. Finished with the grim task, Taryn wiped her hands on her fatigues and set her sights on the dirty white pickup. She tried the handle and found it locked. Without pause, she put the butt of her carbine through the passenger-side wing window.

A few feet away Wilson was clambering up onto the side of the black wrecker. He was scaling the boom out back when Taryn called over to inform him that finding the keys to the truck wouldn't be necessary to move it.

"Best news all day," said Wilson as he stepped from the truck's rear bumper and planted his feet on the oil-stained diamond plate decking. *Didn't want to go into that dark-ass building, anyway,* is what he was thinking as he negotiated a tangle of chains and cables to get to the towing boom. Fighting gravity and his own questionable sense of balance, he inched up the boom on all fours, hand-over-hand, monkey-like, until he was within arms-reach of the cinderblock wall. Knees knocking, he rose and teetered there like a high wire act.

"You got this," said Taryn.

Grimacing, Wilson pitched forward and arrested his fall by slapping both palms against the wall. Then, by stretching to full extension, he managed to get four fingers of one hand hooked over the top edge of the roof's narrow parapet.

Stomach muscles burning, he looked down at Taryn. "Gonna catch me if I fall?"

She nodded.

"I'm not so sure about this *Spider Man* wall-crawling shit," he conceded, going for the parapet with his other hand. Now gripping the parapet tenuously with both hands, he found himself in a position he imagined would look like a poorly executed pushup from the ground.

Inches from his face was a window inset with a single pane of wire-reinforced safety glass. In the split-second glance, he saw what looked to be the office and customer receiving area of the shop. *Nothing to see here.* Only your typical office accoutrements: threadbare furniture, a pair of desktop computers, dented metal filing cabinets, and a lone desk with an open phonebook-size catalog, its parchment-thin pages showing line drawings of parts necessary to save foreign and domestic iron from the car crusher.

Sensing hesitation, Taryn said, "Just do it, Wilson."

He shot back, "This isn't a Nike commercial," and launched vertically off the boom. *Success!* He got enough elevation to hook his left arm over the edge. M4 banging against his tailbone, he dug deep and found the strength to pull his weight up to where he was able to get the other arm hooked over the parapet. The rest was easy. Feet scrabbling against the wall, he pushed up with his arms, twisted his torso, then crashed to the roof, ending up on his back and staring at the clouds scudding across the gray winter sky.

He lay there on the cool, wet roof and listened to Taryn softly calling his name from below.

After a long three-count, which he used to catch his breath, he sat up and leaned over the ledge. First thing that registered when he swung his gaze groundward was the worried look parked on Taryn's face.

"I'm good," he insisted, then forced a smile.

Speaking softly, she asked, "What do you see?"

He went to his knees and looked south. "We've got group of rotters near the junction." He craned north and saw only Main Street spooling away. "North is clear," he called down. Lastly, he rose and looked the length of the single-level section of the building he was on. Partially hidden by the distant parapet, on the street fronting the body shop, was the big black Ford. He couldn't hear the usual engine rumble and exhaust note. Only the whoosh from a surprise gust of wind bringing with it the stench of death reached his ears. On the road down below Cade and Duncan were talking. They'd already moved the Cadillac to where it blocked most of the two-lane. Cade nodded then turned and walked past the Cadillac. Tow cable in hand, he knelt by a compact pushed up against the near curb and disappeared from sight.

Wilson turned back and filled Taryn in on what Cade and Duncan were up to. Then he blew her a kiss. "I'll be alright up here," he said confidently. Nodding toward Main Street, he added, "Hustle back to the others. They're going to need your help."

Still peering up, Taryn dropped her hands to her sides and mouthed, "I love you, Wilson."

Before Wilson could reply to that, she *was* hustling through the cars in the shop's back lot. "Be careful," he whispered after her.

Wilson watched Taryn until she was out of sight. Then he turned his attention to finding a place to set up his overwatch position.

The wall to the garage on his right rose up another twenty feet. It would afford the best view, but was smooth and too tall for him to scale without a ladder. Only heating and ventilation equipment and a row of glass skylights shared space with him on the roof.

With no way to attain a higher vantage point, he opted for a spot beside the south-side parapet with a decent view of the intersection of Main and Center and propped his rifle against the garage wall to his right. Pressing his back to the cool cement block wall, he slid down to his butt and inadvertently sat in an inch-deep pool of standing water.

"Damn you, Murphy," he cursed softly. "Damn you."

From the driver's seat in the Ford, Duncan watched Cade unhook the cable from the four-door Hyundai. This time he was ready for the bang when Cade again tossed the coiled wire and hook onto the hood. Following the clatter of metal on metal, Duncan heard a female voice off of his left shoulder call out to Cade and tracked the younger man with his gaze as he strode to the sidewalk where he held a brief conversation with Taryn.

Mission accomplished, thought Duncan upon seeing the young woman's calm demeanor. Knowing that her presence on Main meant that Wilson was in position and not being eaten by the dead, he flicked his gaze to the body shop roof and was pleased that he couldn't see hide nor hair of the youngster he knew was somewhere up there.

After Cade and Taryn held a brief conversation, Duncan watched the pair part ways. She disappeared through the tangle of cars in the body shop's north-side lot while he looped around back of the F-650 and climbed inside.

Once Cade's door sucked shut, Duncan asked, "Success?"

Cade nodded.

"What now? Do we deal with the rotters ... or finish the job?"

"Let the Zs come," answered Cade. "Less distance we have to drag them the better. Plus, that'll cut down on the blood trails." He hooked a thumb over his shoulder. "Drive around back of the shop."

***

Thirty seconds after having observed the conversation on the sidewalk, Duncan had the F-650 nosed in next to the white Silverado pickup in the shop's south lot. Behind the Chevy's grimy driver side glass, he saw Taryn directing an expectant look his way.

In less than a minute, Cade had the cable secured to one of the Chevy's frame-mounted tow hooks.

Once Cade was out from under the truck, Taryn was to throw the transmission into Neutral and disengage the parking brake.

240

Seeing Taryn flash a thumb his way, Duncan reversed the Ford out of the lot the way he'd driven in, taking the Chevy along for the ride just ahead of a jogging Cade who broke right and took a shortcut to Main Street through the shop's south lot.

Peering over his sore shoulder, Duncan drove in reverse gear around the south end of the block to Center where he wheeled the rig east. At the intersection with Main, he slowed but kept moving east until Back In The Saddle Rehab's south-facing wall loomed over both pickups.

Inside the Silverado, Taryn began to brake before its front end had cleared Main's northbound lane. A beat later she stopped the rig completely, leaving a foot of the nose of the truck blocking the sidewalk and corner curb cut.

After hastily setting the brake, Taryn leaped to the sidewalk and sprinted to the Ford, where she slipped behind the wheel and settled into the still warm driver's seat.

"See you in a bit," Duncan said, closing her inside.

Cade climbed up on the running board. He could feel the thrumming of the engine through his boot soles as he waited for the window to pulse down. Once it seated into the channel, he said, "Keep your radio on."

She nodded. Checked the safety, then passed her M4 butt first to him through the open window.

"No matter what happens to any of us—" he began.

"Stick to the plan," she finished.

He nodded and jumped to the road. Then, drawing the Gerber, he did two things. First, he craned left and told Taryn to get going before the Zs could clog the nearby intersection. Then he passed the M4 and a pair of thirty-round magazines to Duncan. "Building should still be clear. Sure you won't listen to reason?"

Duncan shook his head. "Whites of their eyes."

Cade shrugged. "Go on up, then. I'll meet you in two mikes."

Without a word, Duncan slung the rifle, hefted his Saiga, and strode off toward the rear of the rehab place.

Cade waited in the middle of Center Street as Taryn wheeled the Ford past the throng of living dead and continued to watch her retreat south down Main. Once he saw the rig turn off 16 and disappear from sight behind the wrecked school bus, he drew the Zs' attention back to him with a few choice catcalls. Then, with all eyes on him, he clapped his hands and chanted "Come and get it" until the whole rotten lot of them were locked on and coming at him like the meat-seeking-missiles they were.

With the entire baker's dozen shambling across the intersection, Cade went light on the balls of his feet and extended the Gerber level with the street.

"For Brook," he said through clenched teeth and lunged for the leader of the pack—a stick-thin and very road-weary twenty-something male. Clearly it had been dead for a long time. Maggots spilled from a gaping neck wound as the hissing beast met the knife thrust head on with a nonchalant vigor only the hungry dead could show against an armed man.

The honed steel clinked off orbital bone and the twice-dead corpse crashed over sideways, a hundred and fifty pounds of rotting flesh propelled fast to the road by its own hunger-driven momentum.

Cade slowed the surge with a boot to the chest of rotter number two. While the portly female was pin-balling backwards into the Z behind her, Cade killed her with a roundhouse knife strike to the temple. As number two smacked pavement he backed away in a crouch, muscles coiled and mind going a mile a minute picking out targets and assigning them a number in his order of attack.

Moving left, he crossed the midpoint of Center Street, dragging the lurching crowd with him clockwise. Stopping in the eastbound lane, he grabbed the next Z by the throat and introduced one of its milky eyes to the Gerber's honed point.

Four down, nine to go.

"For Desantos," he said, palming an elderly Z's wispy-hair-covered head and propelling it to the road with force sufficient to open its skull like an egg.

Resisting the urge to stomp its leaking brains to mush, he pivoted left again, crabbed in that direction, and attacked the rear of the group from an oblique angle. To him, as time continued to slow, the temples on the four closest monsters working hard to turn and face him appeared as large as dinner plates. *One, two, three, four* he counted mentally as he struck out with the black steel, scrambling brains and dropping the quartet one by one in quick succession.

Upstairs in Back In The Saddle Duncan was just making the landing. By the time he had cleared the upstairs rooms, approached a south-facing window, and was looking down on the road below, Cade was surrounded by truly dead rotters and being pursued by only two of the original group. His jaw dropped when he saw Cade turn his back on the flesh-eaters and begin to walk slowly toward the Chevy. He banged on the glass and let out some choice expletives, all directed at Cade and earned from the stupidity on display as the camo-clad man placed his bloody dagger on the rig's hood and, inexplicably, turned back to face the rotters with his fists clenched and held up defensively before his rage-twisted face.

"They're not gonna punch you, Cade. One bite is all it takes," said Duncan, the words echoing off the pitched ceiling and heard only by the twice-dead corpses of a hanged woman and what appeared to be her asphyxiated child.

A split-second glance south told Duncan that Taryn had already parked the Ford out of sight behind the school bus. And catching his eye at the tail end of the brief glance was a flash of white as the Raptor came out of the last curve on 39 vectoring toward its intersection with 16. As the rig began to slow, he cast his eyes on the street below the window and saw that Cade had both remaining rotters by the neck and, like some kind of pissed-off bouncer who'd tired of taking drunken lip, was bashing their skulls together repeatedly. Then, displaying strength Duncan didn't know Cade possessed, the young man lifted the corpses off their feet and threw them a yard or two in the direction of the far curb. Next, as the corpses struggled to right themselves, Cade grabbed them both by the meager amounts of hair left on their pallid skulls and dragged them the rest of the way to the curb where, one at a time, he positioned their pistoning maws on the sharp cement edge and stomped down hard. The result: splintered teeth, visible against the black asphalt, shot out in all directions. Like dice on a craps table the yellowed incisors and molars bounced off the curb wall and came to rest in a random pattern around the Zs' still writhing forms. The intense downward pressure transferred through the Danner's soles broke the creatures' jaws before seeing them ripped free—tendon and muscle still attached—by the follow-on outward snap of the man's hip.

Thankfully the morbid sounds from the coup de grâce skull stomping was mostly insulated from his ears by the window glass. The sight, unfortunately, was not. Both creatures' will to rise ceased and their bodies went slack as their collapsed skulls vomited gray chunks of meninges and what little viscous fluids remained in the crushed brain pans.

The word *abyss* again sprang to mind as Duncan watched his friend deliver a solid kick to the head of one of the corpses. A spritz of detritus rose and spattered to the roadway. *Thankfully*, thought Duncan, *I wasn't exposed to that sound, either.*

Both hands on the glass, Duncan watched his friend stalk to the Chevy and collect his blade. After a brief pause to surveil all points of the compass from the corner of Main and Center, the man disappeared around front of Back In The Saddle.

Chapter 39

Upstairs in the rear of the two-story house turned commercial property, Duncan heard the crack of wood from the front door being kicked in. The noise of the brass knob punching a hole in drywall downstairs was not lost on him either.

"Cade, close the door behind you," he called out ahead of a chuckle. Hoping the man had left a majority of his rage outside, he made his way to the top of the stairs to give the younger man a proper reception.

The sound of a door being forced shut and some general scuffing noises preceded the clomping of boots on decades-old wooden treads.

"Why'd you destroy the front door?" asked Duncan the second Cade reached the middle landing.

Pausing mid-run, Cade fixed his gaze on Duncan. "It was locked and I didn't want to walk around back is the smart ass answer I'd expect from you. Truth is, if you insist on this being the place you're going to be when Iris's friends show up, you *will* need the extra few seconds you're going to save by not having to work the lock and throw a deadbolt. Especially hard to do in a hurry with one of your old buzzard wings giving you problems. I left a chair under the knob. You need to egress that way, just kick it aside and you're in business." He raised a brow and regarded the Saiga and suppressed M4 resting against the wall.

Following Cade's gaze, Duncan said sharply, "I can shoot just fine with my 'old buzzard wing giving me problems'. Doesn't matter. If Bridgett's—"

"Iris," interrupted Cade.

"Whatever," said Duncan. "If her friends get past us, all is pretty much lost anyway."

"You're willing to *martyr* yourself?" said Cade, a hint of incredulity in his tone. "Don't you think it's a better proposition to disengage if you have to? Maybe live to fight another day? To see Glenda again?"

Duncan removed his Stetson. Running a hand through his thinning hair, he said, "Look what my strategic withdrawal got us at Bear Lake."

"That was *empathy's* doing."

Shaking his head, Duncan countered vehemently, "No! I truly wanted that bitch to get eaten. Swallow some of her own medicine, so to speak."

"And the people you let go? They can't *all* have been prisoners destined to grace the dinner table."

"No telling how many bodies and guns they had," said Duncan sharply. "And no telling where they were going, either. Could have had back-up real close. And *I* didn't exactly have the army I was expecting." *Hell, he thought*, bitterly. *I didn't even have you.*

"Exactly," said Cade. He walked to the south-facing window. "You just proved my point. If the Bear Lake force proves to be more than the six of us can handle, you're going to need to get out of here real quick. You also have to consider another what if—"

"And that is?" Duncan interrupted.

"What if a large herd of Zs breaks from Bear River and start coming this way? If that happens … by the time we see them coming, we're going to have only a couple of minutes to get you and get to 39. Even then we risk being seen by the Zs. And if they do see us and take chase, we can all kiss Eden goodbye."

"All but the latter are chances I'm willing to take if it gets me the results I want."

"And those are?"

"Same as you: kill them all."

"We can do it here. We can do it there." Cade shook his head, "Wherever we do engage them it *has* to be on our terms."

"I already climbed those stairs," retorted Duncan. "I'm staying until I ain't."

Cade said, "A last stand?"

"Won't come to that."

"Let's hope so."

Simultaneously, from deep inside cargo pockets, both of the men's two-way radios vibrated to life and began emitting muted electronic trills. A beat later Taryn was on the radio and announcing Lev and Jamie's arrival.

"You picking up, or me?"

Cade fished out his radio. Thumbed the Talk button and replied, "Have them snug their truck in next to yours. I'll be there in a couple of minutes."

Cade put the radio away and noticed Duncan staring at him.

"What?" he said, defensively.

"You're not going to try and stop me?"

Cade looked over at the corpses. They were locked in a post mortem embrace. No way they ended up that way on their own. Someone had to have posed them like that, he conceded to himself. Someone showing great empathy for the mom and daughter relationship they likely shared when they walked among the living. After a prolonged moment of silence, he regarded Duncan with eyes wet with emotion. "Trying to impose my will didn't work on Brook. Hell, it hardly has any effect on Raven these days. No way anything I'm going to say is going to steer you away from the iceberg you're steaming toward."

"That's some heavy shit, Delta."

Cade said nothing.

Duncan swiped at his eyes. "Help me move this dresser to the window."

Together they moved the chest-high item to the window nearest the southeast corner of the room. Duncan stood up, rubbing his back. He opened the curtains wide and peered below. He saw that Cade had laid the dead bodies across Center from the left rear corner of the Chevy all the way to the far curb. Five of them were positioned toes to head—or what remained of the latter. The rest were stacked clumsily atop the first row to create a knee-high flesh and bone speed bump of sorts.

"Why the corpse roadblock?"

"First thing any person does when they see a human body on the road is hit the brakes to slow down."

Duncan nodded. "Guess so." He gestured to the Chevy. "And the two you put in the truck?"

"Hoping to provide a momentary diversion. Maybe even get—"

"—the dirtbags to dismount," drawled Duncan, the words coming slow and deliberate. He removed his Stetson and set it atop the dresser where it would be seen easily by anyone looking up.

"Diversion," said Cade, nodding. "What's the towel and foam cube for?"

"You'll see. Help me move the desk from the room down the hall in here."

Cade followed Duncan through the doorway and padded down the hall after him. "Let me check something first," he said, fishing out the radio and continuing past the room on the right containing the low table and chairs. At the end of the long hall there was a west-facing window. He parted the curtains and spotted Wilson at once. Which wasn't a problem from this angle. The young man was set up behind a three by three by two cube fashioned from some kind of dull metal—an air conditioner unit, he presumed. Thumbing the radio to life, he said, "Good position, Wilson. Just stay still and out of sight until the cue."

Thirty yards to the west, the redhead slowly panned his head from due north to due east and, to show he copied the message, flashed a thumbs-up.

Satisfied, Cade made his way to the room where Duncan was waiting. Taking matters into his own hands, he turned the table on its side and dragged it to the south-facing room containing the corpses.

Duncan followed silently, a chair with chrome legs and wrapped in red vinyl in tow.

"This," said Duncan, putting the foam cube and towel atop the table, "is to be used as a rest for that rifle of yours. The shotgun, I'll only use as a last resort."

Cade finished pushing the table up against the window farthest from the door and adjusted it to be able to accept the chair facing the window. "Two guns are better than one," he said, placing the M4 on the table with the other items.

"Three," quipped Duncan, patting the Colt model 1911 hanging low in its drop leg holster.

Cade looked at his Suunto. "Gotta go," he said. "Less than twenty minutes."

Again Duncan looked at his bare wrist.

Steeling himself against what he was about to do, Cade crossed the room and knelt next to the mother and child. Gently, he lifted the dead woman's right arm away from the incredibly small corpse it was clutching. Thanking her under his breath, he worked the band on the watch she had worn through all phases of her journey to this final resting place. Where the skin on a woman's wrist was usually most supple, hers was cool and leather-like to the touch. He removed the digital watch and examined its rugged plastic case. It was large for a woman's watch, but small in his hand. It had also taken some abuse. It was scuffed on the bezel and crystal, but still displayed the accurate time and date.

"Take this," he said, tossing the watch across the mostly empty room. "It's only twenty seconds ahead of mine."

Like an outfielder saving a homerun at the wall, Duncan caught the watch above his head left-handed. "Just my size," he quipped, turning it over and inspecting the face. "Thanks, Santa. Now you better get."

Chapter 40

Roughly twenty miles west of Woodruff by crow Glenda was wheeling the Eden group's lone Humvee into the first leg of what was going to prove to be a very sloppy K-turn. She was dressed for the mission: BDUs from the eighties in the dark woodland pattern. Combat boots that fit her just right. On her head was a boonie hat in woodland she had found hanging from the bedpost in Duncan's quarters.

In the passenger seat next to her, Seth was holding on tight. One hand was clamped to the roof while the other steadied an AR-style rifle muzzle down between his legs. His attire was more REI Co-Op than U.S. Army. Jacket and pants were a lighter shade of brown than his dark leather Timberland boots. All were supposedly waterproof and lined with shiny material purported to possess a magical wind-stopping technology. Great as a sales pitch. Not so great in a vehicle with a drafty gun turret up top and no heater to speak of.

Glenda wore a constant grimace put there by the gnash and snap of bones breaking under the tall off-road tires as the former Utah National Guard rig crawled over a trio of splayed-out corpses.

The recent kills were leaking thin runners of blood onto the damp roadway. Left where they had fallen, it was obvious without voicing it in the jostling Humvee that these former Americans were dispatched earlier in the morning by Cade and Raven—likely the latter, though, because it was common knowledge among the older Eden group members that the recently widowed dad was hell bent on infusing his daughter with the skill sets necessary to survive the apocalypse should he suffer the same fate as their beloved Brook.

As Glenda straightened the wheel and prepared to reverse, the hollow pop of a human skull losing out to tons of steel and Kevlar sounded inside the cabin.

"I'll never get used to that sound," said Seth grimly, lips pressed into a white line.

"Nor should you," she said soberly. "Though they look like horrors from a movie, they *were* our neighbors and loved ones." Before the comment had finished crossing her lips, she was back in her home, in the upstairs bedroom with the deck overlooking a burned-out Huntsville and the expansive reservoir west of the small town glittering like fool's gold in her mind's eye. For a split second between thoughts she was elbows deep into her husband's rib cage and about to do something (even by horror flick standards) that had been wholly unthinkable before that last Saturday in July when her world was turned on its ear and she lost all communication with both of her sons. Now, a little more than three months removed from Omega's rapid sweep up the valley from Ogden, Salt Lake and points beyond, she was widowed and knew for certain her youngest, Oliver, had left this earth. Her other boy, Pete, and his family, as far as she knew, were gone forever too.

Seeing the faraway look in Glenda's eyes, Seth said, "I'll just picture a healthy-sized watermelon under the tires next time I hear that."

"Watermelon," said Glenda, the word coming out slow and syrupy, as if it were saliva-coated. "What I wouldn't—"

Sensing the woman was back among the living, Seth said, "Stop here." He was looking at the wall of fallen timbers to his right. The trees were bowing down in the middle. Nubs of broken branches jutted out at him. Some of the sharp spikes protruding from the trees comprising the first couple of layers wore a coating of glossy detritus from where mindless automatons in search of imagined prey beyond Daymon's makeshift barrier had impaled themselves. "I want to take a look. Just to make sure Bridgett's friends didn't pull some kind of forest-service-road-end-around and get stuck over there."

"Doubtful," said Glenda. She applied the brakes anyway. "Knock yourself out."

Seth stepped from the passenger seat, looped around back and then climbed up into the cramped, armored cupola with the .50 caliber Browning heavy machine gun. He reached his hand toward Glenda and was rewarded with the weighty feel of a pair of Bushnell binoculars. Without saying a word, he looped the strap over his head and pulled his lengthening beard aside so that he could bring the eyecups to his eyes. He remained silent and standing straight in the open top turret for nearly a full minute.

"Any cannibals waiting on the bridge and ready to storm over this, this ..." She went quiet for a tick, then continued, "environmentalist's worst nightmare?"

"Nope," he conceded dryly. "All we have over yonder are about thirty or so of our 'fellow former Americans.'"

Craning and looking up in order to make eye contact, Glenda asked, "What are they doing?"

"Dry humping one of our backup rigs," he said. "There's also a few of them snagged on the barrier. They're just marching in place. No threat whatsoever."

A stiff wind rolled over the barrier from the west, bringing with it the hair-raising calls of the dead and their sickly-sweet odor. The upthrust branches on the barrier rustled and the tall pines crowding the road began to sway.

"If Bridgett's people came from Huntsville and then turned around on that side," Glenda called over the diminishing gale, "the rotters wouldn't still be there. They would have followed the food."

"Good point," said Seth, letting the binoculars rest atop his beard.

"We better get to where Cade wants us," she said, goosing the engine and grimacing as more pops and the resulting wet noises filtered up from the roadway. "Coming down?"

"I'll stay here," he said. "What's a few more minutes going to hurt?"

Glenda shrugged and then backed the Humvee in the direction of the right-side guardrail near where she had begun the multi-point turn. She braked and cranked the steering wheel left, muscling it hand-over-hand until the tires were pointing mostly east. One last stab on the pedal got the wide front end past the mound of withered corpses and branches piled up against the left-side ditch and guardrail.

***

Five minutes after deeming the blocked western approach to the Eden compound clear of threats, Glenda was pulling the Humvee to the right shoulder of State Route 39, two miles past the hidden entrance, at a point in the road where she figured Seth would have an unobstructed view of anyone approaching from the east. She killed the motor and set the brake.

Only when the engine growl had died away and the softly blowing west wind had taken its place did Seth relax and thumb the Talk key on his Motorola radio. "Tran, this is Seth. We've got the approach covered. You need to keep the girls on their toes and your eyes on the feeds."

"Copy that," came Tran's reply. "All's clear right now. Max is running free outside. The girls are in the Grayson quarters."

Craning to see Seth, Glenda said, "You sure you are up to speed on that cannon?"

In reply to that, Seth stood tall and yanked the Ma Deuce's four-inch-long charging handle towards his gut. There was a metallic *schnik-schnik* sound as the first massive linked bullet entered the chamber and the bolt slammed home behind it.

"That must be a yes," said Glenda, brows meeting in the middle.

He handed down the binoculars. "You're my eyes," he said. "Are you ready to fire on them if they do come?"

She patted the black AR-style rifle the thirty-something had left propped on the seat opposite her. "Ready as an old lady can be," she answered ahead of a soft, sad chuckle.

Chapter 41

Cade had hustled down the stairs without a word. After leaving Back In The Saddle Rehab through the back door and locking it behind him, he hustled east to where Center was bisected by another cross street and settled his gaze on the inert Silverado. Satisfied the corpses he'd placed in the cab were clearly visible from nearly a block out, he walked back to the 39/16 junction, along the way pacing off a few different distances and committing them to memory.

Three hundred and fifty yards and five minutes later, Cade was rounding the front of the overturned school bus and being greeted by Jamie and Lev—the latter, while dropping the Raptor's tailgate—quickly bringing him up to speed on the goings on at the compound.

"Thanks for grabbing this," said Cade as he spun the long, hard-plastic case a hundred and eighty degrees so that it was oriented lengthwise with its half-dozen plastic catches facing him.

There was a series of clicks as he threw the push-and-pull latches.

There was another noise nearby as the door to the F-650 opened and Taryn jumped down to the spongy ground.

Ignoring the familiar sound, Cade lifted the lid and examined the contents of the Pelican case.

"One MSR rifle," intoned Lev. "I would have assembled it for you—"

"But you knew better," said Cade, with a conciliatory nod to the former Eleven Bravo. "I would have afforded you the same courtesy." He began removing the pieces from the precise cutouts in the charcoal-gray foam they were snugged into.

Taryn formed up next to Jamie, who was cradling a scoped long rifle of her own and looking on with rapt attention. "Ten minutes," she noted, the slight waver in her voice revealing her nervousness.

"Noted," said Jamie. "You better get your rifle and take cover."

Watching Cade thread a suppressor on the Remington, Taryn leaned in and whispered to Jamie, "Are you sure I should leave the keys in the ignition?"

"Short of leaving the trucks running, Cade wants both ready to roll," replied Jamie in a stage whisper.

Taryn looked a question at her.

"If, God forbid, one or both of us should fall"—Jamie began, turning from the action on the tailgate to look directly into the younger woman's eyes—"*someone* is going to have to do the driving. And if the keys happen to be in one of *our* pockets—." She let Taryn fill in the morbid blanks.

***

A minute after opening the Pelican case, Cade had the modular sniper rifle chambered in .338 Lapua fully assembled. On the top rail sat a Leupold high-power scope. Up front was a Titan suppressor, the stubby cylinder giving the no-nonsense bolt-action weapon a more menacing appearance. With a ten-round magazine seated into the well and the telescoping stock fully collapsed, he ducked his head through the attached sling and moved the rifle so that it rested diagonally across his back.

Next, Cade fetched his plate carrier and MOLLE gear from the Ford and filled the available front-facing pockets with fully loaded thirty-round magazines for his M4.

Going sans the tactical bump helmet, which he had inadvertently left in his quarters back at the compound, he snugged down his camo ball cap and spun the bill around so that it faced backwards, partially covering his neck. Lastly, he stuffed the pair of Steiner binoculars into his Multi-Cam jacket, nestling them safely inside an interior pocket.

Leaning against the front part of the tipped school bus's sloping roof, he pointed to the distant blocked intersection, reminding the others individually of their specific roles and his rules of engagement which, compared with what the lawyers and politicians had handcuffed the military with before Omega, amounted to little more than him urging them to wait until either he, Duncan, or Lev initiated contact. "If for some reason you start taking fire before one of us engages," he said, "return fire at once. We have to make them think the six of us are a much larger force."

"How do we achieve that?" asked Taryn.

"We do that through violence of action," said Lev.

"What Lev means," Cade said, looking first at her, then slowly panning the others, "is you *do not* show mercy once you start hitting them back." He paused and looked at his watch. "Eight minutes. Remember your assigned sectors." Regarding the trio—but mostly singling out Taryn—he asked, "Straightforward enough?"

After blinking twice and swallowing hard, Taryn nodded slowly.

Jamie slung her rifle, adjusted the war tomahawk hanging off her left hip, and then finished the gear check by verifying by feel that the Beretta was snugged safely in the holster on her hip. "Lead the way," she said, surreptitiously gripping Lev's bicep and going to her tiptoes.

"Good to go," said Lev, accepting a kiss on the cheek from Jamie and acknowledging with a subtle nod her whispered plea for him to "Be careful."

Cade lifted the radio to his lips and thumbed the Talk key. "Comm check."

A beat later, one at a time, Duncan and Wilson responded, both assuring anyone listening that they were '*Good to go.*'"

Pocketing the radio, Cade set off for the nearby stretch of State Route 39 with Jamie on his heels. MSR held in check with one gloved hand and M4 thumping his chest with each stride, he led her across the wide expanse of grass north of the wrecked bus, both lanes of 39 to the curved wall of cement Jersey barriers where he hooked a sudden left still on the run. Keeping to the foot-wide strip of dirt sandwiched between the frost-heaved shoulder and barriers to their right, they sprinted up the gentle slope. After roughly thirty feet, the Jersey barrier wall was replaced by a steel guardrail supported by creosote-stained wooden posts. The guardrail ended a couple of hundred yards west where the slight incline flattened out and the trees and scrub began to crowd the two-lane from both sides.

"Here," said Cade. He was still breathing evenly when he cut right and crashed through the underbrush.

A little winded, Jamie followed suit. Eyes locked on the exotic-looking rifle on Cade's back, she gripped the wooden buttstock on her slung long gun and brushed aside the grabbing branches with her free hand as she pushed in after him.

Cade kept muscling through the bushes until he made it to the copse of trees he'd spotted from the road. Once the going got easier he broke to his right again and ranged ahead until they were just inside the tree line. He stopped briefly, looked left and right, then led Jamie to a similar spot a dozen feet farther north.

The location he finally settled on for them to conduct their overwatch was nearly identical to the patch of bare dirt secreted within the woods overlooking the Eden compound's hidden gate. And like the hide some twenty-plus miles west, there was a slight downslope here before it reached the target area. However, unlike the Eden hide, this vantage point afforded much more than a lonely stretch of state route and dense wall of trees and assorted foliage to stare at. The view from here was stunning and stretched left to right for two-hundred-and-thirty degrees. The church steeple at the north edge of town was clearly visible. Hidden behind a picket of mature trees, the auto parts store and nearby church rectory was not.

Straight away the lower flanks of the Bear River Range were sandwiched between low cloud cover and rambling wide-open range. Home to groves of pine and scrub, Cade placed the foothills at roughly ten miles out.

Just below the hide was what appeared to be unused grazing land. The grass was competing with mounds of muddy dirt pushed up by an industrious colony of moles and still recovering from the beating doled out by the previous week's snowstorm.

Atop a rise abutting the dirt road that ran north/south behind the auto body shop's lot was a massive burn pile. Mixed in with the shriveled husks of radial tires and board ends that hadn't totally been consumed by fire were dozens of soot-blackened skeletons. On the periphery of the pile, as if someone had cared about them even in death, more bodies had been laid out in a neat line running away from the hide. For some reason, the bodies were arranged with their heads pointing west. A number of the skulls seemed to be staring uphill at him; the hollow shadowed sockets casting silent accusations his way.

Why us and not you?

Why Brook and not you?

Why Desantos and not you?

After the few seconds spent scrutinizing the morbid scene, Cade closed his eyes and threw a shiver.

Upon reopening his eyes, he came to a conclusion: The simple act of trying to dispose of the infected corpses of loved ones had backfired horribly. Hence the unfinished business. Cade had seen the effect a roaring fire and the associated smoke had on the Zs. It was akin to hollering *come and get it* at the top of your voice just as he had done at the intersection. Yep, he thought. These people did themselves in and the cinderblock building and cars and bushes surrounding it bore the brunt of the undead surge that had either consumed them or run them off. He prayed it had been the latter.

"You OK?"

Cade lowered the Steiners. Sounding tired, he said, "I'm just over all of this."

"Me too," answered Jamie.

Still feeling badly for the people who probably hadn't a clue as to the ramifications of their noble actions, Cade raised the binoculars and glassed the handful of buildings flanking Main Street.

Rising up more than thirty feet over Main and threatening to cast the two-car roadblock out front in shadow, Back In The Saddle Rehab was a wall of weathered white paint home to darkened windows. The south side of the building stretching west to east was much the same. *Closed for business.* And best of all: There was no sign of Duncan moving around behind the south-facing upper windows.

Cade panned the binoculars down a couple of degrees and locked his gaze on the auto body shop. From this viewing angle, the building resembled an L that had been knocked flat on its back. The foot of the L rose up over a rear lot full of piled-up tires and cars left for repairs that would never happen. The rectangle of dry gravel where the Chevy pickup had been parked stood out starkly against the dirt- and moss-streaked cinderblock wall rising above it. The trio of windows inset in the wall were mirrored and offered no clue as to what was going on inside. And though Cade couldn't see the younger man because of said wall, he could still imagine him sitting on the roof, legs crossed with the AR-style rifle laid out lengthwise across them.

Breaking the strained silence, Jamie said, "Looks convincing enough."

Cade lowered the Steiners again and looked a question her way.

"The rotters in the white pickup." She cracked a half smile. "Spitting images of me and Lev."

"It is what it is," replied Cade, resuming the recon by panning the Steiners south. Pausing his sweep at the school bus where the only part of the two trucks visible from his vantage was the roof of the Raptor and its extended tailgate, he said, "Lock and load."

There was a smooth rasp of metal on metal followed by a soft click. The rasp was repeated and the familiar sound of the bolt closing and throw clicking home reached his ears.

Cade pulled out the radio and pronounced to the others that he and Jamie were in place. Then he requested individual situation reports from them.

A barrage of squelch preceded a trio of replies.

"Copy that," said Lev. "I'm inside and all alone."

"I'm ready," stated Taryn. "Road's still clear to the north for as far as I can see." There was a long second of silence. Then, in a voice full of concern, she added, "But I do have rotters coming at me from the south."

"If it comes to it," Cade responded, "put them down with the suppressed pistol."

Taryn made no reply because Duncan jumped on the channel and asked Cade where he was in relation to Back In The Saddle.

"We're sitting up the hill to the west with a good angle of deflection," replied Cade. "I put us at about three hundred yards out."

"Save the sniper lingo for someone who cares," said Duncan gruffly. "Give me your *twenty* in layman's terms."

Cade was back on the channel. Voice calm and even he said, "Call the intersection at Main six o'clock. Taryn's position will be ten. And we have eyes on Wilson at your twelve. That would put me and Jamie at your eleven o'clock. Maybe even eleven-thirty. A freak ricochet is the only way anybody is getting dinged by friendly fire. Is that *layman* enough for you, Old Man?"

Voice betraying his eagerness to get the show on the road, Duncan drawled, "Bring it."

Satisfied they were as *set* as they would ever be, Cade put the radio aside. Then he went prone and snugged the MSR to his shoulder, planting its deployed bi-pod in the soft earth before him. Seeing Jamie mimic his actions, her barrel coming to rest on a scrap of decaying tree trunk she had scavenged from the woods nearby, he flashed her a thumbs-up and settled his crosshairs on the stretch of road where the state route became Main Street.

261

Chapter 42

Five Minutes Prior

Once Lev had finished reciting Cade's orders to Taryn one final time, he grabbed her gently by the shoulders, looked her in the eyes, and said, "No different than the house on the lake. You're only responsible for watching our six. Just observe and report. That's all. When we get back, you do what you do best … you *drive*."

"I shall do my best," she answered as she clambered into the F-650's crowded bed, hauling an M4 along with her.

"Good enough for me," said Lev as he shed his parka, revealing that he had on a black, long-sleeved thermal top with a tan loadbearing MOLLE rig riding over top of it. A half-dozen magazines for the inherited Les Bauer AR were snugged vertically in the vest's pouches and secured with flexible nylon cord.

"Cade wants you to have this," he said, threading a suppressor on a backup Glock and placing it on the snowmobile seat next to her.

Taryn was on her knees on the black seat and leaning against the bus's skyward-facing driver's side. She reached down and picked up the weapon. "What's this for?"

Lev pointed at a medium-sized group of shamblers just coming into view south of them where 16 took a slight bend. "For them," he said calmly. "And anything else you have to put down with discretion."

She blinked and nodded, the severity of her exposure finally dawning on her.

"I'm running late," he said, taking off at a full-on sprint.

As Taryn watched Lev go, the clouds decided to part to the south. For a brief moment, just as he changed direction toward the corner of Main and Center a hundred yards or so north of Taryn's position, a bright bar of light lanced diagonally across the nearby stretch of 39.

By the time Lev was at the spot where both state routes came together, the clouds had snuffed out the ray of sun lighting his way and a cool sheen of sweat was breaking out on his brow and upper lip.

Looking sidelong to his left, he spotted Cade and Jamie just as they were leaving the road and entering the woods. Shoving Jamie's wellbeing from the forefront of his mind, he broke right and crossed a wide expanse of mud dotted with clumps of grass and home to hundreds of oblong, water-filled footprints left there by the walking dead.

The open ground disappeared behind Lev and he scaled a low fence ringing the backyard of the tiny single-story home half a block east of where Main and Center crossed paths. Since there was no time to burn conducting the typical knock and five-count pause to listen for rotters moving around inside, he scaled the short stack of cement stairs and hit the back door behind a full head of steam.

The locks and doorjamb lost the battle with Lev's shoulder and all two hundred pounds of flesh and gear behind it. *This is going to hurt* was just crossing his mind as he careened headlong into a tiny kitchen amongst a shower of paint chips and splintered wood. As he bounced off a tiny white refrigerator and came to rest staring at a sink full of soiled dishes he did a quick check of his extremities. *Good to go.*

Nothing was out of place.

Praying that the front door was marked with a big white X and the home wasn't booby trapped with dead things, he closed the compromised door one-handed and leveled his rifle at the nearby doorway.

After what seemed like an eternity standing there with his heart hammering in his chest, Lev ticked off in his mind the knowledge gained from what was in reality only a two-second pause. First thing that struck him was that the smell of death wasn't riding the still air inside the tiny house. Nor was there present the sound of shuffling feet or telltale moans and rasps of a hungry rotter wanting to make a meal out of him.

Convinced by two of his five senses that he was likely alone in the house, he set off to confirm the hunch visually.

A quick sweep of the four remaining rooms told him the house was indeed empty. Everything had been stripped from the place save for the horizontal blinds, a dirty plunger, and a knee-high mound of summer clothes sized for a very small man.

Cade's voice emanated from the radio in Lev's pocket at the very moment he was parting the blinds covering the living room window. He scanned the yard and street and listened as Cade confirmed that he and Jamie were in position.

Letting his gaze wander Center Street left to right, Lev thought: *Good field of fire?*

Check.

Hearing Cade's request for a SITREP, he thumbed the Talk button. "Copy that," he said. "I'm inside and all alone."

When the channel was clear, Taryn came on and issued her report.

While Lev listened to Taryn state that their six was clear save for the dozen or so dead things homing in on her from the south, he was walking to each window, parting the blinds, and looking out over the surrounding yard.

Cade and Duncan dominated the channel next, going at each other as they discussed firing angles and where each group was located in relation to the intersection. When the conversation concluded with Duncan's two-word challenge directed at the Bear Lake cannibals, Lev was back in the front room, opening sliding windows and punching out the screens fronting them.

Recollecting the dozens of human corpses he had stumbled upon in the basement of one particular house at the Bear Lake compound——some of them in the process of being bled and others already rendered of their flesh—Lev narrowed his eyes and nodded agreeably.

Bring it, indeed.

Chapter 43

The far-off rumble of a hard-working engine hit Cade and Jamie's ears first. Then came the thrum of tires on blacktop—a high-pitched bees-in-a-hive-like buzz that spoke of something other than the off-the-lot pickups and moving vehicles he had been told were the chosen modes of transportation of the Bear Lake cannibals.

Cade swung his rifle left by a few degrees and peered through the scope. At once the stripe of blacktop and acres of fields and barbed wire fence crowding it on both flanks loomed large in the optics. As the sounds grew nearer he seemed to feel the vibration in his gut. Impossible due to the distance, so he chalked it up to the nervous anticipation he always felt before going into battle. Some called it combat tingle. Others simply a case of the nerves. He knew it as an old and constant friend. One that was always with him through armed conflict beginning to end. And taking to heart advice given to him long ago by his late friend and mentor Mike Desantos, the day he stopped experiencing the anticipatory pre-contact jitters would be the day he had to seriously consider hanging up his spurs.

"They're coming over the rise," said Jamie. She was sitting cross-legged with her face glued to the Steiners and her elbows braced on her knees.

"I see them. Three pickups, two passenger cars, and an SUV."

The first two pickups were not stock. They rolled on massive monster-truck-style wheels and sat high on long-travel suspensions. The rig in the lead had a snowplow-like blade mounted up front. It had been constructed from a pair of rust-streaked four-by-three sheets of plate metal. A thick vertical weld

267

line was evident where the pieces came together in the middle. The opposing plates were perpendicular to the road and swept back at a shallow angle. That they were both left flat instead of made to be concave like a plow's blade suggested to Cade that these were intended to split and repel herds of Zs at low to medium speed.

A female driver and passenger rode up front in both of the trucks. In each of the high off the road beds sat a pair of men brandishing AR-style rifles.

The silver Toyota pickup Cade had seen earlier by the compound was third in driving order. Though he wasn't a hundred percent certain, he figured the two women in the cab were the ones he and Raven had spied on at Daymon's roadblock.

The next two cars behind the trucks were late model Dodge Challengers, their neon-green paint strikingly similar to that of Daymon's prized Scout, Lu Lu.

A quick headcount told him the Challengers held four bodies each—men and women—with no rhyme or reason as to how seating order was doled out. Definitely no boy-girl-boy thing happening here. The lead Challenger carried three women and a man. The women were dressed in black and wore their hair short. The man was bearded and sported a safety-orange trucker's hat. The black barrel of a shotgun protruded through his open passenger window.

The second vehicle was a 50/50 affair. The driver and passenger were women, full in the face, their hair shorn close to the skull. The passengers were men. Their tattooed arms were thrown over the front seatbacks and both wore expressions full of bored indifference.

The gun-metal gray Dodge Durango bringing up the rear was driven by a woman whose hair was a shade of platinum one notch south of a sun going supernova. She was pale in the face and, though the dark clouds hadn't broken fully, wore a pair of sunglasses with lenses that could have been honed from obsidian. Next to her sat a man with a tree trunk for a neck and hands like shovel blades. He wasn't holding a weapon that Cade could see.

With mitts like that, he didn't need one. *Hulk Smash* came to mind as the man filling up the front seat clasped those hands and grinned, showing off a mouthful of stainless-steel-capped teeth. If there were passengers—which Cade didn't doubt for a second—he couldn't see them.

Cade thumbed the radio on and relayed the information he'd gleaned from glassing the six-vehicle convoy.

Without slowing, the lifted pickups entered Woodruff, passed by the cross street leading up to the church, and then forged ahead on Main Street for a couple of blocks. A half-dozen car lengths north of the roadblock the lead truck slowed and the bee-like noise from its tires subsided to a soft hiss.

"I think they're going to stop short," said Jamie, quickly trading the Steiners for her scoped rifle.

"As expected," whispered Cade. "Be lazy, dirtbags. Come on… *be lazy.*"

No sooner had Cade begun to chant the words of encouragement than the whole procession lurched to a halt a few yards shy the Cadillac.

The heavily tattooed men riding in the back of the trucks braced themselves, but still rocked back and forth as the rigs swayed before coming to a full stop. A beat later, surprising Cade a bit, the men were taking a knee and aiming their rifles out their respective sides. A quick look at the twenty-something in the rear of the lead truck revealed roving eyes and decent control of his weapon: muzzle pointed at the body shop lot and trigger finger braced alongside the trigger guard. Put together, these brief observations told Cade their training was above average.

Well-tuned V8 engines rumbled as discussion ensued and some kind of decision was being made by those in charge. Then, all at once, the vehicles shuddered as transmissions were thrown into reverse. The Durango started rolling backwards and continued to do so until it was at the intersection two blocks north of Center and Main.

The other vehicles followed suit until the truck with the plow had cleared the street one block north of Center and ground to a halt. In a reversal of the previous maneuver, the six-vehicle procession negotiated the left turn and one by one disappeared from view, moving eastbound on a street whose name Cade hadn't taken the time to learn.

Atop the body shop Wilson had fought the overwhelming urge to steal a peek over the edge by replaying images of the many human bodies he'd seen destroyed by rifles like the ones Cade was describing. For a long minute he had stayed out of sight with only the air conditioner unit between him and the gun-wielding cannibals.

Wilson used Cade's play by play and the sounds of the engines revving to formulate a mental image of what was happening so close to his position. Still, though curiosity was digging its claws ever deeper into him, he didn't budge from cover until the whole herky-jerky affair of the convoy backing up and rerouting east was completed. Only when Cade indicated over the radio that the rear vehicle was lost from sight did he crawl on his stomach to his preordained spot at the right front corner of the rooftop where his only cover would be the foot-tall parapet.

He replayed the instructions in his head: *If things go sideways*, Cade had said. *Keep low and move to better cover.* Sound tactical advice easier said than done once the bullets start flying. However, having already witnessed the man wield the sniper rifle of his with great precision against bad guys in vehicles moving at high rates of speed, Wilson took great comfort in knowing that these targets would likely be stationary when the highly trained shooter engaged them.

And if he *did* have to run for it, there was always Cade's reassuring promise that should anyone give chase he would see to it that, in his words, '*A lethal dose of lead poisoning will befall them.*'

Smiling inwardly at Cade's growled statement, Wilson made himself as small a target as possible and waited for the fireworks to start.

Chapter 44

Upstairs in the rehab place Duncan was standing beside the south-facing window with his back to the wall. He was holding the borrowed M4 at his side with his left hand and pulling the blinds away from the window with the other. Peering one-eyed into the sliver of daylight he witnessed the noisy convoy round the gravel lot behind the business and nose west onto Center. Through the gap, he saw all three pickups and the two cars Cade had described. The gray SUV, however, was nowhere to be seen. Which was troubling in and of itself. Because the coin he had flipped in his head as to whether the rehab place was going to receive another round of scrutiny from the Bear Lake cannibals came up *Heads*. His assumption was that the group were novices at this survival thing and whoever showed for the preplanned meeting would become preoccupied with the vehicles and dead bodies in their way and not give *Back In The Saddle* another round of scrutiny. It was beginning to look as if his choice of *Heads* prior to the flip, he thought glumly, was about to be proven a losing proposition.

"There you go gambling again, Old Man," he muttered. "At least it's only your waste of a life this time."

For reasons unknown, the iconic black and white photo of Black Panther leader Malcolm X brandishing a rifle and peering out a window in a similar last stand kind of pose popped into Duncan's head. Then, inexplicably, as he wondered if that shot had been staged for the photographer, he let the blinds go, reached into an inside pocket, and caressed the sealed half-pint of rotgut bourbon he'd lifted from the watcher.

Thankfully, the craving was gone as quickly as it had reared its ugly head. And as the cunning, baffling, and powerful urge to do some *forgettin'* slinked away to whatever dark corner of his mind it called home, he was gut-punched by the stark reality that there was nothing staged about the situation he had so willingly gotten himself into. Nope, this was as real as a heart attack and was about to end with the same result unless he adopted the attitude the Malcolm X photo was supposed to evoke. No sooner had the words *by any means necessary* entered his train of thought than a loud bang and the screech of splintering wood from downstairs shook him to the core.

It was nothing like the noise Cade had made breaching the front door earlier. That would be akin to comparing a mouse fart to a shotgun blast. This noise gave the latter a run for its money and definitely signaled the demise of the locked door leading to the parking lot out back. Which meant whoever was responsible for the dramatic entry had maybe twenty stairs to climb and less than five feet of hallway to traverse before they were right outside his door.

Aware that his worst-case scenario was coming to fruition, Duncan release the blind and slipped the radio from his pocket.

Backing away from the window, he thumbed the radio alive. Words coming rapid-fire, he spoke in a near whisper, filling the others in on his situation. Finished, he dialed the volume down and put the radio away.

Standing in the center of the room, eyes searching desperately for somewhere to hide, he heard the heavy footfalls from the person or persons negotiating the stairway echoing in the hall just outside the door.

"What now, genius?" he tasked himself as it dawned on him that the lone closet and dresser drawers were his only options for concealment. He didn't even approach the former. One glance told him it was way too shallow to cram his old carcass into with any chance of getting the door closed behind him. The latter, though it had been built at a time when hardwood and dovetail joinery trumped fiberboard and staples and would likely absorb a few rounds, was a no go because moving it to the window in the first place had taken the combined efforts of both he and Cade.

Behind the door it would have to be.

He pressed his back to the wall on the hinge side and shifted his slung M4 to his left side. In the next beat the footfalls were sounding right outside the door and his Colt was in his hand.

Fully aware that he would be kissing his hearing and the element of surprise goodbye by going with the semiauto hand cannon, he thumbed back the hammer, drew in a deep breath, and lowered his gaze to the doorknob.

Cade was training the MSR on the driver in the truck fitted with the makeshift plow when his Motorola transmitted Duncan's whispered warning. Knowing words alone couldn't save the man from his own decision at this point, Cade scooped up the radio and paused for a couple of seconds.

"That man is hardheaded," said Jamie, shooting a questioning look Cade's way.

"Tell me about," he replied, drawing the Motorola to his mouth. "Lord knows I tried to talk him into staying with Wilson." After a slow wag of his head, Cade dropped his chin to his chest. A half-beat later he was back on the open channel instructing Lev to open fire if anything he saw or heard led him to believe Duncan had been compromised.

After receiving an *affirmative* from Lev, Cade delivered modified instructions to Wilson. Finished with the updates, he put his eye back behind the scope, settled the crosshairs on the driver, and drew up most of the trigger pull.

Just as Cade was about to let fly the first round and spring the ambush prematurely, the second radio that once belonged to the watcher at the Thagons' home came to life with a squelch of white noise. Next, a voice, strained and hoarse but definitely possessing a feminine quality, emanated from the speaker.

Behind the wheel of the lead truck the driver went rigid. In the next beat, she was elbowing open her door and stepping down to the road.

Though Cade couldn't initially attribute the voice coming from the watcher's radio as that of their escaped mole, the proof came when the dismount put a radio of her own to her mouth and, lips moving in sync with the words broadcast by the radio near Cade's elbow, answered by saying, "Iris, is that you?"

While keeping one ear cocked for anything sounding remotely like a suppressed gunshot coming from the direction of the rehab place, Cade kept the dismount in his crosshairs and listened to the woman named Iris lament the fact that she was injured badly and nowhere near the rendezvous point.

Nothing happened for a few long seconds as the dismount walked and harangued Iris for more details—none of which included mileposts or signs or distinguishing landmarks. "Forest" and "hills" and "purged" is all Cade caught as he watched the dismount kneel and inspect his assembled pile of corpses.

Abruptly, the dismount ended the conversation without making any promises. And just as unexpectedly the female passenger of the lead truck was on the road and approaching the dismount waving a black brick-sized item sporting a foot-long whip-antenna.

Already two truck-lengths ahead of the convoy and craning to see inside the white pickup, the dismount turned and accepted what Cade took to be a long-range radio. Whip antenna still bobbing beside her head, the dismount did two things. First, her mouth moved as she seemed to issue instructions to her short-haired lookalike. Then she was speaking into the item, her words relayed clearly through the speaker of the long-range radio Cade had found in the attic.

The call lasted ten seconds.

During the first three Cade and Jamie learned that there were people up north expecting the dismount and her group to find the U-Haul trucks stolen from them or die trying.

I'll be more than happy to oblige, thought Cade as he watched the passenger hustle past the plow truck to deliver the head honcho's orders to the other cannibals.

The middle three seconds consisted of the disembodied voice telling the head honcho that the southernmost watcher wasn't answering.

274

Ain't that a shame, thought Cade, drawing back a bit from the scope and blinking to keep his eye moist. In doing so, in his side vision, he caught Jamie looking his way.

"Soon," he said. "Real soon."

The final three-second snippet of conversation consisted of the disembodied voice telling the dismount that to return empty-handed would require the entire party be sacrificed to the purged and mean a three-day stint in the stocks for her own failure.

"Bingo," said Cade. "Proof of life."

"Adrian," noted Jamie.

Cade said nothing to that.

With his stubborn friend dominating his thoughts, Cade said a quick prayer and drew in a breath. Crosshairs settled firmly between the dismount's shoulder blades, he exhaled slowly and caressed the trigger between beats of his heart.

Chapter 45

Duncan heard snatches of conversation outside the door. One voice was deep. A male. No doubt about it. The other was whispering, so he couldn't place a guess. When the conversation ceased, the loud footfalls against the wood floor in the hall began anew. As the heavy thuds moved off toward the front of the building, the doorknob jiggled back and forth and then turned clockwise—away from the striker plate.

As the door swung inward, the change in pressure caused the blinds to rattle against the sash. Which in turn drew Duncan's attention to the dresser where his Stetson was sitting like a big white beacon saying *Someone's been here recently, Baby Bear.*

Hoping his hat would be more distraction than warning to whoever was about to step over the threshold, he sucked in his gut and tried to become one with the wall.

The muzzle of a small caliber pistol broke the plane first. Next, Duncan saw the toe of a hiking boot swing past the door's edge. Not one of those expensive jobs Cade and his special ops buddies favored. This was a run of the mill item sold by every sporting good outfit before the fall. It was soiled with clumps of wet mud and speckled with black dots he took to be spattered blood.

Sure enough, the person entering the room was immediately fixated on the out of place Stetson. *Stumped,* would be a better description, thought Duncan as the door stopped moving and the person froze. Not wanting to squander the element of surprise, Duncan lashed out with his left hand and clamped his fingers around the weapon, effectively blocking the hammer open. Straightaway he felt a stab of pain as the web of skin between thumb and pointer finger stopped the hammer fall and the gun from discharging.

Enlivened by the adrenaline dumping into his system, he clamped down harder on the gun, twisted the barrel away from him, and yanked hard, drawing the weapon toward his breastbone. Fingers crushed between Duncan's palm and the pistol's grip, a woman a hundred pounds lighter and a full head shorter than he came along for the ride. He locked eyes with the platinum blonde whose mouth was forming a silent O. Without hesitation, Duncan brought the butt of the Colt down hard on the crown of the woman's head.

The blow was vicious and unexpected. It froze the scream forming on her lips and sent her eyes rolling back in their lids.

Game over.

As the mousy woman's legs turned to jelly, he threw his right arm around her shoulders and dragged her limp form away from the door swing. He let her down to the floor gently, plucked the Ruger revolver from her grasp, and, for good measure, gave her a swift kick to the temple.

With the door still yawning open, the noise of the footfalls halting and then quickly reversing course was not lost on Duncan. Nor was the distinct chatter of an AK-47 and instant return fire from a different caliber rifle coming from the street below.

"Joy. Joy. Joy …" the man in the hall called repeatedly between labored breaths. There was worry in the tone and he went on about how they were under attack until he reached the doorway and the gaping muzzle of Duncan's .45 shocked him into silence.

For half a heartbeat Duncan sized up the man filling the doorway. He was half a head north of six-foot and three hundred pounds, easy. Legs like tree trunks. Arms like anacondas. Fingers thick as a Chicago bratwurst. And somehow the big man had worked one of them through the trigger guard of the revolver he was dragging up from beside his leg.

Finger tensing on the trigger, Duncan stared into those deep-set eyes for the latter half of the beat, meeting hatred with hatred.

Was it hatred? Or were this breather's eyes already consuming the flesh off of his bones? Tiny here with his mouthful of chromed choppers was well fed. That was for damn sure. A *biggun* considering the *lean* times they were all surviving in.

Oh well, thought Duncan as he took a quick step to his right. *The bigger they are, the harder they fall.*

Mid-step he squeezed the trigger and saw surprise dawn on the man's fleshy face. The single slug left the semiauto pistol at eight hundred feet per second and smacked the man's forehead with enough force to open wide his heavily lidded eyes.

Undetectable to the human eye, the energy transferred as the bullet split bone and breached the man's oversized cranium started a mini tsunami that rippled through pockets of cellulite and started the jowls and folds of skin encircling his neck to vibrate wildly like room temperature Jell-O.

The man's collapse happened faster than Duncan could have imagined. Thankfully he had taken the extra half step that removed him from harm's way. Because the man's weight and forward lean had basically nullified the hurtling slug's kinetic punch, he landed face first and still twitching on the exact spot Duncan had hastily vacated.

Less than ten seconds had elapsed between Duncan's knockout blow to the woman and the gunshot that had incapacitated the monster of a man who was still flopping around on the floor, jaw clenched and eyelids aflutter.

The gunfire below was showing no sign of letting up. Using the din to cover a second report, Duncan put another bullet into the man's head, stilling him forever. Ears ringing from the pair of thunderous discharges, he bent over and grabbed the chromed revolver. A hard tug wasn't enough to gain possession, so he emptied it of all six shells and left it trapped in the dead man's hand.

Duncan unslung the M4 and crossed the room in a crouch. As he passed by the prostrate woman, her hand lashed out and her fingers caught hold of his pant leg.

An action that earned her another kick to the temple.

Point of the boot dead on.

No holding back.

Last thing he wanted was for her to come to a second time and get in the way of all the killing he still had to do.

By the time Duncan reached the dresser, pulled the shades back a few inches, and jabbed the M4's suppressor through the open window, large volumes of fire were being poured into the house across the street that Lev was holed up in. Heartened by the sight of orange licks of return fire coming from the house under siege, he braced his left elbow on the dresser top, trained the EOTech's red pip on the roof of the middle truck, and squeezed the trigger six times in quick succession. Shiny, nickel-sized patches of bare metal materialized in a diagonal line as he raked the roof right to left.

Leaning farther over the dresser top for a better firing angle, he targeted the third pickup. Behind the windshield, he saw two women wearing looks of shock and surprise.

Whites of their eyes.

The passenger leaned forward and glanced up a tick before the barrage of lead spewing from the M4 spidered the glass and punched her back into the seat, leaving her with a shattered breastbone and frothy blood spewing from the closely spaced entry wounds. In a panic, the driver pinned the accelerator. Transmission obviously stuck in *Park*, the engine merely revved and continued climbing into the higher rpm band until the next pair of 5.56 hardball fired from the M4 ended her poorly executed escape attempt.

Finished with his major tasks of stalling the convoy, Duncan swung the rifle left and engaged the men firing on the house from the bed of the rear truck. Before he could get off a shot, the two bearded men were cut down by someone out of sight.

So he started firing on the men clambering out of the middle truck. After riddling the two across the backs and seeing them go face down on the brass-littered road, both dead or well on the way, what sounded like a swarm of angry hornets suddenly inhabited the airspace around his head.

Respecting the buzzing noise for what it was—the sonic signature of bullets barely missing their mark—he ducked below the sill and dove for the center of the room.

Half-dollar-sized bullet holes appeared in the ceiling, showering him with a white talc-like dust for the second time in as many hours. Through the gun-smoke haze, he watched a second barrage shred his Stetson. The offending bullets continued on in their upward trajectory and punched gaping holes in the lathe and plaster above the door, adding more dust to that already clouding the air.

Instinctively going to all fours, eyes seeking out the door, Duncan found himself face-to-face with the platinum-haired woman. Up close she looked much older than he had at first thought. By two decades at least. Nearly his age instead of Cade's. Her eyes were closed and the features of her narrow face unmoving. Once flushed red from the struggle to retain her gun, her cheeks were now rapidly approaching the color of her hair. The observation caused him to stop briefly and press his fingers to her neck on the way out the door.

Dead.

"Better you than us," he spat.

With the gunfire directed his way dropping off sharply, he grabbed the Saiga then crawled on hands and knees and made it to the doorway unscathed.

After a quick listen divulged nothing riding over the gunfire-induced ring in his head save for continual discharges coming from somewhere outside, he holstered the .45 and turkey-peeked around the doorjamb.

Clear.

Using the door frame for support, he rose on shaky legs.

After spinning the M4 around to his back, he took one final look at his handiwork.

By whatever means necessary, indeed.

Saiga snugged tight and finger on the trigger, he crept toward the stairs, eager to face whatever lay beyond.

Chapter 46

The moment Cade felt the MSR punch back against his shoulder he was moving his hand from the stock to the bolt-handle and working it up and back. The rapid *snik-snik* of the fresh .338 Lapua round leaving the box magazine and being pushed into the breach by the finely honed bolt was lost on him as he tracked up and right, searching for his next target. Also unnoticed by the focused operator was the spent shell casing that spun away, dragging with it a gossamer tail of white smoke.

The dismount's sudden death did not go unnoticed. In fact, the simultaneous puff of crimson and violent spasm of her body doubling over on itself from the bullet's violent impact *did* make a blip on his give a shit radar. While he didn't enjoy killing, sending her and those like her to hell, it was strangely satisfying knowing she would never again be part-and-parcel to the kind of wanton violence on display at the Thagon spread.

But he was well-aware her death alone wasn't going to solve the problem. Nor would killing the others on the road below. It would be a good start but only delay the inevitable. The people the dismount was answering to were more worrisome to Cade than the two dozen cannibals currently being smacked in the face with the cold reality that they were now the hunted. And when he was done here, he was going on safari. For Adrian and her ilk possessed the GPS coordinates to the place he and his daughter called home, and he wasn't going to rest until he was certain his bird was no longer in any danger.

By the time his second carefully aimed .338 slug was blazing downrange, several of the cannibals were aware their leader had just been stricken by an unseen enemy. A tick later, after said bullet pitched another one of their own backward from the bed of the lead truck silent and limp as a rag doll, all hell broke loose.

Which is exactly what Jamie had been waiting for. And while Cade was shifting his aim and cycling a third round into the suppressed rifle, she was squeezing off her first carefully aimed shot from the Winchester Model 70. Without a suppressor of its own, the .308 caliber proved to be much louder than her 9mm Beretta. And before she saw results through the scope, the sharp report belching from the bolt-action rifle caused her to start.

As the gunshot rolled down from the hide, one of the cannibals brandishing a rifle with a wooden stock and curved magazine went to one knee beside the lead pickup and sprayed the house Lev was holed up in with a sustained burst of gunfire. Then, from out of nowhere another man armed with an AR-style carbine fired a dozen shots non-stop into the rehab place's upper story window, causing the blinds to jerk and briefly part in the middle.

Cade heard Jamie's gun bark and saw the lead vehicle's front end dip as its left front tire was destroyed by the screaming hunk of lead.

"Good shot," he said as a round of his own found its mark, killing the passenger as she stepped from behind the second truck's open door.

As Jamie cycled another round into the breach, she saw people piling onto the street from the two cars. Three of the four from the first car headed for the fence and trees in front of Lev's position. The people exiting the second vehicle split up. Two heavyset women were lost from sight in the vehicle clutter while a pair of men—one wiry, the other overweight—loped off for the far side of the house and then disappeared from sight.

Seeing the middle truck's windshield spider and buckle, Jamie dragged her crosshairs from the truck's left front tire and chased a female runner with them until she slid behind a tree and came up on one knee, rifle barrel swinging for the small house.

No thought went into what she did next. The woman was trying to kill her man and she wasn't having it. *Besides,* she thought, *the trucks are going nowhere.* Duncan had done his part, flushing the ones from the second truck and leaving the third with dead occupants and a shattered windshield. She squeezed the trigger with no regret and very little up-front remorse.

Since she blinked when the bullet struck the woman, she failed to see the kinetic energy spin her body clockwise and to the left. The massive damage to the woman's torso was known only to her as she went prostrate, screaming and clutching her right side just above the hip.

When Jamie's eyes snapped open and the image in the scope was relayed to her brain, the only thing she could discern was that Cade's previous two shots had cut down a pair of women who had sought shelter from Lev's return fire between the pickups and the rehab place's south-facing wall.

Inside the house, it was all Lev could to restrain himself from opening up on targets so near to him. He stood by and watched two of the cannibals eliminated by a killer they couldn't see.

He even remained disciplined as a passenger slipped over the side of the second truck, knelt beside the open door and fired a dozen rounds through the back window of the decoy truck.

He didn't push the Baer's muzzle through the open window and sight on the enemy until the moment he heard the boom from what he guessed to be Duncan's .45. Mentally, from that moment on he was back in the sandbox. He squared up to the opening, peered through the optics, and squeezed off a dozen rounds into the personnel climbing from the second and third pickups.

A split-second after giving up his position, he was on the move and the window he had been firing from was disintegrating into a hundred jagged shards. Bullets crackled the air, making the fabric curtains dance and jerk in his wake as he hastily relocated to the furthermost window on the home's northeast corner.

As he huddled by a wall and swapped mags he replayed the initial contact in his mind. Fairly certain he had two kills to his name—both the man who opened up first on the decoy and another fleeing the back of the truck near him—he hinged up and stole a peek at the road.

The two men were still down where he remembered them falling. Both prone forms had lost a fair amount of blood. The one nearest had a halo of crimson encircling the patch of road where his head had come to rest. Lev craned and looked past the bodies. Through the picket of trees growing up from the parking strip, he saw the grievous damage inflicted on the pickups' occupants. Some were slumped over in the cabs, dead. Others were sprawled on the road where they'd been gunned down trying to escape the ambush. Behind the third pickup the cannibals were frantically extricating themselves from the two cars.

Before Lev could lay any kind of accurate fire on them, they were sprinting across the road and taking cover behind the trunks of the pair of trees furthest from his position. As he continued to train his M4 on the trees in hopes they would leave cover and advance on the house so he could kill them, two things happened. First, in his right-side vision, he saw a pair of squirters cross the road east of the trees and disappear from view. Then, coinciding with a single gunshot, there was screaming from the direction of the trees out front.

Fairly confident that Jamie was the shooter responsible, he used the distraction and pulled away from the window. Being careful to slide his feet to keep from crunching the broken glass underfoot, he started off for the bedrooms in order to counter the pair flanking him.

On the move, Lev radioed a quick SITREP to the others.

Cade came back at once. "Do you have eyes on Duncan?"

Lev entered the tiny rear bedroom. There were two windows, one facing east and one south. He stepped over the pile of clothes and made his way to the south-facing window first. He parted the blinds to look out over the backyard and saw only brambles crowding the chain-link fence. As he padded to the east-facing window, he radioed back saying that he hadn't seen or heard anything from inside the rehab place since one of the cannibals raked the upstairs windows with automatic rifle fire.

Equal measures of exasperation and worry evident in his voice, Cade said, "Copy that. Everyone be advised, I'm coming down."

"Roger that," said Lev. "I've got a pair of tangos trying to flank me. Once I'm done here I'll check on Old Man."

There was no response to that. Lev guessed Cade was already on the move. Quickly pocketing the radio, he pressed his body against the wall next to the east-facing window, and parted the blinds with his rifle.

What Lev saw next was wholly unexpected. One of his would-be flankers was already in the yard. Inexplicably, the man was face down in the tall grass and as still as a store mannequin. A second man—fully bearded and wearing a black stocking cap—was straddling the fence with a trio of rotters draped over him. The black nylon strap on his slung rifle was hung up on the chain-link. Which was why he was rather unsuccessfully staving off the monsters with his left arm and foot.

In the handful of seconds Lev spent watching the spectacle unfold, things went from bad to worse for the man. One of the rotters worked its gnarled fingers into the man's shoulder-length hair and clamped down with cracked and jagged teeth on his left ear. Another wrapped its arms around the man and worked its fingers into his gaping mouth.

Finally, as the man craned over his shoulder and yelled for help, his tenuous hold on the fence failed and he was dragged back onto the sidewalk. Which was all the opening the third reanimated corpse needed. As the others piled on and tore at the man's denim jacket and tee shirt to get at the flesh underneath, the third rotter wormed its pallid face into the scrum and rent a fist-sized plug of flesh from the man's neck.

Shrill, animalistic howls came from under the squirming corpses.

Lev heard Jamie's rifle discharge again.

Then the dying man called out for Adrian.

He did so three times then went quiet.

Lev watched one of the rotters feed a rope of steaming intestine into its mouth and chew hungrily on it.

Having forever lost his appetite for bratwurst, he let the blinds snap shut and set off for the back door.

Chapter 47

Once the shooting started, Wilson didn't have a target, and wasn't being shot at, so he did exactly what he had been told to do: sit tight and watch their flank to the north.

While the sporadic gunfire continued to his right and carefully aimed shots sounded from the hide at his six, he kept his head on a swivel, going from the road looping behind the auto body shop, to the length of Main scrolling away to the north end of town, then finishing on the east/west-running street and sidewalk bordering the rehab place's north side.

Each deliberate left-to-right sweep lasted roughly three seconds. On the end of the first sweep he heard coming from the rehab place the boom of a large caliber handgun he hoped belonged to Duncan.

Midway through the second pass, Jamie's long gun entered the fight and he was witness to the gun battle being waged between Lev and whoever was firing on him.

On the fourth sweep, with the itch to contribute in some way gnawing at his guts, a second boom sounded from the upper story of the rehab place across the street.

As Wilson sat on the roof with his gaze momentarily locked on the rehab place, three things happened in quick succession. First, his radio came alive and he heard the exchange between Lev and Cade. Next, over the sounds of a battle dying down, he heard the plaintive wails of a man dying. Finally, as he was about to set his gaze roaming back to his left and try to spot Cade on his downhill approach, he saw a person peek around the corner of the rehab place and then quickly disappear.

A cold chill tickled his spine as he snugged the M4 to his shoulder.

The old adage *be careful what you wish for* came to him as he flicked the selector from Safe to Fire and snaked his finger into the trigger guard.

Employing some of what Brook had taught him weeks ago on the sprawling Air Force base in Colorado, he took a calming breath, trained the EOTech 3x magnifier's crosshairs on where he thought the face had emerged, and slowly drew up most of the trigger pull.

When the head reappeared and a barrel-chested man presented himself, Wilson adjusted his aim down a degree and sealed the deal.

The single gunshot started a low buzz in his left ear.

The single bullet crossed the street on a diagonal downward trajectory and smacked the man several inches lower than where the redhead had been aiming. Instead of striking center mass as Brook had taught him to aim when it came to breathers, the round punched into the man's guts an inch north of his belly button. Which was a good thing, because unbeknownst to Wilson, had the bullet hit any higher the ballistic vest underneath the man's parka would have minimized the damage—perhaps even stopped it altogether.

Seeing the blood start to darken the band of the man's blue jeans, Wilson dragged the scope up and caught a glimpse of the pain-filled look twisting his face as he pitched sideways like a felled tree. Hands scrabbling at the wound, the man craned his head and called out something indecipherable on his way to the ground.

It was the beginning of the end, no doubt.

And then another person came to his aid. A big-boned woman with closely shorn hair. Almost a clone of the first one to die.

She was fully silhouetted next to the building.

Wilson aimed for center mass and caressed the trigger two times—barely a second between shots. This came at the same instant the woman was bending forward and reaching to grasp the man's outstretched arms. A slight tremor shook her body and the collar of her jean jacket jumped where it draped across her clavicle. Wilson didn't see her face after that. Only the top of her head was visible as the second 5.56 round struck it. The damage was instantaneous and catastrophic, causing her hands to curl into fists while slamming her straight down onto her ample butt. Chin to chest, she wobbled for a moment in the seated position before finally folding over backwards.

Wilson was certain he had just killed two people. This was nothing like the ambush on the road outside of Green River that he had been on the winning side of weeks ago. He wasn't the only one firing on the bandits and their cars that day. Cade, Brook, Taryn, and Sasha were all contributors. And since then, whenever his thoughts wandered back to the surprised looks on the faces of the people that died on that lonely stretch of sunbaked road, he was quick to remind himself that his bullets weren't the only ones crashing into the bandits' vehicles and bodies.

When the visions got really bad, late at night, his thoughts racing wildly, he would think of the executioners in a firing squad. Not every one of their weapons held a live round. Therefore each and every one of them had plausible deniability. That was far from the case here. He saw the blood bloom on the man's shirt. He watched what looked to him like entrails push out from the entry wound. Then there was the woman. Her brains were on full display on the ground all around her. No disputing that.

Wilson stabbed his fingers into his red mane. Then he vomited without warning. There wasn't the usual flood of bitter saliva. His jaw just locked up and out came the mostly liquefied remnants of Heidi's cooking.

The remorse came next, hitting like a tidal wave that started tears to well in his eyes. The pair hadn't even seen it coming. Breathing one second; lives snuffed the next. Three pulls of the trigger sent them to a place they would never return from. And he was solely responsible for sending them there.

Wilson was rocking on his butt with his gaze locked on the tangled corpses when he heard a gruff voice calling his name. Turning an ear in the direction of the north parking lot, he heard it again. No disputing it was Cade and he was calling up from somewhere below the parapet to his left.

As Wilson rose to investigate, Taryn's calm call informing everyone listening that she was completely surrounded by rotters emanated from his radio.

After leaving the four corpses alone in the upstairs room, Duncan had made his way down the back stairs. He had paused at the bottom for a tick and listened to the gunfire coming from the west. The two evenly spaced gunshots sounded hollow at first then finished with a noise like sheets of paper being torn. Suggesting the shooter was some distance away, the reports crashed around for a second or two before tailing off.

Deciding that friendlies still owned the street out front, he made his way through the wide-open room once used as a place to administer various forms of physical therapy. Instructional pamphlets lay scattered about the floor along with therapy balls and foam rollers. Muddy boot prints were everywhere.

As he padded through the great room on his way to the door to the parking area, more gunfire rang out to his right. In the floor-to-ceiling mirrors dominating the wall in that direction, he saw his reflection moving with him. He noticed he was walking hunched over and favoring his right arm a bit. The way he carried the Saiga on that side suggested it was made of solid lead.

Suck it up, buttercup.

Chapter 48

Looking away from the decrepit image of himself in the mirror, Duncan crept down a narrow hall and took up station beside the back door. Once his eyes adjusted to the change in light, he saw the damage Tiny had inflicted. The wooden jamb on the handle side was completely blown out. The casing where the hinges were set was pushed in a few inches. And in the sliver of daylight stabbing through, he saw several empty holes where the screws holding them in place used to reside.

As Duncan reached out to test the door's swing, he heard harried voices coming from the other side. Car doors clunked shut and then the distinct sound of feet crunching gravel drifted away to the left and to the right.

He tugged on the knob and found the door wedged tight. Probably due to Tiny using the same force to close it in his wake as he had employed on his way in. He paused there and listened hard for a long five-count. During that time, he heard more gunfire and screams coming from Center Street and beyond. A tick later, from that same direction, the unmistakable sounds of someone dying a horrible death started up. Since he had heard no calls for help from the others coming from the radio in his pocket, he told himself he was hearing one of the cannibals get what he or she deserved. Through the crack by the hinges he could see a slice of the gravel lot. There was an SUV parked sideways to him. It was gray and American-made and both passenger doors were open. The rear cargo area door had been popped and remained in the up position. Aside from a lone zombie approaching from the right, nothing was moving in the general vicinity. And as he watched the roaming creature shuffle past the SUV, he wondered why the death warbles and calls for

Adrian and Mom had no effect on the thing. Whatever the rotter was stalking was somewhere beyond the rehab place's north side.

Once the dead thing was out of sight, Duncan slung the Saiga next to the M4 and pulled his pistol.

Using the wails of the stricken man for cover, he squared up to the door, grasped the knob left-handed, and yanked inward. There was no immediate swing. Instead, there was a great deal of resistance from contact between the bottom of the door and the sill plate at the threshold. He put a boot on the wall beside the knob and leaned back, bad wing be damned. The extra leverage caused the door to break free. A harsh grating noise echoed in the hall as he dragged it open and peered out onto the pothole-riddled lot.

Duncan had a wheelchair-friendly ramp and short stack of stairs to choose from. He chose the ramp and looped back around to the left to see who the dead thing was after. He was about a yard from the corner of the house when he heard a single gunshot. *Rotter down*, he thought at once. Then, as he was taking another step closer to the edge of the building, where he intended to steal a quick peek, he heard moans comingling with a woman's voice. As he inched forward with the .45 in a two-handed grip, a pair of closely spaced shots from the same direction as the first froze him in his tracks.

Taking a second to listen, he grasped the two-way radio in his pocket and thumbed the Talk key. *Nothing.* There was no electronic beep or hiss of white noise usually preceding a connection being made.

He glanced at the tiny LCD screen and saw the battery strength indicator showing nearly a full charge. The channel and sub-channel were correct. Then he examined the volume knob and found that it was still dialed down to zero. Exactly where he had put it when Tiny was breaking and entering.

He rolled the volume up. "Anyone copy?" he called. Eyes roaming his surroundings, he waited for an answer. What he heard first was a single gunshot. It was fired from a suppressed weapon and had come from just around the corner from him.

"Duncan. Cade here—"

Duncan was already looking for cover when he heard Cade's voice coming from the radio's speaker. "Was that you shooting just now?" he interrupted.

"Just a straggler Z. That's all. Jamie and Taryn have eyes on Center and Main."

Once the channel opened both women chimed in back to back confirming that save for a few rotters drawn by the gunfire, the roads were clear in all directions.

Cade asked, "What's your twenty, Duncan?"

Duncan thumbed the Talk key. "I'm in the parking lot behind the rehab joint. Looks clear to me." As he released the button to hear the expected reply, he heard Cade announcing his presence from just around the corner. Relaxing a bit, Duncan called back and rose up from beside the SUV where he had been crouched.

After sweeping around the corner with Wilson in tow, Cade clapped Duncan on the shoulder. "We're not done here," he said. "Wilson"—he motioned toward the house on the other side of Center—"I want you to go and help Lev search the bodies."

Wilson asked, "What are we looking for?"

Duncan said, "Just follow Lev's lead until we get there."

Wilson set off toward Center Street, M4 at the ready. He took a few tentative steps, then stopped and looked over his shoulder. Face screwed up with worry, he asked, "How is Taryn?"

"She's well out of their reach," answered Cade. "I think she'll weather the storm until Jamie gets there to help. At least that's what her words said. She sounded pretty confident to me. You were listening in, too."

Wilson delivered a subtle nod, then turned and hustled across the street, boots clomping as he ran.

Cade turned to Duncan. "You had me worried there for a second, Old Man. Thought you finally got your ticket punched. You certainly set yourself up for it to happen."

Duncan grimaced. Then there was a long, strained silence as he stared at his boots. Finally, he leveled his gaze at Cade and started in on what had taken place upstairs. He recounted everything in full. Every last grisly detail. He admitted to pistol whipping the woman and then delivering the pair of kicks to her temple that had killed her. With a flat affect, he described how the big man had flopped around before a second slug from the .45 had finally stilled him. Brushing bits of plaster from his unruly ring of gray hair, he talked of killing the man in the truck bed and then taking return fire from his buddy, putting emphasis on how close he had come to truly having his *ticket punched*.

Cade said nothing. Every so often he would scan their surroundings, giving extra attention to a dozen or so Zs wandering Center Street a couple of blocks east. He remained silent and watchful until his friend admitted to rolling the volume down on his radio and forgetting he had done so.

"Shit happens," said Cade, locking eyes with the man. "You're still on the right side of the dirt. That's all that counts."

Duncan was speechless. He had expected to be dressed down. Or, at the very least, given the cold shoulder while the Delta soldier stewed.

Cade removed his hat and ran a hand through his lengthening hair. "I'm partly to blame," he admitted. "I've been meaning to ask Beeson or Nash for a half-dozen sets of hands-free comms. I'm still hesitant to do so. No doubt Beeson's teams are running nonstop ops against the scattered Chinese forces." He snugged his hat on and turned his attention from the approaching Zs to the sidewalk beside the house across the street. Pointing to three forms standing in a loose knot in the shadow of the trees bordering Center Street's south side, he said, "Looks like we have a visitor."

Duncan's gaze followed. He squinted and a soft chuckle escaped his throat. "Well I'll be dipped in shit."

Holstering his Glock, Cade began a slow walk toward Lev and Wilson and what, from fifty yards away, appeared to be a man-shaped topiary brandishing a very familiar weapon.

Chapter 49

Cade sent Lev and Wilson off to police up the cannibals' weapons, ammunition, radios, and gasoline. "And check and see if the plow on the truck is worth taking," he added before they were out of earshot.

Duncan nodded toward the prostrate forms littering the road near the shot-up vehicles. "Sure they're all dead?"

Without a trace of emotion in his voice, Cade said, "I killed seven." He pointed to his right. "Jamie dinged the two over there. Three dead are still in the pickups. The others ... the ones that you and Lev caught in a crossfire on the street that didn't die outright, I was lucky enough to watch draw their last breaths." He nodded to the rehab place. "Wilson stepped up and took out a pair of breathers trying to flank me and Jamie."

"Beat me to 'em," said Duncan, shifting his gaze from the dead rotters on the sidewalk to the pair of recently deceased men laid out side-by-side in the street before him. Mostly drained of color, their faces stared up longingly at the darkening sky. The thirty-something man on the left was fair-haired and of medium height. He had on blue jeans with skinny legs, the cuffs of which were rolled up to the tops of his black leather Doc Martens boots. The once sandstone-colored Carhartt jacket was stained dark crimson from the chest down. The corpse itself bore crude black tattoos on its neck and hands. There were swastikas and spider webs on the latter. On the former, nearly hidden within a collage of grinning skulls, was a pair of lightning bolts similar to those worn by Hitler's Waffen SS. Though Duncan wasn't inclined to check, he was fairly certain the prison ink didn't stop there. The second man had been borderline obese when his days of eating human flesh were cut short. His graying hair was stretched tight into a ponytail that reached the small of his back. A sharp ridge of cartilage was all that remained of his nose. And snaking from the bloody sockets where his eyes should have been was a tangled mess of muscle and the stringy remains of the filament-like optic nerves. On the left side of the man's face, the dermis was torn and riddled with raised purple bite marks. Adding insult to the injuries he had suffered as a result of the three-versus-one melee, the vital organs meant to be cradled in the protective confine of his ribcage had been ripped out and consumed with hasty indifference by the hungry rotters.

"He didn't stand a chance," observed Cade.

Duncan smirked. "Who's the proud papa of these two?" he asked, shooting Daymon a knowing look.

Daymon was dressed head to toe in an over-the-counter ghillie suit. Made up of strips of fabric torn in random widths and lengths and colored in mostly lighter earth tones, up close, the camouflage garb truly did make him look like a six-foot-tall walking and talking shrub. The bow cradled in one arm was a high-tech item. The matte-black recurve arms looked as if they were made of some kind of exotic carbon fiber. There was an adjustable stock—cheek weld, pad and all—out back. Offset to one side and riding atop a Picatinny rail was a no-nonsense high-power scope.

"I caught them flanking the house," he said, gesturing at the tattooed corpse. "I dropped that one as he went over the fence. Must have pierced a heart valve or something. He didn't even say a word when it hit him here"—Daymon pointed at his ribs underneath his left arm—"just the whoosh of his breath leaving him and he fell mid-step face down in the grass on the other side of the fence."

Duncan was eyeballing the hat to Daymon's outfit. It bristled with flora that looked to have been freshly plucked from the fields and briar patches bumping up to the rear of the nearby house. He regarded the taller man and gestured to the twice-dead rotters. "And pony boy with no guts? Your doing or the stinky three here?"

"I pulled my shot," said Daymon, with a shake of his head. "Hit him in the hammy, though. Slowed him down enough to let the roamers get him. Pretty damn satisfying getting to watch 'em finish the job up close and personal."

Cade asked, "Where were you set up? You have a stand?"

"No stand. Hollah has one in the garage back at the house. That's where I found this suit and the bow. And if you want to believe the photo in Hollah's den, he took down a grizzly in Alaska with this thing."

"That little car-sellin' runt had to have been in a tree stand," said Duncan, "Begs the question, Slim. Where'd you hit 'em from?"

Daymon put a hand on Duncan's shoulder. He pointed the bow at the brambles behind the house. "Crouched down behind the berry patch. Rotters weren't paying *me* no mind so I just popped up and hit the first breather as he's going over the fence. Dumb ass number two is whirling around and looking for me as the stinkies are drawing near. He goes over at the last minute. That's when I winged him." He glanced at the approaching rotters. Though they were still nearly a block away, their rasping calls and toxic stench were evident.

Cade clapped Daymon on the shoulder. He said, "I figured you were listening in when I took that call back at your place."

Daymon nodded. "I couldn't help but hear the time and place. I also couldn't resist crashing the party."

"Thanks for getting our backs. You did good."

"Kudos from the Delta soldier," said Daymon, smiling broadly.

"Don't let it get to your head," shot Duncan. "It's already too big."

Daymon flipped Duncan the bird.

Cade caught the taller man's eye. "You better hustle back to Heidi and hunker down. Things are bound to get crazy in the coming hours. Bear River is under siege by the dead. No telling when that dam will break and they start moving again."

"If the walls don't fall first," Duncan observed soberly.

"You also have Adrian's people to worry about," added Cade, his eyes locking with Daymon's. "Sooner or later they'll come looking for their people. And when they do ... you better not be on the move. Might find yourself cut off from getting home."

"You'll be stuck between the proverbial rock and a hard place," added Duncan.

Daymon opened his mouth to speak but was preempted by a shrill voice coming from a radio in Cade's pocket. He pursed his lips and shot the operator a questioning look.

Cade dragged the radio into the open.

They all crowded in and listened to a woman trying to hail someone named Joy. This went on for a few seconds until the woman said, "Iris, can *you* hear me? Can *anyone* in Woodruff fuckin' hear me?"

Save for the growls and snarls of the rotters still closing in on the group, silence dominated their little huddle. A couple of seconds slipped into the past before the radio finally came alive again and Iris blurted that she was alive and wanted to know where in the hell Joy was.

Hitching a brow, Duncan mouthed, "Joy is *no mas.*"

Incredulity showing in her tone, Iris was back on the radio and again pleading for help. "I know how many people are there," she added. "I even know what *kinds* of weapons they have. Adrian *will* get her food back."

There was no reply.

Eventually, voice gone hoarse, Iris ended her one-sided conversation with a whispered, "I'm a *doer*. Tell Adrian I am finally a *doer.*"

Squaring up to the shambling clutch of undead, Daymon said, "I got this." He set his bow down and reached for his right thigh. A second later his hand emerged from underneath the ghillie suit's fabric strips clutching Kindness. Machete held out in front of him like a miniature jousting pole, he strode confidently toward the rotters.

Wilson and Lev were just returning from their task and missed Daymon's declaration. They set the rifles cradled in their arms down gently on the grass strip. Lev took a trio of pistols from his belt line and laid them out next to the assortment of carbines and bolt-action long guns.

Wilson shrugged off the last of the rifles he'd slung crisscross over his shoulders. Looking to Cade, he said, "No wallets. No maps. There's two cans of gas we can fetch on the way back to our rigs." He nodded toward Daymon, who was just drawing near to the dead. "Shouldn't one of us give him a hand?"

Cade shook his head. "He can handle twice as many as that with one arm tied behind his back."

"And the girls?"

"They'll be alright," is what Cade said. *They'll sink or they'll swim*, is what he was thinking. The time for coddling and scolding was over. That all ended the moment he sank the black blade into Brook's brain. He looked to Lev. "Any radios?"

"Just the leader," he said. "Same type as the one from the Thagon house."

Cade said, "Same channel, I presume."

Lev nodded. "I got a good look at the cowcatcher thing on the lead truck."

"And?"

"Not worth taking for one of our rigs," said Lev. "It's just thin steel tacked on haphazardly by a novice welder."

Cade said, "That explains why they didn't try to run the block."

Lev nodded, then regarded Duncan. "Damn, man. You did a *number* on those two upstairs. The big guy ... one to the chest and one to the head. *Savage*. Looks like an effen alien chewed its way out of his chest."

"Went about it backwards," conceded Duncan. "His Neanderthal forehead diverted the first slug."

"Then you shot him direct in the sternum."

Duncan nodded, then glanced at Daymon. Watched as the gangly looking bush decapitated three of the rotters in quick succession. Saw the decaying bodies crash vertically like snipped marionettes, the severed heads bouncing and rolling in different directions. Imagining the jaws still working piston-like, he shuddered at the thought of those dead eyes continuing to dart to and fro on the lookout for fresh meat until the brain finally rotted away to nothing.

Wilson had been hanging on the words. His jaw dropping incrementally with each sweep of his gaze.

"The woman," said Lev, snapping Duncan back to the conversation. "Did you choke her out?"

Duncan threw a shudder and tore his eyes from the dance of death down the street.

"Choke her out," stammered Wilson. Jaw on his chest, he took a step back from the man he considered to be more of an uncle or grandpa figure than a stone-cold killer.

"It's a long story," drawled Duncan. Frowning, he added, "I don't know my own strength. Let's just leave it at that."

Breaking up the jawing session, Cade said, "As soon as Daymon is finished, we need to scoot." He quickly selected three of the rifles—all AR platforms—and placed them aside. They were pretty beat up and likely ill-maintained. Still, he figured they could be used for practice, or cannibalized for their parts.

"Mine," said Duncan, snatching up the lone AK-47 in the mix. He checked the safety then pulled the curved magazine from the well. "Old boy expended every last round before I killed him."

"Spray and pray is more like it," said Cade. "No accuracy involved. Half of them froze up under fire. Majority of the rest went into panic mode." He picked up a spare magazine for the Soviet Bloc weapon and tossed it to Duncan.

Fumbling the toss, Duncan said, "Gotta love the spoils of war."

Cade said, "Speaking of spoils of war. Which truck are you taking?"

Duncan shook his head. "Two out of the three are resting on flat tires. I raked the cab of the other with the carbine."

"There was a person in there when you did," said Lev. "The passenger." He looked the older man in the eye and added slowly, "And she bled out and died in there."

"Crazy the amount of blood a human body has in it," noted Wilson.

Duncan chuckled. "Better her than one of us."

Pulling his gaze from Duncan, Wilson plucked one of the pistols off the grass. It was a semiautomatic clone of the venerable Colt Model 1911 that Duncan favored. Staring at the weapon, he asked, "Can I have this one?"

"Don't ask," said Cade. "Assert yourself. Claim it."

Wilson nodded and tucked the pistol in his waistband.

Lev said, "What do we do with the rest of the rifles? They're pretty much junk."

Cade picked out a bolt-action item pitted with rust. He laid it across the curb and stomped a bell curve into the barrel.

"That'll take it out of the fight," said Lev, following suit with another of the long guns.

Daymon let out a war whoop that carried the half-block to the trio of men disabling the weapons. "Shit never gets old," he called across the distance.

"Need a ride home?" asked Cade.

Daymon sauntered back to the others, machete in hand. He wiped off the blade in the tall grass. Then, sheathing Kindness, he said, "No, but thanks. I'm going to do a little exploring east of here to get a better lay of the land."

"Killing and running?" quipped Duncan.

"Hey now ... I saved Lev's bacon," replied Daymon.

"Thanks," Lev said dryly as he picked up the bow and gave it a once-over.

"Just effin with you," said Daymon, smiling and slapping Lev on the shoulder.

Throwing a visible shiver, Duncan said, "You gonna go off and leave those heads in the road so they can eye-fuck every piece of fresh meat that comes along?"

"That can be our new calling card," answered Daymon. "Let people know we have *eyes everywhere*." His expression went serious. "Reminds me. I'm working on setting up some more perimeter defenses at the house. Better give me and Heidi a heads up next time you pay us a visit."

Cade slung the three ARs over his shoulder. "We'll be sure to. Regular channel."

Daymon nodded. Held up both hands fingers splayed and mouthed, "Ten." Then he folded all but the pointer on his left hand and said, "One."

Cade nodded. "Thanks again for the snowmobile. I owe you."

"More where that came from," said Daymon. "We only need two." He donned the hat to the ghillie suit, arranging the strands of burlap so that only his eyes were visible.

Cade grabbed Daymon by the arm and led him a few yards away from the group, talking as he walked.

Wilson looked to Lev. "Wonder what's up with that."

"If Delta Boy tells us, he'll have to kill us," cracked Duncan.

Lev watched the two finish talking and when they returned, he approached Daymon and handed over the crossbow.

Daymon took the bow and without another word set off eastbound on Center.

Cade and the others watched him go for a beat, then struck off on foot, walking single file in the direction of the 39/16 junction.

Chapter 50

The girls were sitting sidesaddle on the snowmobile in the box bed of the F-650 when Cade and the others returned carrying the spoils taken off the dead cannibals. Like spokes on a wagon wheel, nearly twenty rotter corpses lay in a ragged semicircle in the long grass next to the Raptor. The nearer Cade got to the Z corpses, the more it became evident to him that a fair amount of them had been felled by someone attacking from the bed of the Raptor. Which told him that the person engaging them hadn't been afraid to get their hands dirty. Some of the prostrate Zs nearest to the Raptor bore puckered, inch-long stab wounds to the temple. Suggestive of point-blank blade strikes from above; others were left with an eye socket weeping scrambled brains.

"What took you so long?" shot Jamie, feigning a look at the wristwatch still hidden underneath her shirtsleeve.

Cade glanced at his Suunto, then looked up at her. "All that and we still have nearly two hours of daylight left."

With the others already stowing their gear, Cade picked his way to the rear of the F-650 carrying a jerry can full of gas in one hand and an M4 in the other. Along the way, he scrutinized the corpses littering the ground on the Raptor's right flank. It was obvious to him that the ones felled farthest from the truck were Jamie's doing. Though he hadn't been witness to the attack, the deep chasms to the rear of their skulls told him she was learning to wield her war tomahawk with great precision. He guessed her footfalls were drowned out by the plaintive calls of the hungry dead as she crept up to the late-to-arrive Zs and culled them from behind.

He placed the gas can on the F-650's open tailgate. Shoved it forward until it was wedged in tight next to the snowmobile and protruding wheel well. He opened the Pelican case and quickly broke down the MSR, snugging each component into its dedicated slot in the gray foam padding.

One at a time, Duncan slid the liberated rifles into the bed next to Ray and Helen's shrouded corpses. Finished, he looked up at Taryn, who was still lounging on the snowmobile and watching the men load the trucks. He said, "While the mice are away the cat do play."

"Held the fort down," she said.

Moving his gaze to Jamie, Duncan said, "And you let that axe of yours loose, I see."

"Taryn didn't *need* my help," replied Jamie defensively.

Duncan raised his hands in mock surrender and slowly backed away from the open tailgate.

"I don't think that's where he was going with his comment," said Cade.

Jamie apologized to Duncan for snapping at him. She regarded Lev and Cade. "I'm just looking out for the fairer sex. Us girls have to stick together."

Cade squeezed between the F-650 and school bus and opened the rear door. He stowed the Pelican case behind the front seats, closed the door, and then slapped the sheet metal. "Mount up," he called. He took hold of the grab handle and stood on the running board. Whispering to Jamie across the Ford's roof, he said, "Thanks for taking Raven under your wing while I was gone."

"She's a great kid ... but—" Letting the word hang in the air, she stepped from the snowmobile and clambered into the Raptor's bed.

Concern creeping into his voice, Cade called, "What do you mean by that?"

"She's taking the loss of her mom pretty hard. She punched a mirror and cut her knuckle."

Cade nodded. "It's to be expected. I take it Glenda patched her up."

Jamie was already opening the Raptor's passenger side rear door. She paused. Part of her wanted to mention the *other* blood, but she held back. Instead, she simply assured Cade that his daughter was in "good hands."

Still standing on the running board and staring across the F-650's roof, Cade said, "I appreciate you." He saw a word begin to form and a brief spark of recognition show in Jamie's eyes. Then she frowned and swiveled her head to the left.

Cade looked a question at her.

She put a finger to her lips.

On the far side of the Raptor, Duncan was watching a pair of rotters staggering up the state route when he also cocked an ear and started a slow pirouette to the north.

A few yards away, Wilson was climbing into his usual seat—the one minus pedals and a steering wheel—when he also went rigid and turned his undivided attention to the north.

Oblivious to what was going on around him, Lev stowed his rifle on the floor behind Wilson's seat. When he emerged, he went stock still and said, "Who is it?"

Hearing the sound of rumbling engines at the same time as everyone save for Lev, Taryn had slowly risen up off the snowmobile seat and, so as to not give them all away, poked just the upper third of her head over the school bus.

Cade stepped from the Ford, bringing his M4 with him. He looked up at Taryn. "What do you got?"

Without establishing eye contact, she answered by showing him her hand, fingers and thumb fully extended.

Five, thought Cade. Grabbing the Steiners from off the seat Taryn was kneeling on, he scrabbled over the side of the bed and slowly rose up next to her. Cognizant of the fact the radio in his pocket tuned to the cannibal's frequency was still silent, he glassed the formidable-looking convoy.

In the lead was the Jackson Police Department Tahoe Alexander Dregan had recently gifted to Ray Thagon. The needle antenna quivered as the tuned SUV sucked up a dip in the road near the north end of town where 16 became Main Street. Once sporting the letters BRPD to denote it belonged to Bear River's fledgling security apparatus, the black and white was now emblazoned with the letters AVPD. The new markings were stenciled in silver over the top of the old. Speaking to a rushed job, the paint had run and then dried, looking like so many icicles hanging off the letters.

Without taking his eyes off the rapidly approaching Tahoe, Cade asked, "The initials AV mean anything to you?"

At once Taryn said, "Adrian Ville. Saw it spray painted on the signs up north."

"They were either poking around in Randolph when we sprang our ambush and were called in over another channel, or they were just down the road and acting as a quick reaction force of sorts."

"If it was the latter," Taryn said, "why didn't they come when the shooting started?"

"Good question," answered Cade. "I'm pretty sure I killed the leader before she got a call out. And Duncan took out the only other person with a radio. Since the shooting started up near simultaneously, I doubt *she* got a call out."

"Who called in the cavalry then?"

"If the lead element missed the check in time—" Cade began.

"Then the backup comes rolling in automatically," finished Taryn.

"Exactly," said Cade as he focused his attention on the other vehicles. Two late-model Chevy Suburbans were tucked in close to the patrol Tahoe. Both SUVs were black and fitted with whip antenna, brush guards, and bright blue HID (high intensity discharge) headlights. Through the front windshields, Cade saw a mix of men and women openly brandishing rifles. Next in line and hanging back from the Suburbans was a blacked-out and jacked-up Ford Excursion, its driver and any occupants hidden behind heavily tinted windows. Bringing up the rear of the procession was a full-sized van that looked to have been stored in someone's garage since the late seventies. It was black with tinted windows and rolled on mag wheels painted red. It was outfitted with a black grill guard that followed the contours of the bumper and headlights. However, the aftermarket add-on was flimsy looking. All show, no go. A thin red accent stripe stretched from the front fenders to the rear of the sliding door where it doubled in width and then shot up on a diagonal toward the roof-mounted rear-spoiler. The van was adorned with a copious amount of chrome that shone in spite of the gray sky overhead.

"Looks like someone invited the A-Team to tag along with the Presidential motorcade," quipped Duncan, who was standing on the tailgate and peering through a pair of Bushnell binoculars.

"Thank God those aren't armored Secret Service rigs," replied Cade as he looked away from Duncan and fixed his gaze on Taryn. "You good to drive?"

"It's in my blood."

"Everyone mount up," Cade said at the top of his voice. He helped Taryn down from her perch on the snowmobile seat. "Keep your motor off until I start the 650." He went on, giving her the Cliff's Notes version of his plan, and then stressed that she was to stay close on his bumper "no matter what happens."

Taryn took it all in, nodded once, then jumped from the tailgate to the spongy ground.

Duncan had been giving a play-by-play as he watched the convoy cross the street leading to the church and rectory at the far end of town. He tracked the five vehicles for a couple of blocks until they slowed and came to a full stop adjacent to the post office. He saw the blue headlights snap off one pair at a time until only the Tahoe's were lit. He lowered the field glasses and glanced sidelong at Cade. "You sure that's how you want it to go down?"

Lifting the Steiners to his eyes, Cade said, "There's no other way."

Duncan noted, "They're going to be dangerously close to the compound."

"They already have the GPS coordinates. That's as *danger close* as it can get."

Duncan was silent for a long five-count. Finally, he clucked his tongue and began the arduous process of climbing down from the F-650. Once on the ground he looped around the open tailgate and crabbed between the two trucks. Drawing even with the Raptor's rear passenger door, he cracked it open and peered inside at Jamie and Lev. Locking eyes with the latter, he said, "Cade wants you and me to light them up from the junction. But"—he drew in a deep breath—"we are to disturb the nest *without* killing the hornets."

"Roger that," Lev replied. "Shots across the bow it is."

From the front passenger seat, Wilson blurted, "What the hell good is that going to do? It's just going to piss them off!"

Taryn reached across the front seat and rested her hand on Wilson's thigh. "Cade's plan is sound," she insisted. Then she went on, describing the vehicles to him and what was expected from each of them once the plan was set into motion—all of which seemed to do little to assuage Wilson's fears.

Duncan grimaced at Wilson's reaction. Without comment, he closed the door, spun a one-eighty, and clambered aboard the F-650. He aimed the Saiga at the floorboard, removed the curved magazine, and cycled the live round from the chamber. From the bag stowed behind his seat, he retrieved the fully loaded thirty-round drum-magazine Daymon had provided along with the new shotgun. Departing from his usual practice of staggering shot and slug shells in the high capacity mag, Duncan had instead opted to go with all 12-gauge rifled slugs.

The heavy drum seated with a solid click. The act of racking the first round into the chamber filled the cab with a satisfying sound. *Ready as I'll ever be,* crossed his mind as he looked out across the nearby Raptor's hood and locked his gaze on a herd of rotters just cresting a rise in the state route a half mile or so south on 16.

Back to glassing the unmoving convoy, Cade imagined a counterpart in one of the rigs doing the same. If they saw the top of his head cresting the bus, they weren't letting on. Then, as absurd as it seemed, a mental image of Adrian with her injured leg in a makeshift cast sitting inside one of the vehicles and berating the driver popped into his head. *God, I hope so*, he thought. And though he hadn't seen Adrian with his own eyes, going by the smattering of descriptions from those who had, he figured a short-statured woman possessing the girth of a pro-wrestler would only be comfortable in the full-sized van—especially if it was a true *stabbin' cabin* and outfitted with the requisite bed in back.

Chapter 51

The enemy convoy remained in place on Main Street, Woodruff for five long minutes.

Periodically, Cade would glance over his shoulder at a column of Zs approaching from the south.

Every other minute Wilson would call through the Raptor's open window and ask what was happening with the cannibal convoy.

Through it all Cade said nothing.

Finally, the patrol Tahoe pulled away from the other vehicles. It was lower to the ground than all but the van. It was also equipped with a souped-up V8 engine and was outfitted up front with a frame-mounted bull bar. Perfect for an occasional PIT maneuver—the art of using the bull bar to nudge a fleeing perp's vehicle into an unrecoverable spin—the wraparound steel cage was also suitable for clearing disabled vehicles from a roadway.

At first the driver of the Tahoe seemed to be content to allow the idling engine to propel the squat SUV forward at walking-speed. Once the post office was a block behind the creeping vehicle, a puff of exhaust formed near its rear tires, the front end rose up and, with a corresponding roar of the engine that reached Cade's ears over the distance, rapidly picked up speed. Holding a die-straight southerly heading, the black and white blazed by the street where the first convoy had diverted. With barely three truck lengths to go before what was looking to be an awful collision with the Cadillac and import blocking Main, the unseen driver employed the beefed-up brakes and black stripes of smoking rubber were spooling out behind the SUV's rear tires. The Tahoe stopped just shy of the angled cars, rocked on its springs one time, then—with the tire smoke wafting right to left across Main—repeated the drag strip theatrics in reverse.

Exhaust puff.

Nose dip and throaty engine roar.

Then the whine of the lower range reverse gears winding out as the three-and-a-half-ton rig reeled the road back in. When the Tahoe finally ground to a halt a dozen feet from the lead Suburban's front bumper, there was none of the previous drama. No black stripes were laid down. And no white smoke billowed up from the high-performance radials.

Cade thought: *They're trying to draw fire.*

The Tahoe remained still, the tick of its engine barely audible from what Cade guessed amounted to about four long city blocks.

***

A quick glance at the Suunto told Cade that ten more minutes had slipped into history. During that time, the lead element of the approaching zombie herd had crested the hill to the south, doddered through the roadside ditch and surrounded the Raptor on three sides.

Up ahead on Main Street the cannibal's convoy remained in place, dark and silent.

Ignoring the stench and scrabble of fingernails on glass and metal, Cade took a hand from the Steiners and rubbed his neck muscles. As time passed he'd come to the conclusion that he had chosen a far from ideal spot from which to conduct any kind of prolonged recon. He found he was too tall to use the snowmobile seat in the same manner as Taryn without his head constantly breaking the horizon. As a result, a dull ache had taken root in his neck and shoulders from holding his upright body in the same bent-knee posture while trying to keep his head out of sight and his Danners from slipping off the F-650's narrow bed rail.

As Cade passed the binoculars between hands and tended to the muscles running up the left side of his neck, the headlights on the lead Suburban flared on and burned bright like twin blue suns. Then, in quick succession, starting with the second Suburban, three more pairs of headlights snapped on.

Cade watched the Tahoe go into motion. It wasn't reenacting the slow creeping roll forward. Nor was it a mad tire-smoking dash to the roadblock. Exuding an air of confidence on the driver's part, it motored purposefully forward at a steady pace, falling somewhere between the two.

Cade continued tracking the Tahoe with the Steiners only long enough to be sure the driver was not going to turn off Main and go behind Back In The Saddle. Once the rig was slowing with the bull bar on a collision course for the narrow gap where the front ends of the Cadillac and import came together, he tucked the Steiners away and snatched up his M4. He made a slow pirouette on the bed rails in the direction of the tailgate where a pair of Zs were wedged into the narrow gap. He leveled the suppressed M4 and put a 5.56 hardball round into each of their skulls. Six clear, he dropped down to the ground and crabbed sideways between the F-650 and school bus roof.

Stepping over the pallid hand reaching for his foot from under the truck, he latched onto the grab bar and slipped through the door Duncan had been holding open for him. In one fluid move, he sucked the door in behind him, threw the rifle on the floor, and fired up the engine.

The rumble of the Raptor's tuned V8 turning over let Cade know that Taryn was on her game.

Duncan asked, "They weren't at all deterred by the roadblock?"

Eyeing the half-dozen grabby Zs forming around the front of the rigs, Cade said, "I'd call what I saw cautious persistence that's evolved into confident action." Throwing the transmission into gear, he leaned forward and shot a glance at the other pickup. Behind the wheel, Taryn wore an expression that relayed equal measures confidence and trepidation. A good thing, in Cade's book.

Next to Taryn, Wilson was leaning away from the Zs batting at his window. As always, his camo boonie hat was pulled down to its lowest setting: narrowed eyes mostly hidden. Ears tucked up under the floppy brim. Only tufts of his bushy red mane showing around the edges.

In the back seat behind Taryn, Jamie wore a mask of grim determination. The barrel of her carbine was pointed at the roof. Next to her, Lev was holding his Les Baer AR left-handed with his extended trigger finger pressed against the smooth metal above the trigger guard.

On the back end of the quick visual sweep, Cade saw a snapshot of Duncan. The man was holding the Saiga left-handed and close to his chest. His trigger finger traced a slow counterclockwise circle next to the shotgun's trigger guard. Behind the softly tinted aviators his eyes were far away and distant.

Over the tinny bangs of cold, dead hands slapping the hood and fenders, Cade heard the Raptor's engine revving. Figuring he'd given the Tahoe driver enough time to get into the act of pushing the inert vehicles aside, he gunned the engine and nosed the big Ford through the throng of Zs and out from behind the makeshift hide. As the truck bounced onto the state route, the sun, already low in the sky due to the season, reached that perfect azimuth in its run toward night where its rays were seemingly swallowed up by the landscape to the west. With the creeping wall of shadow darkening Main and the adjacent killing grounds, he brought the Ford to a halt in the center of the two-lane and alerted the Tahoe driver to its presence with a single flash of the high beams.

Chapter 52

There was no immediate reaction from the convoy. The Tahoe was moving forward slowly and just about to punch through the roadblock when Cade hit the high beams on it. As the westbound stretch of 39 came parallel with the F-650's left front fender, Cade saw the Cadillac shift on axis and imagined the screech created by its buckling panels. He cranked the wheel left and stopped their forward roll at a forty-five-degree angle where the state routes came together in their less than perfect union.

In the passenger seat, Duncan had already motored down his window. Elbows braced on the channel, he had the Saiga's muzzle and bulky drum magazine hanging out of the vehicle. Keeping the weapon level with the road looked to be a chore. Cade watched the jagged muzzle brake waver slightly until Duncan took hold of the stubby foregrip—a vital component in keeping the bucking shotgun on target.

"Slugs?" asked Cade.

"Nothing but," responded Duncan.

Down the road, the second Suburban began to break ranks. Its wheels turned hard right and it rolled up next to its twin. Blocking for the others, Cade presumed. He said, "Do it," and took his hands from the wheel and clamped his palms over his ears as the cab was rocked by a half-dozen thunderous booms. Spent shells trailing wisps of smoke tumbled from the Saiga's ejection port. Duncan's hunched back jerked and rose with each concussion.

Cade glanced in the passenger mirror. Saw brass pirouetting from the open window and orange licks of fire lancing from the right side of the Raptor. Swinging his gaze to the convoy, he imagined what they were thinking. If some of them had had their windows even partially opened at the onset of the one-sided engagement, the distinct crackle-whizz of danger-close lead cutting the air would not have been lost on them. In the event their rigs had been sealed tight, three seconds into the faux attack the roar of the Saiga would have caused them to break their necks trying to discover its source.

Five seconds after Cade's two words set his plan into motion, there was no doubt the cannibals knew they were being fired on. All at once the vehicles were moving forward. Some were zigging and zagging. *A solid tactic*, thought Cade.

The import had gotten tangled with the Tahoe's bull bar and was stuck fast. But the Tahoe didn't stop. It limped forward and once clear of the Cadillac slewed right, then stopped with the Hyundai partially blocking Main.

Message received. The lead Suburban was picking up speed and angling straight for the rear quarter of the tiny four-door.

Cade didn't wait to see the result of the collision. No need. The big SUV would certainly emerge the victor. Instead, he ducked low to the wheel, turned it left a hair and matted the gas pedal.

After the opening roar of cool air being sucked into the V-10 tapered off, the pickup's rear tires found traction and it shot forward. A half-beat later Black Beauty—as Raven had taken to calling the Ford—was tracking for the distant curve where 39 dove into the forest.

The only place Cade figured the cannibals' return fire could do him or the others any harm was the short stretch near the junction where the vegetation was sparse and the only thing standing between them and the convoy was the Jersey barriers and twenty or thirty feet of steel guardrail. So snowmobile be damned, for the entire quarter mile of two-lane between the junction and where it entered the trees, Cade hauled the wheel left and right, zigging and zagging the Ford in hopes of evading any return fire directed their way.

A handful of seconds removed from sending the flurry of bullets downrange at the cannibals two things happened. First, day seemed to turn to night as the trees crowding the road blocked out the late afternoon light. Then the Motorola locked onto the group's shared channel issued three words spoken by Wilson that started a cold ball of dread to form in Cade's stomach.

Duncan answered the frantic call at once. "Jamie's been hit?" he blurted. "How bad?"

Chapter 53

In the Ford Raptor, Wilson keyed the Talk button and thrust the radio toward Lev so he could answer the question and continue to tend to the injured woman. Shouting to be heard over the engine growl, Lev described the wound as flesh and muscle damage to her right cheek and ear. He grunted and muttered something, then plain as day stressed that the blood loss taking place was his biggest concern.

In the F-650, Cade looked away from the road just long enough to fix Duncan with a concerned look. "Ask him if he has a QuikClot."

Duncan spoke rapid fire into the radio. A tick later Wilson said, "Lev's got what he needs to keep her from bleeding out. He's saying that shock is his next biggest concern." There was a two-second pause during which road noise and pained whimpers—no doubt coming from Jamie—bled from the tiny speaker and filled the F-650's cab. When Wilson finally spoke again, he said, "There's so much blood."

Duncan inclined his head and bounced it off the headrest a couple of times. Muttering, "Why her?" he looked a question at Cade.

"Ask Wilson if the tangos were in pursuit when Taryn turned onto 39."

As if it weighed a hundred pounds, Duncan slowly dragged the radio to his mouth and asked the question.

Wilson said, "Three of them that I saw. When Jamie got hit, I ... *we* all ducked down. Then we were in the trees and calling you."

Cade shot a quick look at the right-side mirror. Though the other rig's reflection was a little jittery he could still see a full two-thirds of the Raptor that was now seemingly glued to his bumper. The word FORD that dominated the center of the matte-black grill was mostly visible. Then there was Wilson in the passenger seat holding the radio to his mouth with his left hand. His right arm was pressed hard against the window, the knuckles on that hand no doubt white from gripping the grab bar near his head. Neither Lev nor Jamie were visible. Which didn't surprise Cade. He grimaced as he imagined the former hunched over the latter and trying to staunch the bleeding. And just as Cade had on that fateful night with Brook, Lev would be whispering calming words into Jamie's ear. Only Lev was saving a life—not the other way around.

Cade swallowed hard and cast a cursory glance at the snowmobile in the back of the F-650. He saw it shift a few inches to the right as he came out of the long sweeping right-hand curve. That Taryn was not following his orders precisely was a good thing. Should the spirited driving shake the cargo loose, not only would the snowmobile be a total loss, but so might one of the group's more reliable vehicles.

Always thinking for herself. Taking the initiative without having to be micromanaged. Definitely attributes that endeared Taryn to him. In fact, she was a little like Brook in those regards. And as the apocalypse entered its fourth month, Cade was starting to see some of those same traits manifesting in Raven. His hand went to his neck and he pinched the chain between two fingers. He dragged it through his hand until his fingers found the wedding ring. Oblivious to the action and unaware Duncan was looking sidelong at him, Cade drew the reminder of his recent loss to his lips and kissed it.

"What's on your mind?"

"Just watching our six," Cade lied, blinking back a tear. "Call ahead and make sure Glenda has what she needs to go to work on Jamie when we get there."

"On the side of the road?"

"No choice," said Cade. "Have the girls take the 4Runner and drive whatever Glenda needs out to her."

"They have to deal with the gates. And any rotters that might be on the road. Not to mention the fact that without a stint on a medieval rack Raven is not gonna be able to reach the pedals."

Cade glanced at the rearview. "Then Sasha is going to have to rise to the occasion."

Duncan shook his head. "I don't like it. Why not have Tran run the stuff up to Glenda?"

Cade shot Duncan an incredulous look.

"You're right," Duncan conceded. "Wouldn't be smart to leave the eyes and ears of the compound unattended. Hell, Tran would probably need the rack treatment, too. That or wood blocks for the pedals."

"Set it in motion," said Cade. "We're less than ten minutes out."

Duncan made the call to Glenda first. Then he hailed Tran and had him call Raven and Sasha over.

A few seconds ticked into the past before the speaker hissed and Raven said, "Dad?"

"No honey, it's Uncle Duncan. Your dad is driving. But I'm going to hold the walkie talkie and he's going to talk to you." He lifted his thumb off the Talk key.

"It's a two-way radio," corrected Raven. "Walkie talkies have longer range."

Duncan shrugged and held the radio in the airspace between him and Cade.

"Raven. This is Daddy." He paused for a moment to steer around a Z, a maneuver that caused Duncan's thumb to slide off the Talk key.

"Are you coming back now?" asked Raven as the channel cleared.

Grimacing, Duncan depressed the key.

"Yes, we are," answered Cade. "It's complicated though. Here's what I need you and Sasha to do. Is she listening in?"

Duncan relaxed his thumb.

"She's right here," said Raven.

Cade heard the teenager say, "Hi."

Skipping the formalities, he nodded to Duncan and said, "Do you have your learner's permit?"

Duncan lolled his head animatedly as he let off on the Talk key.

"I'm *fourteen*," shot Sasha. "I was supposed to get one next summer. But the *Rapture* had to happen and screw it all up for me."

Ignoring both the teen's snotty tone and her ongoing *Rapture made the dead rise* theory, Cade waited for Duncan to do his thing then said, "Next summer just arrived eight months early." While Tran and the girls listened, he rattled off detailed instructions.

Duncan mouthed, "Thumb's getting tired."

Finished, Cade said, "Did you get all that, girls?"

Though the connection with the base unit back in the compound was far from crystal clear, the exuberance evident in Raven and Sasha's tone when they accepted the task was unmistakable.

Chapter 54

Seeing a roadside sign with the universally recognized symbol indicating a series of switchbacks lay ahead, Cade eased off the pedal and tapped the brakes. "See anyone shadowing us back there?"

Duncan hunched over and peered into the side mirror. After a few seconds had elapsed, he said, "Just Taryn driving her truck like Danica Patrick."

Might as well be the woman herself, thought Cade as he muscled the F-650 through the final two opposing turns preceding the pair of quarry feeder roads.

"Snowmobile is still with us," declared Duncan.

"Yes it is," said Cade. "Unfortunately, it shifted and that's about *all* I can see."

On the left side of 39 the bullet-pocked sign marking the lower quarry road slid by. A tick later they passed by the overgrown road leading to the upper quarry.

Near the end of the long run of gradually descending S-curves, just prior to the two-lane straightening out, a woman's voice emanated from the liberated two-way radio. At first the signal was weak and garbled. Once the F-650 was out of the trees and tracking straight for the westering sun, they heard, clear as day, the same voice ask, "Is that you, Joy?"

Cade looked to Duncan, who was already wearing a puzzled expression.

"Think you can fake a woman's voice?"

Duncan made a face. Running a hand through his hair, he said, "Not without sounding like a Texan."

"Do your best," prompted Cade. "Just make sure to keep the channel locked open and cover the microphone grill when you're done saying your piece."

Duncan looked a question at Cade.

Cade said, "Just pretend you're Joy and tell Iris we're close."

Which wasn't far from the truth.

Back at the ambush site the engine noise of the first group of arriving vehicles had travelled all the way to Cade's hide from the far edge of town—eight to ten normal city blocks by his estimation. He recalled the rule of thumb was twenty city blocks to the mile. Which after doing the math in his head, converted to roughly four-tenths of a mile from the hide on the rise to Woodruff's northern limits. Call it half a mile, he decided.

Figuring that the trees lining the stretch of 39 dead ahead would act as a natural funnel and carry the engine noise faster and farther than a two-lane bisected by cross streets and dotted with buildings, he concluded that Iris had detected their approach from more than a mile out. Maybe two, if one considered that both the F-650 and the Raptor were not equipped with a typical dirt-hauler's motor and exhaust.

Next to Cade, Duncan cleared his throat and thumbed the button on the radio. In a choked falsetto he said, "We're almost there, Iris," and then kept the Talk button depressed.

With the channel the cannibals were using to contact Iris—and vice versa—locked out, Cade hoped to insert a wedge of confusion between the two parties. He noted where the needle hovered on the speedometer and performed a rough calculation based on the estimated distance to Iris's position on 39. Then he quickly dropped his gaze to the odometer and noted the mileage down to the tenth of a mile.

"Sometime in the next ninety seconds we're going to come into contact with Iris," he declared confidently.

"And you know this how?"

"Trust me," Cade said.

***

326

Duncan had been keeping the radio channel open with his thumb and pressing his palm to the microphone grill for just south of a full minute when he spotted far off in the distance what looked to him like a pile of clothing laying smack dab in the middle of the road. In the next beat the dark object stirred and grew arms and a head. Then, moving slow and deliberate, the strange-looking form twisted around and assumed a kneeling position. After a brief pause the form leaned forward, pushed up off the road, and staggered a few feet to the right of the dashed yellow centerline where it inexplicably froze in place.

"Think that's Iris?"

"Has to be," said Cade, confidently.

"Looks like she's injured," added Duncan.

"Or got bit and is in the process of turning."

Duncan looked sidelong at his friend. "Well, whatever the hell is going on, you're about ten or fifteen seconds from making a hood ornament out of her. You may want to deviate left a hair so we can roll her up and squeeze her for info."

Steering the rig to the left by a degree or two, Cade said, "There's nothing she can tell us that *we* don't already know."

Sweeping his gaze to the fore, Duncan saw that barely two hundred feet now separated the F-650 from the form wavering in the road. From this distance, he could see that its clothes were soiled and shredded in places. Also, one of the pants legs had ridden up to mid-calf exposing a horrible mud- and blood-caked wound. The softball-sized fissure was ringed by a tangle of frayed skin with shiny red muscle bulging from its center. Mind made up that the thing in the road was a live human and not a rotter, Duncan said, "Enlighten me then, Cade. What *do* we know?"

Cade put a finger in the air. Universal semaphore for wait one. He plucked the radio tuned to the group's channel from the center console and ordered Taryn to fall back a couple of truck lengths. Then, to curtail another one of Wilson's question and answer sessions, he set the radio aside and looked to Duncan. "*We* know that Adrian's gang have the patrol Tahoe Dregan gave

Ray. Therefore *we* know that they slaughtered the Thagons and also butchered the Bear River wood cutting crew for their meat."

"That's not much of a stretch," said Duncan. "Maybe Iris can tell us how many more people remain up north. How well they're armed. Where the weak link in their chain is so we can exploit it."

"I wouldn't trust a word she says," said Cade, glancing at Duncan. "I trust the map I found in the attic."

"The what?" asked Duncan, incredulous.

"I had my motives for keeping it to myself," he said. "Anyway ... I looked it over. And it shows the location of their main compound as well as where they set up their listening posts up and down the Bear River range."

As Cade returned his gaze to the road, Duncan saw the Delta operator's eyes narrow and noticed his squared-off jaw take on that damn granite set. Taking a cue from the sudden change, Duncan swung his gaze forward and saw that the form in the road was now less than three truck lengths away. In that snapshot in time he got a clear look at its facial features. Though streaked with dirt, the wide forehead, full cheeks, and thick lips were familiar to him. And instead of the usual jaundice-eyed, faraway stare of the dead, he detected in those eyes a measure of recognition which prompted him to blurt, "Stop the truck."

Cade moved the wheel to the right a hair. "What are you going to do, Duncan?"

"Make her pay for running Oliver down like a dog."

"I was wondering when you were going to put the pieces together," Cade shot. "Too much of a coincidence her showing up on the tail of all that had happened between Woodruff and Bear Lake."

As Cade's words were sinking in, Duncan felt the truck pick up speed. With both hands wrapped around the two-way radio and no way to brace for impact, the only thing he could do was trust the shoulder belt and watch Iris get exactly what she deserved. He saw the cannibal's eyes go wide and her mouth form a silent O. In the next beat, she was falling to her knees, both

328

arms thrust in front of her as if embracing fully what was to come.

At the last second, Cade pulled the wheel to the left and stepped on the brakes.

In the F-650's bed the snowmobile straightened out and with a bang snugged in tight to the rear of the cab. A beat later two thuds rang out as the Thagons' bodies followed suit.

In the passenger seat, Duncan lifted up off his seat and tracked the kneeling woman with his eyes as the truck skidded to a halt. After losing her behind the rear fender flares, he swung his gaze forward and picked her up again in the wing mirror. Throughout the entire evasive maneuver her arms had remained outstretched. Duncan saw that she was still assuming that pose and held a two-way radio in one hand.

In the Raptor, Taryn had reacted to Cade's calmly delivered instruction without pause. She had lifted her foot from the accelerator, tapped the brakes gently, and steered the pickup into the oncoming lane and watched the bigger Ford slowly pull away.

In the back seat, Lev had been oblivious to the call coming in over the radio. The sudden change in speed and direction also failed to register. He was focused solely on holding Jamie upright and maintaining constant pressure to the blood-soaked three-by-three squares of chemical-treated fabric covering up what was in danger of becoming a life-threatening wound.

Seeing the truck carrying Cade and Duncan abruptly steer into her lane and the brake lights flare red, Taryn slowed accordingly and steered her rig farther left until the tires on her side were tracing the white fog line. No sooner had the black truck stopped completely than the driver's side window motored down and Cade was waving her closer.

Pulling the Raptor alongside the larger truck, Taryn flicked her eyes to the rearview. *Nothing.* The road was clear all the way back to the last bend in the road.

Wilson's window seated into the full-open position at the same time Taryn was stopping the Raptor abreast of the other truck.

Face showing concern, Cade asked, "How is Jamie?"

"Hanging in there," Lev said from the back seat. "But we need to go."

"I need a radio and a roll of tape from the first aid kit."

Wilson scrambled to police up the items. As he did, he asked, "Is that her?"

"I think so," answered Cade truthfully.

Wilson placed his radio and a roll of white tape on Cade's upturned palm.

Singling out Lev, Cade said, "Get her to Glenda. Once she's stabilized you know what to do."

Wilson asked, "What are you going to do with *her*?"

"That's up to Duncan," answered Cade. Eyes locked with Wilson's, he nodded west down 39. "Now go."

Chapter 55

Cade watched the Raptor speed off to the west, dive into the turn ahead, and disappear from view. He regarded Duncan. "Has she moved?"

Still staring into the wing mirror, Duncan shook his head. "Not a muscle. What's the surgical tape for?"

"You tired of holding that channel open?"

Duncan nodded. "My thumb was already cramping from holding it down before."

Cade peeled off a foot-long strip of tape and tore it off with his teeth. Then he repeated the process and came away with a second piece barely two inches in length. Next, he thumbed a live 9mm round from one of the Glock's spare mags. Nodding at the radio in Duncan's hand, he handed the bullet and tape over. "Put the bullet lengthwise on the Talk button and then wrap the long strip around a couple of times so the channel stays open. Use the short strip to cover the microphone."

As he prepped the radio, Duncan said, "And Wilson's radio? What do we need that for?"

"You'll see when you get back from dealing with Iris."

Dealing with Iris, thought Duncan as he placed the taped-up radio in the center console cubby. He elbowed the door open and stepped to the road. Swinging his gaze right, he saw that Iris still hadn't lowered her arms. He began a slow walk in her direction, the .45 clearing holster before he reached the truck's bumper.

Keeping the muzzle trained center mass on Iris, he walked a counterclockwise arc away from the truck, stopping only once he was head on to her.

Her eyes were closed, that much was clear.

He said, "What the hell are you doing outside the wire?"

She made no response.

He thumbed back the .45's hammer. On the desolate run of road, the metallic *click* of it locking in place was loud in his ears. He said, "I've always had a soft spot in my heart for strays. Well, no more." He paused. "I know who you really are. Your name isn't Bridgett. It's Iris. Like the flower tattooed on your arm."

Her eyes snapped open. Then, as she lowered her arms, slowly her eyes tracked up and right and locked with his.

"North of Woodruff, the same day we found you back there"—he nodded east down 39—"you ran over a man on a bike with your car, didn't you?"

She blinked one time.

Duncan saw a tear roll from the corner of her eye and follow the established streaks in the dirt on her face. Then he noticed her pulped hand. It was jutting bones and beginning to palsy. For a couple of seconds, it thumped against her hip uncontrollably.

Finally, in a hoarse voice, she said, "I don't know what you're talking about."

"Eventually, you and your friends were going to *kill* our friend and *eat* him, weren't you?"

Her eyelids fluttered. Simultaneously, she looked up and to her left and said, "I told you the truth when you picked me up the other day. I ran out of gas trying to get to Huntsville."

"Tell me your name?"

Again, with the flutter and subtle eye roll, she said forcefully, "My name is Bridgett."

Seeing the signs for what they were—Iris engaging in wholesale deception—he squeezed the trigger.

The report was thunderous. It crashed across the road and flushed a dozen crows from a nearby copse of mature firs.

Cade watched the whole encounter unfold in the passenger-side wing mirror. He saw the lick of flame and the brass shell casing tumble through the air. The single mule kick folded Iris's upper torso over backward, leaving her legs still bent at the knee and her feet trapped under her ample backside. Even viewed from a distance as a reflection in the wing mirror, the smoking hole below the woman's sternum was crater-like in appearance. The impact from the speeding projectile left a six-inch gash in the threadbare shirt. Crimson tendrils spiraled outward from the wound and played connect the dots on the periphery with the blood droplets deposited there.

Moving slowly, as if he'd just emerged from a saloon throw down, Duncan holstered his pistol, bent at the waist, and dragged the limp body to the shoulder, where a nudge from his boot sent it rolling into the tall grass.

Cade saw Duncan retrieve Iris's radio from the road. Then the older man planted his hands on his hips and stared east down the length of 39.

Cade used the time to ready Wilson's radio. Finished, he swung his gaze to the rearview just in time to see Duncan turn a one-eighty and begin the lonely trudge back to the truck.

Cade dropped the transmission into gear.

Duncan reached the open door and paused there looking into the cab over the top of his bifocals.

Cade handed the jerry-rigged radio toward the open door. He said, "Hide this face up in the grass right next to the shoulder."

"Our very own unmanned listening post," noted Duncan as he hinged over and secreted the radio behind a baseball-sized tuft of grass.

Nodding, Cade said, "And it should give us a few minutes heads up that the motorcade is coming."

"*If* it's coming."

"Get in," prompted Cade. "We're pushing our luck sitting here."

Hand shaking from the adrenaline still coursing through his body, Duncan gripped the grab bar and hauled himself into the passenger seat. Emitting a pained sigh, he dragged the door shut and pressed his head against the headrest.

Cade noted the time down to the second on his Suunto. Matting the pedal, he heard the F-650's engine roar transmitted over the open channel of the roadside radio. "You did the right thing," he said. "We've got to stop leaving loose ends."

"I already owned my part in that," drawled Duncan. "As for doing the right thing … guess I'll find the truth to that when I get to the Pearly Gates." He paused for a tick then went on, "Hell, Iris was number five today. Six if you pin the woman at the Thagons' place on me."

"That's not on you," insisted Cade. "She committed suicide." He cast a quick glance to the rearview. Saw the black raptors floating from the trees on wings spread wide. A beat later, coinciding with the F-650's engine growl fading from the two-way's speaker, the crows' cawing was back and coming in loud and clear over the open channel.

Cade noted the elapsed time on his Suunto then flicked his eyes to the speedometer needle. Working the calculation in his head, he took one last look at the black mass no doubt already digging sharp beaks and claws into their newfound meal.

Oblivious of this, Duncan lamented, "I caused that woman to fall through the ceiling, though."

Cade took his eyes from the opportunistic carrion feeders and steered the truck into a long left to right sweeper.

"She was dead the moment she swore allegiance to Adrian." He pushed the Ford's speed to double the limit as trees crowded in on both sides of the long straightaway. After putting a full mile behind them in a little under a minute, he braked hard and threw the rig into another gradual left to right sweeper that ended in a wedge of daylight where the underbrush thinned and the trees backed off the snaking guardrails.

Coming out of the turn the transmission geared down and 39 straightened out again and began a gradual climb to the next sweeping turn a quarter of a mile distant. On the left, beyond the white guardrail, the grass-covered ground fell away at a steep angle. On the right was a head-high wall of red dirt wearing a mohawk of scrub brush the color of muddy water. The earthen berm hosted a phalanx of juvenile aspen growing up through a footing of verdant ferns. It followed the laser-straight run of road for a thousand feet before rounding off and again merging with the state route's undulating shoulder.

Where the two-lane started off to the left at the top of the rise, Cade could see a roadside sign planted in the dirt next to the guardrail. Barely visible behind the white state route sign was the box-like roofline and squat turret mounted atop the desert-tan National Guard Humvee.

Letting his gaze wander both sides of the road, Duncan raised the radio to his mouth and announced their arrival.

Still giddy from being selected for the very important mission outside of the wire, Raven closed the middle gate and, with a spring in her step, hustled back to the idling Toyota 4Runner. Closing the door behind her, she said, "Step on it," and smiled wide.

"I don't know why you're smiling," Sasha said sharply. "This doesn't mean we're done with dish duty."

Raven frowned.

"There was nobody else in the compound," declared Sasha. "I betcha if Max could drive he would be in this seat instead of me."

Hearing his name uttered, Max poked his head between the front seats and received a scratch behind the ears from Raven. She said, "No, Sasha. My dad wants you to learn to drive. He wouldn't have said it if he didn't think you have it in you. Just this morning he told me that he wants both of us to start pulling our own weight. Doesn't mean we're freed from daily dish duty, though. You're right about that." She paused for a beat as the hidden gate came into view at the end of the long straight. "Gotta admit," she added, "sneaking out without telling anybody where we were going *was* pretty stupid."

As if contradicting Raven's positive assessment of the situation, one of the SUV's front tires met a pothole. Which in turn caused the wheel to jerk from Sasha's grip and the rig to shimmy wildly and slew sideways on the washboard gravel road.

"Happens to Taryn all the time," said Raven reassuringly. Ignoring Sasha's sour look, she pushed the bag of medical supplies in the footwell aside with her boot, reached down, and picked her mom's rifle up off the floorboard.

Having regained control of the wheel, Sasha asked, "Think there will be any rotters at the gate?"

Raven shook her head. "There weren't any when Glenda and Seth went through."

"You can call Tran if you want and ask him what he sees on the cameras."

"I got it," said Raven, patting the stubby black rifle trapped between her knees.

Sasha jumped as a thick branch raked the 4Runner on her side.

***

There were no dead things roaming 39 near the hidden gate. Using every last ounce of strength Raven was able to open the gate wide enough to allow Sasha to drive the Toyota through. However, closing the gate after was another story. She needed Sasha's assistance to get it seated correctly and looking like the rest of its surroundings instead of a garden-variety steel gate festooned with both real and imitation foliage.

***

The drive east to where the Raptor and Humvee were parked was short and uneventful. Though Raven hadn't been paying close attention, she guessed they had traveled a mile, maybe two at the most.

Sasha was pulling the Toyota to the shoulder a few feet shy of the squat military vehicle when Raven caught sight of the reason they'd been given a list of supplies to pull from storage and rush to Glenda outside the wire.

Lev and Glenda were kneeling beside a person laid out on the road behind the Humvee. That it was a woman was undisputable. The white shirt underneath the unbuttoned camo blouse was red with blood and adhering to her breasts.

336

Sasha fumbled with the transmission for a second before finally getting it set to Park. "Is that Taryn?" she asked.

"I don't think so," said Raven. "The hair's the right color, but way too long." Bag of supplies in one hand, carbine in the other, she elbowed open her door and stepped to the shoulder.

Sasha remained behind the wheel with the engine running.

As Raven closed her door, she looked around the pillar and said, "You coming?"

Sasha nodded, pried her fingers from the wheel, and stilled the engine.

The familiar growl of the F-650's engine reached Raven's ears at about the same time she saw Wilson and Taryn emerging from behind the Raptor. Guns in hand and wearing serious expressions they split up, Wilson making a bee line for Sasha, and Taryn going forward to meet the approaching vehicle.

Raven rushed to Glenda's side and set the bag on the road next to her. "Everything is in there." She cast her gaze to Jamie and looked her over from head to toe. The only obvious injury was to her face on the right side where Lev was holding a bandage of some sort.

Without acknowledging Raven or Sasha, Glenda tore into the bag and came out with a bottle labeled *Iodine*, a small tube tapered at one end, and a stainless-steel hemostat.

Raven cringed when Lev lifted up the skin that used to be Jamie's cheek. She felt her salivary glands go into overdrive when he tugged the underlying bandage up. Upon hearing the wet sound it made and seeing the corded muscle and bone the action revealed, her jaw locked open. With the pale, half-moon flap of skin jiggling in Lev's shaking hand like a slice of bologna, Glenda clamped down on something out of sight with the scissor-like tool and then poured the dark red iodine into the wound.

Having seen way too much, Raven backed away a couple of paces, spun around and dropped to her knees on the road. Simultaneously, she pitched forward and a torrent of hot bile spattered against the cold blacktop. The next thing she remembered was someone pulling her hair back from her face and helping her to stand. She dry-heaved once then leveled her eyes at the person who had one gloved hand on her elbow and the other bracing her hip.

"Daddy," she said, the drawn-out word bookended by a pair of wet burps.

Seeing the bandage on Raven's hand, Cade said, "What happened there?"

"I punched a mirror," she admitted, wiping a strand of drool from her lip.

"Mom?"

Raven nodded. Her eyes were moist. Cade couldn't decide if it was caused by emotion or a result of her having just purged everything from her stomach.

She looked him square in the face. "Is Jamie going to be OK?"

Inspecting the bandaged hand, he said, "Did Glenda wrap this up for you?"

Again, Raven nodded.

"Then Jamie is in good hands," he said, meeting her gaze. "Because this is a damn fine job she did on your injured paw."

This brought a half-smile to Raven's face.

Cade looked past the Humvee and regarded the distant bend in the road. "Bad people are coming." Slowly bringing his gaze back to Raven, he added, "I need you and Sasha to get back to the compound right now. Get there and go to the dry storage. Don't unlock the door until you hear my voice."

Raven nodded. She said, "I forgot and left your helmet in the Toyota."

"That's OK. Thank you for remembering to bring it, sweetie. Have Wilson deliver it to Duncan." He hugged her and kissed her forehead. Then he handed over her carbine and shooed her along to the 4Runner where Sasha was already behind the wheel and engaged in conversation with Wilson. He watched until she was aboard, then upped the volume on Wilson's radio and strode off to reposition the vehicles.

Chapter 56

Having already pulled the pair of pickups a dozen yards farther west on 39, Cade hopped behind the wheel of the Humvee and started the motor. With Duncan walking alongside the multi-ton vehicle, Cade backed it off of the hill's apex and let gravity pull it down the lee side until he figured that all but the very top of the turret and pair of whip antennas would be hidden behind the military crest of the hill.

He killed the noisy diesel engine and relinquished his seat to Duncan.

As Cade was dogging down the antennas sticking up from the Humvee's rear corners, Lev approached him. In one hand was the MSR rifle. In the other was a two-way radio. They discussed the best place for Lev to set up his overwatch; then Cade asked how Jamie was doing.

"The QuikClot bandage stopped most of the bleeding," said Lev. "Still, it burned the hell out of her cheek."

"Glenda's done with her?"

Lev nodded. "She cleaned the wound and put in a few sutures. Finished it all off around the edges with *Super Glue*." He paused and moved his gaze from Cade to Duncan then back to the former. "She wants to stay and fight."

Holding the Humvee door open with his knee, Duncan inclined his head and asked, "How is she doing mentally?"

"As good as can be expected for a person who just took a bullet fragment to the face," replied Lev.

"Can she see to shoot?" asked Duncan.

Lev jumped on the radio and asked Glenda to send Jamie over. He looked to Duncan and said, "Ask her yourself if you're so concerned."

Jamie appeared from behind the Raptor a few seconds later. She was carrying the bolt-action rifle and a bottled water. The right side of her face was swollen and mostly obscured by a white bandage tinged reddish-orange by the iodine Glenda had so liberally applied.

"Duncan wants to ask you something," said Lev, hitching his brow.

Stopping beside the partially open door, she said, "What?" The word came out sounding more like *wood*.

Duncan made a peace sign with his right hand and held it up for Jamie to see. "How many fingers am I holding up?"

In response, she flipped him the bird. "How many do *you* see?"

Acting as if he didn't see the upthrust middle finger, he said, "Sure you don't want to go back with Glenda and put your feet up for a spell?"

Jamie's eyes narrowed. She said slowly and carefully, "Don't you *fucking* patronize me. I just took a piece of lead to the face."

In a show of surrender, Duncan raised his hands off the wheel. "So what do you want?"

"I want to get even with the people who did this"—she gestured to her face with the bottle—"and I'm not letting some wannabe father figure stand in the way of me achieving that goal."

While Duncan was getting his ass chewed, Cade had been standing beside the rig and glassing the distant bend in the road with the Steiners. To save his friend any more humiliation, he looked over at Jamie and asked her nicely if she would like to accompany Lev into the woods.

Just the words she wanted to hear. She about-faced and began to stalk off in Lev's direction.

"Wait," Cade called. He reached into his pocket and came out with a couple of oblong pills. "Pop these. You'll thank me for it later."

She reached out hesitantly. "What are they?"

340

He dropped them into her palm. The creases there were still caked with blood which made the white pills look large in her hand. "Grunt candy," he said, pointing to his mostly healed left ankle. "Ibuprofen. Eight hundred milligrams each."

After swallowing the pills dry, she said, "Thanks," and hustled to catch Lev.

"Same rules of engagement as before," Cade called after the pair. Then he turned and addressed a red-faced Duncan. "What do you think?"

"I think Lev has his hands full. You think she's scary now … just wait until she has that scar-faced scowl down pat."

Cade hung his head. "Not Jamie. I was talking about the distance and angle of deflection to the bend in the road," he clarified.

"It's a Browning," drawled Duncan. "What's the distance … a quarter mile or so?"

"To the turn—give or take a few—should be about four hundred and fifty yards."

"*Sheeit*," said Duncan. "The old gal's not even breaking a sweat at that range. She could probably reach out and touch Woodruff if those trees weren't in the way. Just let 'em come until you see the whites of their eyes. Then let her eat."

Cade glanced over to see Lev and Jamie pushing into the forest off to the right of the Humvee. He swung his gaze back and said, "What if the column stops short before all their rigs are exposed?"

"We cross that bridge when we get to it."

Cade passed the binoculars back then clambered aboard and took his spot behind the cupola-mounted heavy machine gun. Grabbing the fifty's grips, he peered through the circular sight and trained the weapon on the first visible point at the bottom of the hill. From there he simulated strafing the entire length of the road by slowly walking the barrel along the solid yellow centerline to the point where it curled left and disappeared from view. To test the turret's range of motion, he popped the locking lever by his right knee into the down position and grabbed hold of the crank handle by his left knee. A few turns counterclockwise started the vented barrel swinging around to the right. Reversing the process, he swung the Ma Deuce over to the left shoulder and then brought it back on line with the center of 39. Satisfied with the commanding fields of fire the high ground afforded, he dropped down into the turret, leaving just the top of his head showing, and surveyed the Humvee's left and right flanks through the opposing pairs of rectangular windows. Though the ballistic glass distorted everything a bit due to its thickness and was spotted with dirt (a problem easily rectified), it would do just fine in the bullet-stopping department.

As if he had been reading Cade's mind, Duncan said, "Like shooting fish in a barrel."

"We've definitely got the advantage," agreed Cade.

"What about the Kids ... Wilson and Taryn?" asked Duncan. He had donned Cade's tactical bump helmet and left the straps dangling by his cheeks.

"They've seen and done enough killing today to last them a month of Sundays."

"Sending them back with Glenda?"

"They're taking her and Seth back in the Raptor," said Cade as he started counting the .50 caliber rounds Phillip had so dutifully linked by hand weeks ago.

The helmet straps danced and bounced off of Duncan's graying beard as he nodded agreeably. "Good call," he said, dropping his gaze to the center hump on his right. Positioned there in a neat line smallest to biggest were three two-way radios and the single long-range handheld CB taken off the woman at the Thagons' home. The first radio was tuned to the same channel as the radio Duncan had positioned by the roadside ditch to the east. It was broadcasting a steady stream of white noise interrupted now and again by caws from a murder of crows hanging out somewhere nearby.

The second radio was powered on and locked on the channel Iris had been using to communicate with her people. Since freeing up the channel a few minutes ago, the radio had been silent.

Radio number three was a Motorola handheld tuned to the same channel shared by all of the Eden survivors as well as Tran, who was manning the base station back at the compound.

The long-range CB was powered on but hadn't broken squelch since earlier when Adrian's shrill voice had emanated from its speaker as she berated her followers.

Looking up at Cade, Duncan asked, "How long you figure it's going to take them to get here?"

Finished counting the linked .50 caliber bullets, Cade ducked into the cupola. "They'll be moving slow," he said. "Being extra cautious at every blind turn and long straightaway."

"Which is exactly what we have in front of the compound entrance. Why here instead of there?"

There was a brief starter whine followed by a low rumble as the Raptor's engine turned over. Cade and Duncan turned and watched the white pickup swing a wide left. A hand poked out the passenger window and waved at them as the truck motored toward the next heavily wooded stretch of 39. A handful of seconds passed, the brake lights flared red, and then the Raptor was swallowed up in shadow.

Cade looked at the sky above the trees. It was a dark shade of gray shot through with bars of red and orange and yellow. One glance at his Suunto told him the sun was just minutes from sliding behind the curvature of the earth well beyond the distant Wasatch Range.

As the engine noise died to nothing, Duncan repeated the hanging question.

"It's complicated," Cade said quietly, his hand going to the necklace and then finding the wedding band resting on his tactical vest.

"Pretty vague, my man," pressed Duncan.

"I chose this spot because I didn't want to set up beside the graveyard and have to stare at Brook's final resting place as dusk gathered."

Duncan began to deliver a few words of empathy, but was preempted by engine noises broadcast from radio number one.

Chapter 57

Duncan snatched up Wilson's radio and rolled the volume to the stop. He reached his right arm back and held the radio, speaker facing up, in the airspace between the middle console and the framework supporting the cupola.

A second after the faint rumble interrupted Cade and Duncan's conversation, the noisy birds on the other end went nuts, cawing and squawking, the volume and pitch of their calls increasing in conjunction with the approaching rumble of internal combustion engines. In the next beat, an explosion of sound Cade took to be feathered wings beating the air came from the speaker as the birds relinquished their newfound meal and took flight. He looked at his Suunto, noting the time down to the second.

They listened closely to the sounds on the open channel.

Thirty seconds after the birds took flight, the growl of engines under load lessened. A second or two later there was a squeal of brakes and the low-end engine noises gave way to the steady ticking of lifters and subtle whirring of serpentine belts and occasional whine of power steering pumps moving static tires against dry pavement.

Cade said, "They're loitering at the bend."

Duncan said nothing.

Ten seconds after Cade's proclamation, gears gnashed and an engine revved. For a few more seconds the noises grew louder and then the low rumble of engines at idle were the dominate sound.

Duncan broke the silence. "Sending a point vehicle ahead."

"I concur," said Cade.

345

Barely ten additional seconds had slipped into the past when the engine sounds changed and clearly the convoy was once again on the move.

The time elapsed between the procession getting going again and the engine sounds and exhaust notes finally fading away to nothing was forty-five seconds on the nose. During the first fifteen seconds, from the subtle rise and dip in volume from each distinct engine, Cade determined that four additional vehicles had passed in front of the two-way radio.

Shifting his gaze from the road to Cade in the turret, Duncan said, "Including the point vehicle, I count five total."

"Roger that," said Cade.

"How fast do you gather they get going on the straightaway?"

Cade worked the equation, taking into account the distance from bend to bend and the time it took for the sounds from the passing convoy to diminish to nothing. "Ballpark, twenty miles per," he said. "That gives us six to ten minutes before they get to the start of the incline."

"There's two turns between here and there," proffered Duncan. "We have to assume they're going to pause before each one so the point vehicle can perform another recon."

Duncan snatched up the Motorola and passed along the news, upping the estimate from six to ten minutes.

"Roger that," replied Lev.

Back at the compound, actively monitoring both the video coming in over the closed-circuit cameras and the shared radio traffic, Tran replied, "The girls and Max are safe and sound inside the wire. I'm watching them *park* the truck."

In his mind's eye Cade saw the jostling likely taking place as Sasha struggled to park the SUV among the handful of vehicles remaining in the depleted motor pool. Instead of answering verbally, he clicked the Talk button one time to indicate he had a solid copy.

***

346

Seven minutes into their wait for the point vehicle to arrive, Cade turned off the radio tuned to the same channel as the one Duncan had planted just yards from Iris's corpse. Though he usually liked the mountain birds and had even named his daughter for them, the noise they made as they fed was beginning to make his skin crawl. And though he couldn't make out individual sounds, his imagination conjured up an audio track to go along with the macabre mental movie in which the birds were actively burrowing into dark, empty sockets to get to the plump treat within. He was still visualizing the beady eyes rolling back as the blood-slickened beaks pistoned in and out of the dead woman's skull when the sound of approaching engines dragged him back to the lonely stretch of Route 39 deep in rural Utah.

Instinctively, he ducked deeper into the cupola, hands on the Ma Deuce's vertical grips. Locking his gaze on the bend where the lead vehicle would eventually emerge, he said a silent prayer that when it did the shadows hanging over the road would conceal the Humvee from view.

The first clue that the order of travel in Adrian's convoy had been changed was the blue-white aura lighting up the ground-hugging scrub and guardrail to the right of the distant curve. This was confirmed when the blacked-out Excursion nosed around the corner and the first hundred or so feet of 39 were bombarded by piercing blue cones of light beamed from both the quad HID headlights up front and the half-dozen lights mounted on a bar riding atop the cab. As the towering SUV slowed and came to a full stop, Duncan said, "I'd have killed those Klieg lights on that rolling lighthouse until I really needed them."

Cade said, "I think they're hoping to ratchet up the intimidation factor."

"X gets a square," said Duncan. "And they're framing the windshield wonderfully for you."

Cade made no reply. He was wondering what the occupants were doing behind that blacked-out rectangle. Were they arguing about turning around and coming back this way during the day? *Likely.* They'd already proven to be mostly inept and prone to cowardice. Was the garishly painted van still bringing up the rear of the convoy? More importantly, if it was still tagging along, was Adrian inside and currently receiving a situation report? Cade hoped so. For that would spare him from having to go north to perform the much-needed decapitation.

Lastly, given the fact that the Thagons' house had been stripped of all the gear and weapons they had collected from National Guard posts early on in the apocalypse, were the passengers in the lead vehicle presently scanning the road through night vision goggles or just binoculars?

After pondering the former question for a second, he ruled out that night vision technology was in play. If so, they would be traveling with lights extinguished. From years of experience going up against enemies in all types of conditions, the edge one gained from seeing prior to being seen trumped every form of intimidation short of bringing on station an AC-130H Spectre gunship complete with Gatling guns, Bofors cannon, and 105 howitzer a'blazing.

After arriving at this conclusion, Cade's confidence was further bolstered by the two things besides the element of surprise that were in their favor. First off was the knowledge that the trees behind the Humvee, which were completely blocking any light from the westering sun, would serve to soften any hard lines breaking the horizon. Then there was the fact that the scrub and dirt beside the road was nearly the same color as the paint on the rig. And a quick glance confirmed that both were changing in accordance with one another as darkness descended on the valley.

Beyond that, he was praying that the continual starting and stopping without being engaged by hostiles had sufficiently worn down the point driver to the extent that hubris was edging out caution. Like hounds on the scent of quarry and in a complete bloodlust after seeing their brethren slaughtered, he knew that they were likely aware of how close they were getting to their prey and wanted nothing more than for them to cut the recon short and bomb down the straightaway into his kill zone.

Only time would tell.

He ran a hand over the linked .50 caliber rounds, jingling them a bit in their box which was attached to the left of the weapon.

During the handful of seconds the big rig sat blocking the road with its diesel engine idling discordantly, the east/west swathe of sky overhead changed from dark gray to a light-swallowing shade of purple.

With twilight in these parts a very short-lived affair, Cade willed the convoy forward.

Chapter 58

A full thirty seconds passed before the Excursion started moving again. The rattle clatter of the diesel picked up and a black cloud roiled from the driver's side exhaust pipe. Ten more seconds elapsed as the point truck crept forward.

It was a full minute from the time the Excursion entered the scene and the trees flanking the curve behind it were again being bathed in the ghastly blue-white glow. A half beat after the Excursion vacated the loiter spot, its diesel exhaust note was drowned out as the rest of the vehicles made their grand entrance. The pair of black Suburbans were in the two and three position and racing to catch up with the Excursion. Tucked into the four position and falling behind was the patrol Tahoe. And lastly, bringing up the rear with a two- or three-car-length following distance, the black and red A-Team van crept slowly around the far bend, its headlight wash cutting the darkening state route into tiny wedge-shaped slices.

Duncan caught himself unconsciously ducking his head below the top edge of the steering wheel. Straightening up, he grabbed a radio and let everyone listening know that the enemy vehicles were on the move again. As the convoy rounded the curve he gave a play by play of what he was seeing. Once all five vehicles were committed to the straightaway, he signed off with a reminder for Lev and Jamie—more so for the latter since she was so fired up after being shot—to hold fire until Cade opened up with the big gun.

A handful of seconds after the van cut the corner, the unthinkable happened. Or, as Cade was wont to say, Mr. Murphy inserted himself into the equation.

The gunshot-like sound that emanated from somewhere near the middle of the procession was sharp and not all too unlike the report from a Glock or Beretta. In the blink of an eye, it affected the ambush in two ways.

First, assuming she was taking fire, Jamie instinctively thrust her finger into her rifle's trigger guard and squeezed off a shot of her own.

In the Humvee, Duncan jabbed his thumb down on the Talk key and blurted, "*Backfire. That was just a vehicle backfire.*"

Too late. He heard the crack of the long gun discharging in the woods somewhere off his right shoulder. Muttering an expletive, he dropped the radio between his legs and reached for the ignition start lever.

Down on the road, still trying to determine the true source of the first report, the driver in the Excursion saw the wing window to his left spider and without pause ducked down and matted the pedal to escape the kill zone.

Hearing the backfire and near simultaneous crack of the premature shot, Cade yelled "*Engaging!*" and depressed the Ma Deuce's stamped-steel thumb paddles.

A harsh vibration coursed through the Humvee as the heavy machine gun spit a dozen rounds downrange. After crossing the distance travelling nearly three thousand feet per second, the thumb-sized hunks of hurtling lead found their mark in the A-Team van, punching the windshield in and leaving fist-sized holes stitched horizontally in the sheet metal from the driver's side door to mid-chassis where they walked vertically and then traversed the roof in a ragged diagonal line.

Cade let up on the paddles, silencing the booming reports and ending the tinkle of metal belt links and spent brass impacting all around his feet. He saw the van's headlights sweep across the two-lane as it slewed left, clipping the Tahoe's rear quarter in the process. And though there was a low buzzing in his ears from the hammering of the Ma Deuce, the squealing of tires and resulting crunch of metal still registered.

With the Browning silenced momentarily, the low rumble and vibration of the diesel engine idling in the Humvee underneath him became evident. Also, in between the sharp cracks of Jamie's rifle discharging somewhere to his right, he picked out the soft reports of the suppressed MSR spitting lead. In the time it took Cade to acquire his second target—three seconds at most—all order was disintegrating where the convoy was concerned.

Propelled by the impact from behind, the patrol Tahoe surged forward and then listed hard right when both passenger-side tires jumped the shoulder and carved deep furrows into the roadside ditch.

As the Tahoe continued to roll forward while scraping against the earthen berm, the A-Team van hit the guardrail nearly head on and came to a sudden grinding halt, its headlights and engine cutting out simultaneously.

In the middle of the column the second Suburban cut left in what Cade guessed was a poorly thought-out attempt at conducting the first leg of a three-way turn.

And finally coming into Cade's sights, the point vehicle was zigging and zagging and nearing the original spot in the road he had wanted to start the engagement.

Leading the Excursion by half a truck-length, Cade waited until its front tires turned away from the guardrail and the rig was tracking toward the earthen berm before depressing the paddles. The bullets struck the slab-sided vehicle at an oblique angle, starting a geyser of steam from the engine compartment and shredding both thin-skinned doors on the driver's side.

With the pebbled glass from the destroyed windows tumbling and bouncing and glittering blue in the Suburban's headlight wash, the Excursion, moving much faster than the trailing vehicles, hit the berm at a forty-five-degree angle and travelling well over thirty miles per hour. However, instead of spearing into the dirt or being redirected back to the shoulder, the SUV's massive off-road tires and long travel suspension absorbed the impact, which in turn allowed the rig to summit the sloping wall.

No sooner was the Excursion straddling the thin strip of scrub-covered soil atop the berm than gravity and Newton's law and the top-heaviness of the vehicle, all working together, was dragging it back to earth—roof first.

Cade saw flames lick from the undercarriage up front, twin rooster tails of red dirt arcing away from the free-spinning passenger side tires, and a woman ejected forcefully through an open door.

The small form cartwheeled rag-doll-like through space ahead of the still-moving vehicle.

From all four corners of the Excursion's partially flattened roof, sparks shot horizontally across the road.

The body struck the asphalt ahead of the vehicle, bounced once, then ended up slithering limply down the two-lane for another twenty feet before coming to rest face-up, spread-eagled and unmoving.

After raking the overturned SUV with another short ten-round burst, Cade brought the Browning online with the nearest of the two Suburbans. The damage his compatriots had already wreaked on it and the occupants was immediately obvious. The windshield was spidered, the meandering web-like cracks interconnected by a trio of small, puckered holes. The driver was clutching his throat and bucking against a taut shoulder belt. Blood, black and shiny in the failing light, was pulsing between his fingers. On his face was an expression that could only be construed as shocked disbelief.

A millisecond after setting eyes on the macabre sight, Cade saw two things happen in quick succession. First, a single round fired from the silenced MSR snapped the driver's head back, ceasing the man's struggle with the seatbelt and sending his body into a violent death spasm. Then, before the body up front had stopped quivering, someone in the back of the Suburban stuck a rifle barrel through a six-inch gap in the blacked-out window and opened fire.

The star-shaped muzzle flash drew Cade's attention; he panned the Browning right and hunched over the weapon.

Well-aimed bullets crackled over the cupola. Then a pair found their mark, impacting the cupola's top edge with hollow thunks.

"If you can't play nice, you die," said Cade, caressing the paddle triggers ever so lightly.

At once, the muzzle flashes stopped and a human form enveloped in shadow was thrown backward as the window glass and driver's side passenger door bore the full force of the new salvo.

Knowing that counting rounds fired by a weapon with such a high cyclic rate was a task not even Charlie Babbitt of *Rain Man* fame could accomplish with one hundred percent accuracy, Cade added a ten-round buffer to the fifteen he'd just fired into the Suburban and combined those with the running tally in his head. He quickly subtracted the accumulated spent rounds from his starting count and, considering the damage doled out by the venerable weapon, came up with a number he could live with.

Seventy rounds left. More than enough to tie up these loose ends.

As if reading Cade's mind, Duncan called up, "You're down to about sixty rounds."

Incredulous, Cade said, "How'd you come up with that number?"

"I used to be really good at counting cards."

"Sixty it is," conceded Cade as he walked his gaze and the Browning's muzzle the length of the column.

With one vehicle fully engulfed in flames, and three more shot to hell and unmoving, only the Tahoe was still a viable threat. It was in the process of jockeying back and forth in an attempt to extricate itself from the trailing vehicles when Cade raked it front to back and back to front with a sustained twenty-round burst.

Feeling the warmth radiating up from the spent brass casings crowding his boots, Cade banged on the hood and bellowed, "Drive!"

Chapter 59

The Excursion was burning and the Tahoe just beginning to catch fire when the Humvee made the flat and coasted to a stop. Cade saw the Tahoe's rear passenger door hinge open and a person dressed in all black and brandishing what looked to him to be some kind of light machine gun stepped onto the road. Backlit by orange and red flames, making out much more than the individual's intent was next to impossible. Feeling nothing but hatred for the waste of skin, Cade let loose with what he hoped would be only a five-round burst—anything more would be overkill, and an unnecessary waste of ammo.

The bullets hit the form center mass, picked it up off its feet, and sent it flying head first into the rear quarter of the now bullet-riddled SUV.

The person in black hadn't made a sound. Just folded at the waist for a split second and seemed to leap backwards with a dexterity usually reserved for the hero in a cheesy late night Kung Fu movie. But Cade knew better. The cannibal was dead. One less loose end. And it felt kind of good. Which, surprisingly, didn't bother him one bit. For if rage was one of the seven stages of grief, he was going to embrace it and let it fuel him until every last threat to him, Raven, and the others was erased from the face of the earth.

Duncan said, rather tongue in cheek, "Tango down."

Cade made no comment as he kept the still-smoking weapon trained on the Tahoe.

"Want to dismount here?"

Cade ducked down into the turret so Duncan could hear him over the engine and transmission noises. "Take us closer. I want to assess the damage." As the truck began to move, he heard Lev come on over the radio and report that he saw nothing moving in or around the disabled vehicles.

Duncan glanced up at Cade.

Cade said, "Doesn't mean they're all dead."

Duncan said, "Roger that," and brought the Humvee to a complete stop a dozen feet from the woman who had been ejected when the lead vehicle rolled over. "Want me to get on the Deuce?"

"Not if I'm anywhere downrange," replied Cade. "Wouldn't want to catch a stray round."

"You have plates under that vest?"

"Affirmative," said Cade, as he climbed down from the vehicle.

"M4 or Saiga?"

After a second of thought, Cade said, "Give me the Saiga."

Duncan opened the door and passed out the weapon.

Cade said, "Cover me with the carbine. And be sure to keep one eye on the van. No telling if anyone is alive in back of the thing."

"Roger that," said Duncan. "Eyes peeled and frosty." He hailed the pair on overwatch with the radio, telling them to cover Cade as he checked the wreckage for survivors. Before signing off he told Lev to not hesitate to speak up if he saw anything move.

"A blade of grass?" quipped Lev.

"*Anything*," stressed Duncan. "If a mouse farts downwind from us, I want to know about it."

"Copy that."

Cade hefted the black shotgun. He liked its solid feel. He worked the action. Spotting a shell in the breach, he ejected the drum magazine, inspected the load, and then reseated it in the well.

"You've got twenty left in the drum and one in the pipe."

"All slugs, right?" confirmed Cade.

"Like I said … one and all."

Cade flicked off the Saiga's safety and approached the unmoving body. Before he made it three steps closer, he could feel the heat coming off the burning vehicle warming his entire left side. Which in turn made him wholly aware of the effect the evening chill was having on the rest of his body.

Throwing a shiver, he thumbed on the tactical light attached to the shotgun and parked the white cone of light on the prostrate form. At first glance it looked as if the woman had lain down face first and was taking a quick nap.

He nudged the body with his toe. *Nothing.* Confident she was no immediate threat, he knelt down, wormed the fingers on one hand into her matted hair, and plucked her head off the ground. Everything moved real easily. Too easily. There was total range of motion. Like *barn owl* range of motion. Which wasn't natural. Catching a glimpse of her shredded face made him remember wrecking his bike as a kid and ending up with skinned knees and elbows. "Street pizza" is what he and his friends had called those kinds of wounds. This woman was lucky, he decided. Looked like her neck was broken well before her face acted as landing gear for her brutal return to earth.

"Dead," he called back.

He walked as close as he dared to the burning Excursion and went to one knee and eyed the vehicle's interior. Or what was left of it. Fire had already consumed the headliner and tops of the seats. Hanging upside down from their lap belts, the driver and front seat passenger were both dead and slowly cooking. Due to the crushed-in roof, both bodies were bent over sideways with their arms raised as if frantically trying to ward off the inevitable.

After skirting the Excursion's front bumper, Cade stopped, bent low, and performed a turkey peek around the passenger-side front fender. All he saw were pockets of darkness and long, dancing shadows. He swung the Saiga around the fender and put some light on the subject. For as far as his beam could reach (nearly the length of the earthen berm), where he figured to see a person waiting in ambush, he saw only fields of sparkling glass and pooled oil and water.

Moving on to the first Suburban, Cade found the driver staring straight ahead, eyes devoid of life. The man was in nearly the same position as when Cade first spied him and still clutching his neck which was awash in blood.

The passenger was a different story. She was still alive, but fading rapidly from blood loss and a noisy, sucking chest wound. Eyes darting about and lips moving a mile a minute, she reached one hand up and batted at the airbag draped over her lap.

Cade snugged the Saiga to his shoulder and settled the sights between the woman's roving eyes. "Live by the sword"—he squeezed the trigger and held it briefly—"die by the sword." He felt another tingle of satisfaction as the automatic shotgun bucked blindingly fast against his shoulder. He felt nothing as the three slugs caved in the cannibal's face and sent her upper body crashing violently against the door pillar. She was already forgotten to Cade as her body slumped against her seatbelt and greasy clumps of pulped detritus started calving from what remained of her face.

Lips drawing back into a snarl, Cade tracked the muzzle around and drew a bead on the backseat occupants who he quickly learned were shredded from having caught the full brunt of at least half-a-dozen .50 caliber rounds.

The five occupants of the second Suburban were bloodied and sprawled across their seats. Only the driver—albeit nearly decapitated—was somewhat upright, having been restrained by his shoulder belt.

Low moans were coming from the backseat area. To silence them, Cade poked the Saiga's muzzle between the front seat headrest and B-pillar and let loose a six-round salvo into the passenger compartment.

The moaning ceased.

Cade moved on.

Three cleared, two to go.

Padding past the burning Tahoe, he saw that both the driver and passenger had been killed by smaller caliber rounds. After seeing nothing moving in the smoke-filled passenger compartment behind the melting front seats, he let his gaze settle on the dismount. Once a strapping man of about forty, he had been nearly cut in half despite the black and white's open door having slowed down the massive bullets before they found his flesh.

He fought the law, and the law won.

After nearly tripping over the weapon dropped by the disemboweled man, Cade stooped over, took hold of the angled handle riding atop the barrel, and plucked the seventeen-pound M249 LMG from the blacktop. He gave the light machine gun he knew all too well a shake and determined the attached two-hundred-round ammunition box was nearly full of linked 5.56 x 45 mm hardball. A cursory glance told him the scope was unbroken and there was no damage to the weapon that he could see.

Looking down the length of 39 toward the van, he slung the Saiga on one shoulder and moved on with the business end of the liberated weapon leading the way.

Crossing the road with the M249 tucked in tight to his shoulder, Cade cast a critical eye on the A-Team van. Out back, the bumper looked like a J lying over on one side. The chromed end farthest from him was bent down hook-like and nearly touching the road. The rear doors were bowed in from the collision and the seam where they came together was far from straight.

Slipping by the passenger side rear quarter, he paused and peeked through the head-high bubble window. Trying to illuminate the inside with the tactical light only threw a glare off the smoked glass. Undeterred, he lowered the LMG, cupped his hands, and pressed his face to the curved surface.

Nothing.

Finding the tint too dark for him to see anything inside the back of the van, he peered one-eyed around the passenger-side window pillar.

The passenger seat was empty. But the driver's was not. The man wedged against the steering wheel was middle-aged and heavyset. He was still buckled in and gripping the wheel one-handed. Light from the burning vehicles was reflected off the dozen or so rings jammed onto his sausage-like fingers. Strapped to his wrist and sparkling like a disco ball was a diamond-encrusted gold watch. From the looks of the damage done by the opening salvo, his death had been opposite than that of the man at the wheel of the first Suburban. From his right ear on up a good portion of skull was missing. The contents of the cranium had been splashed onto the headliner and inside of the driver's side window and had already finished the slow downward slide and collected in the space between the armrest and the man's thigh. Strangely, spattered with blood, hair, and brain matter, a military-grade gas mask rested on the man's lap. There was also a second entry wound roughly six inches below the first. Though the destruction rivaled that of the kill shot, the lack of blood from the fist-sized hole told Cade that the man's heart had ceased pumping blood well before the bullet caused the damage.

Another of the lucky ones, he thought as he craned to see into the rear of the van.

Nothing.

All that was revealed in the wash of the tactical light was the dark blackout curtain strung from roof to floor behind the front seats.

Retracing his steps to the back of the van, Cade heard a soft scraping sound coming from within.

Using hand signals, he alerted the others.

"Adrian," he called. "You in there?"

The noise grew louder. In his head, he pictured the woman mortally wounded and thrashing about on the floor covered in what was most likely shag carpet in some putrid shade popular in the era the van was a prized ride.

"Come out with your hands where I can see them."

In response to the order, something inside thunked solidly against the rear doors, causing the van to judder subtly on its suspension.

Cade stood staring at the rear doors and mulled over the possibility that a neutral noncombatant was inside the van. In the next beat, his inner voice was reminding him that the line had been drawn with Iris. Letting her come into the fold without any way to verify who she was or where she had come from was a mistake of monumental proportions that he had been part and parcel to. Never again, he thought as he put a dozen feet between him and the rear doors.

"Last chance!" he bellowed.

Hearing nothing close to a declaration of surrender from within, he snugged the LMG tight to his shoulder, flicked the selector two stops forward, and took hold of the front hand guard. Sighting on the lower half of the doors, he leaned into the gun and squeezed the trigger.

Countered by an internal piston, the weapon's recoil was minimal as the sustained burst left its barrel at three thousand feet per second. Two dozen neat little holes appeared in the sheet metal. Brass and pieces of the breakaway links jangled and skittered across the road as Cade cut a Z pattern in the air before him with the muzzle. He was on the trigger for two, maybe three seconds at the most. Long enough, though, for the LMG to spit out forty rounds.

Illuminated by the flames and propelled by the east wind, the resulting cloud of gun smoke drifted slowly over the inert convoy.

Cade waited and listened hard for a long five-count before moving in to take a look.

Five steps from the van the sound was back. Not as loud as before, but it was no doubt emanating from the rear of the van. Patience eroding quickly—something he wouldn't have given in to days ago—Cade stalked forward and gripped the handle on the right-side door. SMG held in his left, he flung the door to the right and found himself back on his heels to avoid its sweep.

Easily overpowering the stench of burning plastic and rubber and cooking human flesh, the pong of death wafting from inside the van brought with it a gut-tensing toxicity.

Without warning, a hunched-over Z materialized from out of the van's gloomy interior. Skin and flesh and fat, putrefied from a long stint underwater, sloughed from the pale arms reaching for Cade's face. Backpedaling to avoid the scrabbling fingers, he collided with the van door already two-thirds of the way through its return trip. In the next beat—already weighed down by sixty pounds of armor, ammo, and weapons—Newton's Law came into play and he unexpectedly found himself propelled into the Z's slimy embrace.

Chapter 60

Alexander Dregan's breakfast had consisted of cigarettes and coffee. The decision to skip lunch, his body had made for him. Now, just minutes after sunset and with every muscle in his upper body aching from days of nonstop coughing, the idea of eating what passed for dinner in the apocalypse was the furthest thing from his mind.

A fresh round of coughing wracked his body. Hunched over the coffee table with his butt only halfway on the low sofa, he fished out a kerchief and spat into it a ropy plug of phlegm dredged from deep within his cancer-riddled lungs. One glimpse at the quivering blackish-red mass served to further beat down his already suppressed appetite. So much so that even if the pork-and-cabbage-heavy aroma of his mother's famous Kapusniak came wafting from the darkened kitchen in the rear of the house, he doubted it would arouse so much as one drip from his dried-up salivary glands.

He folded the square of fabric and tucked it away in a pocket.

An oil lamp sat on a nearby table. Its flame danced as it burned brightly, causing the shadows on the walls to shift and distort in unison. For hours, the citizens of Bear River had been practicing the highest level of noise discipline. No one was to drive. Wood cutting was not allowed. Kids were kept inside lest the sounds of play carry to the outer walls. And much to the chagrin of a small percentage of the fledgling community's population, the only legal watering hole in town was shuttered—both literally and figuratively. It was all necessary to keep the dead from getting overly excited. Which would begin a chain reaction of bodies crushing against each other and cause the cement freeway sound barriers to come crashing down. Which in turn would lead to multitudes of hungry dead pouring into the town. A catastrophic turn of events, indeed.

Hearing the lone exception to the rule round the far corner, Dregan rose from the sofa and went to the windows overlooking the driveway and street beyond.

As he pulled back the drapes, he inadvertently licked his chapped lips. Grimacing at the coppery taste still dancing over his tongue, he watched twin cones of light paint the mailbox and sidewalk in a dim yellow light as the borrowed vehicle rounded the corner. After a brief squeal of brakes, the ungainly beast bounded up onto the driveway, jumping the curb and crushing the unkempt parking strip grass in the process.

That's my boy, thought Dregan, letting the drapes fall back into place.

He heard the engine cut off, then continue running on for a spell in fits and gasps before finally going silent.

Vapor lock. Not a good sign for a vehicle he supposed was maintained regularly during the summer months before the Omega virus killed everyone from the CEO on down to the fleet mechanics.

After stealing a long look over his shoulder at the place he'd called home for several weeks, he grabbed his rabbit fur Ushanka hat and knee-length duster off the coatrack. Moving toward the front door, he plucked his gun belt off the side table and grabbed his sword from its stand on the narrow fireplace mantle.

Out on the porch, Dregan looked over the rail and spotted Gregory crawling underneath the vehicle.

"Is it even going to get me to the north gate?" he quipped.

Not yet committed to the task at hand, Gregory paused with his face partially obscured by the vehicle's undercarriage. "It will get you much farther than that," he called back, the beam from his headlamp illuminating the elder Dregan. "And that's all we're asking from her. A dozen miles or so and then—"

"All is well in Bear River," finished Dregan. He doubled over the rail as a spasm rippled through his body.

366

Wearing a worried expression, Gregory wormed out from under the vehicle and rushed toward the ladder leaning against the elevated porch.

Dregan spat over the rail and drew a deep breath. "Go back to what you were doing," he said. "I'm on my way down."

Brow knitted and worrying his beard with one hand, Gregory watched his father buckle his gun belt and shoulder the ancestral steel. Concern rising, and favoring his right arm, Gregory braced the ladder and kept his comments to himself as his father descended on shaky legs.

Once his feet were on terra firma, Dregan said, "You're going to make one hell of a helicopter parent when the time comes."

"Gotta find the woman, first," grumbled Gregory. He looked to the north and began to rub his shoulder vigorously.

Dregan shrugged off the sword and presented it to Gregory. "Hold this for me while I'm away."

Nearly fumbling the sword, Gregory said, "No you don't, Dad." Eyes filling with tears, he went on, "Peter needs you to come back. I ... need you to come back. Even if you have only days to live ... come back to us. *Please*." He wiped his eyes on his sleeve.

"Where *is* my Thor boy anyway?"

"Waiting for you at the north gate."

The elder Dregan took a step forward, wrapped Gregory in a bear hug, and held him in it for a few seconds. Releasing his grip, he took a step back and looked his boy up and down.

"What?" asked Gregory, his eyes glassy and red.

"Are you OK?"

"I'm sore on my right side."

Dregan shot him a questioning look.

"The pain starts where I was bitten." He turned to his right and pulled his collar aside, revealing a mass of hardening tissue roughly the circumference of a tennis ball.

"And?"

"And it radiates down my arm and ribcage. Ebbs and spikes with my pulse, too."

"After you alert Brook ..." Realizing the slip, Dregan looked away for a second, shaking his head. "After you alert *Duncan* of my impending success, be sure to talk to the nurse."

"Glenda is her name. I'll see what she has to say."

"Don't sugarcoat things," growled Dregan.

"I won't," promised Gregory. He fixed his gaze square on his dad. "Will you do *me* a favor?"

Dregan put a hand up to ward off the headlamp beam. "What is it?"

"Give my regards to the Thagons when you pass by their place."

Always the realist, Dregan replied, "They won't hear it."

"It's the thought that counts," said Gregory. "Nobody needs to die like they did."

Eyes narrowing, Dregan said, "*Nobody?*"

"Maybe those assholes up north do. They *earned* it."

"Maybe those assholes up north *will* get what they deserve." As if party to the conversation, a chorus of ghastly moans erupted just outside the nearby wall. "If I succeed in getting the dead moving in that direction," added Dregan. "Those assholes might get their just deserts thousands of times over."

Continuing to rub his shoulder, Gregory made his way back to the vehicle. He went to the ground and inched his way underneath the driver's side running board.

***

By the time Gregory had given the fuel system a complete once over, night had fully enveloped Bear River.

Arms crossed and leaning against the porch support beam, Dregan said, "Good to go?"

Gregory rose. "I didn't see anything wrong under there. Took out the inline fuel filter just in case it was gummed up by the old gas."

"We'll know when I fire it up."

Wiping his hands on his jeans, Gregory said, "Keys are in the ignition. Let's go."

"This beast can't be more temperamental than the old surplus Blazer," said Dregan. He opened the door, paused for a second and said, "What did you have to promise Hodges to get the keys?"

Gregory paused before rounding the rear corner of the slab-sided vehicle. "I had to promise him you'd be bringing it back in one piece. He's pretty attached to her."

Climbing in, Dregan said, "To be honest, it doesn't do a thing for me."

***

The drive to the north gate was a short one. Along the way, Dregan heard Judge Pomeroy's promises in his head. Chain of command had been established in the early afternoon meeting in chambers with Deputies MacLeod and Hunt as witnesses. Should the elder Dregan not make it back, Gregory would take over his duties for as long as he was healthy. If something should befall Gregory, two things would happen. First, the community would vote on a successor for Sheriff—with Dregan's nod going to MacLeod. Second, should Dregan's brother Henry survive his battle with the flu, he would become Peter's guardian. However, if both were to happen, leaving Peter an orphan, he would be allowed to either stay in Bear River alone, or take whatever belongings he wanted and be escorted to Duncan's compound where he would remain until he was sixteen and mature enough to make his own decisions.

Thoughts swirling around mortality and family, Dregan stopped a block south of the wall and left the engine running.

The gate was easily wide enough to allow the large vehicle passage. It was flanked by two guard towers that were taller by half and showed no signs of movement. Blackout curtains had been rolled down to keep the zombies from catching sight of the guards Dregan knew were inside what amounted to little more than sandbag-reinforced plywood cubes perched atop a framework of two-by-fours. Knowing he would soon feel their vulnerability, he threw a shudder.

Seeing Peter running from the left-side tower, mane of blond hair flowing behind him, Dregan smiled wide. Before the boy had covered half of the block, he put the shifter in Neutral and set the foot brake.

Peter skidded to a halt in front of the vehicle and looked up. Mouth agape and having forgotten entirely about his father, who was staring back through the windshield glass, the stunned youngster began to walk a clockwise circle around the vehicle.

Dregan watched his boy in the passenger side mirror until he disappeared around back. He then picked him up in his mirror and kept his eyes glued to him, memorizing every crease and freckle on his face before finally locking his gaze with the youngster's ice blue eyes.

"What do you think?"

"Does *everything* work?"

Dregan looked to Gregory, who was just climbing from the passenger seat.

Gregory nodded. "Sure does," he said, then turned and struck up a conversation with one of the gate guards.

Dregan put a hand on Peter's shoulder. "Your brother says it will. Now climb aboard. But don't touch any buttons."

Peter climbed through the open door and sat sidesaddle on his dad's lap. He floated his hands over the controls without touching them. He craned around and stared into the dark, cavernous compartment behind the front seats. Finally, he returned his attention to his dad and said, "When will you be back?"

Dregan said nothing. He wrapped the boy up in a gentler version of the bear hug Gregory had received earlier.

Without warning, Gregory showed up outside the driver's door. "Come on down, Peter," he ordered. "Dad has a very important job to do."

Dregan looked to Gregory. "Distractions in place?"

Gregory nodded.

"Are the dead clearing away from the road?"

"Mostly."

"How many still in front of the gate?"

"Cleo said he figures there's a hundred or so. He's going to hit you with the flashlight when it's time."

"Get ahold of our friends to the west as soon as it's clear the horde is on the move." He paused for a moment and looked away. When he turned back his eyes were going red. "Do not forget to talk to Glenda," he stressed. "Do not be like me."

A tear traced Gregory's cheek and fell to the road. "Stubborn?"

Dregan nodded. He reached down and tousled Peter's hair. "You take care of your brother until I return."

Peter had been following along with the conversation, eyes darting left and right to keep up with the rapid-fire question and answer session. Instinctively, he reached up and put a hand on his dad's knee. "I love you, too."

Dregan grimaced, then began to cough. The attack lasted thirty seconds and resulted in another blood- and mucus-soaked kerchief. "Love you too, boy." Eyes moist more so from the emotion of the moment than the coughing fit, Dregan closed his door and fixed his gaze on the man by the gate.

Seeing the flashlight beam swing his way and the inner gate start to roll aside, Dregan nudged the transmission into gear and let up on the brake. By the time the borrowed vehicle had picked up some forward momentum, the inner gate was open wide and the yellow school bus keeping the dead at bay was beginning to roll slowly right-to-left under its own power.

Chapter 61

Eyes tearing up from the wall of stench pouring from the rear of the van, Cade contorted his body to escape the bloated, living corpse tumbling through the open door. Beginning to fall backwards, he regarded the male Z through what amounted to slits for eyes. Bodily fluids leached from numerous lesions crisscrossing its bare chest. At the front of its neck was a near-perfect fist-sized rectangle where skin and flesh and trachea had been excised with some kind of surgical blade. Giving in to gravity's pull, a torrent of writhing maggots spilled from the opening, their cold smoothness pelting Cade's chest and neck and face. Adding to the olfactory overload and growing toxic soup, putrefied tissue and unidentifiable internal organs sluiced from a pair of gaping bullet wounds to the monster's lower abdomen.

Willing his eyes open, Cade let go of the M249 mid-fall and ripped the claw-like hands away from his face. In the next beat, he impacted the road and experienced a breath-robbing stab of pain as the slung shotgun bit into his back.

Before he could collect his thoughts, the weight of the dead thing hammered his shoulder and pinned it to the ground. With his left arm immobilized, he went for the Gerber strapped to his thigh. As he thumbed the snap, releasing the black blade from the scabbard, he saw the Humvee's headlights rise up and the beams cut across the road.

As the clatter of the diesel engine reached his ears, he came to realize that there was a complete absence of sound where the Z was concerned. Instead of the growling and hissing and raspy calls indicative of a first turn whose vocal cords had dried and atrophied, all he heard was teeth grinding and clicking excitedly an inch from his ear.

Arching his back with all his might freed his left arm. Drawing his face away from the creature's chattering maw, he wrapped the fingers on his left hand into its greasy hair, drew its head back, and buried the Gerber to the hilt in its right temple. As Cade felt the Z go limp and slide sideways from his body, he firmed his grip on the hair and blade and stared into the lifeless eyes of the thing that nearly saw him joining Brook prematurely.

Veins on his neck showing, he bellowed, "Not today, motherfucker! The Reaper can't have me until my work is finished."

The Humvee came to a stop a yard from his head.

Cade let go of the Z's hair, released his grip on the Gerber, and flung the corpse off of him. As he rose up off the road and was bathed in the headlight wash, he looked down at his chest but didn't bother to wipe away the detritus accumulated there. The maggots inching between the magazine pouches and crawling upward on the exposed skin of his neck didn't seem to register to him, either.

Duncan stepped from the idling vehicle, leaving the door hang open. "I distinctly remember you telling *Taryn* to watch for beasties springing out from behind closed doors."

Cade said nothing.

Peering down on the rotter, Duncan noted, "This one has no vocal cords." He went to a knee and adjusted his glasses. "It's been silenced. Damn cuts look real precise. Exactly how Daymon described the work on the critters Taryn and Wilson ran into in Woodruff."

Still, Cade made no reply. He was squared up to the rear of the van, hands on hips, letting his eyes roam the interior, and learning that his earlier assumptions had been all wrong. There was no plush carpet or velvet headliner. There wasn't a bed or even a pair of captain's chairs in back. Judging by the welded metal cage between the cab and cargo area and that the floor and walls were covered in gore, the van was used solely for hauling the "silenced" Zs Adrian's band of cannibals liked to use to booby trap buildings after thoroughly looting them.

Giving up on getting a reply from Cade, Duncan worked the Gerber from the rotter's head. Then he rooted in his jacket pocket and found a stack of napkins taken from the greasy spoon south of Bear Lake. He wiped the blade and rose with it in hand.

"What's spinning that hamster wheel of yours?"

Still staring into the van, Cade answered, "Adrian isn't here."

Duncan craned to see around Cade. "No, sir. Little Lotta did not grace us with her presence." Seeing that dropping the derogatory pet name for the cannibal leader had no effect on his friend, he chucked the napkins to the ground and added, "What else is churning around inside that analytical mind of yours?"

"There's nothing left to analyze," said Cade, turning away from the parted doors.

Duncan turned the black dagger over in his hand and shot his friend a questioning look.

Finally, Cade relented. "I'm pissed that Adrian's up north all safe and sound while Helen and Ray are about to be buried and the Bear River woodcutters"—he stabbed a finger east—"are incubating maggots inside that barn."

"Can't change the past," drawled Duncan. "But we *can* change the future."

Cade shook his head. "Thanks to Iris, they know *exactly* where we are. Sure, we took out a sizeable number of them, but rest assured, she's still coming for her stuff. And when she does it'll be with more of these silent meat missiles and her best shooters." He let his gaze settle on the Humvee.

Reading his mind, Duncan said, "We're nearly winchester on ammo for the Ma Deuce, too."

Cade nodded agreeably, then looked over his shoulder.

Duncan followed his gaze. Saw Lev and Jamie moving wraith-like in the shadows cast from the flames, picking their way down the road, periodically pausing to inspect the wreckage and bodies.

"Because of the way the van door swung closed on you, I don't think Lev and Jamie had an angle when the thing pounced." Duncan acknowledged the approaching pair with a nod and then turned back to face Cade. "And I won't mention it to them, either." He handed the dagger back, handle first.

Cade shrugged off the Saiga and returned it to Duncan. "I only expended nine rounds."

"To great effect," conceded Duncan ahead of a soft, mournful chuckle.

Sensing that Duncan had exhausted his line of questioning, Cade turned the tables. "What are *you* thinking?"

Duncan looked up and spotted a tiny point of light zipping steadily across the southern sky. After watching the satellite until it was lost behind the tops of a nearby copse of trees, he said, "I'm thinking I want to be done with this nonstop killing." The Vietnam vet lowered his gaze and regarded Cade. Saw on his friend's face a thousand yard stare the likes of which he had seen last on shell-shocked grunts clamoring for that final spot on the blood-slicked floor of his Huey.

Seconds ticked by.

Lev and Jamie arrived and paused by the Humvee's open door.

Finally, just as Duncan opened his mouth to greet the pair, Cade said in a low menacing tone, "Done killing?" He held the Gerber in front of his face. The reflected flames made it look like some kind of medieval weapon imbued with magical properties. "Hell, Duncan, I'm just getting started."

Chapter 62

"Slow down, girl," said Dregan.

Wanting to shoot the gap with just inches to spare—or maybe even leave some paint on the nose of the yellow school bus—he tapped the brakes and firmed his grip on the steering wheel. Still twenty yards from the front gate and with the borrowed vehicle moving just above walking speed, he saw the dead beginning to spill through the man-sized opening. To the right of the widening gap, standing in a ragged line, were a dozen helmeted men and women wearing various pieces of sporting goods for armor. Clutched in their gloved hands and held near horizontal to the ground were slender, twelve-foot pikes fashioned from lightweight aluminum pipe and tipped with throwing javelins taken from the equipment room of a nearby high school.

As the speedometer reached twenty miles per hour, Dregan saw the pikers step forward in unison and thrust their pikes head-high into the zombies lurching into the gap. As the first wave of twice-dead creatures fell vertically to the road, the pikers turned their weapons to the right to make room for the speeding vehicle.

Two ticks after seeing the pikers swing their weapons north, Dregan felt their eyes on him as the front bumper cleared the threshold where the paved road became a rutted dirt lane feeding into a nearby orchard. In his left-side vision he saw the woman driver hunched over the wheel of the bus. Her arm was extended and she was flashing him an encouraging thumbs-up.

The weak beam of the twenty-year-old headlights picked up the snarling faces of the second wave of dead at about the same time they were being sucked under its squared front end.

Instinctively, Dregan leaned away from the side window and matted the accelerator.

As the truck exited the breach moving north of thirty miles an hour the combined thumps of bodies being bowled away and peal of nails raking its flat sides caused Dregan to cringe. The wheel jerked in his hands and the right side rose up as the tires ground soft, fleshy things into the mud.

Grimacing at the follow-on sound of bones snapping under the vehicle's weight, he fumbled in the dark with his right hand trying to find three specific and very important switches on the dash. As he continued the search, he started tooting the horn with the palm of the hand he was steering with. Near simultaneously, with the blaring horn drowning out all else, he found two of the switches. Depressing the first started the hazard lights flashing. Toggling the second, newly installed item, sent red and blue light lancing in all directions from the truck's flat roof.

A half-beat after Gregory's cobbled-on addition to the vehicle illuminated the orchard, making the skeletal trees seem to pulse and sway, he found the third switch and activated the vehicle's most important feature.

Looking down from the right-side guard tower, Gregory and Peter had been witness to the heroics below. The tower vibrated underneath their feet as the school bus rolled forward, closing the gap and mashing a trio of monsters against the cement walls.

Shouts rose up from inside the walls as the pikers, joined by a dozen more Bear River citizens, surrounded the twenty or so rotters that had gained access before the north entry could be completely sealed off.

A hundred feet left of the guard tower, the half-dozen citizens who had volunteered to dangle from ropes outside the wall above the assembled dead to act as live bait were being reeled back in.

Two hundred feet outside the gate, the white truck, lit up like a police cruiser and emblazoned on the side with the words Brady's Tasty Treats, ground to a sudden halt.

Though he was worried for his dad, Peter rubbed his hands together. This was the moment he had been waiting for. And he only had to wait a second until the familiar ditty blared from the roof-mounted speakers at full volume. The Pavlovian response to the sight and sound of it all was near instantaneous and he found himself craving one of those multicolored, jumbo rocket pops. As the dead peeled away from the walls below to investigate, despite the awful stink rising off of them, Peter could almost taste the frozen treat.

"Look," said Gregory, pointing west.

Peter turned and gazed the length of the wall. Even in the dark the undulating movement of the dead things wasn't lost on him. He saw brief flashes of tattered clothing and upturned faces as someone in the corner guard tower walked a bright light back and forth over the gathered horde. Then, as the ice cream truck with his dad at the wheel sputtered and began rolling along the dirt feeder road, he witnessed the entire undead mass swing their heads in unison and mount a slow shuffling pursuit.

State Route 39

Working in silence, Cade and Lev walked the road collecting the weapons and ammunition and anything else valuable to survival in these trying times.

As Lev rifled through the shot up Suburban's glove box, he said, "When these two groups don't return—"

Finishing the sentence, Cade said, "We're going to have visitors. I've been thinking about that."

"They'll come during the day."

Cade slipped the keys from the ignition and dropped them into a pocket. "I agree."

Lev took a map of Utah and stack of papers from the glove box and folded them in half. He looked up. "Tomorrow?"

Cade said, "I would if I were in their shoes."

"Then we don't have much time to waste." Lev stuffed the map and papers in his pocket to read later in better light. He elbowed the door open then regarded Cade again. "We better get back to the compound. The rigs need to be gassed up. Guns have to be cleaned and oiled. Plus, we're gonna have to get fresh batteries for the radios and some MREs for the ride. I figure an hour at most and we can be gunned up and Oscar Mike."

"No '*we*' this time," said Cade. "I'm going alone."

Lev looked west down 39. Saw Jamie, M4 in hand, standing watch near the F-650. Scanning right he picked out Duncan's head protruding from the turret atop the Humvee. Squinting from the glare of the two sets of headlights aimed his way, he said, "Duncan will *never* go for that. And neither will Glenda. Even if nobody else presses the issue, she *will* call for a vote."

Cade shouldered a pair of semiautomatic rifles and stuffed the spare magazines for them in his cargo pockets. He looked to Lev. Said, "I can appreciate your enthusiasm," and strode off toward the waiting vehicles.

Lev took one final long look at the destruction, letting his gaze linger on the tangle of enemy corpses Cade and Duncan had shoved none too gently into the rear of the van. Finished, he double timed it to catch up. After running a dozen yards, he slowed and walked shoulder-to-shoulder with the Delta operator. "You can't go it alone."

Without breaking stride, Cade said, "This is no longer a democracy. I can … and I will."

Chapter 63

Dregan braked hard and brought the ice cream truck to a full stop for the third time since his mad dash through the north gate some thirty minutes prior. The trees lining the dirt road on both sides of the Brady mobile pulsed orange with each new strobe of the hazard lights. Peering into the elongated side mirror, he saw gnarled branches bathed in blue and red reaching down from the moonless black void above. And hugging the ground behind the vehicle was a foot-high layer of exhaust fumes. Hell, he thought, throw some Abba in place of the current song on rotation and replace the zombies with Lycra-clad twenty-somethings and the whole experience wouldn't be far from the euro discos of his youth. And as fond of the drug and drink as some of his contemporaries had been in that era, the closing time exodus sometimes resembled the motor-skill-challenged assemblage he had driven through just outside the north gate.

After sitting there for a long five minutes with the engine idling and *Sweet Georgia Brown* blasting for what seemed like the hundredth time from the multi-directional speaker, Dregan was starting to think he was in the stands at a Harlem Globetrotter's game, not playing the Good Humor Man attempting to lure tens of thousands of abominations away from Bear River.

The new attack started as a shooting pain deep within Dregan's lungs. A second later he couldn't breathe. It was as if he had been gut punched on the tail end of a long drawn-out exhale and the follow-on breath was never going to happen.

With stars dancing in front of his eyes, the dam finally broke and, like a person on the receiving end of a successful Heimlich maneuver, he spit a wad of mucous, salty with blood and who knows what else, onto the windshield.

There was a noticeable rattle in his chest when he drew in the much-anticipated lungful of crisp night air. Arms wrapping the steering wheel in a loose embrace, he leaned forward and rested his forehead on its cool, smooth surface. Once he got his wind back and the fireworks had abated, he sat up straight and dragged his sleeve across his mouth.

Stealing a look at the side mirror, he spotted the horde's front echelon. Heads bobbed and lolled and their contorted faces changed to an eerie shade of purple as they emerged from the inky black a hundred feet down the road. Hundreds of zombies poured into the light spill as he watched. Soon they inhabited every square inch of the packed earth road behind the Brady mobile. And as he continued to wait for the first among them to reach the noisy prize, he spotted the long shadows of what he guessed to be hundreds more marching through the trees on both sides of the road.

***

Thirty short seconds after emerging from the dark, the dead on the road were shuffling through the carbon monoxide haze trailing the truck, causing it to roil and begin to dissipate. A tick later hands were slapping the sheet metal and the faint screech of nails raking paint were rising over *Sweet Georgia Brown*.

Dregan waited until the first ashen face mashed against the sliding window to let up on the brake. Goosing the throttle, he said, "Let's go, party people. It's closing time. You don't have to go home ... but you can't stay here." As the ice cream truck gained traction in the shallow mud and began to putter forward, he picked up his radio and let them know back at Bear River that he was on the move again with the Washington Generals in hot pursuit. He released the Talk key and chuckled when the woman on the other end asked him to repeat the last part.

Ignoring the query, he locked his eyes on the road ahead so that he wouldn't miss the left turn that would see him and the undead horde west through a sloping pasture to where it came to a T with State Route 16.

In the guard tower at Bear River, Gregory and Peter were watching the dead streaming north. The majority of them that had been crowding in on the northwest corner and north gate area when the music started up were now angling toward the exact spot in the orchard where the ice cream truck entered. Many more, perhaps numbering in the thousands judging by the grunts and moans and ongoing swishing of wet grass against tattered clothing, were suddenly forgetting about the meat behind the walls and striking off to catch up with the source of the sound most of them had associated with something desirable since early childhood.

Talking loudly so as to be heard over the din of the departing dead, Peter said, "Are they *all* going to follow him?"

Gregory picked a distant spot to the west where he thought the north/south-running state route should be. He pressed a pair of high-power binoculars to his face and concentrated hard. Finally, after catching fleeting glimpses of the undead horde surging north over the pastures and along the nearby stretch of 16, he said, "That's the plan."

"And then Dad loops back around by Ray and Helen's house?"

"That's the plan," Gregory lied.

In the pitch-black of the enclosed guard tower, Big Brother's pained expression was lost on Peter. Misted-over eyes still glued to the field glasses, Gregory cocked his head and listened to his dad's voice coming from the nearby guard's radio. Smiling at the last part of the encouraging report, he tousled Peter's blond locks and handed the binoculars back to the guard.

"The truck's sound system is stuck to playing only the Harlem Globetrotter's theme," he explained to the female guard. "Dad used to take us to see them whenever they came to the Salt Palace." Though he missed the guard's quizzical expression, he went on, explaining, "The Generals are *always* their opponent. And they're always the visiting team. They *never* beat the Globetrotters."

"Understood," replied the guard, a former United States Marine. Her smile was lost on the brothers Dregan as she spoke into the radio, telling Alexander Dregan, "Godspeed, sir. The Generals' losing streak must *not* be broken."

Chapter 64

Twenty minutes after leaving the killing fields roughly two miles east of the Eden compound, Cade was wheeling the F-650 into the clearing. Instead of nosing the rig in between the Raptor and haphazardly parked 4Runner, he drove past the Winnebago, then continued on to the lower part of the clearing where the tarp-covered Department of Homeland Security Black Hawk sat all alone.

As soon as the Ford's headlight beams had swept over the darkened RV, everything that had happened inside there came rushing back to him in a dizzying flurry of sights and sounds and smells. He was still reliving that night of horror—the worst in his thirty-five years on Earth—when he pulled the Ford in broadside to the helo, but just outside of the reach of its drooping rotor blades. As he sat there mulling over the what-ifs and should-haves, the Humvee driven by Lev swung past the Ford's open tailgate and stopped broadside to the helicopter with its headlights trained on a small copse of mature pines bordering the clearing.

After seeing Lev and Jamie exit the Humvee ahead of Duncan, who took some time extricating himself from the gunner's position in the turret, Cade did a J-turn and backed the F-650 in until its tailgate was awash in the other vehicle's headlight spill.

Killing the engine, he climbed from the Ford and felt the night chill through his Crye Precision top. Throwing a shiver, he called Lev over.

"Help me with Ray and Helen."

Lev nodded and grabbed ahold of the curtain shrouding the bodies.

The men carried the corpses one at a time and placed them inside the helicopter so the animals wouldn't get to them during the night.

"I'll bury them in the morning," said Cade to nobody in particular. He donned his pack and helmet. Heavy from the plate carrier and spare magazines he had transferred from the soiled chest rig, the pack hung low on his back. Leaving the chinstraps to his bump helmet dangling by his cheeks, he started removing items from the F-650's crowded bed, starting with the ruined and reeking Multi-Cam blouse and MOLLE rig—both candidates for the burn pile.

A dozen feet away, Duncan was stretching and rubbing his right shoulder. Hearing the telltale creak of the compound's steel door—always a candidate for a fresh spritz of WD-40—he turned his attention across the clearing and picked up a trio of headlamps bobbing in the dark. Though the approaching survivors were only partially front-lit, as they drew near Duncan gleaned from the snippets of silhouette who they were. The lanky form on the left wore the headlamp over a floppy hat. *Definitely Wilson.* The dead giveaway that the person in the middle was Taryn came from the periodic contact happening with Wilson. An occasional brush of the hip by her. Instant reciprocal contact by him. Clearly the two had no problem with sharing personal space.

The form on the lovebirds' right was much shorter and moved with an economy Duncan recognized at first sight. If Tran was here in the clearing, he thought, then Seth was in the security pod acting as the eyes and ears of the group.

Leaving Cade to unload the liberated weapons from the rear of the F-650, Duncan walked to meet the trio. Putting a hand up to shield against the competing headlamp beams, he said, "Where's Glenda?"

Taryn stepped close and adjusted her lamp so the beam lanced skyward. Finished, she said, "Glenda is hanging out with the 'incorrigibles.'"

"Her word or yours?" asked Duncan.

"Her word," replied Taryn. "She caught the two of them gorging on the last of the Halloween candy—"

Wilson cut in. "They ate every last piece. And when she asked them why they thought it was acceptable to do so, they both said they didn't want to carry it out with them when the cannibals came."

Incredulous, Duncan shot, "*When*? Not, *if*? Lot of confidence those two have in the rest of us."

"Raven just lost her mom," reminded Tran. "Sasha did, too. They're forming a bond. The talk is all false bravado."

"Well la-tee-da, Mister Freud. You gonna install a couch in your quarters? Charge a fee for listening to folks blather while you work a mental Rubik's Cube?"

Tran shook his head, intermittently blinding Duncan with his headlamp beam. "Just stating the obvious. What do you need help with?"

"I'm half-strength," said Duncan.

"What's new?" quipped Wilson.

"You need extra muscle to unload the snowmobile," guessed Taryn.

Pointing at her, Duncan said, "X gets a square, young lady."

Yawning, Wilson said, "And it can't be done in the light of day?"

"I'm Cade's emissary," said Duncan. "All I know is that he's itching to get the thing out of there." He paused. "Maybe he's thinking along the same lines as the girls. Our location has been compromised, after all. Found one of those silenced rotters and cables and hardware in the back of that red and black van."

Wilson started walking toward the F-650. "Everything you need to booby trap a place after you loot it and dispose of the people."

"That's their calling card," said Duncan as he fell in behind Wilson.

***

Using a couple of sheets of muddied plywood as a makeshift ramp, the six survivors, well, five and a half considering Duncan's injury, managed to unload the Arctic Cat without breaking it or anyone getting hurt.

Lev looked to Cade. "Where do you want it, boss?"

Indicating a spot under the trees, Cade said, "Right there. And tarp it real good, would you?"

While Lev and the others manhandled the snowmobile across the damp soil, Cade slipped the slings of half a dozen rifles over his shoulders, *Zapata*-style. Rifles hanging off his back and weighing him down considerably, he stooped and picked up the Pelican case containing the MSR with one hand and the M249 with the other. Pulling Duncan close, he said, "Walk with me to the compound," and strode off into the dark.

State Route 16

Much to Dregan's surprise, he had negotiated the gently sloping pasture without letting the heavily rutted strips of dirt passing for a road pitch the ungainly vehicle over onto its side. Twice he had come close to losing control due to mushy shocks and its top-heavy nature but had saved himself both times from a painful death to gnashing teeth and clawing hands with a simple lean-countering-jerk of the oversized steering wheel.

Now, forty-five minutes after leaving Bear River behind and having covered a mile at most, he brought the vehicle to a juddering halt where the dirt road came to a T with the paved two-lane.

Looking left, he saw only a hundred feet of SR-16. It was lit up much like the orchard had been. Beyond the roadside ditches it was bracketed on both sides by barbed wire fencing that shot off die-straight before finally disappearing into the pure black of night. Straight ahead a dirt berm lit up by the ice cream truck's weak headlights glowed an otherworldly shade of orange. Beyond the fence rising and falling with the berm was open pasture devoid of life. Peering over his right shoulder, Dregan saw more of the same: northbound two-lane and dual runs of fencing all lit up in the undulating red and blue and orange light being thrown off by the rig's pulsing lights.

Consulting his wing mirror, Dregan saw that the horde was just beginning to draw within his self-imposed danger zone—a guesstimated distance equal to the length of an American football field. Pulse picking up speed, he reached over to the seat next to him and took hold of the handheld spotlight Gregory had procured from one of the gate guards. After making sure it was plugged into the utility receptacle (also wired in by Gregory) he stuck his arm out his open window, checked to see that the spotlight's lens was clear of the mirror, and threw the thumb switch.

At once, the dancing colored lights on his side were swallowed up by the million candle-power beam as the road stretching for what seemed like more than a mile south of the T was bathed in a detail-revealing bluish-white light.

The sight of thousands of pale, walking corpses surging up the road and over the pasture, the barbed wire fencing and gnarled wood posts falling like dominos, caused Dregan to draw in a deep breath. Which he paid for as the stabbing pain returned to remind him that the deaders were not the only thing trying to kill him.

As he gaped at the contorting faces of the dead lit up like a thousand full moons by the spot, he pondered whether he was going to fall first to total lung failure brought about by the Big C, or have his bones stripped clean by the dual hordes about to merge and become one of the fabled mega-hordes he'd heard mentioned in hushed tones around campfires but had yet to see in person.

The slap of feet hitting pavement and hollow sucking sounds of the dead negotiating the pasture preceded the horde moving on Dregan from to the south. With their hungry calls starting to blend with those of the horde about to spill from the pasture and become one huge sonic tempest, Dregan pegged the volume to the Brady Mobile's sound system and steered right onto SR-16 northbound.

Chapter 65

Eyes locked on the security pod's metal ceiling, Seth said, "You don't have any pants on."

Displaying the sheathed Gerber in his hand, Cade said, "Had to cut them off before coming in."

"Rotter guts?"

"Rotter and breather both," replied Cade. "Mostly rotter, though. The pants and blouse were beyond saving. I'll burn them tomorrow."

Seth fiddled nervously with the satellite phone on the desk.

Risking life and limb, Duncan tugged on the cuff of Cade's underwear. "Wardrobe malfunction notwithstanding," he quipped, "we now know the answer to the all-important question: and *boxers*, it is. Hell, Cade, I had you pegged as a banana-hammock-wearing kind of guy."

Even in the pale light thrown by the lone sixty-watt bulb hanging from the ribbed ceiling, Cade's glare was unmistakable.

Stifling a laugh, Seth said, "I have something I need—"

Cade silenced him with a raised hand. "Lev is going to take over for you as soon as he finishes stowing the snowmobile Daymon gifted us."

Duncan looked Cade up and down one last time. He said, "I'll leave you two fellas alone. If I don't have the boss look at this bad wing, she will not be a happy camper."

Cade grabbed his friend's uninjured shoulder. "Get a good night's sleep," he said. "We'll brainstorm about this in the morning."

"You sure about that?"

Cade nodded. "Thanks for pulling your weight out there." Careful to not further aggravate the injury, he gave Duncan a weak one-armed man hug. Fully cognizant of his state of dress, he made sure to avoid any lower body contact.

Reciprocating, Duncan joked, "I'm feeling vulnerable all of a sudden."

Pulling away, Cade thought he detected alcohol on the man's breath, but gave him the benefit of the doubt. No sense opening another Pandora's Box when there was already one open that needed immediate attention and definitive closure.

"Night, Delta."

"Night, Old Man."

Cade watched Duncan retrace his steps and take a right before the entry foyer. He heard a knock and a creak and voices spilling out into the passageway. Turning his attention to Seth, he said, "You were saying?"

"As you were parking topside I received a call on the long-range CB from Gregory at Bear River."

"The horde is on the move?"

In a low voice, Seth said, "It's breaking north as we speak." He went quiet and twirled the sat-phone on the desktop.

"And?"

Seth looked up to meet Cade's gaze. "It's now a full-on *mega-horde*."

Eyes narrowing, Cade said, "How many?"

Seth was stroking his beard now and staring at the monitor where in one panel dark forms were flitting by the stationary Humvee's headlight beams. Returning his attention to Cade, he said, "Dregan told Gregory that once the two hordes merge there will be at least a hundred abreast."

A door opened to Cade's left and he heard Sasha and Raven chattering. He said, "How deep is the column?"

Seth said, "A mile or so. Damn, I hope to hell Gregory's wrong with that assessment."

While Seth was talking, Cade had grabbed a Sharpie and scribbled the channel the radio placed by Iris's body was locked on. Finished, he did a double take. "A *mile* deep?" Still staring at Seth, he began employing a formula for determining crowd size taught to him by former Secret Service Special Agent to the President, Adam Cross. He shook his head after coming to a rough estimate of the mega horde's size that, even if halved, would be impossible to get around once it ranged north of the 39/16 junction.

"Yep. A mile or so," confirmed Seth, returning his attention to the monitor on which the individual rectangles were now all the same dark shade of gray. The only thing pointing to the fact that the cameras were still up and delivering a current image was the green letters and digits at the corner of each pane denoting the camera's location and current time.

Cade heard the door to the Kids' quarters close and silence returned. A tick later a whispered conversation was filtering down the passage. Ignoring the discernable snippets, he looked back to Seth and asked, "How does Dregan know this?"

"Because he's the one leading the pusbags away from Bear River." He paused again. "In an ice cream truck, I guess." He went on to detail the rest of the plan relayed to him by Gregory.

As soon as Seth stopped talking, the door to the Kids' quarters hinged open and quickly closed again. A beat later the sound of footsteps echoed in the corridor.

Cade clamped down on Seth's shoulder and craned his head so they were nearly eye-to-eye. "Keep these cards close to your vest for now. Can you do that?"

Seth nodded affirmative at the very moment Raven rounded the corner holding her bandaged hand above her head and wearing a conspiratorial grin.

Releasing his grip on Seth, Cade scooped up the sat-phone and slipped it into his pack. Turning toward the foyer, he put on a happy face and locked eyes with Raven.

Smile leaving her face, Raven glanced down and said, "*Dad*, you have no pants on."

He said, "Long story," and bent and picked up the Pelican case. "I'll give you the short version after I unload this gear." He moved to the T and paused there. After Raven had passed and was preoccupied with opening the door to the Grayson quarters, Cade looked to Seth and pressed a finger to his lips.

Stub tail twitching spasmodically, Max was curled up and waiting for them when they entered the Grayson quarters. Cade closed and locked the door behind them. He set the Pelican case aside and propped his M4 against the head of the bed. After shrugging off his pack and plopping it on the floor, he gave Max a quick scratch behind the ears.

Catching sight of his daughter's Brook-like posture—hands on hips, eyes boring into the back of his head—he rose and quickly slipped on a pair of Army-issue sweatpants taken from the foot of the bed.

Raven said, "Did you find Bridgett?"

"Her real name is Iris and she is dead," he said, showing zero emotion. *The bitch is feeding the birds*, is what he was thinking. He went on to relay a sanitized version of the day's events to her. He finished by mentioning the "heightened presence" of rotters walking the roads, stressing that though he had let her and Sasha venture outside the wire to deliver the supplies, she was not to leave the compound without an adult.

"Not even to go to the bathroom?"

Cade shook his head. "You have to go now? I'm going to take Max out and clean up a bit."

Raven yawned, then shook her head. "I'm tired."

He began, "Do you want one of your—"

"Mom's melatonin pills?" she finished. "Sure. They make me dream a bunch. Good dreams, too."

Cade grabbed two bottles from the table. Choosing the one labeled *5mg Quick Dissolving*, he rattled one onto her palm.

"Water?"

He pulled a bottle from his pack and passed it over. Going back into the pack, he came out with the map and, while Raven was washing the pill down, stuck it into his waistband. He reached into the pack and pulled out his Glocks one at a time.

"Come on, Max."

The dog sprang up and spun a circle.

Cade stooped over and gave Raven a hug. Kissing her atop her head, he said, "I love you, Bird."

Regarding him with liquid, sleep-filled eyes, she reciprocated. "Love you more, Dad."

Starting the *Big Nutbrown Hare/Little Nutbrown Hare* routine from a book he had read to her a hundred times when she was a toddler, he said, "Guess how much I love you."

She stretched her arms out to her sides and said, "This much?"

Cade shook his head. "More." He touched the low ceiling. "I love you all the way up to here."

After they one-upped each other a couple of times with Cade getting the last word by looking to the ceiling and saying, "I love you all the way to the moon and back again," Raven retreated to her upper bunk and crawled under the covers.

Cade tucked the covers under Raven's chin and kissed her on the cheek. Seeing her eyelids already beginning to flutter, he turned away and grabbed a threadbare towel and his M4. By the time he extinguished the light and was working the door handle, his girl was beginning to snore.

Chapter 66

Cade took Max outside to do his business then returned and left him guarding Raven in their quarters. Satisfied Raven was out for the count, he retraced his steps to the T where he caught sight of Lev sitting on a folding chair, upright and alert in front of the monitor. Seeing that there was a trio of radios spread out on the desk before the younger man set Cade at ease.

"Any movement?"

Looking away from the monitor, Lev said, "Nothing yet."

"I don't expect that to hold," admitted Cade. "Wilson's radio?"

"Just white noise."

"At least the batteries are holding."

Lev nodded. "Let's hope Wilson put fresh Evereadys in the thing this morning."

Ignoring the quip, Cade said, "Any more Adrian rantings come over the CB?"

Lev shook his head. "They've gone radio silent. Which makes sense. After all, they lost about three dozen of their Jay-Vee team in half a day."

"What made you think the rendezvous team and quick reaction force—if you can call it that—were populated by their bench players?"

"Had to be," stated Lev. "They had zero tactical sense. Even after we pulled the first ambush ... and the QRF saw its aftermath, their actions stayed the same. They gave chase and continued, for the most part, to drive bumper-to-bumper."

"I concur," said Cade. "Adrian seems to have a huge sway over them."

"Like a *cult* type of sway?"

"Exactly. And that's why I have no doubt she's keeping her best and brightest close to home."

Lev glanced at the monitor for a moment. When he returned his attention back to Cade, he asked, "Where *is* home?"

Cade unfolded the map and laid it flat on the desk over the radios.

After giving the area north of Bear Lake a once over, Lev put his finger on State Route 16 near Woodruff. He traced the squiggly line denoting the road south to Bear River, stopping a hair north of the dot denoting the tiny town's location.

"I've already crunched the numbers," said Cade. "I figure the horde is nearly to the Thagons' house by now."

Lev looked up from the map. "That means even the slowest among them will be pouring into Woodruff in half an hour."

Cade nodded. "Unless Mother Nature comes through with an instant cold snap, I won't be able to drive north."

"Definitely not tonight," agreed Lev. "But that's a good thing, right?"

Cade shot him a look that said *go on*.

"If the horde is moving north, then Adrian's people probably won't be coming south any time soon. Maybe the horde will find them and eat them. Karma's a bitch. Stranger shit has happened."

Cade shook his head. "Too many variables. They know exactly where we stay. We have their stuff. If her group is what I think it is, then we're dealing with a cancer here. Cut out some of the tumor—"

"The group south of Bear Lake and the two convoys," stated Lev.

"Was a good start," finished Cade. "However, if you don't get rid of *all* the cancer it's going to metastasize and then you're fighting it on multiple fronts."

After stabbing a finger at each of the half-dozen tiny red Xs scribed on the map between Bear River in the south and Bear Lake to the north, Lev said, "These would be their observation posts. They would have to be eliminated first."

"That they are. And, yes, they pose a big problem. At least half of them do." Cade tapped the X farthest south in the string. "Thagons' home." He dragged his finger north, passing one X east of the 39/16 junction, and stopped at the next X which was situated on Woodruff's northern boundary.

"The church rectory?"

"Has to be," Cade agreed. He moved his finger to the X on Bear Lake's southwest shore.

"That's the compound with the cul-de-sac," said Lev. "No doubt about it."

Cade nodded and took a black Sharpie from the cut-down Pringles canister. He popped off the cap and circled the three Xs he and Lev had just identified as known observation posts. "The two near this so-called *Adrianville* could be satellite colonies similar to the cul-de-sac outpost and contain like numbers of personnel, or, if I'm lucky, they're just one-person affairs like the church and the Thagons' place."

Lev tapped his finger on the X east of the 39/16 junction. "And this?"

"If I didn't know any better, I'd say that's Hollah's mansion."

"You mean Daymon and Heidi's new place?"

Before Cade could say that Daymon had already been informed of his findings on the map nor add that he had just tried hailing the man when he was outside with Max, Lev was snatching up the base station's handheld microphone with one hand, and changing to a new channel with the other. Thumbing the call switch, he said, "Daymon? Heidi? This is Lev. Anyone copy?"

Cade stood still and silent for a long while as Lev tried multiple times to raise their friends. Finally, during a lull, he said, "I told Daymon earlier. If he was worried, he didn't let on. He's a big boy. You'll just have to keep trying. If he doesn't pick up tonight, you'll probably get ahold of him at the agreed-upon time tomorrow."

Lev tossed the microphone unceremoniously onto the desktop. "They still need to be warned about the mega-horde."

"I wouldn't worry too much," said Cade. "The dead should stick to 16. They haven't deviated yet." He refolded the map and, ending up with a finished product far from what he began with, tucked the rumpled mess into his waistband. He grabbed a two-way radio from the shelf and powered it on.

Lev scooped a Motorola from the desk top. "Seth and Tran are patrolling the clearing," he said. "I'll let them know you're going to be out and about, too."

Already through the foyer and reaching for the handle on the door to outside, Cade held his radio aloft and said, "Copy that."

SR 16 North of the Thagon Home

As promised, Dregan said some words for the dead when he motored by the Thagons' place. As the Brady Mobile crested a hill a few hundred yards past the dirt road servicing the white house on the hill, he saw an orange-red glow a couple of miles distant north by east. It was exactly how Vegas appeared to him the first time he approached Sin City at night by car. Only then the glowing multicolored blob had been evident on the horizon for miles and miles and was caused by neon lights, not flame licking skyward. He stared at the distant inferno for a few seconds then shifted his gaze back to the road in order to negotiate an upcoming S-turn.

After steering the ice cream truck along the serpentine stretch of road, the headlight wash picked up reflectors in the distance. Figuring that what he was seeing was likely the side markers on one or more vehicles positioned across the road, he grabbed the spotlight off his lap and sped toward them.
***
Two minutes after spotting the reflectors in the road, Dregan had the Brady Mobile parked in the middle of 16 and was illuminating his surroundings with the handheld spotlight. Dead ahead, where the state route became Main Street as it shot through Woodruff, a pair of cars partially blocked the road. The foreign compact on the left was nearly half the size of the other—

a decade-old Cadillac with broken-out windows and a corpse at the wheel. The gap separating the two cars looked to be a yard narrower than the ice cream truck.

Off to the left, barely a hundred feet behind the idling truck, State Route 39 snaked away west into the dark night. Running away to the east off of Dregan's right shoulder was a two-lane street. The sign on the corner read *Center*. And resting on flattened tires, rendering the entire block-long run of two-lane unnavigable, was a long line of bullet-riddled pickup trucks and passenger cars. On the sidewalk adjacent to the vehicles were what looked to be nearly two dozen corpses. All had been stripped of their clothes and the majority of their flesh. The work was precise, done by someone with the tools and stomach for rendering a human corpse. Bone glistened white and pooled blood appearing as deep as a sea trench gleamed black even in the stark white cone thrown by the spotlight.

Throwing a shiver, Dregan swept the beam from the gruesome scene to the building with the *Back In The Saddle Rehab* shingle hanging out front. The wall facing him was bullet-pocked. Most of the windows held only shards of glass, if any glass at all. The front door was cracked down the center and hung open. The wide painted piece of doorjamb opposite the hinges was loose at the top and leaned across the doorway diagonally.

Dregan shifted in his seat, leaned out the window, and trained the spotlight beam on the distant S-turn the mega horde was just beginning to navigate. Taking into account the speed at which the front of the mass was moving, he figured he had five minutes at most before the leaders caught up to him.

Chapter 67

Eden Compound

Stepping into the night air started an eruption of gooseflesh on Cade's exposed arms. Feeling the sensation working its way down his ribcage, he closed the compound door and, working with one hand, pulled the towel tight around his shoulders.

"Good job, Lev," he said aloud to himself after seeing the pair of Ford pickups and military Humvee backed up to the forest's edge nearby. Sure it would make finding the compound's hidden entrance easier if someone were to come calling, but a fast egress and the ability to quickly bring the Ma Deuce to bear on bad guys using the feeder road trumped any disadvantage.

Standing there on the edge of the clearing with his teeth threatening to chatter, he looked skyward into the inky black and thanked God for the moonless night and high clouds. Couldn't have asked for a better set of circumstances in which to prosecute a solo attack on an enemy whose numbers and resolve remained an unknown quantity.

After thumbing the headlamp switch, he stuffed the Motorola in the pocket opposite the Thuraya and pulled the Glock 19 from his waistband. He checked the magazine and action, pressed the pistol to his leg, then struck off into the woods on a heading that would see him to the outdoor latrine.

***

Raven's handiwork gave away the thrown-together outhouse as the beam from Cade's headlamp swung up from the worn dirt path. Still in the frame, the slivers of mirrored glass sparkled bright above the cobbled-on wash basin.

As Cade stepped up to the sink, he saw drops of crimson blood. When he looked up, he noticed a haggard-looking fella staring back at him: pronounced crow's feet. Downturned mouth hidden in a thicket of whiskers. He couldn't will that frown upside down even if Robin Williams appeared out of thin air and started in on a standup routine. He was run down and doubted the cold water was going to help. Still, he had to try.

But first he had to set his plan into action. He set the Glock on the narrow shelf above the sink and plucked the satellite phone from his pocket. The phone screen lit up when he pushed a random button. After thumbing in the digits to unlock the handset, he scrolled to the messaging feature and banged out a lengthy message. Finished, he hit Send and placed the phone on the shelf next to the Glock.

He wet one corner of the towel with water from the container hanging on the latrine wall beside the broken mirror. Taking his time, he wiped the cold, damp fabric over his entire upper body, starting with his face and ending with his hands.

Five minutes after sending his message, he thumbed the phone on and glanced at its upturned screen. *Nothing.* No missed call. No new SMS message. He took the Glock off the shelf and, leaving the phone behind due to the old adage that *a watched pot doesn't boil*, turned the corner and yanked open the latrine's flimsy door. Instantly, his headlamp beam illuminated the plywood sheet passing itself off as a toilet seat and revealed the sloppy contents of the fifty-five-gallon drum below it. No sooner had the door cleared his face than the newly awoken flies attacked the beam's source. Having no doubt recently been at rest atop the feces and soiled toilet paper, the shiny black pests took station around his head.

No stranger to the insects and other beasties the foreign lands he'd spent time in had to offer, Cade ignored the shit kamikazes and took care of his business.

***

A minute after utilizing the plywood "throne," the flies followed Cade and his beam out of the latrine.

Cade eyed the satellite phone as he washed up. As he was drying his hands off on a clean corner of his towel, the screen flared to colorful life, stayed lit for a half-beat, then went dark again.

Blinking the tracers from his eyes, he grabbed the phone off the shelf. Then, with an upward swipe of the back of the hand clutching the Glock, he angled the headlamp's beam to the heavens and thumbed the phone to life. There on the screen was the response to his SMS message. It was short and succinct. It read: *Timing is everything, Wyatt.* A string of GPS coordinates was below the text. Then below it all, the number *0200* sat all alone.

Main Street, Woodruff, Utah

Dregan had waited until the staggering juggernaut of rotted flesh and tattered clothing reached the 39/16 junction before making his move. Praying for his estimation of the gap between the cars to err in his favor, he stomped the pedal and tightened his grip on the steering wheel.

The truck lurched as the V8 spooled up and forward momentum was established. The steering wheel wobbled in Dregan's grip as the transmission geared up. Soon the centerline was rushing under the front bumper and the two vehicles loomed.

Aiming the Brady Mobile's squared-off front end at the opening, he took the lesser of two evils approach and steered left by a degree or two so if he had to hit something, it would be the smaller import instead of the boat-like slab of American iron.

With two truck-lengths to go, the headlights revealed the gap to be even narrower than Dregan had guessed.

With one truck-length to go, he made a final micro-adjustment with the steering wheel, narrowed his eyes, and braced for impact.

As the barreling ice cream truck came even with the roadblock, its front bumper on Dregan's side met the import's right front fender. There was an explosion of sound: bending metal, tinkling glass, and the screech of unwilling rubber moving against the grain.

In a fraction of a second the ice cream truck had punched through and *Sweet Georgia Brown* was again top billing.

Dregan checked the rig's gauges. The oil pressure looked normal. Voltmeter needle was hovering where he remembered. And most importantly, the water temperature seemed to be holding, the needle parked firmly in the green zone.

Seeing is believing being important to Dregan, he inched up in his seat and peered over the wheel. When he saw there was no steam pouring from the hood, he exhaled sharply. Because if anything up front save for a headlight or blinker were to fail, it was likely going to be the radiator. Which would stop him in his tracks well before he led the dead out of Woodruff and got the lot of them going exactly where he wanted them to: much farther north into the Bear Lake basin.

Adrian's territory.

A "no-go zone" according to the late Ray Thagon.

Fighting back a rising urge to hack more spongy lung tissue into the already bloodied kerchief, Dregan swallowed hard and steered the raucous, rolling dinner bell through Woodruff.

***

Barely a minute after turning the import into a mass of compacted tin, Dregan was pulling to the shoulder and running his gaze over a roadside sign admonishing him not to litter and threatening a hefty fine for doing so.

Letting a rare grin crease his face, he shifted his attention to the side mirror, stared off into the dark, and waited patiently for the inevitable arrival of the ever-persistent Washington Generals.

Chapter 68

After reading the brief message, Cade had spent a few minutes in deep thought all alone in the dark.

Having come to a hard-fought decision, he retraced his steps to the compound entrance, along the way throwing the soiled towel on the heap of camouflage clothing destined for the fire pit.

Passing through the security station, he stopped to inquire about Daymon and Heidi.

"Still not a word," said Lev, his voice suggesting defeat.

"Duncan been out and about?"

Lev was silent for a few seconds. Finally, he said, "He went outside briefly. When he returned, Glenda headed him off in the foyer. He said a couple of words I couldn't make out. Next thing I know she's lighting him up. That goes on for a few seconds and then they passed through here all quiet and icy."

Having a good idea what was brewing, Cade said nothing. Instead, he pulled up the message on the satellite phone and showed it to Lev.

"Where there's a will ..." began Lev, meeting his friend's steely gaze.

"There's a way," finished Cade, his jaw taking a hard set.

"Still hell-bent on going solo?"

Cade nodded.

Lev offered Cade a fist to bump. "Stay frosty, friend."

Cade touched knuckles with the former soldier. Then he took a pad of paper and pen from the desk and continued on his way.

SR-39

Dregan had to wait just south of two minutes for the dead to again show their faces in his side mirror. At first, the glimpses of arms and legs pistoning mechanically as the front ranks staggered into the splash of multicolored light made him think he was on some studio back lot and staring at horrors made up in a special effects shop. He was dragged back to reality a half-beat later when angry-sounding snarls rose over the music being piped through the speaker. And as the mega-horde drew nearer, shrubs and hedges growing up beside the narrow sidewalks folded over and disappeared from view, victims of its steady, unstoppable advance.

Spurred on forcefully from behind, the expanding edge of the lead element met a two-story house head on, causing it to shudder and slide from its foundation. Gunshot-like cracks resounded as mature trees in front and back of the house knuckled under to tremendous pressures when the walking corpses surged around the home as if it were a stone in a fast-moving stream.

With a bone-jarring bang, a dead thing smashed against the passenger side glass. It had come out of the dark and the resulting shock caused Dregan to jump in his seat and drop the spotlight on his lap, the heated glass lens singing his skin through the fabric of his pants.

Letting out a yelp, he brushed the spotlight from his leg and inadvertently let his foot slip off the brake pedal. Whereas the Brady Mobile should have started a slow roll forward under power of the idling V8, it didn't move an inch.

Dregan's stomach relocated to his throat as the realization hit him that he could no longer feel the vibration of the engine through his boot soles. Somehow it had stalled out. And between the ditty coming from the speaker and the noise of the horde destroying everything in its path, its untimely death had gone unnoticed.

As he cycled the key in the ignition and listened to the starter crank futilely, the lone zombie gave up on the passenger window and started a slow shuffle through the headlight beams.

Dregan glanced at the gauges again. Saw that the needles were all parked in the acceptable ranges. Strangely, though he'd logged roughly ten miles—some of them over questionable terrain and had left the motor idling for substantial periods of time—the gas gauge was still pegged at *Full*.

When Dregan tapped the gauge with his finger, three things happened simultaneously. In unison, both the gas needle and his stomach started a freefall, with the former hitting the stops at *Empty*. As the latter began to do acrobatics, the flimsy glass slider to his left shattered and a cold, gnarled hand took hold of his beard.

Leaning his upper body hard to the right, Dregan shot his left hand toward the window and grabbed the creature by the neck. Cursing himself for letting his guard down, he straightened his arm and drew the .45 from its holster. As he thumbed back the hammer, in his head he heard Gregory's voice saying *It was full when Hodges gave me the keys*. And when he jammed the pistol's blued barrel between the deadhead's snapping teeth and pulled the trigger, he was also cursing himself a second time for believing the recent retiree would part with the only link to his past life *and* deliver it to the self-professed Gas Baron of Salt Lake with a full tank of the precious commodity.

The resulting discharge was deafening inside the cab. Because of the barrel's angle relative to the zombie's throat, the expanding gasses exiting the muzzle caused its cheeks to balloon to Dizzy-Gillespie-like proportions. A microsecond later everything from the lip up was being rearranged by the 230-grain slug.

Like a scene from a cartoon, the thing's milky eyes bugged out an inch from the sockets and its nose ripped away at the base and smacked against its forehead.

Dregan watched the monster slip from view. There one second. Gone the next. Then he was aware of the steady ringing happening between his ears. The one positive takeaway from discharging the weapon at close range and in confined quarters was that the cacophonous duel between the looping song and calls of the clamoring horde was now replaced by the constant high-pitched tone.

Causing Dregan to wish his olfactory had also been compromised, the stench of death and decay riding a surge of air enveloped the truck. The gunpowder nose was quickly usurped as tendrils of the carrion-heavy air entered the cab through the broken window.

Eyes locked on the side mirror, he grabbed hold of the spotlight, hung it out the window, and switched it on. The sight that greeted him was not good. True to the admonition etched into the mirror, the objects were truly closer than he had anticipated.

"Damn you, Hodges," exclaimed Dregan as the slow-moving wall of walking dead slammed hard into the Brady Mobile from behind and sent it rolling forward. With the engine stilled, the power steering wasn't working. Which stopped Dregan from correcting the truck's trajectory before the right-side wheels slipped off the shoulder and found the ditch.

The roll was slow at first, but picked up speed as the horde slammed into the truck's rear end a second time.

Dregan was propelled forward out of his seat. Then, when he should have been coming back down on the cushion, he instead crashed face first into the windshield, his ribs taking a beating from the steering wheel. In the serving area behind him, metal items clanged together as drawers and cupboard doors opened, spilling their contents on the floor which was quickly trading places with the ceiling.

As the truck settled on its roof in the roadside ditch, Dregan found himself curled in a ball and staring up at the seat he'd just been bucked out of.

Before he had a chance to drag himself to a sitting position, hands were probing for him. In no amount of time the hands pulled back and the face of a long dead woman filled up the space.

There was a prolonged groan of buckling panels and the truck was forced deeper into the ditch. As a result, dirt spilled in around the wriggling corpse.

Ducking down and peering over the upended dash afforded Dregan a true read on the fix he was in. He saw dozens of faces mashed against the windshield. Behind him, more sneering faces filled up the passenger glass.

After saying a quick little prayer asking for his boys to be happy and safe from harm for the remainder of their lives, he took his .45 from its holster, pressed the gaping muzzle to the flat underneath his chin, and squeezed the trigger.

Chapter 69

Raven was snoring louder than ever when Cade entered the Grayson quarters. Apparently the melatonin was doing its job. As he closed the door, Max approached and nuzzled the Glock in his hand.

"Don't want to do that again, boy," he whispered. He set the pistol on the table by the door and spent a minute lavishing the dog with attention. Finished, he knelt on the floor and slowly pulled the foot-locker-sized Pelican case containing his gear out from behind the bunk that Brook—when she wasn't involved in a body-warmth-seeking incursion to his side—used to call her own.

Sitting on his bunk, he popped the latches and hinged the top over. He took from the box his black kit: fatigues, plate carrier, chest rig, backpack, and tactical bump helmet. He fished out a pair of night vision goggles and spare batteries for them. Wading through the gear at the bottom of the box, he selected batteries in the correct sizes for his M4's tactical light and EOTech optics. Lastly, he plucked out the orange bottle of Hoppes No. 9 gun oil and some clean rags and set it all on the table with his Glock.

With Max supervising, he spent an hour preparing his kit. He stripped, cleaned, and oiled his weapons, checking every moving part twice along the way. The batteries in everything he would be taking north with him were replaced with new items taken from packaging stamped with the best *Use By* dates.

He broke the MSR down, seated the pieces in the foam, closed the case and set it by the door with his suppressor-equipped M4, Glock 19, and Gerber dagger.

Cade moved the chair to the table by the door and sat down. He spent a few minutes writing on the pad, then tore the sheets off, labeled them, and folded them neatly. Next, he removed the ring from the chain around his neck and placed it neatly atop the folded pages. After setting the Suunto's alarm for 0100, he killed the light and stretched out on the bunk. A few short seconds of listening to his daughter's calm breathing put him out like the bulb he had just extinguished.

***

Cade awoke from a light slumber and, despite the impenetrable dark inside the Conex container, kept his eyes sealed shut for a long ten-count and listened hard to the goings on around him. First thing he detected was the slow, steady cadence of Raven's breathing. Then he heard a low groan and faint scrabble of nails on wood that told him Max was underneath his bunk somewhere and likely engaged in a doggy dream.

Next, he thumbed the Suunto's light button and learned he had five minutes to spare before the alarm was set to sound. Which was a good thing. First, it meant he had twenty minutes instead of fifteen to get his ducks in a row prior to the agreed-upon extraction time. Second, it meant he could use that extra five minutes to make sure he and Lev were both on the same page.

After strapping on his helmet and powering up the attached pair of night vision goggles, he dressed in his black fatigues and collected his gear and weapons.

He stooped to collect the Pelican case and felt a cold nose brush his wrist that earned Max a ten-second scratching behind the ears.

Standing there in the dark, he let his gaze roam the room. Seeing the place he had called home for several weeks bathed in the soft green glow of the NVGs was eerie. Seeing his daughter lying on her bunk, blissfully aware of his presence, was disconcerting, to say the least. For when he usually saw people in this light, both literally and metaphorically, he was usually killing them in their sleep. Blowing her a kiss across the distance, he crept out of room and closed the door at his back.

Out in the corridor, Cade left the NVGs powered on but swiveled them up on their mount.

Squinting against the light thrown from the bulb in the security area, he rounded the corner and greeted Lev.

"Any word on Daymon?"

Lev shook his head. "Nothing. I've been trying them every hour on the hour. All of these—" he indicated the trio of radios and lone long-range CB handset lined up on the desk before him"—have been silent as a brick since you were here last."

"Five and a half hours and nothing coming out of Bear River?"

"Nothing," said Lev. "For now, I'm taking it to mean there's nothing new to report." He shrugged. "Which is a good thing, I guess."

"I concur," said Cade. "We'll know for sure real soon." He nodded to the sleek black handset atop the desk. "Keep an eye on the Thuraya. I'll send you a SITREP after I get a bird's eye view of the 39/16 junction."

"Roger that," said Lev.

"Who's on perimeter duty?"

"Seth and Tran. They called in an hour ago and said the rotters are beginning to show in pretty big numbers up by the road."

"They're culling them, I trust."

Lev nodded. "Watched Tran take out a few of them on the closed circuit. Seemed pretty confident."

"Sets me at ease a little," admitted Cade. "It's always hard to leave Raven behind."

Brow knitting, Lev asked, "How long are you planning on being gone?"

"If all goes well I should be back before noon. If things go sideways I'll try and give you a heads up." He paused for a beat. "If Murphy intervenes and I don't come back—"

Shaking his head vehemently, Lev interrupted, "You can't take that kind of thinking downrange with you."

Cade stared at his friend for a long ten-count then went on, saying, "If I don't return, I left instructions on the table in there. The envelope is from Brook. The folded sheets are from me."

In a funereal voice, Lev said, "You're doing this for her, aren't you?"

"I'd put my body in front of a speeding train to keep Raven from being harmed."

Lev said, "I take that as a yes." He rose and spread his arms wide.

Cade set the Pelican case on the plywood floor and, right then and there in the cramped confines with a lone bulb swinging and casting wild shadows, accepted the offered embrace.

Chapter 70

Before leaving the compound, Cade flipped the NVGs down so that they rested in front of his eyes. Suspended by the mount on the front of his tactical helmet, they moved wherever his head went and gave him the ability to see without being seen.

After having Lev lock the compound's outer door once he stepped into the crisp night air, Cade made his way to the edge of the clearing where he caught sight of a lone figure sitting on a camp chair underneath the RV's metal awning. He paused for a second and scanned the tree line. Seeing nothing there to cause him alarm, he strode off across the clearing.

Nearing the dirt airstrip, Cade stopped walking and looked skyward. The clouds were high and through occasional breaks in them he saw stars winking. A light wind kicked up from the west as he continued on. The aroma of pines and dewy grass and mineral rich soil carried on it reminded him of long nights spent in the mountains in hostile lands. Nights just like this when his sole aim was to find the enemy and kill before being killed. Only then he had had the luxury of a squad of likeminded warriors to fight alongside. Tonight he was venturing into truly uncharted waters. Waters that could just as easily swallow him up before the mission's objective was complete.

As he continued his slow steady pace across the wide expanse of knee-high grass, he saw the form on the chair seem to stiffen. Two dozen yards from the RV, he said, "Thunder," to announce his presence.

"Lightning," said the man in the chair in a soft drawl.

Cade approached Duncan in silence. He set the Pelican case on the ground and took a seat on a folding chair across from his friend.

Duncan switched his headlamp on for a spell and looked Cade up and down. Switching it off, he said, "Suppressed weapons. All black BDUs. Vest and loads of extra mags. Helmet and night vision. Looks to me like the quiet one is fixing to cut fence and sort some bastards out."

Cade didn't nod. It would have been lost on Duncan in the dark. Instead, he said, "Loose ends need to be tied."

"Even a person putting a bow on a gift needs an extra finger now and again."

"I'm not wrapping presents," shot Cade. In the green glow of the NVGs he noticed the pint bottle clutched in Duncan's hand. "Glenda caught you drinking, didn't she?"

Duncan nodded toward the RV. Drawled, "Yep. Why I'm sleeping in there tonight."

Cade said nothing. He glanced at his Suunto, noted the time, then shifted his gaze to the far end of the clearing where he needed to be in five minutes. On the exact spot he was deposited days ago immediately before making the longest uphill trudge of his life. At the end of which he had forced himself to perform the hardest task he had ever faced in his life.

"She'll get over it," said Duncan.

"Will she?" said Cade. "You're sure as hell going to regret it if she doesn't." He saw Duncan plant his elbows on his knees and slump forward in his chair. He added, "That's all I'm going to say about the matter. You're a grown man."

Changing the subject, Duncan said, "When's your ride gonna be here?"

"Three mikes."

"Better get, then."

Cade rose and snatched up his case. As he shouldered his M4, he placed a gloved hand on his friend's shoulder. He felt the shoulder twitch, then start to jerk in his grasp. Aided by the NVGs, he noticed tears streaming from under the lenses of the man's bifocals. And clear as day, albeit cast in shades of green, he noted the tremors beginning to wrack his doubled-over body.

Leaving the man to deal with his demons his own way, Cade struck out for the far end of the clearing, already roping demons of his own and shoving them deep down into the void where everything important and trivial went before he set foot outside the wire.

***

Cade felt the familiar harmonic vibration signaling the helo's arrival fifteen seconds before the stealth aircraft ripped over the clearing at near treetop level. As it flashed from tree line to tree line, the airframe and whirring rotor blades was but a green blur, the sharp angles softened by speed and Cade's inability to track it fully before it disappeared.

Recon pass, he thought. Flying with the aid of NVGs of their own, the pilot or copilot should have seen him standing in the predesignated area all alone. Either that or the copilot had been working the forward-looking infrared pod during the pass and picked up his heat signature.

***

Twenty seconds after the initial flyby, the helicopter snaked in from the opposite direction at roughly half the speed as before, flared hard overhead, and began a quick vertical descent.

Standing just outside the rotor cone, Cade was buffeted by the wash and the grass at his feet bent over and whipped at his boots. Seeing the landing gear spring from internal bays and the port side door begin a slow crawl backward, he picked the Pelican case up off the ground and ran toward the settling helo. One hand on his helmet and bent low at the waist, he made it to the door just as the Ghost Hawk's wheels settled on the rain-softened soil.

At once the wiry crew chief jumped from the open door and, aided by NVGs of his own, made a quick visual sweep of the clearing. Finished scanning the tree lines, he acknowledged Cade by name, took the rifle case out of his hands, and ushered him aboard.

Chapter 71

The Ghost Hawk's troop compartment was bathed in red light and smelled of sweat, gun oil, and aviation fuel. Feeling the bird go light on her gear, Cade shrugged off his M4 and grabbed the first available forward-facing seat. Just as he was getting his safety harness buckled, the door snugged shut and the turbine whine rose exponentially. With the g-forces from takeoff pressing him firmly to his seat, he cast his gaze around the cabin. Expecting to be alone with the crew chief, he was surprised to see four men that he knew staring back at him. All were clutching various weapons and dressed in full battle rattle: MultiCam fatigues, vests brimming with spare magazines, combat knives, and semiauto pistols in drop-leg holsters. The NVGs adorning their helmets were swung away from their eyes and grins were forming on their faces.

"Take this," mouthed the crew chief, handing a headset to Cade. "And these," he added, placing a set of four-tube NVGs on the seat beside the black-clad operator. "Swap them out ASAP. You can thank me later."

Cade removed his helmet and donned the comms gear. Staring at the SOAR crew chief everyone called Skipper, he said, "Commo check."

Eye sockets awash in the soft white glow emanating from his deployed NVGs, Skipper flashed a thumbs-up and replied, "Solid copy."

Cade felt the helo beginning to spin on axis while in his headset he heard a familiar voice say, "Thanks for choosing Night Stalker Airways."

Leaning to his left and craning his head hard over, Cade spotted SOAR aviator extraordinaire Ari Silver staring back from

421

the right seat. He was wearing deployed NVGs and, like Skipper, his eyes were aglow from the pale white light spilling from the device's ocular lenses. In the left seat was an imposing figure that could be mistaken for no other aviator in the storied 160th Special Operations Aviation Regiment. How the African American Warrant Officer named Haynes poured his six-foot-four-inch frame into the seat was a mystery to Cade. However, what he did know, based on the pair of previous missions with Haynes at the controls, was that the man was Ari's near equal when it came to piloting the futuristic Jedi ride.

"Wyatt," said Haynes, flashing his always ready smile. "How's it hanging?"

Cade raised his hand above his head while holding his thumb and pointer finger an inch apart.

"Don't sell yourself *short*," boomed Haynes, his words morphing to laughter.

Smiling at that, Cade swept his gaze clockwise around the cabin. Off to his left, leaning against the port-side window, was Adam Cross, Navy SEAL turned Special Agent to the President. Sitting adjacent to the blond-haired, blue eyed surfer-boy-looking operator was another SEAL who answered only to Griff. The thick-necked, heavily bearded operator, originally hailing from Boston, shifted his Hecker & Koch MP7 submachine gun aside and bumped fists with Cade. Back parked firmly to the port-side bulkhead and sporting a tangle of red whiskers barely passing for a beard, British SAS shooter Nigel Axelrod nodded and flashed a thumbs-up.

Lastly, Cade fixed a dumbfounded stare on the Delta operator just days removed from a burst appendix. He said, "Last time I saw you, you were on death's door. Shouldn't you still be in a hospital bed recuperating?"

"I was just a little toxified, that's all. Got a few staples out of the deal," replied the stocky Hispanic captain as he slowly patted his gut. "No way I was going to leave you hanging, Wyatt."

Not yet fully grasping the meaning of the last part of Lopez's comment, Cade regarded the operator's MultiCams. Seeing that they were clean and crisp, he cast scrutiny on the rest of the joint team and noted that their uniforms looked the same.

"You guys aren't returning from an op?" he asked.

Slowly, Lopez shook his head.

Cade felt the Ghost Hawk's nose dip and intuitively he knew it was pointed east. A tick later he realized what was up and locked eyes with Lopez. "All I asked Beeson for was a ride north."

Ari interrupted. "What do you think I am? An Uber driver?"

"No idea what that's supposed to mean," conceded Cade. He looked at Cross, who just shrugged and made the universal sign of the idiot by setting his finger on a lazy orbit of his right ear.

"This new ride-sharing startup in Frisco that *was* going to fund my retirement," Ari replied glumly.

"Then the shit hit the fan," said Haynes. "And ... *poof* ... no Uber."

"And no helo tour operation on Oahu for Ari, either," added Skipper.

Cade looked over and saw that Skipper had already swapped out the old NVGs on his bump helmet for the new models.

"Thanks," he said, taking the helmet back and snugging it on.

Lopez slapped his thigh and regarded Cade. "Damn, Wyatt. I almost forgot you." He pulled a round, flat item about the circumference of a tennis ball from his breast pocket and passed it over. "It's Beeson-approved. Slap it on your shoulder and join the club."

Cade glanced at the patch. Dominating the center, red-eyed and cloaked in a black robe, was the Grim Reaper. Instead of the ubiquitous death-dealing scythe, he was clutching in his skeletal hands an M4 carbine complete with optics, foregrip, and stubby suppressor. Stitched in black below the Reaper were the words *PALE RIDERS*. Arcing above the mascot's head in the same black font was the word: *BASTION*.

"Bastion Pale Riders," said Cade as he pressed the patch to the hook-and-loop facing on his upper sleeve. "Has a nice ring to it."

Smiling wide, Lopez said, "I'm glad you approve. I designed it while I was plotting my escape from the docs at Schriever."

"If this whole saving the world thing doesn't work out," said Cade, "you got something to fall back on."

"Five mikes," called Haynes over the shipwide comms.

Skipper killed the cabin lights and urged Cade to power his new "*eyes*" on.

Finding the switch by feel in the dark, Cade threw it and dragged the goggles down over his face and positioned the ocular lenses in front of his eyes. Instantly it seemed as if the helo's interior was lit up by overhead fluorescents. Everything around him was rendered in black and white with gradients of gray thrown in. The depth perception the new NVGs afforded him was unreal.

"What is this sorcery?" he exclaimed.

Goggles deployed and aimed across the cabin, Cross said, "White phosphor technology. Super top secret stuff. Just before the shit hit the fan, DARPA sent two dozen pairs to DEVGRU to have them put them through the wringer."

"Try to break them, basically," added Griff.

"How'd *you* all get them?"

"Beeson pulled some strings," said Lopez. "He's head of JSOC now. And that's why you're getting more than just a ride and an infil. After having to root out the Green River squatters, he's all for cleaning house early and often wherever the bad elements try to stake claims. This is one of those instances. Good for you President Clay thinks along those lines, too. Ounce of prevention is worth a pound of cure were her exact words."

Incredulous, Cade asked, "He's running Joint Special Operations Command out of Springs now?"

Again with the slow side to side wag of the head, Lopez replied, "Negative. Out of Bastion. You should see it now. Heavy lift birds have been coming in and out of Grand Junction every day since you saw it last. President Clay wants it to be Springs West, so to speak. They're already planning on housing essential personnel in Fruita and all the little towns along the Book Cliffs."

424

"Then I assume, if he's the head honcho, he ran with the intel I forwarded and conjured up satellite and sigint on Adrianville."

"Even better," replied Lopez. "I mentioned the possibility that she may be aiding and abetting the PLA. Said it with a wink and a nudge, even. I'll throw up the real-time drone feed once we're pushing north."

"Beats the alternative," said Cade. Mesmerized by the sight of his gloved hand as seen through the new goggles, he turned it over and moved his palm rapidly back and forth in front of his face. "I can't wait to see what the world outside looks like viewed through these."

Ari broke in over the comms. "Wyatt, your wish is my command. Port side, two o'clock, everyone. Behold Cade and the gang's handiwork. Bet you guys hollered *Wolverines* as you lit 'em up."

Cade didn't respond. He was already peering below the craft. At what he guessed to be two hundred feet above ground level the shot-up vehicles looked like Tonka trucks in a diorama. The clarity of the white phosphor NVGs afforded him depth perception in the dark that rivaled what he was used to in the light of day. He could see the pile of spent brass he had cleaned out of the Humvee. He could make out skeletal forms still seated in the smoldering wreckage. Pooled blood actually seemed to glisten. And when he cast his gaze to the van, the legs protruding from its rear doors were easily identifiable as just that—down to the brand of tennis shoes one of them was wearing.

"Stacked them like cordwood," said Ari. "How many did you bag?"

Cade felt all eyes on him. "I've seen enough," he said, still looking groundward.

Lopez said, "Wait until you see the mansion. You sure did a number on that place."

Slowly, Cade swung his gaze up. He fixed a stare on Lopez and mouthed, "What mansion?"

"The one southeast of your first ambush site. Big footprint. Must have been three stories from the amount of debris. Big timbers."

Elbows on knees, Cade asked, "Outbuildings? Garage?"

Lopez said, "The garage had to be at least an eight-car job."

"I spotted what looked to be a basketball court off the port side," added Cross.

Feeling a cold finger of dread trace his spine, Cade said, "Ari, I need to see it."

Chapter 72

The closer Jedi One-One got to the site of Cade's first ambush, the more Zs he was seeing down below on SR-39. During some of the bigger breaks in the tree cover where long stretches of the winding two-lane were revealed, he saw herds of them, some several dozen strong, traipsing west toward Huntsville and an eventual meet-up with Daymon's roadblock of fallen trees. Standing out starkly against the blacktop, Cade couldn't help but think how ghost-like the gray hued forms appeared from his vantage.

The still-smoldering remains of the house were visible from a mile out. Once Ari brought the Ghost Hawk into a tight clockwise orbit over the site, Cade was certain he was looking down on what used to be Casa De Daymon.

Hundreds of Zs drawn in by the conflagration milled about the property.

Daymon's black Chevy pickup remained on the circular drive near the front stairs. Its paint was bubbled and all four of its tires had been reduced to pools of molten rubber. Though he couldn't be certain—or didn't want to be—it looked as if the sides and rear of the pickup were peppered with bullet holes.

"Can you run the FLIR over the site?" asked Cade.

"FLIR coming on line," responded Haynes. "Patching the feed to the cabin monitor."

Underneath the helo's angular chin, the gimbal-mounted pod containing the advanced optics suite came to life.

Inside the troop compartment, Cade flipped up his goggles and watched the moving image captured by the thermal camera on the flat panel affixed to the aft-facing bulkhead.

The inferno had reduced the mansion to nothing but cement foundation, stone fireplace footings, and a few lengths of what had been massive beams that had failed to burn completely.

The garage was a complete loss structurally. All Cade could distinguish from the rubble were the burned metal shells of several vehicles lost in the fire.

"No life," said Lopez.

"I concur," agreed Haynes.

As the helicopter made one last orbit, Cade plucked the Thuraya from a pocket and sent a quick SMS message to the phone Lev was monitoring. In it he detailed the number of dead near the intersection, then, rather reluctantly, he described what he had just witnessed on the ground, stressing that Daymon and Heidi were not accounted for. Finished, he stowed the phone and hung his head.

After a few seconds, Cade looked up and met Lopez's stare, held it for a second, then told him all about the mansion and the missing couple, all the way down to their descriptions and capabilities. Feeling a headache coming on as Ari brought the helicopter around for a second pass, he rested his helmet against the bulkhead and stared into the darkness overhead. He stayed that way for a beat before redeploying his NVGs. Finally, gaze swinging over to the window, he said in a low voice, "We can go now."

***

Overflying the first ambush site revealed to Cade that though the bodies were still lined up in a neat row and the pickups and automobiles were still parked haphazardly and blocking the side street, someone had stripped the former and butchered them for their meat. There wasn't even enough left on the bones to attract the Zs ambling about the side street.

Main Street, on the other hand, was unrecognizable. The import and Cadillac once blocking the road were now half a block north. The former was on its side with its front end speared into a storefront all the way to its A-pillar. The latter, unbelievably, ended up balanced atop the thick trunk of an uprooted tree in a trampled yard fronting a two-story house.

"Lots of dead wankers down there," observed Axe. "Haven't seen that many since Salt Lake City."

Cade cast a glance at him.

"It was overrun, mate. Worse than the District. Way worse."

"I'm sure some of these are one and the same," said Cade. "We've seen a horde moving north and south on the state route for several weeks now. Each time it returns it's exponentially bigger." He felt the helo nose down and watched the buildings lining Main Street glide by.

A few beats later they were nearing Woodruff's northern limits and Cade was seeing the church steeple off the helo's starboard side. Concurrently, the same image, picked up by the FLIR camera, was filling up the monitor to his fore.

"This new FLIR pod Whipper threw on can pick up heat sigs behind walls. They're part of the same DARPA project responsible for the phosphor white NVGs," called Haynes. "No heat sigs in the steeple. You satisfied, Wyatt? Or should we take a closer look?"

"Good money says Adrian's called her flock home," he replied.

"Sounds biblical," noted Cross.

Revisiting the morbid scene at the Thagons' place in his head, Cade said, "Nothing biblical about Adrian. She's doing the same thing to the Bible that the radical Islamists do to the Koran. Her and her kind are evil. Pure evil."

Griffin tapped a finger on his port-side window. "Looks like the Good Humor man had a very bad day."

Cade craned but saw nothing.

Haynes said, "Coming up," and the image on the monitor began to move. The steeple slipped away to screen-right and was quickly replaced by a boxy, wheeled object rendered in muted shades of gray. As more detail was revealed it became clear the image on the screen was of a vehicle resting on its roof.

"That wasn't there earlier," said Cade.

"The motor and exhaust apparatus are presenting as cold," noted Axe.

The image grew small on the screen as the helicopter continued north at a slow low-level crawl.

Ari entered the conversation. "Maybe the mega-horde brought it with them from Salt Lake."

"And maybe it still has some Sponge Bob popsicles in its freezer," said Lopez sarcastically. "You guys remember running after the ice cream man?"

Griff perked up. "That Eddie Murphy skit was the shit."

Cross piped up. "Oh man ... I miss Nestle Crunch ice cream bars."

Throwing cold water on the trip down memory lane, Lopez said, "Haynes, kindly put the latest intel on the monitor."

"Anything for my best customers," he quipped.

A few seconds passed before an overhead image of the location marked Adrianville on Cade's map splashed on the screen.

Lopez said, "Study that for a moment, Wyatt. Then I'll throw on the overlay showing where the other teams are laying up."

Jumping into a mission mid-flow was totally foreign to Cade. Caught flat-footed, he said, "Looks a lot like UBL's compound in Abbottabad."

"It's about ten times the size of Usama's place," Cross proffered.

"It holds ten times as many girlfriends as well," quipped Griff.

Cade shot him a questioning look.

Seeing the subtle tilt to Cade's head, Cross jumped in. "There's goats roaming wild inside the perimeter."

"And pigs in a pen behind a barn," added Ari. "You believe that? In the middle of the end of the world these mutts find time to have a good old-fashioned barn raising."

Griff said, "Maybe we can talk one of the Chinook drivers into taking a couple of hogs back to Bastion. Have us an honest to God hog roast."

Ari flashed a thumbs-up to the customers in back. "Best idea I've heard out of you ground pounders in weeks. We'll have us a full-on luau in the high desert of Utah. Haven't had Kahlua pork since that layover in Pearl before the event changed everything."

Haynes said, "And I haven't had relations with a woman since that joint exercise."

Tuning out the banter, Cade looked to Lopez and asked, "How many other teams?"

"Two Ranger chalks and a pair of ODA teams usually working out of Kit Carson. Both have been running ops out of Bastion for some time and happened to be on stand-down between rotations back to Springs." He went on to detail their call signs and personnel make-up.

"That's a lot of bodies," Cade said, incredulous. "Are the 10th Group Green Berets the same teams Gaines commanded?"

Lopez nodded. "All top-notch pipe hitters. Hell, after the horrors his boys found in Green River, Beeson doesn't want to see any of these monsters slip the net."

As Cade committed the image on the screen to memory, he heard Ari in his headset talking to a two-ship flight somewhere northeast of their current position. Then the comms channel switched and Ari's voice was replaced by the sound of Lopez hailing the two Green Beret teams designated Dagger One and Dagger Two.

Feeling much better about his prospects of returning home to Raven, Cade subconsciously reached for the wedding ring, but instead came up with his dog tags. Seeing Lopez shoot him a furrowed-brow look, he dropped the tags back into the slot between his plate carrier and MOLLE rig. Fighting the sheepish feeling brought about by getting caught showing even a scintilla of emotion, he went stone-faced and mouthed, "Next image."

While Cade waited for Haynes to fulfill his request, he looked groundward just in time to see the southern edge of the small town of Randolph slip by underneath the slow-moving helicopter. There he saw hundreds of Zs crowding the half-dozen blocks making up the blink-once-and-you-miss-it municipality. The structures lining yet another Main Street were damaged, some having been nudged from their foundations. Mere seconds after overflying the southern limits they were crossing the north end of town where a dozen windowless cars with mangled bumpers and dented sheet metal had been deposited in one mountainous tangle.

"Enemy strength estimates coming at you," said Haynes as the satellite image of the triangular-shaped compound was replaced by camera stills shot at night from a hide very near to the walled compound.

Cade addressed Lopez. "I take it I'm not going to need the MSR?"

"We have overwatch teams in place. They're going to hit the guards as soon as we're making our move."

"Roger that," Cade said then continued staring at Lopez.

"You have something else?"

"One of the things I've been worried about is the presence of kids."

Lopez shifted uneasily in his seat.

Cade continued to stare.

"Nothing concrete," replied Lopez. "Overwatch has only been in place since 1900 hours."

"There's sports balls scattered all over the asphalt," said Cross. "Also a few of those plastic playsets are set up on the grassy areas. There's got to be kids on site."

"Rules of engagement?" asked Cade.

"Once boots are on the ground it's operator's discretion to shoot," said Lopez. "And that came straight out of Beeson's mouth and was delivered with a wink."

Cade said nothing. He was already trying to decide what he was going to do to the adult cannibals when he was looking them in the eyes. Figured whatever it was, it was by no means going to be pretty, nor was it going to be humane. For in his mind, these animals didn't deserve to keep stealing air from the good people of the world.

Chapter 73

By crow, the distance between Randolph and Laketown, the latter of which was but a stone's throw from the cul-de-sac compound near Bear Lake's south shore, was roughly eleven miles. Overland via the snaking two-lane, the distance between the two was nearly double that.

From Randolph's limits, US-30 cut north by east for nine miles before coming back on itself and shooting straight north by west to a meetup with Laketown a dozen miles away.

Somewhere along the first nine-mile run is where Cade figured the Ghost Hawk would overtake the shambling mega-horde.

***

Four minutes' flight-time north of Randolph the stench of death found its way into the helo's cabin. Cade's hunch was confirmed seconds later when the FLIR picked up the mega-horde's tail just prior to the dogleg where 30 shot west to Laketown. Consisting of several hundred stragglers, it stretched out for more than a mile behind the main body which had already made the turn and was lurching north by west on a collision course with Laketown.

"Behold, off the port side," said Ari over the shipwide comms. "In all their decaying glory, we have an honest to goodness mega-horde in the flesh ... or, what's left of it."

Haynes made a rimshot-like sound in his mike.

The main body of Zs were stretched out in a long, narrow column for as far as Cade could see. Amazingly they were mostly staying to the road, although here and there the outliers would get caught up in a wire fence and cause a pile-up until either the posts gave or the stray rotters were sliced into pieces and their bodies trampled in place.

As Haynes's laughter filtered back from the cockpit, Cade was struck by how seamlessly the big aviator was meshing with Ari's unorthodox style. At times, it seemed as if Haynes was channeling the late Durant's acerbic wit. Once Haynes quieted down, Ari cracked, "Keep your arms and hands inside the bus at all times. Wouldn't want one of you to get *bit*."

Not funny, thought Cade. He looked to Skipper and asked him if the scientists had made any improvements to the Omega antiserum.

Skipper shook his head. Then he offered his condolences for Cade's loss. "I've been trying to figure a way to say that since I closed the door behind us back at your compound."

Cade bobbed his head, saying, "It is what it is."

"And your daughter—" Unsure of her name, he paused.

"Raven," offered Cade.

"How is Raven taking it?"

"Good as can be expected for a twelve-year-old."

Feeling the helo banking hard to port, Cade went quiet and stared out his starboard window at the cloud cover. A beat later the helo returned to level flight and Bear Lake was visible. Though it was still miles distant, viewed in white phosphor it looked so true to life that he felt the urge to take an eye-opening plunge into its frigid waters.

Snapping him back to reality, the helo's airspeed halved and the monitor filled with the real-time feed from the constantly sweeping FLIR pod.

"Keep your eyes peeled, gents and gents," said Ari. "We have officially entered Indian country."

***

The stretch of 30 running west to Laketown was home only to small groups of walking dead and head-high mounds of moldering, twice-dead corpses.

Twice the FLIR picked up herds of deer, their individual forms presenting as white silhouettes.

"No two-legged beasties," declared Haynes.

"Clear on my front," added Griff as Cross nodded his approval.

"No contacts to starboard," said Skipper.

Silent nearly the whole way, Axe piped up, "I'll take bloody Bambi over getting shot at any day."

"Shot at you may be before the night's over," said Ari.

"From the mouth of Yoda," quipped Haynes. Then, all business, he added, "Coming up on the cul-de-sac garrison. Stay frosty."

Cade smiled as he shifted in his seat. Glancing groundward, he saw the drive-in diner Duncan had mentioned was used as a rallying point when Dregan and his crew came to aid in the assault. Without their timely help, Duncan, Daymon, and the others may have been killed along with Oliver and Foley. Sitting there all alone at the confluence of two westbound roads, the sight ubiquitous to small towns everywhere, made Cade pine for the time before the dead walked the earth, now more than ever.

The cul-de-sac was just as Duncan had described it: several two- and three-story houses distributed evenly around a circular patch of asphalt fed by a paved road, its entry point set back roughly two blocks to the south. The gate and cement freeway noise barriers were gone. Cade presumed they had been carted north and were incorporated into Adrianville's formidable perimeter wall.

***

A short flight north by west had them nearing Garden City. Down below Cade saw that someone had jammed the main road with a number of vehicles. Every one of the north/south-running streets had been given the same treatment. All in all, it looked as if every car registered in the tiny lakeside town had been used to deter passage through it.

During the five-second Garden City flyover, the FLIR picked up what everyone guessed was a raccoon, or, less likely, a very large feral cat picking its way through an alley running behind a row of boarded-up storefronts.

Other than that lone thermal hit, darkness and dead things owned the streets.

***

Continuing on the due north heading took them out over the western edge of Bear Lake for a short while before finally making landfall again on the southern edge of Fish Haven, Idaho.

Over the shared comms, Ari said, "We just crossed over into Idaho where open carry is legal, gentlemen. Next town is Fish Haven. Cade's map doesn't indicate there's a forward listening post. Still, this close to target I'm not going to take any chances on us being fingered before go time. To be safe, we'll loiter here for a spell. When I get the word I'll bring us around south by west. One big loop, real slow." He paused as the Ghost Hawk slowed and stopped in a dead hover over the lakeshore then hailed Skipper over the comms.

Cade saw the crew chief stiffen and shrug out of his safety harness. "Skip here, over," he replied, already rising up out of his usual seat.

"Deploy the starboard mini," ordered Ari. "You see anything down below that's on two legs and throwing a heat sig, shoot it before it can pull an E.T. and phone home."

"Roger that," said the crew chief. Then, without pause, he worked a lever and depressed a button that caused the hatch in front of the starboard minigun to begin parting noiselessly. Grabbing the grips on the weapon capable of spitting three thousand rounds a minute downrange, he swung the barrel downward and lifted up slightly until the swivel-mount baseplate locked with an audible click. A tick later the two halves of the weapons door reached the stops and seated into the airframe with a pair of soft clunks. Cupping his boom mike, Skipper said, "Starboard mini is on line."

"Copy that," said Ari as the helo resumed forward movement. "If Fish Haven is all clear we'll proceed north and follow the same routine at Saint Charles, Bloomington and then we'll just conduct a long-range sweep at our loiter position southwest of Paris."

With the slipstream beginning to tear at his flight suit, Skipper put his head on a swivel and dragged the weapon's six-barreled muzzle wherever his gaze happened to go.

***

There was no sign of a watcher anywhere inside Fish Haven's minuscule city limits. Furthermore, the smattering of homes on the outskirts of town were devoid of life. As soon as the barren, desert-like terrain was again filling up the port-side windows, the ship's turbine whine increased unexpectedly and Ari popped the craft up and over a picket of mature trees. Peering out his window, Cade saw that the trees, likely planted as a windbreak of sorts, ran all the way east to the lake's sandy shore.

Feeling his stomach settle as the helo resumed level flight, Cade shifted his gaze from the landscape scrolling by outside the ship and looked around the cabin.

Arms crossed over their weapons and heads bowed slightly, both SEALs appeared to be deep in thought. Cade concluded they were both stuffing all of the extraneous flotsam and jetsam not pertaining to the task at hand in a place similar to where his were stowed.

Sensing Cade's scrutiny, each operator flashed a thumbs-up and tapped their weapons—shooter semaphore for "good to go."

***

Saint Charles and Bloomington were crawling with Zs but showed no signs of life, human or otherwise.

Soon after bypassing Bloomington, Cade felt the helicopter beginning to slow. Then, a full six miles beyond the northernmost shore of Bear Lake, and barely a mile from the final waypoint where the helo would be just out of earshot from the target, the wind picked up out of the east and began to buffet the stealthy craft.

Cade felt the ship bob and shimmy as Ari made corrections to counter the intermittent gusts hitting them broadside. This continued for a short while until the Ghost Hawk banked hard to starboard and met the wind head on. Knowing that the sudden onset of blustery weather would not only further mask their

437

approach by air, but also act to cocoon any latent noise once their boots hit the ground, he smiled at the good fortune Mother Nature had just bestowed on them all.

Chapter 74

Zero dark thirty.

The witching hour.

Full dark.

Many terms had been coined for the slice of early morning bookended between midnight and four a.m., when a sentry's senses are dulled by sleep deprivation and boredom.

Cade didn't have a particular favorite among the many he'd heard over the years—the majority coming from the mouths of commanders during meticulous assault briefings—of which this operation had none.

As Cade stared at the image from the FLIR on the screen before him, he was seeing proof of that age-old theory. During the two or three minutes Ari had been holding the Ghost Hawk in a steady hover nearly a mile west of Bear Lake County Airport, also known as Adrianville to the killer cannibals, Cade had determined that two of the three guards were either asleep or lulled into an unmoving trance by a job only the most dedicated could endure for prolonged stretches of time. Didn't matter now. Another two minutes and the three armed guards separated by hundreds of yards and stationed in towers equidistant from each other would be asleep for good—all victims of .338 Lapua sleeping pills delivered from silenced rifles of the sniper teams positioned in hides outside the razor-wire-topped perimeter fencing.

As Haynes worked the FLIR from guard tower to guard tower, Cade gazed at the flat panel and soaked up all the details.

The two-strip municipal airport was set on a triangular-shaped plat of land he guessed to be roughly a thousand acres. A narrow river feeding into Bear Lake ran left to right along the airport's west perimeter, while the land behind the airport to the north and southeast was forest for as far as the eye could see.

As per most airports after the 9/11 attacks, Bear Lake County Airport had been fortified with hurricane fencing topped off with triple-strand barbed wire. Sheets of some kind of fabric hung from the fence. Judging by how little effect the wind had on it, Cade pegged it as canvas likely sourced from Army surplus tents.

Paved lanes feeding to the surrounding roads paralleled the fencing on the west and northeast sides. A wide swathe of grass whipped by the wind dominated the landscape southeast of the outer fencing. Beyond the undulating carpet of grass was the Bear Lake Wildlife Refuge, a sanctuary mainly for waterfowl that stretched three-plus miles south to the northern shore of Bear Lake.

Dozens of concrete freeway noise barriers were erected parallel with the three outer fence lines. Standing on end and shored up with milled timbers, they formed a smaller triangle within the vast outer perimeter fencing that completely encompassed the airport's multi-story administrative building and three airplane hangars. The two hangars on the right looked big enough to house several small planes, while the hangar abutting the centrally located administration building's west side was nearly twice as large. Hidden from view behind the smaller hangars were a trio of glass greenhouses. Behind the larger hangar was a newly constructed barn. From the aerial footage put up on the flat panel earlier, Cade knew there would be goats, pigs, and chickens roaming around in pens behind the barn. He had also noted a small fleet of tractors hitched up to plowing apparatus as well as a pair of boxy, Zamboni-looking vehicles he took to be harvesters. He thought: *Someone is planning on being here for the long haul.*

He craned left to get a look at the motor pool situated southwest of the smaller hangars. Parked on the apron was a smattering of cars and pickup trucks, a half-dozen semi-tractors with flatbed trailers still attached, and one lone eighteen-wheeler

440

hooked up to an oversized trailer, the words Custom Prefab Barns emblazoned on its slab side.

Heavy machinery sat in a neat row on the tarmac beside the tractor trailers. Cade counted two dozers, two diggers, and a solitary crane which was certainly the linchpin when it had come to erecting the concrete walls. And on each corner of those inner walls was a lone guard tower. Each rose a good fifteen feet above the tops of the cement barriers and, though Cade couldn't be certain because of the diminished clarity of the FLIR camera, all three looked to have been constructed with two-by-fours and plywood sheets.

Trapped between the outer and inner perimeters, hundreds of Zs roamed freely about the unkempt grassy infields. Small groups of them even doddered along the laser-straight stretches of asphalt runway not trapped within the walled-in perimeter.

Poor man's security guards.

As if reading Cade's mind, Cross said, "Sure beats running active patrols outside the walls."

"Or laying mines and sensors," added Griff.

"I'm just glad we don't have to deal with *demonios*," said Lopez, throwing a shudder that went unnoticed thanks to the slipstream infiltrating the troop compartment.

Smiling, Axe said, "A Screamer dropped into the middle of the *rotties* would instigate one hell of a football match."

"*Soccer!*" bellowed Cross and Griff, in unison.

Nipping the age-old argument in the bud before it had a chance to escalate, Ari said, "Five mikes out."

For the umpteenth time during the hour-plus they'd all been sitting in close proximity to one another, all around Cade his teammates checked weapons, patted pockets down, and tweaked adjustments on their NVGs and comms packs.

Chapter 75

As Ari called the two-minute mark over the shipwide comms, Cade felt the helo nose down and begin a slow crawl forward. Though he wasn't privy to the conversation taking place between Ari and the other aircraft in the package, he was at ease knowing that the steady shooting of three highly trained snipers was about to clear the way for their infil.

***

As Ari called out the one-minute mark, the distance from the standoff point roughly a mile west of the airport had been halved.

The ground below the Ghost Hawk, awash in detail thanks to the phosphor white of Cade's NVGs, was ripping by at a dizzying speed.

***

"Thirty seconds out," called Haynes, his voice calm and even.

Skipper let go of the minigun long enough to start the starboard door running back in its tracks.

Cade took a blast of cold, carrion-laced wind to the face.

No turning back now.

At this mark, the shooters were supposed to engage their targets. All parties involved in the hastily thrown-together planning session attended earlier by Beeson and the teams back at Bastion had concluded that the buffer would be sufficient to keep the inbound helos safe from an errantly fired round or bullet deflection that might occur as the guards were neutralized.

Three long beats later, all at once Cade saw on the flat panel the damage inflicted to the guards and in his headset heard Haynes saying, "Tangos Alpha, Bravo, Charlie are down. Twenty seconds to infil, gentlemen."

Cade watched Lopez perform the sign of the cross over his chest, kiss his fingers and look skyward.

Across the ship, on the port side, Cross and Griffin were already free from their safety harnesses and edging forward on their seats.

NVGs covering his eyes, Axe stared Cade's way and smiled wide. The SAS shooter mouthed, "Get some," and patted his carbine with a gloved hand.

Remembering the ferociousness the Brit brought to the battle last time he was downrange with the man, Cade nodded to show he was of the same mindset—and then some.

Gloved hands again wringing the grips, Skipper kept the minigun trained on the airport's main cluster of buildings as the low flying helo crossed the outer fencing and began to nose up in order to crest the taller inner walls.

Cade heard mechanicals at work underfoot as the landing gear motored out of their housings. Praying that Ari remembered what had happened to the stealth helicopter during the Abbottabad raid, he held his breath as the top of the cement wall flashed by just underneath the still-deploying landing gear.

Unlike the Abbottabad insertion, this one didn't end with an explosion and follow-on whirlwind of debris as composite rotor blades chewed into desert hardpan. Instead, the Ghost Hawk cleared the wall by a half-dozen feet, flared hard in front of the administration building's south-facing side, and alit softly on its landing gear.

As expected, Lopez didn't draw fire from the nearby guard tower when he scrambled through the helo's open door.

Hot on Lowrider's heels, Cade piled out with his head on a swivel and the M4's suppressor tracking with his eyes. Two hundred feet to his right the pair of dual-rotor stealth Chinooks drifted groundward, flared in unison, and settled on the tarmac nose-to-tail broadside to the smaller hangars. A blur of fluid motion, the Special Forces teams, Dagger One and Two, spilled out of the yawning rear ramps. Crouched low and with their weapons snugged to their shoulders, the teams split up and set off

444

toward their assigned hangars, separating the kids from the adults as their main objective. Then, as quickly as the hulking Ghost Chinooks had settled and disgorged the special ops troops, they were rising into the pale-white night sky and nosing off to the west.

"Go, go, go," said Lopez as Jedi One-One lifted off with a turbine whine and quickly peeled away after the retreating Chinooks. In seconds the matte-black helo was passing over the inner wall with less room to spare than when it had come in hot and laden down with the Delta team and all their gear.

Less than twenty seconds after the three helicopters touched down, all were well beyond the outer fence line and Adrianville was again as quiet as a morgue.

In his headset, Cade heard Lopez hail Jedi One-One and identify himself as Whiplash Actual. In the next beat, the stocky operator was on the move toward the administration building and requesting a SITREP from Haynes, who was monitoring the situation on the ground via a live feed being beamed to One-One from a Reaper drone orbiting somewhere high above.

Without a word, the team quickly made their way in the dark to the squat administration building's west-facing front door.

On the run, Cade eyed the structure's features. He spotted a short stack of stairs leading to the front door which looked to be a steel item. Above the door was a short rectangular window. And like the windows to the left and right of the main entry, it was blacked-out—covered from inside, he guessed.

Lopez stopped beside the door and tried the handle. He said, "Locked," and produced a lock gun from a cargo pocket. "Cover me," he whispered as he went to work.

In his headset, Cade heard Haynes assure all teams that the perimeter inside and out was presently clear of tangos.

Feeling Axe's hand on his shoulder and aware that the two SEALs were stacked up behind the SAS man, Cade aimed his rifle at the center panel on the door and nodded to Lopez.

"On one," Lopez called and started to count down from three.

Hearing the count arrive at "one," Cade mounted the stairs in a combat crouch and, weapon tracking left, followed the door's smooth inward swing. As he crossed the threshold the distinctive chatter of an AK-47 rang out from somewhere near the large hangar. Knowing the fire was likely directed at the Dagger teams, he ignored it and continued on. Amazed by the clarity the new NVGs provided, he zippered through a maze of desks and filing cabinets with ease. Putting the would-be obstacle course behind him, he slowed his gait and took a quick peek down a hallway branching off to the building's north side. Seeing only closed doors and muddied carpet stretching away to the right-hand bend at the end of the hall, he went to one knee and declared his sector clear.

While Cade was on the move, Axe and the SEALs had transited the tiled, open-air foyer and parted ways.

The SAS shooter skirted the low table and assemblage of cloth-upholstered chairs making up a waiting room of sorts. At the same instant Cade was calling his sector clear, Axe was training his carbine up the open stairwell off his right shoulder and declaring the same for his.

Before Cade was halfway through his sweep, Cross, Griff, and Lopez had stormed through the doorway in Axe's wake.

Throwing the door closed behind him, Lopez covered the SEALs as they peeled off to clear their assigned sectors.

Stubby MP7s snugged tight, Cross and Griff stalked through the wide-open space to the right of the foyer hunting for targets. Finding only cubicles and desks and tarp-covered windows, one at a time, they called their sectors clear and reversed course.

With the rest of the Rider team ranging his way, Cade took a split-second inventory of the room.

Clues were everywhere that this place had recently been occupied. Near Axe, at the base of the steel and concrete stairs, was a bullet-style trashcan with empty MRE wrappers spilling from its jammed swinging door. Suggestive of constant comings and goings, the tile and carpet surrounding the entry was tracked with dried mud. Viewed through the NVGs, the boot prints showed up as pale gray against the stark whiteness of the floor.

Still standing on the tile entry, Lopez motioned for Cade and Axe to move to the end of the north-side hall—an order that also entailed clearing the rooms along the way.

Drowning out the soft footfalls of soldiers on the move, the sound of bare feet slapping the floor filtered down from upstairs.

Cade kept his rifle trained down the hall and cast a furtive glance at the stairs, barely thirty feet off his right shoulder.

Nearly to the mouth of the hallway, Axe spun a one-eighty and directed his attention to Lopez, who was already moving toward the stairs and directing Cross and Griff to cover him.

The footfalls ceased and a male voice called out, "Adrian? Is that you?"

The operators stood stock still.

More footsteps. They were now hollow-sounding, though.

"What the hell is going on outside?" asked the disembodied voice. "Did some deadheads squeeze through the gate?"

The footfalls drew nearer, then stopped abruptly.

Weapon trained on the second landing, Cross watched a wiry middle-aged man make the turn from above and halt on the flat six-by-six concrete slab. Despite the hour, the man was fully clothed in blue jeans and a long-sleeved shirt bearing the words BEAR LAKE AVIATION. Eyes bugged wide, the man looked more meth freak than pilot. Narrow face wearing a mask of concern and eyes darting every which way in a failing attempt to pick out anything in the suffocating dark, the man called out again. When there was no response, he reached one arm behind his back and pulled a boxy pistol from his waistband.

Cade saw white licks of flame leap from Lopez's carbine. The suppressor swallowed most of the noise of the back-to-back-to-back discharges. In the still, the clatter of the bolt and follow-on tinkle of spent brass on the tile entry was very pronounced. As was the sharp crack of the limp body smacking the last tread head first. Even viewed in the phosphor white of his goggles, Cade knew that at least one of Lopez's bullets had struck the man in the face. For when his wide-open mouth met the sharp edge of the bottom stair, a fist-sized blob of pulped brain oozed from the jagged crater where his eyes should have been.

In all, only five seconds had elapsed from the sound of the first footfalls to the man's gory face plant.

Picking up where he left off, Lopez sent Cade and Axe on their way. Then, shaking his head in disgust, he stepped over the corpse and led Cross and Griff up the stairs.

Cade padded down the carpeted hall to the first of four doors. Lining the hall two to a side, a dozen feet separated the doors, save for the last door on the left that looked to be the only entry to a room double the size of the others. Using the same technique with each door—Axe taking the cover position while Cade did the opening—they cleared the first three executive offices. Finding the rooms darkened and containing only desks topped with blotters, computer monitors, and engraved brass nameplates of long-dead nine-to-fivers, they moved on to the last door on the left.

Pressed to the wall beside door number four, Cade heard movement coming from inside. Just a soft fabric rustle at first.

In a raspy smoker's voice, a man called out, "Is that you, Chet?"

Axe raised the M4's suppressor level with the center of the wooden door and nodded.

In the next beat, there was a soft click and a paper-thin wedge of light spilled from under the door.

Cade tried the knob and found it locked. Shrugging, he rapped lightly.

Again the sound of fabric on fabric. Then a zipper was being worked. The noise was long and drawn out. *Sleeping bag*, thought Cade.

The man coughed. Then he said, "Chet? That you?"

On one knee now, Cade tucked his carbine in tight and slipped his finger into the trigger guard.

The sound of a lock being thrown came as the knob began to rattle.

Cade drew up some trigger pull.

"Damn it, *Adrian*," said the voice through the door. "Next time you take *Toy* to the pisser, don't just take your gun ... take the fuckin' keys, too!"

More so a byproduct from the utterance of the cannibal's name than the fact that the door was now slowly swinging away from the doorjamb, Cade felt his body tense involuntarily.

Chapter 76

As the door hit the halfway point in its swing, two things happened. Cade heard Axe say, "Engaging," and saw the fat, naked man filling the doorway propelled backward violently as a trio of rounds from the Brit's M4 stitched him from sternum to chin. Then, just as he was following Axe into the room, in his headset, he heard Haynes say, "Whiplash Actual, Jedi One-One ... be advised, you have a *squirter* near the Porta Johns. Repeat ... scratch that. You have *two* squirters moving west along the north end of the administration building. One adult and one child. How copy?"

Cade was staring into the wide eyes of a naked pre-teen girl when Lopez responded to Haynes by saying he was clearing the upstairs of the administration building. Hearing Lopez inquire if either of the Dagger teams could intervene, Cade sidestepped the fallen corpse, reached past the dumbfounded girl, and stripped the nearby inflatable mattress of one of its blankets. He was wrapping the blanket around the trembling girl and reassuring her that he was one of the "good guys" when he heard the Dagger team leaders answer back saying that they were currently hands full rounding up squirters of their own.

Cade sat the girl on the edge of the bed and asked for her name.

Voice trembling, the girl said, "Katy."

While Cade was calming the girl, Axe rooted about the messy office-turned-bedroom.

Cradling his M4 in the crook of his arms, Cade knelt in front of the girl and asked, "Who is Toy?"

"That's what Gary"—she gestured to the corpse on the floor—"and Mama call my little sister, Tory."

451

Toy, thought Cade. Highly unlikely the moniker was a nickname. Even harder for him to believe was that they called her Toy only to shorten an already short name.

"Who is Mama?" he asked.

"That's what Adrian wants us kids to call her."

"Where *is* your mother and father?"

The girl tugged the blanket up to her chin and hung her head.

"Did something bad happen to them?" pressed Cade.

"Dad died a long time ago."

"The outbreak?"

The girl nodded. Tears were welling in her eyes.

Cade glanced at Axe, who was rooting in a pile of clothes on the floor. He asked, "And your mom?"

"Mama ... I mean Adrian said she left one night. Abandoned us." She paused for a beat then added forcefully, "But me and Tory don't believe her."

"I don't either," Cade replied grimly. Knowing there was a better chance of headshot Gary standing up and doing an Irish jig, he added, "Maybe she will turn up one day."

Katy was sobbing now.

"Here," said Axe, handing Cade a wadded-up ball of gray fabric.

Cade separated the two articles of clothing and was handing the girl a rumpled shirt and sweatpants several sizes too big when Haynes came back on the comms to inform the three teams that the Porta John squirters had just entered the barn. Casting a furtive glance at Axe, Cade set the clothing at the girl's feet and asked her to get dressed.

Though it was pitch-black inside the room, the NVGs still allowed Cade to see everything. So before the girl removed the blanket from around her shoulders, he quickly put his back to her.

A split-second after giving the girl her privacy, someone upstairs bellowed, "Drop the weapon."

A beat later a booming male voice yelled back, "Fuck you!"

452

A short volley of suppressed gunshots answered the hollered epithet.

As Cade turned to tell Katy what to expect next, Lopez was back on the comms and ordering him and Axe to search the barn for the squirters.

You mean Adrian, Cade thought to himself.

"You and me, mate," said Axe. "What do we do with her?"

Cade motioned for Axe to drag the leaking corpse into the hall. Then he turned back to Katy, who was sitting on the bed fully clothed but still trembling and glassy-eyed. "Someone will be back for you real soon," he promised. Glancing across the room to his left, he added, "Get in the closet and stay there."

Katy nodded and mumbled, "Don't let her hurt Tory."

"I won't, sweetie." Before closing the closet door, he told her to stay put until either he or another soldier came for her. Hearing a mumbled acknowledgement, he closed the door and turned back to face Axe.

Wiping Gary's blood from his hands with the discarded blanket, Axe growled, "Let's get the *cunt*."

Cade said nothing. However, in his head he was already doing unspeakable things to the pedophile waste of skin.

***

Cade followed Axe to the end of the corridor and waited while the SAS shooter peered one-eyed around the corner. Satisfied they were alone, Cade followed Axe down the carpeted hall, passing a half-dozen exterior windows all covered on the inside by black plastic sheeting. Along the way, they stopped twice to check a pair of unlocked closets on their right. The door to the first was labeled *CUSTODIAL* and held the usual: brooms, mops, buckets, and cleaning supplies. The closet labeled *UTILITY* housed the breaker box and some heating and ventilation controls.

Nearly to the end of the hall, Cade spotted the door leading to outside on the left. Because a horizontally mounted metal crash bar bisected it, he concluded it opened outward. Like the rest of the windows in the building, the square item inset head-high in the steel door was also blacked-out.

Cade smelled the Porta Johns before they reached the door. Paired with the eye-watering, ammonia-heavy stench of urine and feces was the pong of the dead things patrolling nearby between the two fence lines.

"It's propped open," observed Axe as he stepped to the opposite jamb and peeked through the gap.

From a yard back Cade felt the cold, steady draft responsible for bringing the stink inside. And though very faint, he could hear the dry rasps of the dead carrying on the wind.

Axe produced a fixed blade and sliced the plastic sheeting. Peeling up the corner, he stole a glance outside.

Crouched low opposite the hinge side, Cade watched and waited.

"Clear," called Axe.

Nodding, Cade pushed through the door, carbine tracking with his gaze. As he crossed the threshold, he nudged the crushed beer can cum door stop aside with his toe so the door would latch behind them. While Axe was exiting the building, Cade was crouched low and surveying the lay of the land.

Extending a few feet from the rear exit was an alcove and gently sloped wheelchair ramp that spilled them into an alley. Fifteen feet to their fore was the row of Porta Johns—at least a dozen total. The outer wall rose up behind the toilets, dwarfing them by at least fifteen feet.

Hustling west past the Porta Johns, Cade sized up the barn. It was slightly shorter than the hangar on its left and stood head and shoulders above the outer wall to the right. Save for what looked to be a metal roof hosting twenty to thirty solar panels, it was constructed entirely with unpainted wood. There were no windows to speak of and entry to the barn was through the double doors facing him.

Cade looked to his left as they covered the hundred feet of open tarmac between the administration building and main hangar. He saw nothing but open ground all the way to the far wall. Glancing right, he saw that the grass from where the tarmac ended to the cement freeway barriers was trampled down and surrounded by post and beam fencing. Eyeing him from within the makeshift pen was a dozen full-grown goats and half as many kids.

Somehow the two men made it from the administration building to the barn at a full run without the goats making a sound.

The metal latch used to secure the barn doors had been thrown open. Expecting to find the doors locked from the inside, Cade grabbed the latch with one hand and gave it a tentative tug. Shocked that it moved freely, he opened up a four-inch gap, went to one knee, and stole a quick look at the barn's roomy interior. Seeing only baled hay stacked a dozen feet off the floor to the right, and miscellaneous pieces of farm equipment pushed against the wall to his left, he leaned back and whispered his findings to Axe.

They spent a few seconds outside the door deciding on the best approach to clear the barn, then Cade widened the gap between the doors and he and Axe slipped inside.

The air in the barn smelled of hay and hewn fir. Like sediment stirred by a scuba diver's fins, dust motes scudded the airspace in front of Cade's NVGs, only beginning to settle once the door was shut behind them.

They stood there in silence for a few seconds letting their senses attune to the sudden absence of the hungry cries of the dead and constant rush of blowing wind.

Chapter 77

As soon as the door sucked shut behind Axe, Cade knew they weren't alone inside the barn. From somewhere deep in the bowels of the massive structure came a pained whimper. Then, between the intermittent groans of support beams under stress, they heard boards creaking.

Cade looked to his left and spotted a piece of equipment whose technical name he didn't know. On its side, however, was the word SKYJACK.

Pretty self-explanatory.

The SKYJACK's chassis was six feet across and three deep with wheels at each corner. The wheels were a quarter of the size of an automobile's and shod with what looked like rubber bands for tires. The chassis supported a four by eight rectangular steel platform. The platform was ringed on all sides by a waist-high safety cage—also fashioned from steel tubing. Between the two components was a fully extended apparatus that looked a lot like an old-fashioned scissor jack. Providing proof that the panels on the roof were in fact for solar collection, a power cord snaked from behind one of the lift's rear wheels.

Cade followed the cord with his eyes. It ran up the wall and was plugged into an electrical box nailed to one of the support beams. He continued walking his gaze to the platform and saw that it was even with the lip of an overhead hay loft, which, thanks to the hay bales stacked near the door, he had initially failed to notice.

Cade looked to Axe. Mouthed, "There's got to be another way up."

Axe pointed to his eyes, then stabbed a finger at a pair of rudimentary ladders leading up to the loft. Basically just a handful of eighteen-inch-long lengths of two-by-four nailed horizontally to the sturdy loft support beams, the rungs looked capable of supporting his weight. That there was no block and tackle affixed to the rafters above the loft helped explain the need for the motorized lift.

Change of plans.

Cade plucked a flashbang grenade from a pocket and showed it to Axe. Returning the black metal cylinder to the cargo pocket it had come from, he motioned for Axe to scale the support beam furthest from the lift.

Nodding, Axe padded away, swinging his carbine to his back as he went.

Cade made his way to the beam nearest the SKYJACK lift, took hold of a rung, and tested it for movement. Secured to the six-by-six beam with four screws, it barely moved.

Solid enough.

Throwing his M4 around to his back, Cade drew the suppressed Glock 19 from the drop-leg holster. Out of habit he checked the action to confirm a round was in the pipe.

Good to go.

Snugging the pistol home, he glanced to his right. Seeing Axe in position and already grasping a rung of his own, Cade stabbed a thumb skyward and started to climb. The lengths of two-by-four creaked under his Danners as they accepted the combined weight of his hundred-and-eighty-pound frame loaded down with fifty-some-odd pounds of gear.

In between rungs, Cade heard a snuffling noise drifting from the rear of the barn. Strangely, it sounded as if it had come from underneath the loft. Writing it off as sound from the loft being distorted by the openness of the structure, he pressed on, slowly, one rung at a time, until there were only two left and his helmet was in danger of breaking the plane.

To Cade's right, clinging to a rung of his own and with the carbine swinging lazily from his back, Axe presented a near mirror image. Left arm wrapped around the beam, Cade plucked

458

the stun grenade from his pocket. Using the fingers of his left hand, he pulled the pin from the grenade.

Cade held the grenade so Axe could see it. Directing his voice toward the ground, he said, "I know you're up there, Adrian."

Nothing.

"There are only two ways this can go," he pressed.

Boards groaned near the back of the loft. That it sounded more distinct to his right ear led Cade to think Adrian was nearly equidistant to the ladders.

Good to know.

"Last chance," he warned.

"Fuck you."

A woman's voice. Shrill and obviously stressed.

More whimpering was followed by the faint, faraway sound of a girl pleading to be let go.

Voice seemingly back to normal, the woman said matter-of-factly, "I am *not* going to be locked up again. Not now, not ever again. I will die first."

So be it.

Cade let the spoon slip from his hand, counted to one in his head, and one-armed the flashbang over the lip. It was a perfect hook shot. One that he guessed Kareem Abdul-Jabbar would let slide without much criticism.

In unison, Cade and Axe looked groundward, both squeezing their eyes shut and covering the multiple lenses of their NVGs with their free arm.

There was a minute concussion followed a millisecond later by a shockwave that Cade felt roll over his head. When he opened his eyes a half-beat later, he found that the washout effect to the goggles from the flash was minimal. In the latter half of that beat he was dragging the Glock from its holster and swinging it over the ledge.

At the exact moment a pair of poorly aimed shots snapped from the hip crackled through the air to Cade's right, he was acquiring the target and bringing the Glock online. As he did so, the adrenaline dump hit his system, which caused time to seemingly slow to a crawl even as a million and one thoughts were jumping synapses.

Cade's first glance at the rotund woman confirmed to him that there was no way in hell she climbed the beam to get to where she was. And the longer he studied her—microseconds at best—the more dumbfounded he became knowing that the platform had even budged from the chassis under her weight, let alone made it to full extension.

The woman's eyes, partly hidden under a deep-set brow, darted about, searching for something in the dark. *God almighty*, he thought as his gaze finished the split-second recon. *She has to be four hundred pounds, if not more*. Bra and panties were all she was wearing, or, more like it, the bra and panties were wearing her. Fat rolls spilled over the straining waistband and pooled under her sagging breasts. In her right hand was a large revolver, curls of gun smoke wafting from the gaping muzzle. Her left leg was bowing inward and sported a dirty cast that looked to have been thrown together by kindergarteners dabbling in papier-Mache. That the naked girl trapped in the crook of the woman's left arm was barely half a head shorter than her captor meant the woman Duncan referred to as "*Little Lotta*" was Brook's height, at best. "*As wide as she was tall*," Duncan had insisted days ago, the statement, at the time, drawing a skeptical look from Cade.

I stand corrected, thought Cade, already weighing odds and calculating angles in his head.

At first blush he concluded a head shot on Adrian would put the girl in grave danger. Then, taking into account the woman's considerable girth, he began to doubt how far the 9mm Parabellums would penetrate her torso if he aimed for center mass. Would they make it to her heart? Or any other vital organ, for that matter?

All of this took a fraction of a second for him to process. Then, suddenly, two things happened back-to-back that simultaneously made Cade's decision for him and sealed the fates of everyone involved.

First, the cast crumbled and Adrian's leg, buckling under her massive weight, started her upper body on a slow pitch backward, her immense head acting as a wrecking ball. Then, the girl Cade presumed to be Tory latched both hands onto the meaty forearm pressing in on her throat and, elbows jutting in front of her pale, nude torso, arched her head back and presented the clean shot Cade needed.

Without further thought, Cade caressed the trigger two times in quick succession. In his side vision, even before the pair of bullets had crossed the distance, he saw Axe spilling over the ledge, suppressed rifle a blur as the SAS vet brought it to bear.

There were two wet slaps as Cade's rounds found flesh. But he didn't see them, for his NVGs momentarily washed out as the pistol in the woman's hand boomed again, lighting up the entire length of the loft.

When Cade's goggles returned to normal a half-beat later, the girl was on her hands and knees at Adrian's feet, Adrian no longer possessed the weapon, and she was pitching backward toward the vertical seam of light behind her. In that snapshot in time he saw her now free hand going for the right side of her face, which was a mass of shredded flesh after having absorbed one or possibly both of the bullets. Didn't matter. With the girl safely out of the way, he snapped off another round that punched a hole above Adrian's right breast.

Having also recovered his vision from the revolver's muzzle flash washing his NVGs, Axe put two rounds from his M4 into center mass, which in this case ended up being the woman's rather distended belly.

While Cade's first two shots had started the ball rolling, the third added to the already spooling momentum, which in turn caused Adrian to spin her arms backward in tight little circles as she fought a losing battle to regain her balance.

The 5.56 mm hardball rounds fired from Axe's weapon had ruptured flesh and released tightly packed innards.

In the end, Adrian's head was the wrecking ball that started the loft doors at her back to swing open.

Axe blurted, "Destination fucked," as the gut-shot cannibal—both arms still frantically rolling the windows up—disappeared through the newly created opening.

Cade lowered his Glock and sprinted the length of the loft, calming words coming from his mouth as he approached the girl in the dark. Finding her shaken, but unharmed, he stole a quick glance over the edge.

The out of place snuffling sounds he had heard from the ladder moments ago now had a face, or, more like it, snouts. And some of those snouts were already buried deeply into the writhing woman's abdomen.

A rope of intestine spooled from the fissure as a large sow backed away from Adrian's flailing arms with one end of the juicy prize trapped between her teeth.

"Destination Hell, is more like it," Cade said, casting a sidelong glance at Axe. "Good shooting."

"Back at you, mate. She was a tough nut to crack."

Nodding, Cade turned away from the gruesome sight. He quickly stripped off his chest rig and plate carrier. Though it was sweat-soaked, he peeled off his Crye Precision top and dressed the young girl in it.

Chapter 78

The pair of stealth Chinooks were flaring and settling on the tarmac when Cade, Axe, and Tory emerged from between the hangar and administration building. Jedi One-One had already landed and was a hundred yards away, near the first of the smaller hangars, its rotor blades still spinning under power. Lopez, Cross, and Griff had collected Katy and were approaching one of the Green Berets, who was standing before a pair of body bags.

Having received the bad news in his ear from Lopez as he was helping Tory climb down from the loft, Cade walked as slowly as possible across the distance with the knowledge of what was to come weighing heavily on him the entire way. He knew that by walking half-speed he was only delaying the inevitable, but that didn't make a blip on his give-a-shit radar. The longer he could go without confirming the death of another of his friends, the better.

Slow walk becoming a plodding slog, Cade watched Tory break from Axe's side and sprint toward her older sister's outstretched arms.

After watching Katy wrap Tory in a tearful embrace, Cade shifted his attention to the two oblong shapes resting on the asphalt beside the idling Ghost Hawk. Having seen enough in the ghostly phosphor glow, he flipped his NVGs away from his face and covered the final thirty feet in the dark. Fully aware of the blades scything the air over his helmeted head, he walked erect until the oblong forms materialized to his fore.

With the words "Dagger One found your friends, Wyatt. I'm sorry, they didn't make it" still resonating in his head in Lopez's mournful voice, he aimed his M4 at the pair of body bags and thumbed on the tactical light.

Instantly the glossy bags were reflecting the light back at him. He set the M4 on the tarmac, the beam from the light only partially illuminating the bags, and knelt next to the one nearest him. He noted that it was filled out more than the other. And though he wasn't a great judge of someone's height as they lay horizontal, at first glance his gut told him his friend was zippered up inside.

Going to one knee, he lifted up the end of the bag and located the zipper. Slowly, he drew it up and over the filled-out area where the corpse's head lay. Once the zipper reached the point where he could see the dreadlocks and the flat of the corpse's forehead, he yanked forcefully on it until he saw more of the upturned profile. And it was all wrong. The thick ratty dreads were the first clue. That the nose was flat and crooked as a lightning bolt from being broken in the past confirmed he was not staring down on a dead Daymon Bush.

After leaning back, looking skyward and uttering a prayer of thanks, he regarded Lopez. "That is not Daymon."

Smiling wide, Lopez flashed a thumbs-up.

Hopes buoyed by the revelation, Cade scrambled around on hands and knees and knelt by the head of the second body bag. Without pause, he grabbed the zipper and drew it away from him. The instant the two halves parted, revealing the aquiline nose, narrow lips, and alabaster skin, his stomach clenched. He didn't need to see the profile right side up. Nor did he need to illuminate the corpse's flowing hair to know he was looking down on Heidi. The split-second glimpse had been enough to confirm the worst.

Thinking, *So much loss in so short a span,* he grabbed his M4, rose, and trudged toward the Ghost Hawk's open door.

Epilogue

In a handful of seconds the Ghost Hawk was free of the clearing and plowing west into the darkness soon to be broken by the coming Utah dawn.

During the entire forty-minute flight to the Eden compound, Cade's eyes never left the black cadaver bag containing Heidi's fleshless corpse. He continued staring at the black vinyl draped over his boots even as Ari was calling out the five-minute mark.

Landing and unloading the incredibly light bag was a blur. He barely remembered opening the DHS Black Hawk and placing Heidi inside with Helen and Ray.

Cade didn't really come to until he was safely in his quarters and slipping Brook's wedding ring back onto the chain alongside his dog tags.

The one thing that did stick indelibly in his memory as he lay down on his bunk, spent and dog-tired, was his daughter stirring and calling down from her bunk to profess her love for him.

"Love you, too, sweetie."

"What about the bad guys?" she mumbled.

"The bad guys won't be bothering us. Now go back to sleep. Tomorrow is going to be a busy day."

###

To be continued in a new *Surviving the Zombie Apocalypse* novel in early 2018

Thanks for reading! Reviews help us indie scribblers. Please consider leaving yours at the place of purchase. Look for books in my bestselling series everywhere eBooks are sold. Please feel free to Friend Shawn Chesser on Facebook. To receive the latest information on upcoming releases, please join my no-spam mailing list at ShawnChesser.com.

Shawn's Facebook Author Page:
www.facebook.com/SurvivingTheZombieApocalypse/

Shawn on Twitter: http://twitter.com/@sdchess

ABOUT THE AUTHOR

Shawn Chesser, a practicing father, has been a zombie fanatic for decades. He likes his creatures shambling, trudging and moaning. As for fast, agile, screaming specimens ... not so much. He lives in Portland, Oregon, with his wife, two kids and three fish. This is his eleventh novel.

CUSTOMERS ALSO PURCHASED:

JOHN O'BRIEN
NEW WORLD
SERIES

JAMES N. COOK
SURVIVING THE DEAD
SERIES

MARK TUFO
ZOMBIE FALLOUT
SERIES

**ARMAND
ROSAMILLIA**
DYING DAYS
SERIES

HEATH STALLCUP
THE MONSTER
SQUAD

www.ingramcontent.com/pod-product-compliance
Lightning Source LLC
Chambersburg PA
CBHW071111290626
47170CB00018B/63